Raised in a farming family in Northamptonshire, England, **Jack Slater** had a varied career before settling in biomedical science. He has worked in farming, forestry, factories and shops as well as spending five years as a service engineer. Widowed by cancer at 33, he remarried in 2013 in the Channel Islands, where he worked for several months through the summer of 2012. He was forced to retire early from laboratory work by ill-health and now concentrates on writing and interests such as gardening, home-improvement, photography and genealogy. He has been writing since childhood, in both fiction and non-fiction. *Nowhere to Run* is his first crime novel and the first in the series of the DS Peter Gayle mysteries.

Also by Jack Slater

Nowhere To Run
No Way Home

No Place to Hide

JACK SLATER

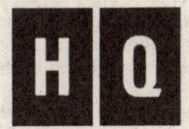

ONE PLACE. MANY STORIES

HQ
An imprint of HarperCollins*Publishers* Ltd
1 London Bridge Street
London SE1 9GF

www.harpercollins.co.uk

HarperCollins*Publishers*
Macken House, 39/40 Mayor Street Upper,
Dublin 1 D01 C9W8

This paperback edition 2024

1

First published in Great Britain by
HQ, an imprint of HarperCollins*Publishers* Ltd 2017

ISBN: 9780008743079

*For Christine, who shone a light
through the darkest times.*

Chapter 1

'Damn it.'

Jerry's knife hit the floor with a thump. He reached for it, tempted to ignore the knock on his front door that had caused him to drop it. Who the hell was going to be calling at this time of the evening, anyway? He certainly wasn't expecting anyone.

Probably Jehovah's Witnesses or something, he thought, checking the knife and the carpet where it had fallen.

The knock came again, louder, more insistent. They must have seen the light from inside. He sighed and got up, putting his dinner to one side.

In the hallway, he could see the silhouette of a man through the glass front door. He checked the chain and opened it a crack. A young man stood there. Clean cut, with neat dark hair, dressed in chinos and a jacket against the chill of the November evening.

'Mr Tyler?'

'Yes.'

'Perfect.' He took a step back and Jerry frowned, confused. From nowhere, something slammed into the door. The chain gave way and the door hit Jerry in the face. He staggered. The young guy leapt in, shoving him back so that he stumbled and fell onto the stairs, the treads digging painfully into his back. Another figure crowded in behind, carrying what looked like a heavy metal pipe with handles along two sides and a black sports bag with a dark gold logo. The first one was leering over him now, his face inches away. 'Now, Jerry. You're going to show us your computer.'

'My computer?' Jerry frowned. 'Why? What are you . . .?'

'We know what you are. I've seen your record.'

'That's—'

The guy's hand clamped across Jerry's throat, cutting off his words. 'It wasn't a request,' he said. 'Where is it? Or do we have to search the place?'

Jerry stared into the young man's eyes and saw no give at all. No compassion. If anything, a cold enjoyment of what he was doing. Who was he? How had he seen closed records?

'You want it the hard way? Fine.' Something hard pressed into Jerry's solar plexus and agony spasmed through his torso. He gasped. Had he been stabbed? He couldn't look down for the hand at his throat. 'Josh, get his trousers.'

The other, larger guy crowded forward. Jerry felt hands at his belt. 'No, please,' he gasped. 'I'll tell you.'

A smile lit up the face above him. 'I know.' The head tilted. The agonising pressure lifted from his torso. 'So . . .?'

'Front bedroom. It's my office.'

'Password?'

'Axminster.'

'Ironic, in the circumstances. Josh?'

Panic flashed in Jerry's mind. 'No. I told you . . .' He cried out as agony flared in his stomach and chest again, so fierce and intense that he barely felt the fingers unfastening his trousers. His shoes were slipped from his feet and his trousers tugged from the bottoms, down and off in one quick motion, change and keys spilling across the wood floor. Jerry was paralysed by the pain in his torso as he felt his underwear tugged down. Tears were running freely from his eyes as he stared up at the young man holding him. 'Please, don't. Don't do this.'

He felt rubber-clad fingers place something around the base of his genitals. It felt like wire. He gasped, his eyes widened in horror. 'No. Fuck!' Panic surged through him, almost overwhelming the pain in his chest and stomach.

The guy shook his head. 'No, no, Jerry. Not wise. What you can feel is cheese wire. One tug from Josh, and bye-bye bits. Do you understand?'

Jerry nodded, unable to speak.

'Good.' The guy's voice was almost friendly now. He pushed himself up. The pain went from Jerry's torso, but he was horrifically aware of the tension around his groin. 'Up you get. But no sudden moves, eh? We wouldn't want any accidents. Awfully messy on this nice, beige carpet.'

Jerry felt horribly exposed and vulnerable. He sat up carefully and got to his feet.

'Up you go,' the first one said. 'I'll be right behind you.' He took the wooden handle on the end of the wire from the bigger guy in the blue surgical gloves and stepped in close, grabbing a handful of Jerry's shirt with his free hand.

Jerry turned, feeling the wire across the top of his thigh as he took a tentative step up. He led the way cautiously up the stairs and along to the front bedroom, which he had converted into an office.

Keep them calm, do what they want, he thought. It was the only way he could see of getting out of this intact. Any wrong move and that little wooden handle would be snatched back and . . . He didn't even want to think that far, but an image came unbidden into his mind – blood spurting, a lump of flesh lying at his feet as he collapsed, ruined forever. He would bleed out, here, on the floor.

'Right. Stand aside, Jerry. Let the dog see the rabbit.'

The big one – Josh – stepped past them and took the seat in front of the computer. He powered it up as if he owned it and a flash of annoyance pierced Jerry's fear. A hand clamped heavily on his shoulder, almost as if the guy standing beside him knew what he was thinking. Jerry felt suddenly crowded, claustrophobic in his own private space.

The computer screen lit up with a pleasant coastal scene, dotted with icons. Josh clicked on the Documents icon and searched until he found what he was looking for. Jerry felt himself go pale.

'Oh, Jesus,' he murmured.

'He won't help you now, Jerry,' the other one said from his side. 'Or where you're going, if the preachers are right. Up you get, Josh.'

'What? What are you going to do?' Fear formed a lump in his throat that was the only thing stopping him from retching. His legs didn't work properly as he was pushed forward and into the seat. He sat down hard, the wire digging into the sensitive skin at the top of his thighs. 'Please. Don't hurt me. I'm not that guy any more. I don't use that stuff. I'd forgotten it was even on there.' Jerry felt the guy's free hand grab his collar and tug it down, then a sharp prick in the muscle between his neck and shoulder. 'What are you doing?'

'Just something to help you relax, Jerry.' He patted him on the shoulder, where the injection had been.

A weird feeling swooped through Jerry's body. He tried to shift his feet under the chair, but couldn't. They wouldn't respond. My God, what was this stuff they'd given him? Jesus! He could clearly hear the TV from downstairs. He recognised the voice of the BBC News anchor. Fiona. Not his favourite. He liked Julie. What the hell was he thinking?

He stared at the screen in front of him. Went to lift his hand to the mouse, to close the image, but his arm wouldn't work either. 'What . . .?' His voice was slurred and he couldn't turn his head to face the men behind him. What was happening? Had they overdosed him? God! He'd never done drugs before, not of any kind – he didn't even smoke – and he never would again. This lack of control was frightening. 'Wha—?'

He felt the guy's presence, close beside him. Felt his breath in his ear when he spoke.

'Of course, in the dose we've given you, it goes a bit further than that. Becomes a paralytic. Stops your muscles from working. You can see, hear, smell, feel, but you can't move. And soon, you won't be able to breathe.' He stood back. 'Best get on, before we lose him. Wouldn't want him to miss the fun, eh?' He laughed and the other one joined in.

Panic filled Jerry's mind as he felt his hand being placed around the wooden handle of the cheese wire. They were killing him. Slowly, so that he would feel every terrifying, agonising moment of it.

The bigger one placed a couple of big, fat candles on the ends of the wall-to-wall desk and lit them.

'There,' the one in charge said. 'A bit of romance. Appropriate, or what?'

A lighter sounded. The candles were lit. Then a third one.

'Josh, check the sitting room, would you? And turn the TV off while you're there. You know what we need.'

Josh left the room.

Jerry tried to look away from the image on the screen in front of him, but even his eye muscles no longer worked. He heard a creak on the landing. 'Ah, perfect.'

Josh came back into the room and dumped a pile of newspapers and magazines on the back of the desk, under the curtain. The top quarter or so of the stack was slid across a few inches and the third candle placed under it.

Jerry gasped. They were going to burn him alive! 'Pwu . . . Nu . . . Hu . . .'

A hand clapped him hard on the back. He coughed, tried to get his breath and found it difficult. 'We'll be off, then, Jerry. Don't worry. You probably won't feel the flames. I dare say the Sux will have stopped your breathing by then.'

Frozen in place, Jerry stared at the stack of papers and

magazines as his attackers walked calmly along the landing and down the stairs. The bottom one of the overhanging magazines and papers was already beginning to brown. Desperately, he tried to shift his body in the chair, but nothing happened. He drew a breath to try to shout, but his chest felt tight and restricted. 'Hel—' he croaked, then struggled to breathe in again. 'He—'

Chapter 2

'Concealing evidence is a serious offence, Sergeant.'

DCI Adam Silverstone's slim hands were flat on his desk as he stared at the man standing stiffly before him.

'I haven't concealed anything . . . *sir*. Tommy's connection to Rosie Whitlock wasn't relevant to the case. How could it have been? He's been missing for six months, he hadn't exchanged any messages with her since April and he's thirteen years old. He wouldn't have been driving the van. So I made a judgement call. As you know, every minute counts in cases like that. It was a question of either/or. *Either* I followed protocol *or* I gave Rosie Whitlock every chance of being recovered alive and well. I chose the latter. Was I wrong, sir?' With difficulty, Detective Sergeant Pete Gayle kept his eyes on the wall above the station chief's head.

'Don't push me, Sergeant. You're on thin ice already. In fact, you're a very small step away from being back on the beat. You've deliberately and blatantly flouted the most basic of rules. You cannot work a case involving a direct member of your family. But, knowing that, you hid your son's connection to the victim and carried on regardless. Did you imagine there'd be no consequences to that?'

'No, sir. I imagined there would be fatal consequences if I didn't

– for a thirteen-year-old girl whose case was all over the press at the time. And the girl's own testimony suggests I was correct.'

'It doesn't matter whether he was a victim or a suspect, Sergeant. The fact that he was involved at all, and you knew it, is enough that you should have handed the case over instead of carrying on regardless. You are not the only competent officer in this nick.'

'No, sir. But all the others were fully occupied on other cases and there wasn't time for one of them to start again from scratch.'

'That was not your call to make, Sergeant. It was mine or DI Underhill's. And I distinctly remember telling you at the outset to keep DS Phillips up to speed so that he could take over if necessary.'

'My understanding at the time was that he'd got to a critical stage in one of his own cases, sir. With all due respect to Simon, he couldn't deal with that and take on Rosie Whitlock's case at the same time, as urgent as it was. And any delay in our investigation would have meant the suspect getting away. To attack another victim. He's already killed at least twice, sir.'

'Which he blames on your son, Sergeant. With, at least in one case, the support of the pathologist's report. And where's *he* now, eh?'

'I think that's a question you should ask Simon Phillips, sir. He's been trying to answer it for six months now.'

'Enough!' Silverstone's hands slapped his desk as he came up out of his chair, face reddening. His dark eyes locked on Pete's, jaw clenched as he pulled a deep breath in through his nose. He held it a beat, then slowly let it out. 'I have been reminded by HR at Middlemoor that, before going back on active duty, you should have had a psych eval. Circumstances prevented it at the time, obviously, but that is no longer the case.'

'Sir, I don't . . .'

'Do not presume on my patience, Peter,' Silverstone snapped, overriding him. 'You'll find it severely lacking. This is not my

8

decision and certainly not yours. You will attend Middlemoor HQ and report to the police psychologist at 0900 hours on Wednesday.' He slapped a piece of paper down on his desk in front of Pete. 'There are your orders. See that they're obeyed.'

*

Silence descended as Pete walked back into the squad room. He ignored it, marching back to his desk, jaw clamped tight with the anger still seething inside him.

Bloody jumped-up, clueless twat. How the hell did the brass ever imagine he was going to be any use to the force? Talk about piss-ups and breweries, as a manager he was as much use as a chocolate teapot and there was no way he'd ever survive in a political environment. They'd wipe the floor with the arrogant, preening dick.

He sat down heavily, yanked open the bottom drawer of his desk and took out the file that he kept there. He slapped it open and stared at the page without focusing.

'You all right, boss?' DC Jane Bennett asked from the desk opposite.

Pete looked up and sighed. 'I'm still here. For now.'

DC Dave Miles straightened up in his chair, next to Jane's. 'Even he's not stupid enough to sack you while the press is still singing your praises.'

'No, but you know what the press is like, Dave. News is only news for a day or three. Then they get bored and move on.'

'Be back for the trial, though, and that won't be for a few months at least. Bit of luck, FTP'll have been promoted out of here by then.'

One of these days, Silverstone was going to catch somebody calling him that, Pete thought. It was just a question of whether he would realise it was him they were talking about. Which would probably depend on whether they used the initials, as Dave had, or the full version, Fast-track Phil. If the latter, what he'd just endured would be nothing in comparison . . .

He shook his head. 'If we get a conviction then he might get his promotion. Not until then.'

'What do you mean, *if*?'

'Nothing's certain in this life, Dave. Anyway, now's not the time to be taking the piss out of the chief.'

'Feeling sensitive, is he?' Dick Feeney, the oldest member of the team, asked with a grin.

'Distinctly tetchy would be closer to the mark. So, what have you lot been up to while I was getting my balls chewed off?'

Pete had explained the situation to his crew before he'd reported the email and text links between his still-missing son, Tommy, and Rosie Whitlock, the victim of the abduction they had been investigating. The team had understood and supported him but they'd all known that DCI Silverstone would not.

It was now just over a week since the girl was rescued and Dave arrested the suspect after a brief car chase through the streets of Exeter. When the tech team at Headquarters had found the link between Rosie and Tommy on her computer, Pete had kept it to himself. He knew it was against the rules, but, as he'd said to the DCI, it was a judgement call. There was no way that Tommy could have snatched her and there wasn't time to waste on following protocol when the girl's life was at stake. Or, at least, that was what he'd told himself.

Thinking it through afterwards, he'd accepted that DI Colin Underhill could have taken over. He was a bloody good copper – had taught Pete everything he knew – but, having only just stepped back into the fold after five months' compassionate leave following Tommy's disappearance, the last thing Pete had wanted was to be pushed straight back out to the sidelines.

And, in the end, he'd been right. They'd nailed the guy. He'd been arrested before he could harm anyone else, including Rosie.

'You know how it is, boss.' Dave leaned back in his chair, fingers linking behind his head. 'While the cat's away . . .'

'Well, I'm back now, so let's get to it, eh? We need every i dotted and every t crossed on this one. No chance of him wriggling out of it for any reason at all.'

Including some smart-arse DS hiding the fact that his son was connected to the victim.

Pete pushed the thought aside as soon as it popped into his mind. As lead investigator, it was up to him what was relevant and therefore what would go to the CPS lawyers. As long as the defence team didn't get hold of it and, more importantly, of the fact that Pete knew of it . . .

'There's no way he's wriggling out of this, boss,' Dave said, sitting forward again and tugging his black waistcoat back into place. 'His van. His barn. The stuff at his house. The girl's testimony. We're safe as houses.'

'Even so. Every i and every t.' Pete wasn't going to allow Malcolm Burton to get away with anything, if he could possibly help it – especially laying the blame off on Tommy, as he'd been trying to do since he was arrested. The boy had had his problems. Pete had been aware of some of them, of course, but had found out a lot more since he disappeared, back in May – and more especially since he'd come back to work the week before last. He couldn't accept that he was a rapist and a killer as Burton and his solicitor were trying to suggest, though. He was only thirteen years old, for God's sake.

Pete's phone rang. He blinked, returning to the here and now, and picked it up. 'DS Gayle.'

'Peter. It's Tony Chambers. I've got something here that I think you ought to see.'

'What's that, Doc?'

'Fatality in a house fire last night, out to the east of the city. Dental records have just confirmed the identity of the victim as the house owner, Jeremy Tyler, aged forty-two. It looked like an accident during an auto-erotic pursuit, but a couple of things don't ring true.'

11

Pete pictured Chambers, small and lean in his green scrubs, his greying hair little more than stubble, sitting at his office desk, his free hand clicking through crime scene photos on his computer while he talked.

'Such as?'

'For one, there's a needle mark in the right trapezoid – which is a strange place to find one – and the fire chaps tell me there was definitely no syringe at the scene. And for another, there was a half-finished plate of food on the side table in the lounge, as if he'd been eating his dinner and got interrupted. Yet, he was found upstairs, seated in front of his computer. I mean, even a sex maniac would finish his dinner first, surely?'

Pete blinked and sat forward in his chair. 'Hang on. Jeremy Tyler, you said?'

'Yes.'

'Are we talking about the registered sex offender Jeremy Tyler?'

'That's right. Why?'

'Name's familiar, that's all. Came up in the Rosie Whitlock case, but he had a solid alibi. And no syringe. We sure on that?'

'That's what the fire investigator tells me. And the needle would have survived, even if the syringe itself didn't.'

'Yeah, that's right. OK, I'll come over.'

'Thanks, Peter.'

'You got something, boss?' Jane asked as he put the phone down.

'Maybe. The doc reckons he might have a murder on his table. House fire, last night.'

'Ooh.' She grimaced.

Pete pushed his chair back. 'I'm off to the mortuary, to have a look-see.'

She flicked her ginger hair back from her face. 'Sooner you than me. I hate the smell of burners. Put me off barbecue for life.'

*

With no alternative, DI Underhill being in Bristol on a course for the week, Pete reluctantly knocked on DCI Silverstone's door for the second time that day.

'Come.'

Silverstone was seated at his desk, reading through a report. He looked up from it as his door opened. 'Peter. What can I do for you?'

'I got a call from the pathologist earlier. Been looking into what he said and it seems we may have a serial killer in the city, sir.'

'In Exeter?'

Pete tilted his head. 'Can happen anywhere, I suppose.'

Silverstone pursed his lips. 'Hmm. What have you got?'

'Registered sex offender Jeremy Tyler was killed in his home around seven-thirty last evening. A house fire was used to cover it up. Clever job, made to look like an accident, but it wasn't.'

'One suspicious death doesn't make a serial killer.'

'No, but the doc detected a pattern. He's looking into it more deeply as we speak. I just heard back from him on another death, a few days ago. A bloke collapsed in the street. No obvious cause. Except, again, there was a needle mark found and no needle at the scene.'

Silverstone raised an eyebrow and sat back in his chair, fingers steepled in front of him.

'The victim hadn't worked in about fifteen years. So, we've got a dole scrounger and a sex offender. And, apparently, there's been a string of others recently. A druggie, a drunk, a prostitute and so on.'

'People like that die all the time.'

'Exactly. Vulnerable. Isolated. Won't be missed. Perfect targets. All died of plausible causes except the one that hasn't been determined. Someone's being very clever about it, but they're out there – killing off the city's undesirables. Doc Chambers is rechecking other cases to confirm. His idea, not mine.'

Silverstone stared at him flatly for a long moment, then sat forward. 'All right. Work the Jeremy Tyler case for now. We'll see about the serial killer angle if and when Doctor Chambers comes up with something concrete.'

What? Pete struggled to hold his tongue. Who the hell did this jumped-up Hendonite think he was? Pete had no idea whether he'd gone into the police training college at Hendon with the right degree or just the right connections, but the fact that he was on the fast track to the upper echelons didn't make him an expert on anything, never mind pathology. Just because he'd been able to waltz in over the heads of far more suitable candidates to be in charge of this station for now, he clearly imagined he was qualified to spout forth on all sorts of subjects that he'd have been better keeping out of.

But Pete was in more than enough trouble with the DCI as it was. He didn't need any more. He drew a long breath. 'Sir,' he said and turned to leave.

Back at his desk, he sat down, shaking his head incredulously. 'What's up?' asked Dave.

'I can't believe that bloke sometimes. The arrogance of the jumped-up, clueless tit. He's calling the doc's judgement into question, now.'

'Why? What's Doc Chambers saying?'

'He's got a suspicious death on the table. Which is now officially ours, by the way. He reckons it's one of a series. Except Fast-track, in his infinite wisdom, has just decided that it's not, until the doc can "come up with something concrete", as he put it. What the bloody hell's that about?'

'Reputation?' Dave suggested. 'He wants to be moving onwards and upwards, ASAP. Doesn't want a serial killer on his watch – unless, of course, we can catch him and he can take the credit.'

'Whoa.' Jane looked at him, green eyes wide. 'I take it all back. You're not just a pretty face, are you?'

Dave tugged at the collar of his open-necked shirt and straightened his waistcoat. 'Well, it's good of you to notice, at last. Women, eh?' he said to Dick. 'Nothing but hormones and make-up.'

'Oi!'

'Ow,' he yelped as both Jane and Jill thumped him. 'Physical violence, boss!'

'Sexual discrimination,' Jill shot back. 'Misogynist pig.'

Dick was shaking his head. 'And you go on at Ben for not learning.'

'I learned one thing on the internet last night,' Ben said, nodding towards Dave. 'He's more Bryan Ferry than Elvis. Only without the looks.'

'Cheeky sod.'

'I'm surprised you've heard of either,' Pete said.

'He hadn't till yesterday,' Dick said. 'Poor, uneducated boy.'

'And he's got you and Dave to teach him? God help the lad.' He shook his head. 'Anyway, we need bodies out to Jerry Tyler's place, to canvass the area and check on friends, family, colleagues – all the usual stuff. The fire guys have given us permission to go in, but we'll need wellies, apparently. It's structurally sound, but a major mess. Dave, I need you to check the records. See what we've got for known associates, family and so on. You find anything, let me know and then go and see what they have to say. Take Dick or Jill with you, as appropriate. Ben, you can come with us,' he said to the spiky-haired young PC as he stood up and grabbed his jacket from the back of his chair.

*

'So, Doc Chambers reckons some sort of drug overdose, then?' Jane asked as they went briskly down the station stairs.

'The lack of soot in the lungs and no abnormalities in the brain or heart told him something was up. The guy wasn't bound, but something stopped him getting out of that chair. Then he found a needle mark in the shoulder, up here.' Pete tapped the muscle between his neck and shoulder. 'Unusual place to inject – yourself or someone else. And there were no other needle marks on the body. He's asked for a rush-job on the analysis, but it'll be later today, at least, before the results come back.'

They reached the bottom of the stairs and turned right, towards the back of the building.

'And how does it get to be part of a series?' she asked. 'This is the first I've heard of it.'

'First anyone has. It reminded the doc of several others recently. Different MOs, if any at all but, taken together, they add up to a spike in deaths of these types of victims over the past few months. He's got another one in the mortuary at the moment, so he's going back and rechecking, see if he can find anything.'

Pete reached the back door, hit the security lock button and pushed through.

'So, for now, we've just got the one,' Jane said as they crossed the car park behind the station.

'That's right. And, whatever we think of the victim, he's still a victim.'

'Don't look at me, boss. I'm with you. We can't leave a killer out there to do it again, no matter who he's targeting.'

Pete pressed the remote and his car bleeped, indicators flashing as the locks clunked open. 'I might have to quote you on that. There's going to be some who need convincing. Including DCI Silverstone.'

Chapter 3

Driving out onto Heavitree Road, Pete turned left towards the edge of the city. A mile or so up the road, he turned left again into an estate of 1940s and '50s housing, the overall impression one of tidy and neat functionality.

'So, what's the aim here, boss?' Ben asked from the back seat.

Pete glanced in the mirror. The baby-faced PC was sitting forward keenly, leaning on the back of Jane's seat. 'Time of death is around six forty-five to seven last night. We need to find out who reported it and if any of the neighbours saw or heard anything out of the ordinary around that time or just before and what they know of our victim. If they saw him coming and going, or anyone else coming and going from his house – friends, family, girlfriend, whatever. Build up a picture that might lead us to who did this to him.'

Pete turned at another junction. Tidy gardens with low brick walls, cars parked on drives rather than on the road, a grass verge between the road and the footpath, dotted here and there with small ornamental cherry trees.

'Nice area,' Jane commented.

'Seems well looked after,' Pete agreed. 'Here we are.' He pulled in outside a house, similar to all the others except for the blackened bricks around and above the broken-out front bedroom window and the damaged roof above it, rafters showing like charred ribs through a large gap in the slates.

'See you in a bit, then, boss.'

'Yep.' Pete went to the boot as the other two headed off down the street. He took out a pair of Wellington boots and a set of blue overalls. After pulling them on, he left his shoes in the boot, locked the car and went up the drive to the front door of the house; his nostrils filled with the smell of wet charcoal.

The door was open but there were two strands of safety warning tape across it. Pete ducked under them and stepped inside. The place looked like it had been through a tropical storm with no roof on. The walls and ceilings were soaked. Pictures on the walls were knocked off-kilter. The banister railing at the top of the stairs was blackened and charred. All the doors were open, upstairs and down. The upstairs appeared to be brighter than expected, but that would be the lack of roof and ceiling, he guessed. He could see through to the kitchen at the rear and into the lounge to his left. It was dark in there, the curtains still closed from last night.

'Hello,' he called. 'DS Gayle, Exeter CID.'

'With you in a sec,' a male voice came from upstairs.

Pete waited in the narrow hallway. A moment later, a pair of black rubber boots with yellow rings around the tops appeared at the top of the stairs and started down.

The man wearing them was in his mid-forties, Pete guessed, and the sort he could imagine on one of those firemen calendars aimed at women of a certain age and disposition. He smiled and held out his hand.

'Pete Gayle.'

They shook hands.

'Steve Patton. Good to meet you.'

'So, have you got it all sussed?'

'Hmph. They used a simple but effective delay method. Enough

18

for the arsonist to be out and away before it flared up.'

'So, deliberate rather than an accident?'

'Oh yeah. Nobody's that careless. It was set up to look like an accident, but . . .' Patton shook his head. 'It wasn't.'

And the victim, if the doc's right, was left sitting there, watching it, Pete thought with a shudder. 'Which leaves us with the job of finding out who did it,' he said. 'Any damage in here?' He jerked a thumb at the sitting room door.

'No. Bit of water might have soaked through the ceiling, but that's all. All the electricals were off in there.'

Pete nodded. 'Any idea who called it in?'

Patton shook his head. 'Anonymous. Just came through on the 999, said, "There's a house fire at this address," and hung up. We've got it on tape, of course, but . . .' He shrugged.

'Have you got the number, though?'

'Dunno. I'll have to check. I'll let you know.'

'OK, cheers.' Pete shook his hand again and they both stepped out.

The fire investigator handed him a key. 'Here. You might as well have this. I've finished here.'

'Thanks.'

Pete took out his phone as the man walked away down the drive. He hit a speed-dial number and waited for the connection.

'Forensics. How can I help?'

'DS Gayle, Exeter CID. I've got a crime scene here that I need you guys to take a look at. Place has been in a fire, so time is of the essence, before the weather damages any evidence the fire crew left. We've got the all-clear for entry. Of particular interest is the sitting room, with a view to foreign fingerprints. The top of the TV and its power-button, a plate of food on a side table and perhaps the light switch. Also, wherever someone might have picked up a stack of magazines from in there.'

'OK. I've got all that. I'll pass it on to the team and they'll be there as soon as they can. Are you currently on-site?'

'Yes, but I won't necessarily be when they arrive. If not, I'll have an officer stationed here for security.'

'OK. And the address?'

Pete gave it, then phoned the station.

'Andy? Pete Gayle. I need a uniform out here to a crime scene. The fire in Whipton.'

When the duty officer had confirmed he would send someone, Pete went back into the living room where he pulled the curtains carefully back and checked for signs of disturbance. There was nothing obvious. A few magazines remained on the coffee table. He glanced through them then checked the DVD collection. The guy seemed to like comedies and action movies. He glanced around the room again, but saw nothing out of the ordinary, apart from the abandoned plate of food.

Closing the curtains, he headed upstairs.

The upstairs front room was utterly destroyed and open to the elements. Nothing remained in there but charred wreckage that stank of burning. Pete was searching the room next to it when his phone buzzed in his pocket. He drew it out and checked the screen.

Chambers.

He pressed the button to take the call and lifted it to his ear. 'Hey, Doc. You got something?'

'I take it you mean apart from backache and sore fingers?'

'I was hoping.'

'The answer is, yes, I have. I've just finished with the other relevant body that's still here and found a single needle mark.'

'Another overdose?'

'Not in the sense you're thinking and we certainly won't get a measurement now, but I did a vitreous glucose analysis. The vitreous humour, the fluid in the eye, is about the only reliable source for biochemical levels in the minutes and hours leading up to death. The blood begins to degrade almost immediately post-mortem, so normal constituent levels in it wouldn't be reliable.

20

The result was 0.4. The only way to get that low is with an insulin overdose.'

'And I'm guessing your victim wasn't a diabetic?'

'Exactly.'

Pete let go a long sigh. 'Best send me the particulars, then, Doc. Victim file and your report.'

'Will do.'

Pete chose not to tell Chambers of Silverstone's reluctance to accept his theory without further evidence. There was no point now. 'What about the other cases you mentioned?'

'All in the ground or cremated by now, I'm afraid. I'll check which is which, but we'll need exhumation orders to pursue any of them.'

'OK. Keep me posted.'

'Of course.'

Pete returned the phone to his pocket.

Two cases didn't make a serial killer, but they certainly started to look like one. And that was the last thing he needed to get tied up with right now.

*

'Andrew Michaels was thirty-four years old, five foot nine and weighed seventeen and a half stone,' Pete read from Doc Chamber's report to his assembled team a little over an hour later.

Dick Feeney ran a hand down his cheek, skin rasping on dark stubble. 'Big lad, then.'

'You really are going have to reset your body clock, mate,' Dave told him.

'Eh?' Jane frowned.

'Well, look at him. If that's not a five o'clock shadow, I don't know what is. And it's only . . .' He made a show of checking his watch. 'Twenty past one.'

'Damn, no wonder I was feeling peckish,' Jane said. 'It's feeding time.'

'Talking of food and getting back to the matter at hand,' Pete said, 'Michaels worked for eighteen months in a bakery, ending in 2001. He'd been on the dole since then, living at home with his parents. He collapsed in the High Street; keeled over suddenly on a seat across from the Princesshay Shopping Centre. The attending paramedics said that witnesses reported nothing abnormal leading up to the collapse. He had just been sitting there quietly one minute and slumped on the ground the next.'

'Presumably not from a heart attack from being a lazy, fat bastard,' Dave said. 'Or we wouldn't be talking about him.'

'Exactly.' Pete stuck his photo – taken on the steel mortuary table – on the board alongside Jerry Tyler's. 'But you're right about the intended impression. Victim two in the doc's theorised series. In this case, the needle mark was in the back of his upper arm, the triceps muscle.'

'So, what was it?' asked Jane.

'Insulin, based on the guy's glucose level, as determined from the fluid in his eye.'

'Ouch.' Jill Evans cringed.

'Why the eye?' asked Ben Myers, across from her.

Dave glanced at him. 'You a poet and didn't know it?'

'Because,' Pete said, ignoring him, 'it's the one place in the body where levels of several blood constituents are stable for a time after death. It's a filtrate of the blood serum, but it's isolated from the bloodstream after death, so it's not affected by the early stages of decomposition like the blood is. Unfortunately, it doesn't help us with the actual insulin because that's only stable for a few hours.'

'And there's nothing else that could cause the glucose level the doc found?' Dave asked.

'No. In the blood, it would drop to that kind of level fairly quickly after death, apparently, but not in the eye fluid.'

'So, insulin jab, staged accident . . . We're talking about a fairly sophisticated perp, here.'

'And one with access to insulin,' Jane added. 'Which suggests a diabetic. Or at least one in the family.'

'Or peer group,' Ben put in. 'He could have borrowed or nicked a dose.'

Pete nodded. 'We should check GP surgeries, the hospital and the ambulance trust – see if any thefts have been reported. It could have come from one of them as well as a friend or family member.'

'That's a big old job,' said Dave.

'I'll do it,' Ben offered. 'What about vets?'

Pete frowned. 'I don't know.'

'I'll find out.'

'Will you never learn, Spike?' Dave asked.

'What?'

'Never volunteer,' Dick told him.

'Right.' Pete grabbed his coat off the back of his chair. 'Jill can give you a hand if you need it, Ben. Dick, check out the victim and see if he's got a record of any kind. I doubt it, but you never know. Jane, you and I'll go see his parents, see what we can get from them. Come on.' He headed for the door, Jane's heels clipping on the lino as she hurried to catch up.

*

Michaels had clearly inherited his height from his father and his girth from his mother. Brian and Kathy sat uneasily in the two armchairs in their lounge, leaving Pete and Jane on the sofa, the TV muted but not switched off in the corner.

'So, why are the police interested in our Andrew all of a sudden?' the dead man's father asked, his hands clasped in his lap as he leaned forward in his chair.

'The pathologist has come to us with some unusual findings,' Pete told him. 'Was Andrew diabetic?'

'Why would you ask that? Because of his size?' demanded Kathy, whose greying dark hair wafted in a curly halo around

23

her as she moved, hands wringing in her lap. 'Not all fat people are diabetic, you know. I'm not.'

'We don't judge, Mrs Michaels. It's not our job.' Pete felt sympathy with her defensiveness. He was still the same way with Tommy, despite all he'd learned about the boy in the last couple of weeks. All parents would be, he guessed.

After a long pause, she sighed and seemed to slump in her chair. 'No, he wasn't diabetic. Why?'

'One of the pathologist's findings suggested the possibility. You say you're not, either. Is anyone in the family, or one of his friends, perhaps?'

She shook her head, unruly strands of hair wafting. 'Why should it matter?'

'Talking of friends, did you know most of Andrew's?'

'He didn't have many,' his father said. 'Quiet lad, kept himself to himself.'

'He was bullied at school,' Kathy said, reminding Pete again of his own son, who was small for his age. 'Never really got over it. We tried to encourage him to get out more, join a club or something, but . . .' Her hands fluttered briefly then went back to her lap, where the fingers resumed their random pattern of twining together.

Evidence suggested that Tommy had reacted differently to the Michaels boy. According to both his peers and his teachers, he'd turned things around to the extent that many of the other kids were frightened of him. Too small to fight, he'd become devious, cruel and bitter. Instead of the brawn that he lacked, he'd used his brains to get back at the kids who'd previously targeted him. Not that Pete had ever noticed any of this, he had to admit regretfully. He'd always been too busy working.

'Did he have a computer?' Jane asked.

'Up in his room,' Kathy said.

'Could I take a look? It helps to build up a picture of him – his associates, his interests and so on.'

'He wasn't into anything mucky,' Kathy said quickly. 'You won't find none of that porn stuff on there.'

'As I said, Mrs Michaels, I'm just interested in who he was connecting with, what his interests were, what he was like as a person. We didn't know him, you understand.'

She grunted. 'I suppose. Come on, then.' She got up and shuffled towards the door.

Pete waited until the door closed behind them, then turned to Brian.

'I'm sorry, but it's possible your son was killed, Mr Michaels,' he said. 'We need to know as much as we can about him, to find out who might have done it. If anyone in his life might have had the opportunity or the inclination. Do you have any other family?'

'I've got a brother and a sister, live here in the city. His mother's an only child. Dave's got no kids, Beck's got a son, five years younger than our Andrew, but they don't see each other except birthdays and Christmas. Her husband don't come round here, either. He works down the industrial estate. Car mechanic.'

'And your brother? David?'

'Retired last year. Done his back in. Been troubling him for years but it finally got too much last spring.'

'And do you see him much?'

'Nah. He got himself one of those disabled cars, but he don't drive it much and we don't drive, me and Kath. Never did. Like she said – keep ourselves to ourselves.'

'I understand Andrew was in town when it happened. Sitting on a bench up by the Princesshay.' Pete's mind conjured an image of the wide, pedestrianised High Street with the glass and concrete entrance to the covered shopping centre off its east side. 'Did he do that much?'

'Every fortnight, when he had to go and sign on, he'd spend a few hours round the centre. Got him out of the house, change of scenery, bit of fresh air, you know?'

Pete nodded. *An isolated, lonely life, broken by sitting alone among the crowds on the High Street once a fortnight. Christ, talk about sad.*

His phone buzzed in his pocket and he took it out, checked the screen and saw the ID flashing up: *Doc.* 'Sorry,' he said to Michaels. 'I need to take this.' He hit the button and raised the phone to his ear. 'Hello, Doc. What's up?'

'I've just heard back from the lab,' Chambers said. 'We have the toxicology from Jeremy Tyler. I was right, unfortunately. He had been dosed. With suxamethonium, so he was paralysed but fully aware as the fire took hold around him.'

Chapter 4

'So, what did she have to say while you were on your own with her?' Pete asked as he pulled away from the kerb outside the Michaels' house.

The sun was low in the sky, hidden behind a mass of heavy black cloud, leaving it near-dark although it was still mid-afternoon. Pete switched his lights on. The beams swept across other parked cars, pavements fronted by stretches of mown grass and low, neat walls protecting tidy gardens in front of suburban houses where situations like this were not meant to arise.

'She loved her son, boss. Wouldn't have a word said against him, even hypothetically. My guess – she was the reason he was so withdrawn. Overprotective, you know? Smothering. But essentially, he kept himself to himself. Had interests that most guys grow out of at about twelve. Trains, planes – stuff like that. The only vaguely social thing he seemed to be involved in was the annual model train exhibition at the local school. Has quite a big following, apparently. Draws people in from all over. As far as the West Midlands. And she was right. There was no porn on his computer, or any sign of it in the history log.'

He drove past the school she had just mentioned – the school his own daughter, Annie, attended. The one Tommy had gone to as well until just over a year ago when he switched to the local senior school. Cars lined both sides of the road outside, parents sitting patiently waiting for their offspring to emerge. The bright railings and heavy metal gates made it look like some kind of junior prison. His mind conjured an image of ten-year-old Annie, sitting at her desk, sucking on the end of her pen as she avidly watched the teacher at the front of the class, absorbing every speck of information they could provide.

In a few minutes, the scene would change completely, the ring of a bell releasing a dark tide of noisy humanity onto the quiet streets like a swarm of angry bees.

'How's she doing, boss? Annie? She all right?'

Pete blinked. 'Yes, she's great. Don't know what I'd have done without her, the past few months, to be honest.'

'And Louise?'

Pete glanced across. Saw the genuine concern in her expression. Jane was more than a junior officer. She was a friend. They had been partners for three years before he got the sergeant's exam. He trusted her like no one else on the force – even their DI, Colin Underhill, who had been both a boss and a mentor through their early years in CID. 'She's . . . She seems to have turned a corner. The fact that Tommy was there with Rosie, that he's still alive . . . It's given her something to focus on. Some sort of hope. I wouldn't want to be Simon Phillips if she ran into him, but . . .'

Jane laughed. 'Not impressed, eh?'

'Not really. It's been almost seven months and the only real evidence he's got is what we gave him last week, from the Rosie Whitlock case. She's bad enough with me. Why could I bring Rosie back and not Tommy? Where is he? Why won't he come home? What are we doing to find him? Not that I can blame her. I just wish I had the answers for her. But, if she got hold of Simon, she'd have his balls for earrings.' He glanced in the mirror, but the school was gone from sight around a bend in the road.

Dave stared up at the castle-like gatehouse of the dark-brick Victorian prison with its huge arch-topped doors of incongruously bright blue.

'Bugger, that took a can or two of paint, didn't it?'

'Just don't say anything about cheap labour.' Pete knocked on the man-sized door cut into the big gates.

'Would I?'

The team had drawn a blank on their search for a source for the suxamethonium and on Tyler's internet history, so Pete had sought Silverstone's permission to talk to other people's arrestees and brought Dave along to lighten the load and speed the job up while the rest of the team continued to search for other clues.

The door in front of them opened and a black-uniformed prison guard asked, 'Sergeant Gayle?'

Pete nodded and flashed his badge. 'And DC Miles.'

Dave showed his own ID.

'Come in, gents.' He stood back.

'Yes, you would,' Pete said to Dave as they stepped through. 'But if you do, I won't try to stop them keeping you.'

The door behind them banged shut and a bolt shot across, then another. Despite himself, Pete shivered.

'This way, gents.' The guard stepped past them and led them across the wide, blue-brick yard.

They signed in at the reception desk in the main block and Pete was led to an interview room more usually used by inmates and their solicitors.

A table stood in the middle of the room – more of a cell but without the fittings – with a plastic chair at either side of it. In one of them sat the lean, scraggy-looking figure of one of the men who had been arrested in the major anti-drug operation that had brought Pete back to active service two weeks ago. His hands were manacled to a steel ring in the middle of the table, which was bolted to the floor.

'Afternoon, Stevie. How's it going?'

'How do you think?' Lockwood's lank blond hair had been cut short, but his attitude hadn't changed and he still managed to look scruffy, even in prison uniform.

'Well, it's not like it's your first visit here, is it? Should be used to it by now. Anyway, I thought I'd come and brighten your day a bit.'

'How's that?'

Pete sat down opposite the drug dealer. 'Might be able to put in a good word, get a bit shaved off your sentence if you can help me out with something.'

'I don't want to get a rep as a bloody snitch, mate. Not while I'm in here.'

Pete shook his head. 'Where's your public spirit, eh? I'm not even asking you to snitch on anyone. I just want a bit of info, that's all. About where I might come upon a certain substance, if I was inclined to.'

Lockwood gave a snort of laughter. 'What, you getting desperate? I hear you've had it a bit rough, lately.'

'I don't need drugs when I've got the likes of you I can go out and use as punchbags, Stevie. Marvellous release for frustration, that is. But, just for now, I need to know if there's somewhere in the city a person might get their hands on some sux.'

Lockwood's eyes widened as he sat back abruptly in his chair. 'What? I ain't into weird stuff like that.'

Pete sat forward in his chair. 'But you probably know who is. Am I right?'

Lockwood frowned. 'Why would I? I don't use the stuff and I don't deal in it.'

'Like-minded people know about each other, though. It's a fact of life. Doesn't matter if you're into drugs, kiddie porn or model railways, you get to know who else is. The club mentality.'

'Well, I ain't the club type. I'm strictly a loner, me.'

'Oh, well.' Pete shrugged. 'You can't help me, I can't help you. But the fact that I've been here, talking to you, what do you want to bet that'll stay secret in a place like this, that thrives on gossip? A guard mentions it to another guard, gets overheard by an inmate and soon the whole place knows.'

Lockwood started to look nervous. 'No, no, no. I'd be dead meat in a week.'

Pete shrugged, pushing his chair back. 'Nothing I can do about that.' He waved a hand vaguely at their surroundings. 'Not my jurisdiction.'

'Yeah, but . . . That's setting me up. That's murder, that is.'

Pete stood up. 'Nah. It's just life in prison, that's all. The way it goes.'

Lockwood peered up at him. 'You wouldn't . . .'

Pete chuckled, pushed his chair in under the table and headed for the door.

'All right, I might have a name I could suggest. But I'd need some sort of guarantee. These buggers don't piss about. They'd skin me alive, then kill me if they found out I'd talked. Or even suspected it.'

Pete paused, turned back. 'OK,' he said slowly. He caught Lockwood's gaze. Held it. The man looked genuinely nervous. 'What have you got?'

'What can you do for me, first?'

Pete grimaced. 'I can make sure you're safe, but the charges you're in for aren't going away, Stevie. They can't. It's not like this is your first time around, is it?'

Lockwood sat back in his chair. 'You can't make sure I'm safe in here. No chance.' He shook his head. 'I talk to you, I'm a dead man. We're done here. Guard!'

'Last chance, Stevie. You tell me or I tell that guard you have done.'

Lockwood's eyes shot wide. 'That'd be murder.'

The lock in the door rattled behind Pete as the key was inserted.

'No skin off my nose. Save the taxpayer thousands in keep.'

'You wouldn't. You're not the type.'

Pete smiled as the door swung open. 'Try me.' He turned to the guard. 'Mr Lockwood and I seem to be done here,' he said. 'Very helpful young man, our Stephen.' He stepped forward. 'In fact, you know, he might just have—'

'Gayle!' Lockwood almost shouted over him. 'All right, you win. Give us another minute, will you?'

The guard looked at Pete and raised an eyebrow. Pete shrugged and he backed out, closing the door behind him. Pete sat back down, hands flat on the table.

'You're an evil bastard, you know that?'

Pete waited silently.

'OK, there's a bloke I'd go to if I was asked for stuff like that. He might be able to get it. Only one I know that could. But you really do need to do something for me now. Another jail, another name, the works, or I'm dead. Understand?'

Pete inclined his head. 'Fair enough.'

'Fair? That's the last bloody thing this is. I'll be looking over my shoulder from now till I peg it. No matter what you do.'

'What we'll do, Stevie, is have the bugger if we can get sufficient evidence. Then he won't be able to come after you.'

Lockwood laughed. 'You're joking. Prison won't stop him, no matter which side of the bars he's on. Like the bloody Mafia, these blokes are, only worse. The Mafia would do what was needed and leave it at that. These buggers hurt people for the fun of it. They find the worst ways to kill you could imagine, then do it to your family first.'

'Except you haven't got any, Stephen.'

Lockwood grunted sourly. 'Yeah, lucky for them.'

'So, who is it you're so scared of, eh? Give me a name. Something to work with.'

'Petrosyan.'

'Petrosyan? What's that? Romanian or something?'

32

'They call him the Armenian.'

'Have you got a first name?'

'Gagik.'

'And where will I find him? Or, put it another way, where would *you* find him?'

'Dunno. He'd find me if I put the word about that I was looking for him. He's got ears everywhere.'

'OK. And he wasn't caught up in the arrests last week, when you were collared?'

'Not that I've heard. But he's the main man, isn't he? You wouldn't have got him.'

Pete smiled. 'But we will. I can promise you that.' He stood up. 'All right. Thanks, Stevie.'

'What, that's it? You're off? What about me? Come on, man. You made a promise.' Lockwood's voice was rising, his fear genuine.

Pete hammered on the door with his fist. 'Don't panic,' he said. 'It's bad for you.'

The lock rattled again and Pete stepped aside to allow the door to swing inward.

'What are you doing, you bastard?' Lockwood shouted.

Pete turned and winked at him, then stepped out. He waited until the door was locked firmly behind him, Lockwood yelling desperately on the other side of it, before turning to the guard. 'Keep him in there for now while I have a word with the governor.'

'Right you are, sir. This way.'

*

Pete scooted his chair around to Jane's side of the desks.

'Ben.'

Myers looked up and Pete nodded for him to come around and join the rest of the team on the other side of their desks. When they were all together in a tight bunch, Pete leaned forward, elbows on his knees. 'Dave, keep half an eye on the rest of them, will you? This is strictly between us for now.' He glanced around his team. He had their full and serious attention now.

'What is it?' Jane asked.

'Has anyone here heard of the Armenian?'

Blank looks and shaking heads gave Pete all the answer he needed.

'Gagik Petrosyan?'

More shaking heads.

'Who's he?'

'Good question. I've been talking to the bloke who gave us Ian Sanderson. He says that Petrosyan is known as the Armenian, and he's the likeliest source of the sux used to paralyse Jerry Tyler and possibly the insulin used on Andrew Michaels. Yet, not only was Petrosyan not arrested last week, no Armenians were.' His gaze went around the team again.

'None?' asked Dave.

Pete tilted his head. 'I checked with the prison governor.'

'And you believe Lockwood?' asked Jill.

'His fear of Petrosyan was genuine. He didn't want to tell me and, when he had, I let him sweat for a minute or two, to make sure. So, yes. I believe him.'

'These Eastern Europeans can be some vicious bastards,' Dave said. 'Armenians, Albanians, Romanians – the gangs up London and so on, they're into all sorts. People trafficking, prostitution, drugs, the lot. And you certainly don't mess with them, that's for sure.'

'Yeah, but for none of them to be arrested . . .' Jane's voice tailed off as the significance hit home. There was no need to put what she was thinking into words. Deliberately or otherwise, there had been a leak. Someone had fed the gang vital intel on an ongoing operation.

Pete nodded. 'Hence the need to keep this between us, at least for now. And I'm going to have to go to Silverstone with it. Meanwhile, all of you reach out. Tap up your CIs, see if you can get anything on these Armenians.' He slapped his knees and sat up straight. 'We might have had to hand the child-sex case off to London, but this one's all ours.'

'Shit or glory,' said Dave.

'Up to us to make sure it's glory, then. Right?'

Chapter 5

'Steve Patton here. Fire investigator. Sorry it's taken so long to get back to you, but I've been kind of busy.'

'Hello,' Pete replied. 'No problem. Thanks for calling. What have you got?'

'Nothing basically. The caller blocked his number.'

'Oh.' That sounded suspicious right off the bat.

'Yeah, so all I can tell you is, it was a youngish-sounding male.'

'Nothing distinctive in the background?'

'Nope.'

Pete grimaced. 'OK. You couldn't send me over a copy of the tape, could you?'

'I haven't got it – the call centre have. But I can get them to do it, yeah.'

'Great. Thanks, Steve.'

'You got something, boss?' Jane asked as he ended the call.

'Nothing useful, no. Just, whoever called in the fire at Tyler's didn't leave their details and blocked their number when they made the call.'

She shrugged. 'Maybe they just didn't want to get involved further than doing their civic duty.'

'Maybe.' But how many people would even think of blocking

their number for reasons like that? Not many. And the fact that it was a 'young-sounding male', made it seem even more suspicious.

Pete put his phone away and headed for the DCI's office.

*

'Again?' Silverstone put down his pen and sat back in his chair. 'What is it this time, Detective Sergeant?'

'I've got some bad news, sir.'

'Strangely, I'm not surprised. What is it?'

'Operation Natterjack, sir.' The DCI's pet project had been a huge force-wide synchronised series of raids designed to wipe a large proportion of the two counties' drug dealers and pushers off the streets in one go. It was the reason that Pete had been recalled two weeks early from compassionate leave, to provide cover here in the station while the raids were carried out.

'What about it?'

'There was a comprehensive and glaring omission from it, sir. I've been speaking to a CI I developed recently and to the governor of the city jail and it seems that there were no arrests at all among the Armenian community, yet there definitely should have been.'

'Explain.' Silverstone's dark eyes turned cold as he sat forward, hands clasped on his desk.

Pete quickly laid out the facts.

'And what does Jim have to say about this?'

DS Jim Hancock was the local drugs expert and the man who had originally arrested Steven Lockwood for possession with intent to supply Class A drugs.

'I haven't spoken to him, sir. In the circumstances, I thought it best to bring this straight to you, as someone who definitely doesn't have an axe to grind.'

Silverstone's eyes widened. 'You're suggesting that Jim Hancock might be . . .?'

'I'm not suggesting anything, sir. I'm eliminating the possibility.

I thought it best, in the circumstances. As I said, not only was the Armenian left out of the frame, so was his entire crew, or family or whatever they are.'

'So, you immediately suspect your colleague, a man you work with . . .'

'I don't suspect anyone, sir. Not without evidence. But there's only one man in this nick that we can be sure has no local connections that might have jeopardised any part of Operation Natterjack. And that's you. So, here I am.'

'Well, thank you for the vote of confidence, Sergeant. I think. But how would you suggest we proceed from this point?'

'Cautiously, sir. Cards close to the chest. My team weren't involved in the operation and we developed this conclusion between us, so they're under strict orders to tell no one else about it. For now, we're intelligence-gathering. Does the Armenian really exist? If so, what connections does he have? Where is he? We have a name for him, but is it real? Then, we go from there.'

'Very well. But, if this gets out, Sergeant . . .'

'I know.' *I'll have your full support – not.*

Silverstone shook his head. 'You don't know the half of it. You'll be a pariah. Your career as a police officer will be over.'

Pete drew a slow breath, fighting down his anger. What the hell had he expected? Silverstone didn't want his record tarnished, his rise through the ranks jeopardised or even delayed. 'I don't want it to be true any more than you do, sir. These are people I've worked with for years. Friends, some of them. But if it is true, then it needs dealing with. And, if I can be frank – from your point of view, it's better dealt with promptly than discovered later, after you've moved on, isn't it? I mean, if someone else came in after you and uncovered it, there'd inevitably be questions asked about why it wasn't dealt with sooner.'

He saw the change in Silverstone's expression and wondered if he had taken a step too far. 'Yes, Sergeant,' the DCI said with exaggerated calmness, his dark eyes glittering with barely suppressed anger. 'But be absolutely clear. If it's true, I want it weeded out, quietly and efficiently. If it's not, then woe betide the man or woman who lets it out. Even a hint of a suggestion of it.'

'Sir.'

'Find what's to be found, Sergeant, tell absolutely no one and bring it straight to me. Clear?'

'Yes, sir.'

*

Walking back into the squad room, Pete saw that Dick Feeney was back at his desk from his afternoon's mandatory training. The other three teams looked and sounded replete with returned bodies, too.

'Nice nap, Dickie?' he asked as he took his seat.

'Well, it comes but once a year. Be rude not to take the opportunity, wouldn't it?'

'Have this lot filled you in?'

'Yes. Bit of a dodgy wicket, isn't it?'

'You haven't heard the half of it, matey. Fast-track is not a happy camper. I thought he was pissed off this morning, but now I'm really off his Christmas card list. We're on our own on this. No one but us must even get a hint of a breath of a clue about it until we've reached a conclusion and taken it to him, in person. He doesn't want it screwing up his promotional prospects.'

Dick laughed. 'And there's the real rub, eh? Never mind any other implications.'

'Well, at least we know where we stand,' Jane said from opposite Pete.

'Yeah, on a cowpat in the middle of a slurry pit,' Dave agreed.

'Doc Chambers called while you were in there,' Jane said. 'He's been on to the coroner and got two exhumation orders for other potential victims. He'll keep us updated, he said.'

'Any news on the foreign fellow we were talking about earlier?'

'Nothing yet,' Dave said.

'Well, keep on it. If he's out there, we need to find him before he gets nervous and does a disappearing act. I'll be back in a minute.'

*

Although there was a staff canteen on the top floor of the station, a small storeroom opposite DCI Silverstone's office had been converted into a kitchenette. White cupboards and a cheap grey worktop held a microwave, toaster and fridge as well as a hot-water geyser above the sink. Pete got six mugs out of the cupboard and spooned in the makings of four coffees and two teas. Then he took out his phone and tapped the speed-dial for home.

It was picked up on the fourth ring. 'Hello?'

'Hi, Button. How was your day?'

'OK. You're going to be late, aren't you?'

Pete swirled the tea bag in the second cup until it looked the right colour. 'Afraid so, love. We've picked up a new case and it's a complicated one. We need to get the basics done before we call it a night. Fish and chips?'

'What time?'

'Half-seven at the latest.' He hooked out the tea bag and dropped it in the pedal-top bin.

'OK.'

'Sorry, Button. I know you miss me. But not as much as I miss you.'

'So you say.'

'What does that mean? Are you taking your mum's side now?'

Louise resented the fact that he'd gone back to work long before she was ready to do the same. It followed on, no doubt, from the arguments they'd been having for some time before their son went missing about the hours he put in, here at the station. He couldn't understand why, as a nurse, she couldn't – or wouldn't – grasp that his job was as much a vocation as hers, the main difference being that, when her shift ended, there was someone there to replace her whereas he didn't have that luxury.

'It means actions speak louder than words, Dad. It's one of the things I learned about at school today.'

'I'm going to have to have words with that teacher of yours.'

'She's right, though, isn't she?'

'Who – your mum?' Pete lifted milk from the fridge and started pouring it into the six mugs.

'No, silly. Miss Jennings.'

He sighed. 'Yes, Button. She is. At least, mostly. Me, I'm conflicted. It's a special case. I've got two places I need to be and I can't be in both at once. Anyway, I love you and I'll be home as soon as the wicked DCI lets us out, OK? How's your mum?'

He finished pouring the milk and put it away.

'She's OK. She's watching *Countdown*.'

Pete's lips pressed together. Louise had started to improve, recently, from the semi-catatonic state she'd inhabited for months after Tommy's disappearance. His showing up in the Rosie Whitlock abduction had helped, even if he did vanish again at the first opportunity. But the fact that he clearly wasn't coming home had knocked her back almost as soon as the fact that he was alive had spurred her on. 'OK, love. I'll see you later. Soon as I can, all right? Tell your mum for me. Love you.'

'Love you too, Dad.'

'Bye.' He ended the call, stirred the mugs and put them all on a tray to take back into the squad room for his team. They were going to need caffeine.

*

'Thanks, boss.'

Jane leaned across to take the last of the mugs from Pete. He stood the tray against the end of his desk and sat down.

'There's news,' she said quietly.

41

'What?' Pete looked up, frowning.

Her green eyes locked onto his with a rarely seen intensity. 'Tommy.'

Pete froze, tension crackling through him. 'What about him?'

'The enhanced CCTV's back from the Co-op where Burton claimed to have dropped Tommy off on the way back into town. Still nothing probative on the car, but the boy in the shop is definitely Tommy and he looks like he's been through the mill. I had a word with Alan Westbury. He also said that they've finally got hold of the assistant from that night. She said he bought plasters and bandages and stuff. Claimed he fell out of a tree. She had her doubts, but she didn't know him, so what could she do?'

Pete slumped back in his chair, feeling suddenly weak. His son was alive and out there somewhere, just beyond reach. The confirmation was a huge relief, but at the same time utterly depressing. The boy was hurt and alone, God knew where, and too scared to approach anyone. He looked up at Jane. 'Hold on. You spoke to Alan about this?'

Alan Westbury was one of Simon Phillips' DCs.

'Yes. Why not? I was following up on a legitimate lead. Burton's our case. He admitted dropping Tommy off there. And, according to Rosie, Tommy's a potential witness.'

'OK.' He nodded slowly. 'But don't push your luck on my account, all right? I don't want you getting into trouble.'

'Heard back from one of my CIs,' Dave said. 'He knows of an Armenian family that's not exactly squeaky clean. He doesn't know them, per se, just *of* them, but it might be a start. I'm going to see him later.'

'Nice one, Dave. Anyone else got anything?' He got no response, so checked his watch. 'OK. If I hurry, I might just catch one of my blokes. Don't stay up too late, kids. Long day tomorrow.' He grabbed his jacket and hurried out.

Traffic was already busy on the Heavitree Road when he stepped outside, but he took the car anyway. Working his way around the one-way system, he reached the city centre in about as long as it would have taken him to walk and turned down onto Fore Street. The high, narrow buildings hemmed the street in on either side, telephone lines criss-crossing between them like a scene from a 1970s San Francisco cop show. The shops on the ground floors were closing up, the bars and restaurants opening. Car roofs gleamed under the street lights. The pedestrians on the narrow pavements were thinning out and getting younger, practical dress giving way to decorative as the evening crowd took over.

Pete found a parking space on the steep hill and pulled in. He walked down past the end of the dark alley that led past a cinema to the scruffy, blue edifice of Mamma Stone's club. A couple of doors further on was the pool hall he was heading for.

The place was still fairly quiet, most of the guys around the tables. Just three stood at the bar, drinks in front of them. There was no sign of Darren Westley.

Back outside, he leaned on a lamp-post just beyond the side street, took out his phone and pretended to play with it. A bus went past, barely fitting between the cars parked down one side and the narrow pavement on the other. A group of girls in short, sparkly dresses stepped past him and turned down towards the cinema and the nightclub beyond.

Pete wondered how on earth they managed to avoid hypothermia with more skin exposed than covered in temperatures that were set to drop near to freezing in the next few hours. Then he saw the distinctive mop of ginger hair weaving through the crowd towards him. He pushed away from the lamp-post and put his phone away as he stepped past the girls and headed quickly down the hill.

He met Westley two doors beyond the pool hall. Put out an arm to wrap around the other man's shoulder and turn him smoothly to one side.

'Hello, Darren. Fancy meeting you here. Do you want to get

a drink somewhere?'

'That would screw my reputation, wouldn't it – being seen with you? What do you want?' Up close, Westley could be seen to be suffering. He looked ill. His always-pale skin was sallow and rough. There were dark rings under his blue eyes and his mop of hair hadn't been washed in a few days. His jeans looked stained, too, as did the T-shirt Pete could see under his brown denim jacket.

'Just a quick word. And I was thinking about somewhere you wouldn't be recognised. Somewhere nice, for example. Like that little place along Cathedral Passage. Plenty of noise, so you won't be overheard if you say something impolite.' Pete pulled him around, arm still around his shoulders, and headed back up the hill. 'Look on the bright side. You look like you could do with a little something. Booze is better than bugger all, right?'

'Yeah, well . . . That's down to your lot, innit – the bugger all.'

'What, the supply's dried up, has it?'

'Almost. And the price has nearly doubled.'

'Supply and demand. The beauty of capitalism. So, it has started up again, then?' Pete guided them across the road and up past the bus stop.

'Yeah, just two or three days ago. It was dead for a week or so before that.'

'So, who's out there now? Anyone I might know?'

Westley shot him a sour look.

'I'm not interested in shutting off your supply, Darren. I just need some information, that's all. And they're the likeliest source.'

'You'll be lucky. Bloody foreigners, ain't they? Barely speak the bloody language, never mind having a conversation with the likes of you.'

Pete turned him into the end of an alleyway that led through to Cathedral Square. 'You let me worry about that. All I need to know is where to find them.'

'I only know one,' Westley said dubiously. His sullen expression reminded Pete of his son, Tommy. The last few months before he disappeared, he'd often worn an expression just like that. Pete's gut twisted. If only he'd spent more time with the boy, taken him out, played with him, even just watched him doing his own thing – the swimming, for instance – maybe things would have been different. He wouldn't be gone. He wouldn't have got tangled up with Malcolm Burton. He'd be . . . at home. Happy. Safe.

They reached their destination and Pete stopped, held out a hand. 'Here we go.' He nodded at the door to the small bar near the far end of the alley.

Darren frowned at him. 'Seriously?'

Pete shrugged and held the door open, nodding for him to enter. One day, hopefully, he'd get to do the same for Tommy. If he could find him. If he could get him to come home.

When he found him, he corrected himself, as the noise hit them like a train. There was no *if* about it. There couldn't be. He was going to bring his son home. Somehow.

The cacophony of raised voices, all trying to be heard over each other, was almost solid, a physical force pushing them back as they as they pressed into the small, crowded room, heading for the bar along the right side.

Pete kept one hand on Westley's shoulder, letting him lead the way. There was no way they were getting through this lot side by side. At the bar, they squeezed in and he raised an eyebrow and jerked his head at the shelves behind.

Darren leaned in close to be heard. 'Vodka,' he shouted. 'Straight.'

Pete nodded and waited to catch the eye of one of the three young guys in black shirts and trousers behind the bar. Raising one hand to cup Darren's ear, he shouted into it. 'Don't worry. Like I said, I don't want to arrest the bloke. Just ask him some questions. He'll be back on the street in a couple of hours, tops.'

He caught the eye of the nearest barman and waved him over. 'Vodka and a Murphy's red,' he called.

Westley was still looking at him sceptically. He leaned close again. 'I need information and I'm pretty sure you can't give it to me,' Pete told him. 'Unless you've heard of somebody bumping off the undesirables of the city?'

'What?'

'Pimps, pushers, prostitutes. Druggies.'

'Getting killed? Are you . . .?'

'Serious? Yeah. And I'm looking for a lead on who's doing it. Your guy might know someone who's supplied them with certain items. That's what I'm after. A link in the chain.'

The barman put their drinks on the bar and Pete slapped a note down beside them. Nodded for the guy to keep the change, not that he guessed there would be much. Then he turned back to Darren, nodded to the drink and picked up his own.

Darren looked from Pete down to the shot glass and back again. Pete could see the decision being made in his eyes. 'OK.' He picked up the glass and downed the contents in one. Slapped it down on the bar. 'The Firkin Angel. Big bloke. Shaved head, chin like an anvil and a nose like a bloody toucan. Some colouring at the moment, too, especially round the eyes. Don't fancy meeting the bloke that did it to him. Must be some kind of bad bastard. Or dead.'

Chapter 6

Ten minutes later, Darren Westley was on his way back to the pool hall and Pete was enjoying the cool and the quiet of Cathedral Square, his phone to his ear.

'Dick?' he said. 'I need you and Ben down the Firkin Angel ASAP. A Zivan Millic hangs out there, who I need a word with. Apparently, he's big and he's hard but he's recently come up against someone harder. Anyway, I don't want him running off when I approach him, so I need the exits covered, OK?'

'You sure, boss? Sounds a bit dodgy.'

'It'll be fine. It's not like I'm going to arrest him, is it?'

'Yeah, but he don't know that, does he?'

'Just bring your truncheons and keep your eyes open and your reflexes sharp.'

'OK. Twenty minutes?'

'Don't be late.'

'You are going to wait for us, right?'

Pete imagined the frown that would be creasing Dick's brow as he asked the question. He laughed. 'Just get there as soon as you can, Gramps.'

'Will do.' Feeney broke the connection and Pete put his phone away and sauntered back through to Fore Street, turning downhill.

The Firkin Angel was on a side street just up from the bottom of the hill, where Fore Street met the inner ring road. Pete leaned on the wall of the old ruins opposite while he waited. There were fewer people coming and going at this end of the street but he concentrated on his smartphone, hoping to blend in. Using the time to look up Zivan Millic on the Police National Database, he quickly found a picture of the guy and his arrest record. It did not make pleasant reading, especially as he was about to confront him. At six foot five, he looked like something out of a horror movie and his record did nothing to assuage the impression. A Polish national, he had been arrested several times over the seven years since he arrived in the UK, on a number of charges including possession with intent, GBH, assault with a deadly weapon and carrying a concealed weapon. His tool of choice appeared to be a knife and Pete was acutely aware that he was not wearing a stab vest.

Still, if the opportunity to talk to the guy was going to present itself, he didn't want to waste it, then have him get wind that the police were looking for him and do a disappearing act. They didn't have time to play hide-and-seek with a possible secondary witness. They needed results – and fast.

Dick Feeney and Ben Myers arrived in a little over ten minutes. They were the opposite extremes of Pete's team – the Grey Man and the spike-haired boy. The oldest and the youngest, experienced and keen, dour and bright. When they pulled up in an unmarked Volvo, it appeared that Dick had been looking Millic up on the PND too. He was carrying a stab vest and an overcoat.

'You'll need these.'

'Thanks, Mum,' Pete said with a grin. But he accepted them. He strapped on the stab vest and slipped the oversized coat over it. 'So, Ben, I need you to go round the back. Dick, you cover the front here, in case he does a runner. I'm going to make it plain that I just want to talk to him, but you never know and we don't want to lose him.'

'Right, boss.'

'I'll give you a couple of minutes to get into position, Ben, then I'll go in. You've both got your radios on, right?'

'Yep,' said Dick. 'On and checked.'

'Right, off you go, Ben.'

Pete took out his own radio and keyed it to make sure it was working before transferring it to a pocket of the coat he was now wearing. 'OK. We're all set. I want this to go nice and smooth, if possible. No fuss, no trouble. But we'll have to see how Zivan reacts, won't we? He's not known for his subtlety.'

Dick lifted his collapsible baton from his pocket. 'It's a shame we're not allowed the old side-bar truncheons any more. But, if he comes my way, I'll be ready.'

'Remember, he's a possible witness, not a perp tonight.'

'Right, boss.'

Pete held his gaze for a moment.

'What?'

'You cause extra paperwork, you do it.'

'You want me to stop him, don't you?'

'Yes. But not at the expense of a hospital visit, if at all possible. All right?'

'Anybody would think I was slap-happy,' Feeney complained.

Their radios crackled and Ben's voice came through faintly. 'In position.'

Pete lifted his radio from his coat pocket and keyed the mike. 'OK. Stand by. Going in.' He returned the radio to his pocket and fisted his badge. 'See you in a bit.'

Pete ambled the thirty yards along to the pub. While he waited, he had seen several groups of people enter and only a few leave, but he was still surprised at how packed the place was. The noise hit him before he even opened the door, swelling out through the closed windows. The place was rammed. It was worse than the bar up by the cathedral. There was no music, just the sound of raised voices. He could barely push his way in. He eased between two young men with pint glasses in their hands who were chatting across the doorway and moved slowly through the crowd to the bar, barely able to hear himself think. How anyone could carry on a conversation in here, he had no idea – apart from yelling like a parade-ground sergeant major.

And he'd thought the other place was noisy!

Finally reaching the bar, he found that it was a Theakston's pub – rare, this far south. He managed to get the attention of one of the barmen and signalled for a half of Old Peculiar. Glass in hand, he turned to survey the heaving throng around him. Taller than most, it did not take long to see a still spot near the far end of the bar. Then the man at its centre straightened up.

'Damn, you are a big bugger, aren't you,' Pete muttered as the top half of Millic's head went from view between the dark beams of the ceiling. He took a swig of his drink – cool and smooth – and stepped away from the bar to make his way towards his target. After some careful navigation, he eased in beside the big man, who was now leaning his elbows on the bar, a pint glass two-thirds full in front of him, his ugly face set in a scowl.

'Zivan,' Pete yelled, slapping him on the back with one hand as he set his glass on the bar with the other. 'How you doing, buddy?'

Zivan turned to look at him from under large brows. 'I know you?' His voice was deep and heavily accented.

'No, but I've heard of you.' Pete eased in closer to the big man's right side – too close for him to be able to draw his knife – and surreptitiously showed him his badge. 'I'm not here to cause you any trouble. I'm told you might know a bloke I'm looking for – again, just for information on another party.'

Zivan's face had closed down at the sight of Pete's badge. 'Why the fuck should I help you?'

'Call it customer relations. The bloke I'm after is killing off your customer base. And that of the man I'm told you can point me towards. So I'm doing you a favour and you'd be doing him one.'

Pete could see the cogs turning in the big man's brain. It was

50

almost painful to watch, but he reached his conclusion in the end. He picked up his glass and drained it in one long swallow, then locked his dark eyes on Pete's. 'Fuck you, pig,' he said flatly and swung the empty glass at Pete's head. Pete ducked. The glass went over his shoulder. He heard it smash behind him and someone yelled out.

Pete stamped hard on Zivan's left foot, ducking his head in close to the bigger man's chest. Zivan howled, hunching over in pain, his chin coming down on the top of Pete's head. Pete pushed back against the tightly packed crowd to make room and swung his foot around to heel Zivan in the back of the leg, aiming to drop him to one knee, but he didn't have the space to make the move count. Zivan's huge hand clamped around his throat and lifted him bodily off the ground, slamming the top of his head against one of the dark-painted ceiling beams.

Pain lanced through Pete's skull, lights sparking in his vision. Then Zivan released him. His feet hit the floor, knees sagging under him as Zivan swung a punch. It caught Pete in the shoulder, knocking him back into the press of people behind him. Zivan turned, pushing through the press of people towards the back door as Pete shook his head, trying to clear it. Pete was pushed forcibly from behind. He saw Zivan wading through the crowd like a bear up to its chest in water, leaving a seething mass of angered patrons in his wake. There was no way Pete was going to get through there after him. He turned the other way. He lifted his radio from his pocket and keyed the mike, hoping the others could hear him over the noise. 'Ben, he's coming your way,' he yelled. 'Dick, go and help him.'

Pete wove his way as quickly as he could through the tightly packed patrons and out into the cool and the sudden, blissful quiet. But he didn't have time to pause and enjoy the contrast. He turned fast to the alley at the side of the pub and ran down it, hearing Dick's footsteps ahead of him. Rounding the far corner, he saw Feeney helping Ben Myers up off the ground. Ben looked up sheepishly.

'Sorry, boss. I nearly had him, but Christ! I've never come across a bloke as big as that. He legged it off up the alley, there.' He nodded towards the narrow path that led through the small residential area and up towards the churchyard.

Pete cursed inside, but waved the confession away. 'You OK?' he asked.

'Yeah, just . . . ego more than anything, I suppose.'

'OK. Too late to go after him now. I'll go back in and have a word with the landlord. Maybe he can help. You two get off home.'

'You sure?' Dick asked.

Pete nodded and Dick shrugged. 'OK. 'Night, boss.'

'Sorry,' Ben said again.

Pete pushed through the back door of the pub and went quickly up the short corridor past the toilets and the door to what he guessed was the upstairs accommodation. Back in the heaving bar, he eased his way through the tightly packed crowd. This time, he took more notice of the three men behind the bar. He quickly spotted the one he needed. He was older than the others by a good twenty years. Could probably give Pete ten, he guessed. His black T-shirt was stretched over a considerable beer gut, his thinning dark hair long and tied back in a ponytail.

Pete reached the bar right in front of him, pushing through between a guy in his mid-twenties, in a shirt and tie, and a young lad in denims. He slapped his fist down on the bar, wrapped around his police badge, and leaned in to shout. 'I need a word, mate. Now.'

The man's too-small eyes rose to meet Pete's. He shrugged, waving at the crowded room around them.

'Here or Heavitree Road?'

The man frowned sharply. 'Upstairs.' He turned towards the far end of the bar. Pete followed as best he could. As he eased through the tightly packed crowd, he thought, *I bet the Health and Safety bods would have a field day in here with access points and so on.*

The landlord waited for him near the rear door, then led the way wordlessly into the corridor and through the black-painted door marked 'Private'.

The narrow, uneven wooden stairs led up to a corridor with several doors, only one of which was open, right at the top of the stairs. Pete saw a kitchen with a small table in the middle. The fat man led the way in and pulled out a chair.

'So, what's this about?'

Pete sat across from him. 'Zivan Millic.'

The man frowned.

'Big bugger I chased out of here a few minutes ago. Looks like a cross between a Neanderthal and a brown bear.'

The man grunted. 'Didn't know his name. What about him?'

'I've got a witness telling me he deals drugs in here. Not that I'm interested in that, particularly. I'm also told he could tell me about a man I'm looking for as a witness in a murder case. Bloke known as the Armenian.'

The landlord went very still. His bulbous bottom lip disappeared briefly into his mouth and bounced back out again. 'Never heard of him. The other one, I see in here sometimes, but that's all.'

'I never suggested you had heard of him,' Pete said evenly. 'I just want to know how to find Millic. And don't tell me you only know him by sight. You wouldn't put your licence at risk for someone you don't know, even if he is as big as a bloody Portaloo.'

'Look, I'm just trying to stay out of trouble. These old places, they're like tinderboxes. I don't want no so-called accidents like the Dolphin last year.'

Pete remembered the old pub, up near the cathedral, which had been burned out in a massive fire one night, several months ago. 'What do you know about that?'

'Only what the landlord told me. Somebody like Millic – not him, somebody else – was dealing in there. He threw 'em out. Few nights later, up it goes. Coincidence? He don't think so, and nor do I. So, yes – I know what he's up to. And no, I haven't reported it.'

'Well, the only way to stop people like him is to help us put them away.'

'Yeah, right. There's no way you'd catch all of them. And as soon as they found out who shopped their mates, what do you think would happen?'

'Look, I told you. All I want Millic for, for now, is a link in a chain that could lead to a killer who might be one of their customers. How can that do any harm? You tell me what you know, I can go talk to him, job done.'

'Yeah, and where do you think he'll imagine you got the information, eh? After you just tried to take him in here?' The landlord shook his head. 'No way.'

'Well, where else does he go then? He's not in here every night, is he?'

'I've heard you can find him in the Blue Boar sometimes, up by the library.'

'OK then. Any idea which nights?'

'He's not usually in here on Saturdays or Mondays.'

'Right.' Pete stood up, clapped the man on the back. 'Thank you. Oh, by the way, do you get any coppers in here that you know of?'

'Eh?' He shook his head. 'That'd be a bloody good mix, wouldn't it?'

Pete shrugged. 'Stranger things have happened.'

'I suppose. But no, not that I'm aware of. Why?'

'If you did, I could ask them instead of you, couldn't I?' *And, more to the point, if there was a link between the Armenian and anyone on the force, it had to have started somewhere. Here was as good a place as any to start looking for it.*

*

Pete was struggling to eat his fish and chips. His mouth felt dry, the food curdling in his stomach. The TV was on at the far end of the room – some mindless rubbish, the volume turned down so that they could talk, though nothing was being said. Finally, the heavy silence was too much. He looked up from his plate. Annie was concentrating on her food, hoovering it up with relish. Louise's head was down. She had eaten some, but her heart was no more in it than his.

'I got some news about Tommy today,' he said.

Annie's head snapped up. 'Where is he? Is he OK?'

'I don't know where he is, love. What I do know is, he's alive. One of Simon's team spoke to a shop assistant who served him in the Co-op on the Dunsford Road. She said he bought plasters and bandages. Claimed he'd fallen out of a tree or something.'

'So, why hasn't he come home?'

'He must have been with Burton all that time. Maybe he thinks he'll be accused along with him.'

'But he won't, will he? He's only a kid himself. He couldn't do all those things they're saying were done to those girls.'

Pete frowned. 'What are they saying?' Annie was ten years old. He didn't want her introduced to the subject of sex at all yet, never mind in this way. She was a bright kid, of course. She was aware of what went on in the world, but he didn't want it brought to her doorstep, especially in this way. He wanted to leave it on the news – at a distance – for as long as possible.

'They're saying he killed two girls and raped that one you found. Rosie. But Tommy's only a kid. It's crazy.'

'Of course it is, love.' Pete was not going to tell her about the evidence they had to the contrary and he hoped that Louise would not mention it either. He glanced across at her. She had stopped eating and was watching him, a strange light in her eyes. They had had a massive row about the forensic evidence against Tommy when it came to light. 'But if Tommy was with Burton all that time – and Burton was a teacher, remember – there's no telling what he could have convinced him of.'

'So, you've got to un-convince him. Make him see that nobody believes he's guilty, so he can come home,' Annie insisted.

A swell of emotion swept over him, its intensity almost overpowering. He dropped his knife and fork, got up and stepped around the table. Taking Annie in his arms, he hugged her like he'd never let go. He felt her slender arms around his waist, smelled the shampoo in her hair as she laid her head against his chest. His grip tightened even further, eyes closing as emotion trembled in his chest. Then he felt her squirm in his grip. He opened his eyes. She was staring up at him. 'God, I love you,' he murmured.

Looking up at Louise, who was watching them now, he opened his arms and reached out to her, too. She hesitated.

Come on, he thought. *Don't just sit there. Please.*

Finally, she left her seat and joined them on the other side of Annie. He drew her in, one arm around her waist, and sighed deeply. 'I don't know what I'd do without the pair of you.'

Chapter 7

Pete switched off the engine and checked the dashboard clock: 6.28 a.m. It was still fully dark, the street lights casting a yellow glow over the houses and parked cars on either side of the steep road. All was quiet. Peaceful.

He felt emotionally drained after last night. He didn't know why. Was he not as ready as he'd thought to come back to work? The intensity of the Rosie Whitlock case had been difficult to deal with on top of everything else. And now this one, just days later . . . It was a lot to handle with the lack of anything concrete on Tommy's situation, the difficulties that Louise was still facing and the guilt he couldn't help feeling over how much he had come to rely on Annie over the past few months and especially since he'd come back to work.

Much as he knew that the police shrink at Middlemoor was going to try to find one, he was aware there was no easy answer.

He shook his head.

Two cars up, on the far side, its nose pointing downhill, he could see Jane's little green Vauxhall. Pete climbed out of his car and pressed the remote as he crossed the road towards Jane's Corsa. The remote locking system clunked behind him.

Dave had called him at home last night, interrupting a

discussion of exactly how they could let Tommy know that it was safe for him to come home, to say that he'd found out where Petrosyan was currently living.

The address he'd got was a few doors along from the next junction up the hill.

Jane's window buzzed down as Pete approached. 'Morning, boss.'

'Any sign of Dave?'

Further down the hill, a car turned a corner towards them, headlights bright and dazzling in the crisp, frosty morning.

'Not yet. Maybe this is him.'

Pete went around the little car and climbed into the passenger seat. Jane left the window down as the other car approached slowly up the hill, eventually resolving into a silver Ford Mondeo just like the one Pete was driving. As it drew level with them, its window slid down and it stopped.

'Morning all,' Dave said brightly from the passenger seat, beyond Dick Feeney. 'What's the plan then? No dark alleys round here, are there?'

'If there are, they're all yours,' Pete told him. 'Meantime, you two take the next street across. Park where you can, facing down-hill like Jane has. I'll go up onto his street and keep an eye on his doorway. When he comes out, I'll let you know, then we'll leapfrog him with the three cars so that one of us has got him in sight all the time. If he's as paranoid as they reckon, that should save him spotting us until he gets where he's going and we can take him there.'

'Sounds like a plan.'

'Right, let's get into position.'

Pete climbed out of Jane's car and crossed back to his own while Dick drove on up the street, turning right at the junction. As they went from sight, he started his engine and followed them up the hill. Their target lived three doors along to the right. Pete turned left, found a space a few cars along and backed into it, lining his side mirror up along the pavement. Then he switched off the engine and settled in to wait.

With two of the car's side-windows wound slightly down to avoid misting up, it did not take long for the inside of the car to get as bitterly cold as the outside. Pete was glad of the heavy police-issue coat he was wearing. His hands were clad in thick gloves, but still the cold seeped into him as he sat there, waiting for Petrosyan to emerge, not even certain that he would.

He remembered Annie, the previous morning, running from the car to meet her friends, bundled up in a thick coat, black gloves and a black wool hat with a pale, furry bobble on top, winter tights under a skirt that, even at ten years old, she was starting to wear too damn short for his liking. But at least she was warm.

He grunted. At this moment, she'd still be tucked up in bed, fast asleep.

What about her brother?

Where was he, and what was he doing? What was he wearing on this icy morning? Was he indoors somewhere? *God, I hope so*, Pete thought. The idea of him hunched, shivering, in some freezing corner of the city, probably with no winter coat, never mind a hat or gloves or enough to eat, no shelter except perhaps from the rain – *And thank God it's not doing that* – made his stomach twist and his teeth clamp together in anguish.

Wherever the boy was, Pete hoped he was at least warm enough. Cold like this could kill a person, especially if they were under-nourished and vulnerable. He sucked air in through a throat clogged by emotion.

He shook his head, refusing to allow the thought to go any further. *Come on, Pete. Focus.* But there was still no activity to be seen in his side mirror. The street was quiet and still.

He caught a flicker of movement, but it was just a dark cat jumping up onto the wall of the house beyond where the Armenian – if he even was one – was living. As he watched, it jumped down onto the footpath and disappeared under a car.

Pete was briefly tempted to switch his gaze to the other mirror, to see it emerge on the road, but resisted. He had to stay alert. This whole operation depended on his spotting Petrosyan as soon as he came out.

He waited a while longer, then checked his watch again. Almost seven. He shivered. Maybe he should start the car and close the windows, just for five minutes, warm himself up a bit . . .

It was incredibly tempting. But, if Petrosyan came out, heard the engine running and saw no one . . . People around here wouldn't leave a car running unattended to defrost the windscreen. It was dodgy enough where Pete lived but here, on the rougher side of the river . . . No way.

He rubbed his gloved hands together briskly and wriggled his shoulders inside his coat.

Movement.

He stared at the side mirror. A door swung open. A man stepped out, breath pluming, closed the door behind him and headed for the pavement. Stocky and bald, his head gleaming under the street lights. His distinctive, thick leather jacket matched the description Dave had provided to a T.

Petrosyan.

He lifted his radio. 'Heads up, people. Engines off. Our man's on the move.'

The target started towards him along the narrow pavement.

'Coming this way,' Pete said quietly into the radio. 'Jane, be alert. Dave, come on round. Gently does it. No rush.' He paused, waiting. Watching from low in the seat, hidden by the headrest.

Petrosyan turned at the junction.

'Jane, target approaching you.'

'Got him, boss.'

'Dave, you're up.'

'Roger that.'

The man in the leather jacket had now gone from Pete's view. He knew that Jane would have eyes on him until he turned another corner or, if not, for a good two hundred yards, so there was no rush for Dave to take up the pursuit.

Behind him, headlights showed, coming up around the junction beyond the target house as Dick Feeney drove slowly up into view.

'Steady, Dick. Jane's got him for a minute or two unless she says different.'

'He's in sight,' she confirmed. Then, 'Hang on. He's gone behind a van.' A pause. 'There. He's crossing over. Continuing down the street.'

They waited.

Then the radio hissed again. 'He's turned. Right, right, right. Gone from view.'

'OK, Dick. Drive straight down the hill. Try to spot him on the way past the road he's turned into, but don't slow down. I'll go down the next one along and come in from the far end so he can't suspect anything.'

'Affirmative.'

Pete saw the headlights of Feeney's car moving towards him in his mirror as he switched on the ignition. 'Which cross-street, Jane?'

'Third one down from here. That's the third one.'

'Roger that.' He pulled out as Dick turned down towards Jane's position, heading further along the road to take the next left. He was approaching the second cross-street down the hill when the radio crackled again.

'Target sighted,' said Dave. 'Right side of the street, still walking.'

Pete relaxed slightly. As he'd suspected, the Armenian was heading for the small group of shops along there. A newsagent's cum post office, a fish and chip shop and a small independent pet shop were set back slightly from the 1950s houses to either side so that three or four cars could park in front of them.

'OK, Dick,' he said into the radio. 'Turn around where you can. He'll be going to the newsagent's. Jane, you can come on down, too.'

He made the turn and spotted Petrosyan walking towards him, about a hundred and fifty yards away. Like the other streets around here, the houses had no drives or garages. It was parallel parking on the street, wherever you could find a space. Pete spotted one and stopped to reverse into it. Ahead of him, Petrosyan turned into the newsagent's, as expected. Pete keyed the radio mike again. 'Heads up. He's in the shop. Move in, move in.'

He finished parking and switched off the engine as two cars turned into the junction ahead of him, one from the left, one from the right. Taking the radio with him, he stepped out of the car.

'Jane, leave your car back a bit. Dick, come in and stop outside the shops,' he ordered, then tucked the radio into his pocket as he headed in on foot. He was just turning into the narrow forecourt of the shops when the door of the newsagent's opened, bell tinkling, and the Armenian stepped out, a newspaper folded under his arm, hands deep in the pockets of his leather jacket.

'Morning,' Pete said with a nod.

Petrosyan glanced at him. His small eyes narrowed.

A car pulled up to Pete's right. 'Good thing I bumped into you, Gagik,' he said. 'I need a word.'

Petrosyan's frown turned instantly to a snarl. 'You're a cop.'

Pete held his calm expression. 'I am, but you're not under arrest.' He heard the door of the car to his right open and close. Jane's footsteps were echoing along the pavement behind Petrosyan. 'Somebody in Exeter is going around killing people. His latest victim, he used what I'm told is very likely your product in the process, so you might be able to help me identify him.'

'Why should I help you?'

'I've got two officers to your right and another one behind you.'

Despite himself, Petrosyan glanced over his shoulder.

'If we wanted you in custody, you would be by now,' Pete went on. 'We just need to talk. The guy we're after is busy reducing your alleged customer base as we speak, so it would be good for business for you to help us.'

'What business?'

'We know exactly what business you're in, Gagik. But, like I said, we don't care. Not this morning. All we need is to find out who's been buying suxamethonium recently.'

Petrosyan stepped in close to Pete. Although he was a good five inches shorter, his bulk and his attitude were enough to intimidate most people and he relied on them now as he tried to stare Pete out. 'Why would I tell you, even if I knew? What would it do to my reputation if I did that?'

'Depends if anyone knew about it, doesn't it?' Pete said, unfazed. 'The way I see it, we've got two choices here. You talk to me or I put out an appeal to the public for information on whoever might have supplied our man with the sux he used on his latest victim. What do you think he's going to do then, eh? If I were him, I'd be coming after the supplier straight away. One, to shut him up and, two, because he fits the profile of the victims we're looking at. So, two for the price of one.'

Petrosyan's thick lip curled. 'You think I'm scared of some college punk? I could have him for dinner and spit out the bones.'

'Oh, I doubt you're scared much of anybody, Gagik. But, looking at his previous victims, I think maybe you should be. He's clever as well as vicious. The last one, he burned alive. That's what the sux was for. To keep him conscious while he burned.'

The sneer had died on Petrosyan's face. Now it twitched in what could have been disgust. 'I don't know who this guy is that you're talking about.'

'But you know he's a college punk.'

'Aren't they all?'

Pete shook his head slowly. 'Not serial killers like this one.'

Petrosyan grunted.

'So, what do you know, if not his name?'

'What, you think I'm some sort of street dealer? I don't know him. I never seen him.'

'But you know who does know him, who has seen him.'

'You want me to give you a dealer?'

'We both know they're ten a penny. You'd just replace him with another. Allegedly.'

'I am not the man you think I am,' Petrosyan said stubbornly.

'OK. I'll just go back to the station and get onto that press release then. Let our killer help us clean up the streets a bit more before we take him off them. Have a good day, Mr Petrosyan.' He saw the doubt flash in the Armenian's eyes as he nodded to the others to back off, let him go. But Petrosyan had face to save. Scowling, he walked doggedly away.

Pete and his crew came together on the narrow forecourt behind the retreating figure.

'He knows,' Dave said.

'Of course he does,' Pete agreed. 'But he can't be seen to back down to us, can he? His reputation could get ruined. And then his hold on his organisation would be gone.'

'You reckon we'll hear from him, though?' asked Jane.

'One way or another. Might be worth getting a tap on his phone, though.'

'With the protection he's got?' Dave snorted. 'Fat chance.'

'So, we're just going to leave him out here as bait?' asked Dick.

'Why? You feeling sorry for him?' Dave countered.

'No, but it does seem a bit . . .'

The low sun flashed on Jane's ginger hair as she swept it back with one hand. 'Harsh? Unethical? What do you think about what he does for a living, then? Pushing poison to our kids.'

'I know, but . . . They have a choice, whether to get into it or not.'

'So did he. And he had a choice of whether to talk to us or not,' Pete said firmly.

Chapter 8

Pete waited until they were all back in their cars, then took out his mobile and dialled.

'Jane. We might not be able to put a tap on his phone, but I want surveillance on that bloke, from now on. I want to know who visits him or where he goes if he leaves the house. Get hold of Jill and Sophie Clewes. I'll clear it with the uniform squad. And don't let either of them tell anyone what they're up to.'

'You seriously think he's got a source on the force?'

'He's still walking the streets, isn't he? I don't know what he's got, but I'm not prepared to risk losing him at this stage, so, bearing in mind his paranoia, be careful setting this up, right?'

'Right, boss.'

He ended the call and dialled the station. 'Bill, who's the duty sergeant today?'

'Andy Fairweather.'

'Patch me through to him, would you?'

'OK.' There was a click, a pause, then a dialling tone. A phone was picked up. 'Sergeant Fairweather, Exeter Police.'

'Andy. Pete Gayle. Sorry for the short notice, mate, but I need to borrow Constable Clewes again.'

'How long for?'

'Not sure yet. Probably just today. Assistance with a surveillance op.'

'All right. I'll adjust the rota and get hold of her. Where should I send her?'

'That's OK. My DC will give her a call.'

'Fair enough.' Fairweather didn't sound too happy at being kept out of whatever was going on, but Pete couldn't afford to be oversensitive now.

'Thanks, Andy. I owe you one.'

'Another one.'

Pete nodded. 'Yeah, I know. I'll return the favour one day, if only by sending Fast-track on his way to an early grave with stress.'

'You won't stress that bugger. Cast iron, he's made of.'

'Damn brittle, that stuff, though.'

Andy laughed. 'Good luck then.'

'See you.'

Pete started his car and headed back to the station.

He pulled into the car park just moments behind Dick Feeney and Dave Miles. They were heading for the back door as he stepped out of his car. 'Oi,' he called.

Both men turned and Pete beckoned them across with a tilt of his head. They gathered beside Pete's car.

'Before we go inside,' he said, 'you realise that what we've done this morning could flush out Petrosyan's contact here?'

'Yeah,' Dave said. 'Or it could just make him run like a scared rabbit.'

'Jane's setting up covert observation on Petrosyan. Nobody outside of us and those directly involved is to know about it. I just told Andy Fairweather I needed someone for a surveillance op.'

'OK.' Dave nodded.

'I don't like this,' said Dick. 'Looking into our own oppos. It feels wrong.'

'If you're not comfortable with it, Dick . . .'

Feeney grimaced. 'It just seems creepy, that's all – that one of the guys is . . . well, bent.'

'It is,' Dave said. 'But there's no point having a force that can't be trusted. Unless you're Robert Mugabe or Bashar al-Assad, I suppose.'

Dick grunted. 'Which Fast-track isn't, is he?'

Dave laughed. 'I reckon he'd like to be though. Only way he's going to get the respect he thinks he deserves.'

'Also while we're out here,' Pete said, bringing the conversation back on track, 'I want someone in the Blue Boar tonight, to see if Millic turns up there. If so, I want him followed. I want an address for him. But there's a lot else to do before that. We've got a killer to catch.'

*

Pete draped his jacket over the back of his chair, sat down and switched on his computer. As he reached for the mouse, his phone beeped. He checked the screen. One missed call. Recognising the number, he called back.

'Morning, Doc. You rang?'

'I did. I have two exhumed bodies on the tables in the mortuary. And I think you ought to get here as soon as you can, Peter.'

Pete felt something swoop in his chest. 'Any particular reason, Doc?'

'Initial examinations suggest that our theory is probably correct.'

'Ooh. OK, I'm on my way.' He ended the call, switched off his computer and stood up again. 'Going to the mortuary. The doc's got something to show me.'

'Careful, boss. Statements like that are what rumours get started on.'

'Well, you concentrate on the other rumour we were talking about earlier and see if you can come up with something useful.' He hooked his jacket off his chair and headed for the door.

Doc Chambers looked up from the steel cart he was working at, the overhead lights glittering on his short stubble of grey hair. He set down the large forceps he was using and stepped forward, stripping off his gloves to shake hands.

'Peter. Good to see you.'

'How's it going?'

Two of the four steel autopsy tables were occupied. The bodies had been cleaned and laid out ready for examination. The pathologist had been in the process of laying out his tools to begin the first of them.

'Interestingly,' he said. 'Basically, we were right. We have a serial killer in our midst, here in Exeter.'

Pete grimaced. 'Show me.'

Chambers extended a hand to the body on his left. 'First, we have the remains of one Donald Tennyson. He was found two months ago. Cause of death was recorded as acute cardiac failure – which, ultimately, is what kills us all, of course – with no clear cause. He had no record of cardiac issues, despite his obvious size, and shows no needle marks, unlike our previous victims. There are a couple of ways that can be achieved nefariously. One of them can still be tested for at this stage. The other can't, I'm afraid, though it is recorded that he had a substantial amount of clear, colourless, non-alcoholic liquid in his digestive tract. He'd taken a large drink, possibly of water, though we'll never know now. I'll take samples in due course.

'The other case . . .' He nodded at the body on the second table. 'A female, twenty-two to twenty-five years of age, identity unknown. Her body shows all the signs of addiction to Class A drugs and the kind of lifestyle often associated with that. In short, she was a prostitute. Tests showed that she was not high when she died. In fact, there were only traces remaining in her system. She was trying to kick the habit. Physical findings are intriguing though. Faint, generalised bruising was noted around her abdomen along with a red mark across her shoulders.'

He crossed towards the body, which was greyish and emaciated by the early signs of decomposition, took a pair of disposable gloves from a box on the side and pulled them on.

'She was found just over a month ago, down on the Marsh Barton industrial estate. Cause of death was recorded as exposure. You can see the bruising around her stomach – probably more clearly than you would have when she was brought in. One of the advantages of a delayed examination.'

Pete looked down at her. No matter what condition a body was in, he always thought of it as a person, not a corpse. A person who was not conscious, but, nevertheless, a human being. A victim. Someone who had had a life, hopes, dreams and all the rest. Someone who needed him to speak for them, and whose friends and loved ones needed him to find justice for the wrong that had been done to them. And it seemed like this girl had suffered several wrongs in her short life, only the last of which had left her lying on this steel table today, her death unexplained, her killer still out there on the streets, walking free.

A diffuse discolouration showed across her stomach and around to her flanks. It started around four inches below her breasts and ended a couple of inches below her belly button. 'That's bruising?'

Chambers nodded. 'Perimortem. Hence the delay in its visibility.' He placed her hand onto her stomach and half turned her over. 'You can see the welts on her shoulders. They're a lot more obvious now than they would have been at autopsy.'

Pete peered more closely. 'Yes. Three of them?' The lines were very narrow and seemed to be evenly spaced across her back. He glanced up at Chambers, who was watching him. 'Vertical. What could have caused them?'

Chambers let the body rest down onto its back again. 'They're pressure marks. Again, perimortem. As if she was pressed or bound against something rigid, made up of very thin uprights. A grille of some sort, perhaps.' He shrugged. 'The other findings were interesting, in the same context, too. There are scrape marks on her upper arms. You can see here.' He extended the near arm out from the body, all traces of stiffness long since gone from the corpse. Reddened graze marks showed faintly on the skin around the arm, a short way down from the shoulder. Chambers laid the arm back down.

'Also, when she was found, her hair was wet, which was put down, at the time, to the hard frost that we'd had that night and its thaw between her death and her recovery by my colleague. You remember we had several frosts in a row in mid-October. Her clothes were also wet, but, interestingly, they appeared to be wet from the *inside*. Her pants were very wet, although she hadn't been incontinent. Her outer clothes, such as they were, were also damp. The impression was of someone who had died in the sweats of a drug overdose but, as I said, she was practically clean. In fact, it was noted that the body was very clean, though the clothes were less so. And you can see for yourself, the clothes show no sign of the sweat-salt deposits that would be associated with that scenario.' He pointed to the meagre outfit that was laid out on the table beside the body. A short denim skirt, a black vest top, thong briefs and a pair of long, cheap-looking boots.

Pete noted the absence of a bra and guessed it had been deliberate. As a working girl on a chilly night, she would have wanted to use her assets to their maximum effect. He glanced at her face. Although emaciated by death, he could tell that she had been a pretty girl. The bone structure beneath the papery skin was well proportioned and delicate.

He looked up at the pathologist. 'So, you're saying that she was out on a cold night, in not a lot of clothes, and got doused with water, so she died of exposure?'

'Dousing, as such, wouldn't do it. She would have had to be kept wet for some time. And the evidence from her clothes suggests that she was naked at the time and re-dressed afterwards.'

'So, restrained somewhere, naked and wet until she collapsed with the cold, then re-dressed and left for dead.'

Chambers nodded. 'That's about the size of it. Somewhere with a hosepipe, so she could be kept constantly wet for at least an hour, perhaps more.'

'Jesus!' Pete shivered as an image of the poor, tortured girl flashed into his mind.

'I don't think he'd have ever experienced the kind of cold this poor girl did. I looked back at the records. It was minus nine that night.'

'This is a sick bastard we're dealing with here.'

'Indeed. I'll get started on Mr Tennyson. Take samples for laboratory analysis and see if there's anything else in evidence with the passage of time.'

'Right. You want me to stay or shall I go and start trying to find who did this?'

'Go ahead, Peter. I'll let you know if I find anything useful.'

Pete nodded and left the big, brightly lit room, the mental image of the tortured young woman still playing in his mind.

*

'So, did he have anything for us?' Dave asked, as Pete draped his jacket over the back of his chair.

Pete looked across. Dave had paused, hands over the keyboard, in the middle of typing something into his computer. 'One more confirmed victim, another probable but waiting on lab tests.'

Dave grimaced, sucking in air through his teeth. 'Fast-track's not going to be happy.' He glanced at Pete's empty hands. 'No files yet?'

'Give him a chance. Meantime, I want to know who attended Marsh Barton on the night of the fourteenth to the fifteenth of October, to the death of a roughly twenty-five-year-old woman, unknown identity, prostitute and former drug addict, who died of exposure.'

'I remember that,' said Dick. 'There was no sign of foul play, so it wasn't investigated.'

Pete turned towards him. 'There was foul play all right. The signs just weren't visible at the time. We're dealing with a very vicious and very clever killer here.'

'Detective Sergeant Gayle.'

Pete turned to see Detective Chief Inspector Adam Silverstone standing in the doorway, a stern expression on his face – not that that was anything unusual.

'Guv'nor.'

'My office, if you please. Now.' He turned and left the room.

Pete glanced at Dave Miles and shrugged, then went after the DCI.

Silverstone was already seated behind his desk when Pete entered his neatly turned-out office and closed the door behind him. He looked up, hands steepled in front of him.

'I've received a complaint, Detective Sergeant. A very serious one. Harassment. Threatening behaviour. Dereliction of your duty of care. Public endangerment. What the devil's going on?'

'Who did you receive the complaint from, sir?'

'What the hell does that have to do with it? I will not have my officers going around, sullying the name of this force. Is that clear?'

'It has everything to do with it. I was making a calculated move towards maintaining the reputation of this force. The point was to find out where any complaint might come from, so that it could potentially identify the source of the leak you asked me to trace.'

'I asked you to identify it. I didn't ask you to go at it like a bull in a china shop. I expected some subtlety.'

'An opportunity arose to kill two birds with one stone, sir. My conversation with the subject of your complaint was also relevant to the murder of Jeremy Tyler.'

Silverstone's hands slapped down on his desk. 'How, for God's sake?'

'He was, directly or otherwise, the probable source of the drug used to incapacitate Mr Tyler while he was burned alive, sir. I judged that, in those circumstances, a little loss of subtlety was justified.'

Silverstone's eyes narrowed as he stared intently at Pete. 'Do not presume to lecture me, Sergeant,' he said. 'Not if you want to keep your job.'

Pete held his gaze, letting the silence stretch for a slow count of four. 'You haven't answered the question, sir. Who did the complaint come from?'

Lips tightening to a thin line, Silverstone sat back in his chair. 'It came from Charles Savage of Bartholomew and Savage solicitors.'

Pete grimaced. 'That's a shame. Still, we've got the subject under surveillance. He could still lead us to someone relevant.'

'You've set up a surveillance operation? And when were you going to inform me of that?'

'In my regular report, sir. Along with the fact that Doc Chambers has confirmed a third victim of Mr Tyler's killer and is waiting on tests to make sure of a fourth.'

The phone rang abruptly on Silverstone's desk, interrupting what he was about to say. He snatched it up. 'Yes?' Listening for a moment, he looked up at Pete. 'Your DC requires your presence,' he said stiffly. 'Another victim has been identified.'

Chapter 9

'The second of the two bodies Doc Chambers dug up this morning has been confirmed as a murder,' Dave reported. 'Digoxin. Heart drug produced from foxgloves. Easy enough to do, he said, and deadly to someone who doesn't need it. Traces in the gut of the victim and in his blood. Looks like he was fed the stuff.'

'It's official then. We've got a serial killer. Dick, look into the background of this new victim, Donald Tennyson. We need to know if there's any possible link between him and Jerry Tyler or the girl, however slight. Our doer encountered all four somehow. Ben, see what a last-known address search gives us on Millic. The sooner we can speak to him, the better. Dave, on the other matter in hand, can you do financial checks on the likely parties? See if anyone's spending more than they ought to. Or saving it somewhere careless.'

Dave's glance slid past Pete, towards the other teams. 'OK.'

'Right, let's try to get this done before anyone else loses their life, shall we?' Pete sat down and picked up the phone. He dialled an internal number. It rang for several seconds before being picked up.

'Andy? Me again. You got a few minutes?'

'Yeah, what's up?'

'I need your duty roster for the night of October fourteenth to fifteenth.'

'No problem. I'll look it out for you.'

'Great. Be down in a minute.'

Andy Fairweather was a big, bulky man. Even sitting down, he filled the space he occupied. His eyes widened when he looked up from the paperwork on his too-small desk to see Pete stepping into his office on the ground floor just moments later.

'Blimey. You're in a hurry.'

'No announcement yet, but we've got a serial killer to track down before he does it again.'

'Ah.' Andy nodded towards the file-stacked worktop along the side of the little room. 'On the printer,' he said. 'Quicker than looking for the paper copy.'

Pete stepped across and took the single sheet of paper from the top of the printer. 'Thanks.'

'What are you looking for?'

'A young woman reported dead of exposure, down on the Marsh Barton estate.'

Andy nodded. 'Yeah. Prostitute, wasn't she? Can't say I was surprised, given how little they wear out there in all temperatures.'

'So, who attended?'

'Here, let me see.' Andy held a meaty hand out for the sheet Pete was holding. He handed it over and the uniformed man glanced down at it. 'Nicky French, I think. Hold on, I'll have a look at the dailies.'

He tapped something into his computer, scrolled down, then looked up at Pete. 'Yep. Here it is.'

Pete made to step around the desk, but Andy stopped him. 'It's all right. I'll print it out for you.'

'Thanks. So, where's Nicky today?'

'At home. Night shifts again this week.'

Pete sucked air through his teeth. He was well aware of how that went. And how popular he'd be if he disturbed the officer in question. Still, needs must. 'Sorry, but I'm going to need to talk to her, soon as.'

Andy grimaced.

'I know. But we need to solve this sooner rather than later and she might have something we could use.'

'If so, I'd have thought she'd have put it in her report. Thorough sort, our Nicky.'

Pete shrugged. 'Yeah, but you know how it goes. The right questions can pull out information that wasn't thought important or relevant at the time.'

'OK.' Andy was already tapping at his keyboard. 'Here's her number and address.' He hit the enter key and the printer clattered and whirred.

Pete stepped across, took the sheet as it came out of the top of the printer. 'Thanks, Andy. I won't take any more of her time than I need to.' He waved the papers in a quick salute and headed for the stairs.

Back at his desk, he sat down and was reaching for the power switch on his computer, preparing to read PC French's report when Dave said, 'The two reports from Doc Chambers came in. On your desk.' He nodded at the two manila folders on the corner of Pete's desk.

'Thanks.' Pete called up the database and entered the details for the body on the Marsh Barton industrial estate. It popped up almost immediately and he read quickly through it. Efficiently worded with none of the stilted, extraneous language that featured in most police reports, it told him nothing that he didn't already know.

OK. Time to put some flesh on the bones. He picked up the phone and, referring to the sheet on the desk in front of him, dialled the number.

'Hello?' A female voice, hoarse with sleep, answered on the fourth ring.

'PC French? This is DS Pete Gayle at Heavitree Road. Sorry

to wake you, but it's a matter of some urgency.'

'Sarge?'

He heard the rustle of sheets in the background as she sat up in bed.

'Fifteenth of October this year, you were on nights. A body was found on the Marsh Barton industrial estate. You attended.'

'That's right.'

'I've just read your report and I hoped you might be able to add a few details in light of the fact that we now know the victim was murdered.'

'Murdered?' That had woken her up. 'But . . . It was an accidental death, wasn't it? Exposure.'

'Exposure, yes. Accidental, not so much. Turns out, she was tortured and left to die, probably there or close by.'

'Oh, shit,' she moaned.

'So, I'm afraid we need your detailed observations of the scene. Anything you might have noticed that you didn't put in the report.'

'I put everything relevant in the report.'

'I'm sure you did. But what we see as relevant depends on what we think has happened, doesn't it? You thought it was accidental. Things that you might have seen and considered irrelevant might now be more than relevant. And might point us towards a killer who, so far, has claimed at least four victims that we know of. Now, I've already spoken to Sergeant Fairweather. He understands the urgency of this.'

'OK. I'll be there in . . .' She paused. 'Half an hour.'

'See you then.' He put the phone down, picked up the top one of the two manila folders from the mortuary and opened it. The details of the unknown young woman's autopsy began with a photo, her eyes closed almost as if she were asleep. 'So, who are you, missy?' he muttered. If she was a prostitute then surely she would have been known to the police. Unless she was relatively new to the game or just a part-timer. There were enough of those in the city these days, with the way tuition fees were crippling the university students financially. Bar work and waitressing paid next to nothing so a surprising amount of them turned to stripping, modelling or even hooking to make ends meet. He would need to look at the police reports to see how much effort had gone into identifying her and where that effort had been directed.

Meanwhile, he concentrated on reading through her file.

*

'Whoa . . .' Jane snatched up her camera and focused quickly. The face of the man walking along the far side of the street, seventy yards away, snapped into sharp, bright focus. 'Yes.'

She lowered the binoculars. 'Jill,' she called. 'Get up here, quick.'

'Coming.'

PC Jillian Evans had arrived no more than fifteen minutes ago and was in the kitchen with the homeowner, making tea. Mrs Collins had offered when she first installed Jane in the small upstairs room, but Jane had declined, knowing that Jill and Sophie Clewes were both on the way.

She picked up the digital SLR camera with its telephoto zoom lens. With a light touch of the shutter button, the camera snapped into focus and she started shooting. The front gate of the house where Petrosyan was staying was just three doors up on the far side of the road and the man walking along the narrow pavement had to be heading towards it. Feet thumped on the carpeted stairs behind her.

'What's up?' the tiny dark-haired PC asked from the doorway.

'Our man's getting a visitor. Zivan Millic,' Jane told her, eyes fixed on the approaching figure. 'Looking as handsome as ever.'

Even as she spoke, Millic opened the front gate of the house where Petrosyan was staying and stepped through. Jane snapped several shots as he approached the pale blue door. She felt Jill leaning over her to watch as the big man waited. Then the door opened. They saw a bulky figure in the shadows then Millic was yanked inside by the front of his Puffa jacket and the door slammed shut.

'Not exactly a warm welcome.'

'No, but he's here. Best tell the boss.'

'Right. I'll go and finish the tea. Sophie should be here soon, shouldn't she?'

'Any minute.' Jane took out her mobile and selected the squad room number as Jill headed for the stairs.

*

Jane leaned her elbows on the old desk and stared through the net curtains. She had not taken her eyes from the front door of Petrosyan's house while she spoke to Pete. She had as close to the perfect vantage point as it was possible to get, here in the old couple's house. She had no intention of wasting it.

She heard the back door open then voices in the kitchen. Moments later, the stairs creaked as someone climbed them.

'Hiya,' Sophie Clewes said from the doorway. 'Tea's up.'

'Thanks.' Jane took the mug that Sophie offered and glanced back at the house across the street before taking a sip. The tea was hot and strong – just the way she liked it. 'Mmm. Our man's got a visitor. Zivan Millic. Known drug dealer and—'

'General bad bugger,' Sophie finished for her. 'Yeah, I've come across him a couple of times. ABH, GBH, that sort of thing.'

'Petrosyan didn't seem pleased to see him, but he invited him in anyway. Actually, more like dragged him in.'

'So, at least that establishes they know each other.' She nodded at the camera on the desk beside Jane. 'Did you get any shots?'

'Yes, but not of Petrosyan. He stayed back in the shadows. I just got his arm.'

'No tats or distinctive watch or anything?'

Jane grinned. 'We're not that lucky.' She went abruptly quiet, staring out through the window as the door across the road

79

opened. A pause, then the big Pole stepped out. 'Millic is leaving.' She grabbed up the camera, started clicking away.

'We need to follow him,' Sophie said.

'And blow our cover? No way.'

'Petrosyan hasn't seen me. I can just walk out the front door.'

'But he didn't see you come in, did he?'

'He can't be watching out the window all the time. Especially not while he's talking to Millic.'

The big man was nearing the front gate. Jane hesitated, not willing to blow their cover but knowing that Pete wanted to get hold of the Pole.

'OK,' she said finally. 'Do it, but act normal. Stop at the gate and wave goodbye to your gran or whatever.'

Sophie nodded and was gone, boots thundering down the stairs, calling out as she went. 'Jill, see me out, would you? But stay out of sight.'

'What?'

'Go with it, Jill,' Jane called down.

'OK.'

There was quiet for a beat then the click of the front door opening. Outside, she saw Millic turn out of the gate, heading away from her, back the way he'd come. Then Sophie came into view. She opened the gate and went through, pausing to close it behind her. 'Bye, Gran. See you soon.' She waved and walked briskly after Millic, buttoning her grey frock coat as she went.

Jane picked up her phone, flicked through the contacts list until she found what she wanted and pressed Call.

*

Walking as quickly as she dared, not wanting to lose him, Sophie heard the buzz of her phone and cursed. Now, of all times? That was the last thing she needed. She thought about ignoring it, but, after three more steps, took it out and checked the screen.

Pressed Accept.

'Jane?'

'Slow down, Sophie. Relax. You're not following anyone, remember. All you need is to keep him in sight and pretend you're chatting with a friend.'

'All right.' She checked behind her and headed across at a shallow angle. 'I can do that.'

'Good. Just remember, if he sees you, you don't take any notice. Don't look away, hesitate, anything. You've every right to be there, you're minding your own business and you don't know him from Adam, OK?'

Ahead of her, the big man turned the corner and went from sight. Sophie felt a flash of panic. What if she lost him? She started to speed up. 'He's gone round the corner. I can't see him.'

'Don't worry about it. It's a long road down there. Relax. You'll see him again in a minute.'

Sophie laughed, trying to make it sound genuine. 'A lot can happen in a minute.'

'True, but he can't vanish into thin air, can he?'

She was past Petrosyan's place now. She fought not to look across at the pale blue door or the window beside it. 'He's a bit bigger than Paul Daniels,' she giggled.

'Are you old enough to remember him?'

'He was on a bit when I was a kid. I think my dad fancied his assistant.'

Jane laughed. 'Yeah, so did mine. So, what are you planning for tonight?'

'Tonight? Well, I'm not going clubbing, that's for sure. I've got to be up in the morning. I reckon a hot chocolate and a movie.' She stepped up onto the pavement near the junction that Millic had turned down. 'Exciting life, eh?'

'I never had you down as a dressing gown and slippers girl.'

'Don't knock it till you've tried it.'

'Oh, trust me, I have. I'm married, remember?'

Sophie laughed and immediately wondered if it had been a little too loud. Her nerves were starting to get to her again as she neared the corner where Millic had disappeared from view. Then she was there.

'Can you see him?' Jane asked over the phone.

'Yeah. You were right,' she said, as she saw the big man several yards down the hill and felt herself relax.

'Good. How far?'

'Oh, thirty-five, forty, I suppose.'

'Metres?'

'That's right.' She ambled down the pavement, head slightly bowed as she chatted into the phone.

'Perfect.'

'That's what I thought.' She paused. Dropped her voice to a murmur. 'He's crossing . . . No, he's going to a car. A black Golf. Can't see the plate yet.'

'Don't concentrate on it,' Jane told her. 'Just keep chatting. A side glance as you go past is fine, but that's all, OK?'

'OK, Mum. I'm not completely daft.'

'Far from it. You're doing really well. Just remember, you're absorbed in your own little world, barely aware of the bloke you're going to walk past.'

'Yeah, yeah. Good job it's daylight, is all I can say. It'd be different at night, wouldn't it?'

She was closing the distance steadily. Forty metres had become twenty. She had heard the clunk of the central locking, seen Millic duck into the car, and heard the slam of the door. The engine started.

Jane must have heard it through the phone. 'If he moves off before you get to him, cross the road behind him,' she said. 'That gives you an excuse to look his way. But keep walking downhill, don't turn around.'

'You sure that'll work?'

'Even a partial plate is more than we've got now.'

'OK. I'll do what I can.'

The car began to pull out of its space.

'Here goes, then,' she said into the phone. She kept walking, waiting for the car to pull out fully and move off. When it did, she stepped between two others and looked down the hill first, then up towards the receding Golf.

'Whiskey Papa, zero five, Oscar Romeo Charlie.'

Chapter 10

'So, let's look at this another way, then.' Pete sat forward, elbows on his desk and set his chin in his hands. 'There has to be some sort of link to the uni, so what do we know about our man? He used suxamethonium on his most recent victim. A drug that medics use. He also used digoxin – another medical drug – and insulin. Is he doing medicine? Veterinary science? Pharmacy? I can't see something like that fire being the work of one person, so perhaps we're after a gang. In which case, they'll have a leader. He'll be charismatic as well as clever. And the target group suggests he's opinionated, maybe even bigoted. And cruel. So we need to get out there and check the science faculties for anyone fitting that profile. Ben, you could do that. I'll send a couple of uniforms to help out. And check the general-use areas, places everyone has to deal with. Admissions, bursar, student canteen, accommodation.'

'Boss?'

'Bit of exercise will do you good. Some sunshine won't hurt, either.'

Pete's phone rang abruptly, cutting off whatever Ben was about to say. He picked it up. 'DS Gayle, CID.'

'It's Jane. We've got something.'

Her cryptic statement made his heart beat a little faster. She always did that when what she had to tell him was particularly good or bad. 'What?'

'Our friend over here just had a visitor. A certain Zivan Millocovic, listed by the DVLA as residing at 45 Fergusson Road in the wonderful city of Exeter.'

Pete felt the grin creep across his face. 'You beauty. How did you manage that?'

'Sophie followed him back to his car and got a licence plate. I just ran it.'

'So, Millic is an abbreviation. It didn't say that on the PND. Well done. When did he leave there?'

'About ten minutes ago.'

'So, another half-hour at this time of day, and he'll be safely home. Ready to receive visitors.'

'That'd be my guess.'

'What does he drive?'

'A black Golf.' She quoted the registration.

'We'll look out for it. Thanks, Jane. And thank Sophie for me.'

'Will do, boss.'

Pete set the phone down and sat back to let a wave of satisfaction wash over him. For the first time in this case, something had gone right and it was a good feeling.

'Got something?' Dave asked.

'Full name, address and vehicle registration for our man, Millic.'

'Oh, yeah!'

'Fancy a ride out to see if he's home yet?'

'You'd better believe it. You want to take some backup this time, though? Just in case?'

Pete stared at him, knowing he was taking the piss and letting him know it was not appreciated.

Dave pushed his straight, dark hair back off his forehead. 'Just asking.'

'And we will. Phone downstairs. We want to be leaving in ten with a van.'

'Love it.' Dave picked up the phone.

*

Sophie Clewes was fifty yards short of the far end of the cross-street when she heard the distant screech of tyres and a heavy, metallic crash.

'Jesus,' she muttered.

It sounded like the accident had happened at the bottom of the hill. She picked up her pace and, seconds later, peered down the street. A cream-sided lorry with a maroon logo was stationary across the end of the road, about three hundred yards away, but from here she could not see why. She checked that the road was clear and stepped out to get a better angle.

'Christ, it can't be.'

Now that she could see the front end of the lorry, she could also see what it had hit.

A black VW Golf.

*

'What?'

'He's dead, Sarge.' Sophie's voice was tinny over the Bluetooth speakers in the car.

'Fu— Christ's sake.' Pete pulled over to the side of the road, not trusting himself to drive safely. 'Are you sure this was just an accident? Petrosyan had nothing to do with it?'

'As far as I can tell, the lorry driver's genuine, Sarge. He's not local. Comes from two or three hundred miles away, so how could he have a connection to Petrosyan?'

'You'd be surprised, Sophie. These immigrants, they've got connections all over the shop. Communities within communities.

86

Just like the Brits in Spain. It's only to be expected.'

'But the driver's English, Sarge.'

'Doesn't mean everyone he knows or works with is. There're all sorts of ways to persuade someone to do something. You don't just have to pay them, or even trust them.'

'Yeah, but . . . he seems genuine, Sarge.'

'OK. I'm on the way. Hold him until I get there, or if the ambulance wants to take him, let me know.'

'Will do.'

Pete ended the call and glanced at Dave, beside him in the car. 'Sounds like an accident.'

Pete nodded. Millic had come out of a junction right under the nose of a lorry. Maybe never even knew what hit him. Maybe. 'Get onto the station, get a warrant for Petrosyan's phone. And get Forensics onto checking the car and where it was parked. I want to be absolutely certain he didn't set this up. It's too bloody convenient for him.'

'Agreed, but it would take some doing. He's had limited opportunity.'

'True, but if he did it, we can forget drug dealing. I want him for murder.'

*

An hour later, Pete was knocking on the pale blue door of number 34 Hillview Road. If earlier events had not worried Petrosyan enough to get him talking, perhaps this would.

Hearing nothing from inside, he hammered on the door again.

'Gagik Petrosyan,' he called. 'This is the police. We know you're in there. Open the door. Now. We have a warrant.'

Finally, he heard movement from inside. The sound of a chain on the inside of the door. Then the latch was released and the door opened a couple of inches. An eye peered out of the shadows. A grunt. 'Oh, it's you.'

The door closed, the chain was released and it opened again, the man stepping back. 'Come.'

Pete stepped in, followed by Dave Miles. Standing to one side of the door, Petrosyan pushed it closed behind them, plunging the hallway into near darkness. The glass on the door and the windows to either side of it was blacked out, all the doors leading off the narrow hallway closed. Petrosyan opened one of them into a back sitting room. He led the way in and turned to face them.

'What you want?'

'We have a warrant,' Pete told him again. 'Where's your mobile phone?'

'Why? What you . . .'

'Do we really have to open all the windows and turn this place inside out, looking for it?' Pete demanded. 'Because we will, if we have to.'

'All right, all right,' Petrosyan moaned. 'What's this about?'

'Your friend, Zivan Millocovic.' Pete used the big man's full name to demonstrate that they knew it. 'He was seen leaving here just over an hour ago.'

'He's no friend.' He moved towards an armchair in the far corner, reached for the small table beside it and held out a mobile phone.

Pete took it and passed it to Dave. 'But you did talk to him here, didn't you?'

'What of it?'

'He's now dead. And I'm wondering if you had anything to do with that.'

'Dead? Are you shitting me? How?'

'His car was smashed into by a lorry, down the road from here. He didn't stop at a junction. Couldn't, it turns out. His brakes had been tampered with while he was here. We found brake fluid on the road where his car was parked.'

'I did not do it. I was here. With him.'

Pete grinned. 'Not much of a witness now, though, is he?'

'I tell you, this was not me.'

'Nothing on here, boss,' Dave reported, looking up from the phone. 'Last call was to Zivan himself, two and half hours ago.'

'And before that?'

'Last night – 21.15.'

'So, we'll check the landline. And, in the meantime, we'll search this place for any other mobile phones.'

'There are none.'

'I hope you're right, Gagik. But we'll see for ourselves, thanks. Dave, check the kitchen while I keep our man company in here.'

'Right.' Dave left the room.

Turning back to Petrosyan, Pete nodded to the chair in the corner. 'Take a seat, Mr Petrosyan. We won't be any longer than we can help.'

Petrosyan's sour expression suggested his doubts on that score, but he sat anyway.

'Actually, talking of that, excuse me a moment.' Pete took out his mobile phone and dialled.

'Jane. Where are you?'

'Boss? You know where.'

'You alone?'

'No, I've got Jill and Sophie here with me.'

'Good. I'm with Dave at Gagik Petrosyan's residence. Number 34 Hillview. Can the three of you get here in fifteen minutes?'

'Uh . . . Yes, we can do that.'

'Right. Meet us here. You can help search the place. Speed things up a bit.'

'If you're sure, boss.'

'I am.' He ended the call and put away the phone. 'So, Gagik, what was Zivan doing here? If he wasn't a friend.'

'Business.'

Pete raised an eyebrow. 'And we both know what business Zivan was in, so is that an admission?'

'I admit nothing.'

Pete shrugged. 'Fair enough. So, why was he here?'

'Because you accuse me before of something I know nothing of. I want to see if he knows.'

'And did he?'

It was Petrosyan's turn to shrug. 'He said he would look into it. But now . . .' He spread his hands.

Pete smiled. 'If I didn't know better, I might even believe you, Gagik.'

'You are sure I am big dealer in this city, no matter what I say. Why ask questions that you don't want answers to?'

Pete shook his head. 'You're wrong, Gagik, I do want answers. I just want honest ones, not fairy tales. I told you before – I'm not currently interested in you and your drugs. I'm looking into several murders. Including that of Zivan Millocovic now. The drugs are just a line of inquiry that could lead me to the killer. Did he get any phone calls while he was here?'

Petrosyan shook his head. 'No.'

'Did he mention where he'd been or where he was going?'

'No.'

'And you didn't get any calls while he was here? A hang-up, maybe?'

'No.'

Pete nodded. 'So, the attack on his car, if it wasn't your doing, was either random or opportunistic. But, if he was targeted, then how did the person in question know where he'd be and where he'd park?'

Petrosyan said nothing.

'They'd have to either know his car or have followed him here,' Pete went on. 'So, then, was he the primary target? Because, chances are, they now know where you live, old son.'

Petrosyan hid it well, but Pete still caught the brief flash of fear in his eyes before it was replaced by bullish anger. 'Then let them come. They will be sorry they ever heard of Gagik Petrosyan.'

'I think I ought to pretend I didn't hear that,' Pete said. 'Threats of violence don't tend to go down well in British courts. Especially when a history can be demonstrated.'

'I have no history,' Petrosyan snapped. 'I have never been charged.'

'Yes, I'd noticed that.'

The doorbell chimed and Petrosyan glanced away.

'Dave, get that, would you?' Pete called. 'It might be DC Bennett.'

'Boss.'

As Dave's footsteps sounded in the tiled hallway, Pete turned back to Petrosyan. 'So, Zivan didn't tell you what you wanted to know?' Pete heard the front door open. Dave said something. A female voice replied. Heels sounded on the tiles. More than one set.

'I have nothing to tell you,' Petrosyan said.

'In here, Jane,' Pete called out.

The door opened and Jane stepped in, followed by Jill Evans and Sophie Clewes, all in plain clothes. The room was suddenly crowded.

'What can we do, boss?' Jane asked.

'Sophie, you help Dave in the kitchen. When you've done, we'll swap places and you can check in here. Jane and Jill, upstairs. You know the drill.'

As they turned to leave, he turned back to Petrosyan. 'We will find what we're looking for. You know it and I know it. So, why make it harder for us and for yourself?'

'For me, how?'

'Co-operation goes a long way towards what charges are brought and what sentence is handed down. And if you're a potential victim here, then the sooner we can find out who's coming after you, the sooner we can catch them and the safer you'll be.'

Petrosyan said nothing, but Pete could see the look in his eyes – the look that said, *If I find them first there won't be any need for you.* 'There's more than your safety at stake here,' he said. 'They've killed at least four people. That's four families that need justice and it's my job to see that they get it. So, did Zivan tell you anything that might lead to them?'

'Nothing.' Petrosyan hunched down in his chair, arms folded across his chest.

Pete grimaced. 'That leaves you with two people coming for you, then, doesn't it? Me and the killer. Just a question of who gets there first.' He turned to his team. 'Change of plan. Dave, get Dick over here to help you finish off the search. Jill, I want you to go to Millocovic's place. Go through it top to bottom. Nothing unchecked. Then talk to the neighbours, check his phone records, his sat nav if he's got one – everything. Jane, you and Sophie go back to what you were doing before. I'm going back to the station.'

*

The chatter of voices, the clatter of keyboards, the scrape of chairs on the floor all faded from Pete's awareness as he hit the pause button and leaned forward, staring intently at his computer screen. He had zoomed in as much as he could, but the seats where Andrew Michaels had been sitting on the High Street were still too distant to make out detail as the group of lads emerged from the side street and started towards him, larking around and pushing each other as they went.

They looked to be in their late teens or early twenties. University age. He could see that one had a leather jacket and jeans. Another wore a brown sports jacket, a third was all in denim and the last one was in dark trousers and a check shirt. Apart from that, all he could make out was hair colour and the fact that they were all IC-1 – white. But at least it confirmed his theory of a gang.

He pressed Play again and watched as they came nearer to Michaels. There was an old couple on the next seat up from him, just four or five feet away as the lads jostled and laughed, surrounding him briefly. The one in denims pushed the one in the brown jacket. He appeared to stumble, but his hands did not go out as you would expect. He contacted Michaels, leaning over him briefly before pushing himself upright, clapping him on the shoulder and reeling away with a light-hearted wave.

This time, Pete let them go out of shot and continued to watch. It was no more than a minute until Michaels slumped forward, clutching his chest. The old couple stood up, the woman's hand going to her mouth. She turned and shouted or screamed while her husband went to Michaels, leaning over his slumped form. Pete pressed Pause, staring at the screen. At the moment a man had died.

Finally, he blinked and reached for the keyboard, winding the footage back so that he could see the bunch of lads on the screen again. 'Eyes front, boys,' he muttered. 'We're coming for you.'

Chapter 11

'OK, I'm here. What do you want to ask? Sarge.'

They were seated in an interview room, tapes running in case Pete missed anything. Nicky French was small and slim – as small as she could be and still get into the force, Pete guessed. Her dark hair was scraped back into a ponytail, which emphasised the hardness of her narrowed eyes as she slouched in the chair. He had called her as soon as the news of Millocovic's death had come in, to put off this interview until mid-afternoon. She had not been happy, but had accepted his order of priorities.

'I want your impressions of the scene. As a person. Not the official police-speak report, but the reality of the place. It was cold, dark. What did you smell, hear and see? Where was the nearest street light?'

'Right over her.'

Pete's eyebrow rose in surprise. That was the exact opposite of what he'd expected. Had the scene been staged as some kind of deliberate message, despite the risks that entailed?

'Was anyone else nearby?'

'Not that I could tell. The girls mostly work towards the other end of the estate.'

'So, this was down towards the far end?'

'Yes. It'd have to be, wouldn't it? Otherwise, there'd have been witnesses. They wouldn't have been able to do what they did to her.'

'So, the immediate surroundings. Where was the hose you mentioned in your report?'

'Dumped on the ground outside a car body shop, between the building and one of those big, enclosed skips.'

'And had it been used recently?'

'Well, yeah.' She looked at him like he was an idiot.

'Don't assume. Did it look like it had?'

'Yes. Water had leaked out of it, was frozen in a puddle around it.'

'What colour was the skip?'

She frowned, not seeing the relevance. 'Yellow.'

'And what about the ground? Was it tarmac, dirt, grass, what? Was there anything other than the hose there? Muck, rubbish, fag ends, diesel puddles?'

'It was tarmac with white lines for parking spaces. Bits of rubbish lying around near the skip. A few fag ends.' She paused, eyes closed, remembering. Then shook her head. 'Nothing else.'

'The body then. Your first impressions when you saw it. What went through your mind?'

'A shiver. It was freezing cold that night and she was wearing next to nothing. Typical working girl outfit. And she was wet. Her hair was stiff with it. Clothes, too. And there was ice beneath her.'

'Much ice or just a little?'

'Not much, but . . .' She grimaced. 'How much would it take on a night like that?'

'So, she was soaked somewhere else,' Pete said quietly.

'Yeah. And moved after.'

'Now we're getting somewhere. So, how did she get where you found her? Is there anywhere we could hope to get evidence from, after all this time?' A thought struck him. He stood up abruptly. 'Fancy a field trip? I'll have a word with Andy Fairweather and get you the night off.'

'OK.'

*

They were approaching the antiques emporium on the industrial estate when Pete's phone rang. He hit the button on the car's Bluetooth system. 'DS Gayle.'

'Boss, it's Ben. I'm done at the uni. Heading back to the station.'

'Any good?' As they passed, Pete saw a huge man with a grey beard and a ponytail carry a large dining table out towards a bright yellow hire van.

'No. Sorry.'

'Well, when you get back, get onto the computer. I need everything we've got on our Marsh Barton victim. We need to ID her. Then we need to know her habits, her contacts, where she lived, where she worked. She might have been found down here – doesn't mean she worked down here. Get some feet on the ground in the other red-light areas, like up around the clock tower. Also, clubs and pubs. She was a young woman. She had to have had some relaxation time. Dealers, too. She was a druggie, or had been. She had to get it from somewhere.'

'OK, boss.'

'Dick and Dave can help you once they've finished what they're doing. See you in a bit.' He ended the call. 'I expect the girls down here were asked about the victim, if they knew her and so on?' he asked Nicky.

'Yes. They were as helpful as you'd expect, but I didn't get the impression that any of them knew her.'

'And if she didn't work down here, she must have been brought from somewhere else. Which suggests a street girl, to have been picked up in a vehicle.'

'Yeah.'

They passed a junction on the left and a dead end loomed

ahead. Galvanised railings marked the edge of the estate. Beyond was an area of scrub and bushes, a mobile phone tower standing tall among the weeds.

'Over there on the right,' Nicky said, pointing.

A car repairer's stood next to a specialist carpenter and joiner's, a large enclosed skip at the far side of the parking area in front of the garage.

He pulled into the forecourt, parked across the front of the VW and got out. Looking around, he could not see any CCTV cameras on the adjacent buildings. There was one more unit beyond the garage – a tyre and exhaust fitters – then the angular, grey metal fence at the end of the road.

The killers had chosen their dumping ground well.

*

'Hey, boss.' Ben looked up from his computer at the sound of the squad room door. 'I reckon I've got her.'

Pete dropped a CCTV disc on his desk, shrugged off his coat and hung it over the back of his chair. 'Already? Nice one.'

It was barely an hour since he had asked Ben to start a data search for the unknown victim. He stepped across. 'Show me.'

'This one fits the description, though we haven't got a photo of her. Reported missing ten days ago by her landlord. She rents a flat down between Western Avenue and the river. He normally collects the rent in person.' Ben looked up at him, eyebrows raised, then focused on his screen again. 'Missed her in October, but thought nothing of it, left it to this month, but missed her again. That's when he got suspicious and reported her missing. She'd always been a good tenant up to that point: paid on time, kept the place tidy and all that.'

'OK, what's her name?'

'Brigit Mostova. Age twenty-four. Originally from Poland.'

Twenty-four, Pete thought. *What a waste of a life. And Polish, the same as Zivan.* 'And the landlord?'

'Anthony Perkins.' Ben read out an address in Topsham.

'Have we got a phone number for him?'

'A mobile.'

'Write it down for me, I'll give him a call.' He took the note from Ben, picked up the phone and dialled.

'Hello?' The voice on the other end was hollow and echoing.

'Anthony Perkins?'

'That's right.'

'This is DS Pete Gayle, Exeter CID. I'm phoning about the Missing Persons report you placed, regarding Brigit Mostova.'

'You've found her?'

'Do you know if she had any family in this country?'

'No. She came over here to work. I know she was sending a portion of her money back to Poland, to her mother. Why? What's going on?'

'Can I come and talk to you in person, Mr Perkins?'

'I'm in the car. How about if I come to you? Half an hour?'

'That would be great. Thank you. Just ask for me at the front desk and I'll come straight down.'

Silence echoed down the line for a moment. 'You're going to tell me she's dead, aren't you?' His voice was heavy with sorrow.

'What makes you say that?'

'You asked if she *had* family over here. Past tense. Plus, if she was alive, she'd be able to tell you herself.'

Pete grimaced. 'We found a body that we suspect is hers. We'll need to make a formal identification. And I need to ask you a few questions about her – things that might help us work out what happened to her.'

He heard Perkins sigh on the other end of the line. 'Bloody shame. She was a nice girl. All right. I'll see you in half an hour or so.'

'Thank you.' Pete ended the call and slipped the DVD that he had left on his desk into his computer.

'So, what's that you've got, boss?' asked Jane.

'Footage from Marsh Barton, just up the road from where our victim was found.'

'You lucky bugger.'

'Aren't I?' He grinned. 'But the question is, why wasn't this checked before? Whose case was it?'

She shrugged. 'There wasn't a case. It was presumed to be natural causes. Exposure.'

'It still should have been checked, if only briefly. Same as we check suicides, to make sure that's what they are.'

'Don't tell I,' she quoted in an exaggerated West-country accent. 'Tell 'e in the big office.'

'The DCI?' He stared at her incredulously.

Jane tilted her head. 'It's his call, isn't it? And you know how he likes to have his figures looking their best.'

'And nobody picks him up on stuff like this?'

'Don't want to interrupt his upward trajectory, do we?' Dave put in. 'Sooner he's gone, the sooner we can get back to proper policing.'

'Maybe so, but you can't run a station like that – cases getting skipped and people walking the streets that ought not to be.'

'It's not our call to make, though, is it, boss?' Ben said.

'Ours not to reason why,' Dick agreed.

Pete was shaking his head. 'I can't believe Colin would let him get away with stuff like that.'

'Yeah, but again,' Dave said, 'it's not his place to criticise, is it?'

'It is, if he sees something going on that's clearly wrong.'

'Who's he going to take it to? The brass, who're trying to push Fast-track up the ladder? I can see that going down well.'

'This gets worse by the bloody day,' Pete muttered and concentrated on his computer screen, opening up the single file on the DVD and pressing Play.

The image that came up was in grainy monochrome, showing a night-time street scene outside the antique emporium on the

Marsh Barton estate. A digital clock counted up in the bottom right corner as a car sped past, heading out of the dead-end road: 16.30. Time of death had been estimated at around 11 p.m., plus or minus half an hour, but he had no way of knowing when she might have arrived down there or how long it had taken her to die. All he could be sure of was that she had arrived there after all the surrounding businesses shut up shop for the night. He pressed Fast-forward, concentrating on the screen.

*

Cars, vans, a couple of motorbikes, a few pedal cycles and several people on foot darted across Pete's screen, almost all from right to left until the time in the bottom right said 6.45 p.m. Then they slowed to a trickle and by 7.15 had stopped altogether. There was no movement until 8.38 p.m., when a fox darted into view and out again. Stillness settled over the section of the industrial estate covered by the camera. After a while, Pete was tempted to speed up the replay even more, but resisted, unwilling to take the risk of missing even the briefest movement.

'Christ, there's no way I could be a security guard,' he muttered. 'The boredom would kill me.'

The fox passed across the screen again at 8.57, then there was nothing but the clock ticking over in the corner of the screen until . . . *Flash.* A vehicle darted across.

Pete pressed Pause and went back frame by frame. A pale-coloured hatchback had crossed the camera's angle of view at 9.32 p.m. The grainy monochrome image showed little detail. The angle gave just a side view of the car. Pete thought it was a Peugeot by the shape, but the only other thing he could make out was that the driver appeared to be male, judging by the hairstyle. He couldn't even tell if anyone else was in the car. He sucked air through his teeth and took a screenshot of the image, then continued the replay, running it more slowly than before.

There was nothing more until the glow of headlights preceded the return of the little car at 10.42. It drove smoothly past the camera position, out of frame and no doubt out of the industrial estate. Again, all he got was a side view and this time no image at all of the driver. He hit Pause and backed it up until the car was mid-frame.

This had to be the killer's vehicle, but what information could he glean from it? *Not a bloody lot*, he thought. A rough year of manufacture, maybe, from the shape. Blowing up the previous image might give him something on the driver, but it seemed unlikely. The best thing to do would be to find out if there were other cameras that might have picked up a better angle on the car, elsewhere on the estate or on the way into it.

He took another screenshot, stopped the DVD and stood up.

Jane looked up from her screen. 'You off home, boss?'

Pete frowned and looked at his watch. It was 5.45. He grunted in surprise. 'No, down to the CCTV room. But I will have to go soon, I expect.'

'You will, if you want Annie to still recognise you.'

'Don't you start. I get enough of that at home.'

She shrugged. 'Just saying . . .'

Dave laughed. 'Yeah. When did a woman ever do that?'

'What?'

'Just say.' He shrugged. 'I'm just asking.'

Pete grinned as Jane threw a sideways punch at the man beside her. 'I'll go see whoever's—' His phone rang, interrupting him. An internal line. He picked it up. 'DS Gayle.'

'It's Mike on the front desk. There's a Tony Perkins here for you.'

'Ah. Thanks, Mike. On the way.' He put the phone down. Jane and Dave were both looking at him expectantly. 'The dead girl's landlord.'

*

Perkins was a solidly built man in his fifties with dark curly hair that was peppered with grey and brown eyes that met Pete's openly. His handshake was firm and dry.

'Thanks for coming in, Mr Perkins,' Pete said. 'If you come this way, we can find a room to talk in.' He led him through to the back corridor and along to the custody suite, where Bob showed them into an interview room. They sat and Pete took out his notebook and pen. 'So, how long have you known Miss Mostova?'

'Since she took the flat in Albert Street. Just over two years.'

'And that's just as landlord and tenant? No other aspect to the relationship?'

'I'm a married man, Sergeant. One woman's enough for me.'

Pete tilted his head. 'I wasn't implying anything.' He drew a breath. 'I've got a picture I'd like to show you. Nothing too unpleasant, but I should warn you, the subject is deceased. Are you OK with that?'

'I suppose.'

Pete took a photo of the dead woman from his inside pocket and laid it on the table, facing Perkins. The man glanced down. His eyes immediately slid away, face drawing into a frown.

'Yes, that's her.'

'Brigit Mostova?'

'Yes.'

Pete put the photo away. 'Thank you. What can you tell me about her?'

'She was a nice girl. Polite. Friendly. Kept the place clean and tidy, didn't annoy the neighbours. Always ready with the rent. Like I said, her family's back in Poland. She sent money to them every month. Her mother's not well. MS or something like that. I don't know anything about her social life. I know she was trained as a secretary. When she first took the flat, she was working at some trucking company, I think. They went bust a while ago, but she never had a problem with the rent, so I suppose she got straight into another job. Don't know where though.'

'And you never met any of her friends or associates?'

'No.'

'Do you know if she drove?'

'Not that I'm aware of.'

'OK. Well, thanks for coming in, Mr Perkins.' Pete stood up, tucked his notebook and pen away and shook the man's hand. 'Oh, by the way, could I have a look at the flat? Just to be sure there's nothing there that could help us.'

'Of course. I'll drop you a key in.'

'Thanks.' He showed Perkins out as far as the front desk then headed for the CCTV room.

He let himself in quietly. 'Graham. I've come to look at your map.'

Graham gulped at his drink and set it on the desk in front of him. 'I wish you wouldn't do that,' he said, turning away from the bank of monitors with a deep scowl on his face.

'What?' Pete asked innocently.

'You know what.'

Pete grinned. 'Caught you by surprise, did I?'

Graham grunted. 'What d'you want the map for?'

Pete turned towards the back wall of the room, where a large map of the city and its surroundings displayed a number of red pins, marking the locations of all the police-controlled CCTV cameras. Blue ones marked speed cameras and white ones showed traffic observation cameras. 'To see what we've got down towards Marsh Barton,' he said.

'Not much. The leisure centre on Alphington Road, but that's about all down that way. Why?'

'I've got a murder that happened down there, mid-October.'

Graham grimaced, hissing air between his teeth. 'We only keep stuff a month, mate. Regulations. Can't go infringing a criminal's human rights, can we?'

'Shit. I'll have to do it the hard way then. See if there's any private systems out there.'

'Bound to be. Trouble is, like us, how long will they keep stuff? And there's three or four different ways in and out of the place.'

'Yeah, but knowing where they ended up, I can narrow that down to Willeys Avenue and Marsh Barton Road.'

'I dare say McDonald's will have cameras over their car park. Can't think of anywhere else though. There might be, but, like you say, it'll be a case of going down there and looking.'

'Yeah. And hoping.'

*

Pete stopped his car at the station entrance. The traffic was queued into the city, way back towards the old hospital site. Two cars passed from the other direction, nose to tail. Pete saw that the road behind them was clear and followed them with his eyes to check again to the left. Something pale caught his eye as headlights lit it. He glanced at the lamp-post just a few feet to his left, directly in front of the station. A poster was wrapped around it.

'Cheeky buggers,' he said, half in admiration. There was a by-law banning such postings in the city, and he had no doubt that whoever had put it there knew that.

With the traffic cleared, he pulled out, turning towards home.

Two streets away from the main road, in the estate where he lived, Pete pulled into the car park of his local Co-op. Annie had phoned just minutes before he left the station, wanting him to stop off and pick up some milk. An A4-sized poster caught his eye on the noticeboard outside, a close-up portrait of a black and tan cat that had gone missing with a mobile phone number underneath and the message, 'Jangles, aged four, missing since 4 November from Hargreave Road. She is nervous but friendly. If you see her, please call.'

She'll have been scared by the fireworks, Pete thought. *She'll go home when she calms down if she doesn't get run over in the meantime.*

He entered the store, found the milk and noticed, on the shelf just a couple of feet away, some cream cakes. They were packaged in twos and fours. Four would have been perfect if . . . He tried to swallow the lump that had appeared in his throat from nowhere, but it wouldn't go away.

Where the hell was Tommy? What was he doing now? Not eating cream cakes, that was for sure. With Malcolm Burton in jail and his house locked up, he'd be out on the streets somewhere, cold, probably hungry. Pete pictured him hunched in a doorway, small and vulnerable. He had to reach out to him somehow, persuade him to come home. That he was loved and missed, and between them, they could fix whatever was wrong. He drew a deep, shuddering breath, shook his head and blinked. As he straightened up, he noticed the small trifles between the cakes and the milk. They were in packs of three. He snatched up a pack and headed for the till.

Back outside, he glanced again at the poster of the missing cat. How the hell had they come up with the name Jangles? Still, he hoped she turned up soon. A pet wasn't the same as a child, but it was still part of the family.

He stopped, his mind returning to Tommy, an image of him walking out of another Co-op on the other side of the city. Like the cat, he was out there alone and no doubt afraid, with no way of knowing what Burton had been saying about him or what he would face if he turned up now. But, with Rosie to testify on his behalf and Burton being a manipulative paedophile who no one would believe anyway, it was . . .

Pete grinned suddenly.

It was just a case of letting him know. And there, in front of him, was the way to do it.

'Yes!' he said aloud, starting back to the car with a spring in his step.

Chapter 12

Annie must have heard him pull into the drive. She had the front door open almost before he locked the car.

'Dad! You're early.' She ran to meet him, jumping up to clamp her arms around his neck and her legs around his waist as he grunted, staggering at the impact.

'Blimey, Button, are you putting on weight?' he gasped, as his free hand went to support her.

She kicked him in the backs of his thighs, making him stagger. 'You could give someone a complex, making comments like that.'

'Some people, yes. Not you – you're far too sensible. How was your day?'

'OK. What about yours? How come you're home so early?' She jumped down and went ahead of him into the house.

'It's not early. It's past six.'

'That's early for you.'

Pete sighed and pushed the door shut. 'True. But we'd got to a stage in the case where there wasn't much else to do until morning so I thought I'd come and spend some time with you and your mum.' He stuck his head through the lounge doorway. 'Hey, Lou. All right?'

She grunted without taking her eyes from the TV.

At least it was an answer, of sorts. He went through to the kitchen, put away the milk and trifles and checked the kettle before flicking it on. 'Who's for a cuppa?'

'Yes, please,' Annie said. He didn't expect an answer from Louise and didn't get one, but set her mug alongside the other two anyway. He made the tea and let Annie carry her own through to the sitting room. He gave Louise hers and sat down next to her.

'You're chipper,' Louise said without taking her eyes from the TV screen.

Wow, he thought. *She might not say much, but she's noticing stuff. Is she getting back to her old self?* God, he hoped so. He missed her strong-mindedness, her sharp humour and lively conversation. Everything about the woman she had been until Tommy disappeared. It was like she'd gone, too, and left a completely different person in her place. Only in the last few days had there been occasional glimpses of the old Louise. 'I think I've got an answer to our problem,' he said.

'Which problem?' asked Annie, who was curled up in the easy chair to his right.

'How to contact your brother. We don't know where or how he's living, but we can be sure he won't be watching TV or buying newspapers. So, the question is, how do we let him know that he's safe to come home? That we want him back and he won't be arrested for whatever he was forced to do while he was with Malcolm Burton. And the answer is posters.'

'Yeah. But what do we say on them?' She turned around so that she was facing him fully, all attention and keen to talk the problem through.

'I thought if we had a picture of him with something like, "Missing. Tommy Gayle, aged thirteen, loved and needed by his family. Anyone with information, please call this number," my mobile and then, "Tommy, we know you have nothing to answer for. Please come home."'

Annie tilted her head to either side. 'How about, "Tommy, we know you're innocent. Please come home"?'

Pete nodded. 'Yes, that's better.'

'What's he innocent of?' she asked.

He hesitated. At ten years old, he wasn't certain how much she was aware of, in terms of sex or crime. Not a lot, he hoped. And, if so, he wanted it to stay that way. 'All you told me last night they were saying at school. Rosie Whitlock said herself that he was another victim, not part of the crime. Or not a willing one, at least.'

She frowned as if she was going to ask something else, but held it back. Then, 'Who's going to do them?'

'What – the posters?'

'Duh.' She looked at him like he was stupid.

'I can get them printed and . . . I don't know. Maybe your mum could put them up around town?'

'I could take some to school,' she said brightly. 'We could put one out by the gates and people could take them home, put them up at bus stops and so on. They'd get all over the place that way, and lots quicker than we could do it.'

He nodded. 'Good idea. What do you reckon, Lou?'

'You seem to have got it all sussed.'

'But what do you reckon to going out, putting them up? Get you out and about a bit. Get some fresh air in your lungs and daylight on your face.'

She was silent for a moment. 'Why are *we* doing this? Why isn't Simon Phillips doing it officially, now there's been another sighting of him?'

'Maybe he will. But this is a more personal approach. From us to Tommy, letting him know that he's not in any trouble. A police notice might have the opposite effect, in that sense.'

'OK. So, if both are around at the same time, wouldn't that just confuse the issue? Make him doubt the honesty of your message?'

'What are you saying? That we shouldn't do it? Or that Simon shouldn't?'

'I don't know. Just . . .' She shook her head. 'Just . . .'

'Mum,' Annie wheedled. 'Come on. Please. This is something we can do as a family – as *his* family – to make Tommy come home.'

Even as pride and amazement swelled his chest at Annie's maturity for her age, Pete reached out to quieten her. 'If it's too much, Lou, then it's not a problem. I just thought you might like the chance to be involved, that's all.'

'Just don't keep pushing me,' she said. 'I'll go out when I'm ready.'

'Nobody's pushing you. I just thought this would be a good reason for you to try.'

'Well, I expect it would, but I don't know that I can, all right? Now, can we drop it, please?'

God, what was it going to take to get her moving? Pete fought the urge to ask the question out loud. He didn't want to argue in front of Annie. She had enough to contend with already. At ten years old, her brother was gone – they didn't know whether from his own choice or having been snatched by someone – her mother had sunk into an agoraphobic depression that left her, most of the time, as nothing more than a silent dummy in the corner, and her dad was back at work all hours, leaving her to not just do her schoolwork but help around the house and support her mother.

He sighed. How the hell did she cope with it all?

She had more than stepped up. She had grown up rapidly and long before she should have had to. Had taken on the mother role in the household to a large extent when she should have been playing like her friends. *With* her friends.

Could Louise not see . . .? But of course not, he thought. She was too sunk into herself to see much of anything. He pushed back the flare of resentment. It wasn't fair. Different people coped in different ways – or didn't, as the case may be. Different histories gave different strengths and vulnerabilities. But still, a small corner of his mind couldn't help thinking, people were intelligent creatures. They could see and assess what was going on around them, could make decisions about what to do or not do. They were not simply creatures of instinct.

He had never believed in excuses like 'I had to, I couldn't help myself.' The namby-pamby do-gooders who made excuses for criminals about their upbringing or their low IQ needed to wake up and smell the shit under the roses, not just the flowers themselves.

He glanced over at Louise. She was watching him, her expression one of such abject pleading for understanding that his heart melted all over again.

The air slipped out slowly out of him.

For better or worse, he thought. He couldn't help it: he loved her.

He slapped his knees and stood up. 'Right. Well, pudding's sorted. What's for dinner, eh?'

*

'Ben. What the hell are you doing here at this time of the morning?'

The young PC grimaced. 'I thought what I'm doing is best done when nobody can look over my shoulder, boss.'

Pete nodded. 'How are you getting on with it?'

'I've broken the back of it, but there's still a way to go. Not found anything incriminating yet though. And, to be honest, I don't know if I will. I mean, there's no one on the force here with Eastern European connections, is there? Not even in civvy support.'

'Well, keep looking. The less you find, the better, in a lot of ways.'

'Yeah, but somebody's on the take and we need to find them somehow.'

'But . . . Hold that thought, Ben. I'll be back in a tick.' Pete headed back out of the squad room and along the corridor. He knocked on DCI Silverstone's door.

'Come.'

Pete went in. Silverstone, immaculate as ever, was seated behind his desk, a stack of files at his right elbow, one open in front of him.

'Operation Natterjack, sir. Who compiled the target list?'

'Good morning, Detective Sergeant. Someone at HQ. I don't know who. Why?'

''Morning, Guv. But it would have been based on data supplied by the local stations, yes?'

'Of course.'

'So, who supplied ours?'

Silverstone stared at him for a long moment. 'Simon Phillips,' he said at last. 'Why?'

'Could I have a copy of it?'

'Of course. What have you found, Sergeant?'

'Nothing definite yet, sir, but we might be a step closer.'

'Very well.' He turned to his computer, called up a file and, moments later, the printer at the side of the small room began to whirr, paper emerging from its top a sheet at a time. 'There you are.'

Pete stepped across, waited for it to finish and picked up the several sheets it had pushed out. 'Thanks.'

'Keep me apprised of your progress, Peter. And remember – even with a bad apple in the mix, we're one team here. Otherwise, we're nothing.'

Speak for yourself, he thought. 'Sir.'

Pete took the sheets and hurried back to the squad room. He and Ben Myers were still the only two people in there. 'Ben. Simon Phillips. Take his life and career apart. Toothpick and paintbrush. No speck left unturned. Got it?'

Ben looked shocked. 'It was . . .?'

'We don't know yet. But if not, he's the next link in the chain, so we need to be sure.'

'OK.'

As Ben turned back to his computer, Pete sat down and began to go through the printout from Silverstone's office.

*

When Dave Miles finally strolled into the squad room at twenty-five to nine, Pete closed the file he was working on and stood up.

'Right. Now we're all here, I've emailed everyone all we've got on our primary victim, Jerry Tyler. Being an ex-con, we know quite a bit about him. I've also sent everyone what we've got on Andrew Michaels, Donald Tennyson, Brigit Mostova and her landlord, Tony Perkins. He's not a victim, of course, but he is a potential link between her and the others. I've excluded Zivan Millocovic because his killing was obviously one of expediency. Tidying up loose ends. Now, so far, we don't have any links between the victims, but there has to be one, however obscure or tenuous. The killer found them somehow. If we can figure out how, that could lead us to him. Or, at least, point us in the right direction.

'Now, limiting factors. Brigit Mostova's only been in the country three years, and in Exeter for just over two, so she clearly didn't go to school with the others, for instance. Where did she live before?

'Andrew Michaels only had the one job, and that was some years ago, so although it's not impossible that he worked with one or more of the others, it's unlikely and easily checked. Also, he's never moved house, so we need to check whether any of the others ever lived in that part of the city.

'We've got very little on Donald Tennyson. We need to do a full background check on him and on Tony Perkins, in case he's the link to Brigit. It could be as basic as they all went to the same pub or supermarket, but if we can find a link, it might well lead us to the killer. And it would be good to get there before they kill anyone else, despite the opinion some might hold that the victims are no loss to society.' He looked at Dave as he said the last sentence.

Dave held up his hands defensively. 'Hey, what are you looking at me for? I haven't said a word.'

Jane gave him a shove. 'We know you so well,' she sang quietly.

'I resent that remark,' he said in a mock-hurt voice. 'In fact, I'm deeply wounded.'

'Aah. Poor baby. Truth hurts, eh?'

'All right,' Pete cut in. 'Dick, you can look into Donald Tennyson and Tony Perkins. Jane, you and Sophie give Petrosyan one more day. We're limited by the fact that we can't get a tap on his phone, but it is what it is. If he doesn't do anything significant today, we'll have to pull back on him for lack of manpower. Ben, you carry on with what you're doing. Jill, you take Brigit, and Dave, see if you can get anywhere on the bakery where Michaels worked.'

'Seems unlikely, boss. It's fifteen years since they shut down, isn't it? Even the taxman only wants stuff kept for seven.'

'Yeah, but we don't need documentary proof, just a reliable witness.'

*

Pete headed out as soon as he had finished allocating tasks to his team. He turned left out of the station entrance, heading out of town. Middlemoor was only about a mile from the Heavitree Road station and, although the rush hour was still in full swing, he was heading in the opposite direction to the bulk of the traffic so it would take just minutes to get to the Devon and Cornwall Police HQ. Not that he cared, particularly, if he was late. He knew it was required, standard procedure, but he couldn't help thinking this was a waste of time – especially now, in the middle of a case.

He was fine. He knew it. The team knew it. Colin knew it, not that he was in the station at the moment. Even Fast-track himself wouldn't have bothered sending him if it hadn't been for those damned emails between Tommy and Rosie Whitlock. Or, more particularly, if it hadn't been for him hiding them for three days while he solved the girl's abduction, he admitted to himself ruefully.

Which meant that, ultimately, this was his own fault.

He sighed.

An hour and he'd be out of there. If he could just persuade the shrink that he was OK and fit to work, he wouldn't even have to come back.

He gave a wry grunt. Fat chance. These time-wasters had to justify their own existence somehow. Especially highly qualified, highly paid time-wasters. He'd just have to try to put his next session off until after this current case was dealt with. Surely, even a psychologist could understand the urgency of stopping a killer.

He reached the junction and turned right down the Hill Morton Road. The police headquarters was a maze of a place. It took longer to find the department he needed than it had to drive here from the station but, by five past nine, he had found not only the department but the right room.

He entered a waiting room where a secretary was typing something into a computer. A handful of chairs were ranged around the other three sides of the room. The woman looked up and stopped typing.

'DS Gayle?'

'That's right. Sorry I'm late.'

'Go on in.' She nodded towards a door opposite the entrance. A sign on it read, 'Dr Abigail White'.

Pete knocked out of politeness and opened the door. The doctor's desk was to his right. She was seated behind it, facing across the room towards a cluster of lounge furniture.

She looked up as the door opened. In her mid-forties, he guessed, she was handsome rather than pretty or beautiful. Her dark hair was worn in a long bob, the sides swept back over the collar of a businesslike blouse. Her brown eyes were cool.

'Morning, Doc,' he said. 'Pete Gayle. Sorry I'm a bit late. Got tied up on a case.'

'And, of course, your work is much more important than mine,' she said.

Touché, Pete thought, closing the door behind him. He might even enjoy this. When he turned back to her, the corners of his mouth were twitching upwards. 'There is a certain degree of urgency involved in tracking down a multiple murderer.'

'As there is in finding a missing young girl, I'd imagine. Or young boy, for that matter.'

So, she'd read his file while she was waiting.

'As there also is,' she continued, 'in ensuring that our officers are fit to carry out such tasks. That they're not going to be a danger to the public or themselves while they go about the duties involved in protecting us all from the dangerous elements in our society.' She stood up and stepped around the desk. 'Tell me, Detective Sergeant, how much complexity would you consider is involved in your job? As compared to, say . . . a lorry driver, for instance?'

'Several times as much.'

Folding her arms, she leaned against the edge of her desk and crossed her ankles. 'And yet, a lorry driver can have a momentary lapse of concentration and cause several deaths. So, what would result from a lapse in concentration in your job?'

In his mind, Pete was picturing the driver of the bakery lorry that had killed Zivan Millocovic through no fault of his own. 'In that sense – and in this case – the same, I suppose.'

'And you would agree with the necessity, for public safety reasons, of the tachograph, yes?'

Pete nodded slowly.

'Then think of me as your tachograph, Detective Sergeant,' she said, pushing herself away from her desk. 'Now, shall we take a seat?'

He made a show of looking around. 'What, no couch?'

She tipped her head. 'I work with policemen, not film critics and dress designers.'

'Fair enough.'

She raised a hand towards the sofa. 'Make yourself comfortable.' She took one of the armchairs opposite. 'So, tell me, why are you here today, Peter? I take it I can call you Peter?'

He nodded. 'Regulations. It's a requirement on coming back to work after what happened with my son.'

'Which was . . .?'

His lips pressed together. 'We don't know. He disappeared. There was no sign of him until about ten days ago, when he popped up in a case I was investigating.'

'You were investigating? Yet, you said yourself it's a requirement, on returning to active duty, to come here.'

'Circumstances prevailed, Doc. I came back a couple of weeks early, just for the day – or at least that was the plan. To cover the office while the rest of the crew were out on a force-wide series of drug busts. While I was in, we picked up a kidnapping case that Tommy turned out to be tied up in.'

'And you took it on.'

'We didn't know Tommy was involved at that stage. And everyone else was busy.'

'Nevertheless . . .'

'Cases like that don't wait for convenience, Doc. Stats suggest that you've usually got about seventy-two hours before the victim's killed. There isn't time to mess about with protocols and regulations, no matter how ideal they might be.'

'And yet, your son had been missing for what – nearly six months?'

'Yes.'

'Which suggests—'

'I'm fully aware of what it suggests, Doc,' he said, cutting her off. 'And it changes nothing. He's still my son, no matter what he's done or hasn't done. And our key witness – our primary victim – says adamantly that he was another victim rather than a perpetrator.'

'But, without that knowledge, you apparently did not take the matter to senior officers when you discovered that your son had a previous connection with the victim. Another regulation breached.'

'As I said before, all the other officers in the station were busy with other cases and, anyway, there wasn't time to transfer the case to someone else. It was a matter of urgency.'

'Which, at this stage, had justified your breaching of at least two regulations.'

'No. It wasn't my decision to breach the first one. I was assigned the case by my superior officers.'

'Only upon your belligerent insistence, according to DCI Silverstone's report.'

Pete laughed. '"Belligerent insistence"? That's classic, that is.'

'Classic?'

'Fas— DCI Silverstone abdicating responsibility.'

'You have a problem with DCI Silverstone?'

'No more than anyone else who works with him. He's arrogant, opinionated and ignorant. Not a good combination.'

'And he's in charge.'

'An even worse combination.'

'Or is that the actual issue, Peter? That he's in charge?'

He frowned.

'It's common enough. Most people have some resentment for those in charge. You see it in every workplace you go into.'

Pete nodded. 'True. But, in this case, not relevant. I respect those that earn it, whether they're in charge or not.' He thought of Colin Underhill. Steady, mature, experienced and respected by everyone in the station.

'Very well.' She recrossed her legs, settling more comfortably into the chair. 'I noticed that you seem to hold some resentment about the lack of progress in your son's case.'

He waited, saying nothing.

'Would that be an accurate assessment, do you think?'

'As an investigator, I'm fully aware that not all cases can be solved. You can't make progress in a vacuum. You need information to build on.'

'And yet, when you said it's not known what happened to him, your expression showed a lack of acceptance of that fact. As if you thought, had you been working the case, things would have been different.'

'Of course they would. I'm his father. I'd have left no stone unturned.'

'And the investigating officer wasn't as thorough as you'd have liked?'

'I've never said that.'

'But you've thought it. Am I right?'

Pete paused. She was good at this. 'I expect any parent would, in similar circumstances. I know that, in just about every case I've worked involving kids, the parents were on my back every step of the way. And, as a parent myself, I couldn't blame them for that.'

'But, in this case, those circumstances were reversed. You were that parent. How did you cope with that? How *are* you coping with that?'

'Better than some, I'd say.'

She nodded. 'Meaning other parents in other cases or other members of your family in your son's case?'

Pete pictured Louise, sitting numbly in front of the TV at home, and annoyance flared. Not at Louise, but at this woman for pushing him in that direction. He met her steady, detached gaze. 'Both.'

'Your wife?'

He frowned, sitting forward, elbows on his knees. 'I thought this was supposed to be about whether *I'm* fit for work, not Lou.' He shook his head. 'That sounded self-centred, even to me. I mean, what's Lou's state of mind got to do with my competence to work, which is what you're supposedly here to assess?'

'Your wife's state of mind inevitably affects yours, Peter. We may try not to bring our domestic issues to work, but it can't be done, except perhaps by a sociopath. Our mood is affected by those we care for whether we like it or not. And our mood affects how we do our jobs – especially jobs that involve mental rather than physical work – both in terms of efficiency and the choices and decisions we make.'

He drew in a deep breath and let it out. 'All right. I can accept that.'

She tilted her head. 'So . . .?'

He smiled. 'What was the question?'

'How are you coping with being the parent instead of the investigator in your son's case?'

'I think any parent would want to be as active as possible in those circumstances. You can't just sit back and let others do everything. It's not in our nature.' *Well, it wasn't in his. Louise seemed to be a different matter, the past few months.* He pictured her again, sitting in her usual spot on the sofa, staring blindly at the TV.

He blinked himself back to the present.

'What were you just thinking, Peter?'

He pursed his lips, feeling disloyal.

'Is your wife – Louise, isn't it? – not coping as well with the situation?'

His eyes narrowed. This was going in a direction he was not happy with. He didn't care what she said to or about him, but when it came to Louise, he wasn't going to sit here and criticise – or allow anyone else to.

'What about your daughter? Anne?'

He blinked. 'She's fine. She's better than fine. She's been an absolute gem.'

'In what way?'

'In every way. She's grown up a lot more than she should have had to over the past few months. And she can—' He stopped himself abruptly.

'She can what, Peter? What can she do, that you can't?'

He hesitated, still not willing to say anything against Louise. This was covered by doctor–patient confidentiality, of course, but still. 'Maybe when I know you better, Doc. For now, let's just leave it that she's a wonderful kid.'

'Very well. Perhaps we should leave it at that until next time.' She uncrossed her legs and sat forward. 'When should we arrange that for?' She raised an eyebrow. Didn't need to say any more.

'As I said, I'm in the middle of a multiple-murder case just now. It requires all my time and attention.'

'And how does that fit in with family life?'

He felt a flare of annoyance. 'Not so well. I thought we were done.'

'We are.' She stood up. 'It's a common problem with your type of work. Many marriages don't survive the kind of strain it puts them under.'

Pete stood up also. 'My marriage is fine, thanks. I love my wife and kids.'

She placed a reassuring hand on his arm. 'I can see that, Peter. I was just saying it takes a lot of effort, on both sides, for a marriage to work alongside a job that's as intense as yours. There are bound to be rocky patches. And that can only be intensified by the disappearance of a child. So perhaps it would be worth treading water for a while, rather than plunging in. Trying to stay within reach of your wife.'

Load of bollocks, he thought. *What planet are you living on? It damn sure isn't this one.* 'In an ideal world, I'm sure you'd be right, Doc. But, sadly, this isn't one. If it was, my job wouldn't be necessary, would it?'

Chapter 13

Pete went from police HQ straight to the printers, where he arranged for the posters to be made. With Brigit Mostova's address in his smartphone and a spare key from the landlord in his pocket, he was on his way there when his phone rang.

He checked the number and hit the button on the hands-free system.

'Jane. What have you got?'

'I got a call from Jill, boss. Tried you at the time, but your phone was off.'

'Yeah. I was at Middlemoor. Appointment in HQ. What's happened?'

'He's gone. Petrosyan. Did a moonlight flit.'

'Shit.' He slumped in the driving seat.

'About half past two this morning, apparently, he got into a dark-coloured saloon, possibly a Mercedes, with a couple of suitcases and was driven away. That's according to a woman who lives two doors down from the observation post, who'd got up to go to the bathroom and saw it from her landing window.'

'So, we've lost him.' He sighed. 'Well, we didn't have the manpower for a twenty-four-hour watch, so . . . He'll have to go on the back burner for now.'

'Yeah. Thought I'd best let you know.'

'Thanks, Jane. I'll be back in a bit. Got another stop to make first.' Pete put the phone down and shook his head.

If Fast-track had taken the case seriously from the outset, they'd have had the manpower to cover Petrosyan 24/7, then this wouldn't have happened. And that was going into the case notes and his report.

Silverstone wouldn't like it, but there was nothing he could do about it. It would be too late by the time he saw it.

*

The flat was in a three-storey Victorian house near the river. He parked in a side street nearby, found the correct house and discovered that she had lived on the second floor. He climbed the steep, narrow stairs and let himself in.

The place was neat and clean, the door leading straight into the lounge with the kitchen and bathroom to his right, at the back of the house, and the bedroom beyond. In one corner of the room was a small folding table with two matching chairs tucked under it and a laptop computer on top. He would come back to that. He headed for the bedroom, where he guessed a wardrobe or bedside cabinet might provide what the lounge lacked in storage. He needed some way into her life, her past and her finances.

Two shoeboxes in the bottom of the wardrobe contained what he wanted: bank statements, council tax and utility bills as well as various other documents. In the bottom one was her passport and her UK work visa, dated two and a half years ago. He put the boxes on the bed and continued the search, but found no more of interest. She must have conducted most of her communications online or on the phone.

He found the charger for a mobile phone in the bedside cabinet, but the phone was nowhere in the flat. She must have had it with her when she was picked up by her killer. He'd seen the latest bill for it in one of the shoeboxes. He would have to get a trace put on it, just in case her killer still had it. They wouldn't be the first to be tracked down through such a basic mistake. He would also get its call records and those of her landline for the three months leading up to her death. Also, the bank statement would help him access her account records and see where and when she had last held a job and if she was claiming any benefits.

Maybe the link between the victims was as simple as the dole office.

Or maybe there really wasn't one and the whole series of deaths was simply a smokescreen to hide a single target.

Pete shook his head as he picked up Brigit's laptop and the two shoeboxes. He hoped to God that wasn't the case. Apart from making his job that much more difficult, the waste of life would be so much worse.

*

'So, how are we doing?'

Pete set the two shoeboxes from Brigit Mostova's wardrobe on his desk and handed her laptop computer across to Jill Evans. 'Here, see if you can get into that.'

'Brigit's?' she asked.

He nodded. 'Anyone cracked the case yet?'

He noticed Ben give a small nod. He'd clearly got something that he didn't want to talk about in present company. 'Dick, any progress?'

'Donald Tennyson, AKA the Prof—'

'That never is,' Ben said. 'Bloody hell. He's been around town since I was a kid. I never recognised him.' He shook his head in disbelief.

'As Ben said,' Dick continued, 'one of the city's longest-standing homeless. He was in the cells downstairs on a regular basis. Sometimes two or three times a week. Rumour has it that he used to work in the university, hence the nickname, but no one's ever verified that.'

'Then, maybe we should,' Pete said. 'It could provide the link we're looking for. If he did work there, find out exactly what he did and when. Anything else?'

Dick shrugged. 'That's about it, so far, on him. Tony Perkins is another matter though. Lots on him.'

Pete tilted his head. 'Well, don't keep us in suspense.'

'Forty-three years old. Comes from Exmouth, originally. As we know, he lives in Topsham now. Has most of his property in Exeter. Mostly flats – student lets and such-like. Doesn't use an agent. He's been in the property business since 2003. He's married. Has been for twelve years. He's financially secure, no vices I could find and no record with us.' He spread his hands.

'OK. Dave?'

'As we said, the bakery where Michaels worked closed down fifteen years ago. Family-run business, owned by the Hendersons since it was started in 1921. At its peak, it had three shops here in the city, one in Exmouth and others in Honiton and Okehampton, but it seems like the rise of the supermarkets killed it off in the end. There's one family member left alive – spinster Lily Henderson, aged seventy-six. Lives in Topsham. I spoke to her a few minutes ago, but she said she never had much to do with the factory side of things. She was more involved with the shops. The only name she could recall from the factory was the transport manager, Bill Williams.'

'Really?' Ben put in. 'William Williams?'

Dave shrugged. 'I've seen worse. Makes you wonder about the parents, but still . . .'

'OK. See if you can track him down, Dave, and find out if he remembers our boy.'

'Right.'

'I've got some more material here on Brigit Mostova, but have you got anywhere with her, Jill?'

'Not so far, boss. She worked for Trent and Son Transport as receptionist and secretary until they closed down just under two years ago. As far as I can find out, she hasn't been in regular employment since, but she doesn't claim the dole and her landlord says she's kept up with the rent and bills, so . . .' She shrugged.

'She's been on the game,' Dave concluded bluntly.

'Yeah, but how do you get into something like that?' asked Ben. 'I mean, how would she have got started in it?'

'Has your dad never told you about the birds and the bees?' Dave asked, poker-faced. 'Dick, you've got kids, how about you give the poor lad a bit of insight?'

Pete suppressed a grin with difficulty. Much as he enjoyed the team's banter, he couldn't be seen to encourage it too much. 'OK. Moving on . . . Maybe there'll be something useful in the stuff from her flat, Jill. Dick, have a word with Bob on the custody desk, see if you can track down anyone who knew Tennyson, knew anything about him, and talk to them. If not, try the university itself. Who wants a coffee?' Each of them raised a hand. 'OK. Ben, it's your turn. I need a leak.'

*

Pete found Ben filling the mugs in the kitchenette across from DCI Silverstone's office a few minutes later.

'I'll help you carry them. You found something?'

Ben looked up from the kettle in his hand. 'I've checked the whole of CID now. Only one anomaly came up.'

'Yes?'

'DS Phillips. He had fifteen grand pop up in his account last month.'

Pete's eyes widened. 'Where from?'

'Bank draft, so it's untraceable.'

'OK. We can't go off half-cocked on this. We need to find out if there's any legitimate reason for it. What's been going on in his

125

life recently? Has he spent any of it in a visible way?'

Ben shook his head. 'He put it into a savings account – not that it's doing him much good, with interest rates as they are.'

'Shame. It could have been a way into finding out where it came from. Still, I'll have a think on that. You carry on checking the rest of the station.'

'Right, boss.'

Ben stirred the drinks and Pete picked up three, including his own.

Back in the squad room, with rain lashing the front windows, he passed a mug to Dave Miles and another to Dick Feeney, then took his seat.

'The doc rang while you were out,' Dave told him. 'Said there's three more he's sure of and another two maybes. He's emailing you the details.'

'Christ, what are they trying to do – empty the damned city?' said Dick.

'It's a hell of spring clean, I'll give them that,' Dave agreed.

'If that's what it is,' Pete said.

'Boss?'

He met four pairs of attentive eyes. 'We haven't established the motive yet, have we? It could still all be a smokescreen to hide one intended victim.'

*

With the rest of the team occupied, Pete downloaded the files from Doc Chambers and began to research the victims he had listed. Like the ones they had known about before, the MOs were all different, the victims a mix of male and female, from all over the city and beyond. Some had criminal records, others didn't, and the sites of their deaths were widely spread and apparently random. There was no discernible pattern at all.

But, as he'd said, there didn't have to be. They could all be a smokescreen or they could all be random or opportunistic choices.

Could the clue be in the locations?

Who would go to all these various places and why?

Pete got up and crossed to the big city map on the wall. He plucked a handful of pins from the collection pushed into the cork backing along the bottom of the map and began to mark the kill sites, using red pins for female victims and blue for male.

When he'd finished, he stood back and surveyed the map. The spread still appeared to be completely random, covering the whole of the city, but he made a list of the addresses and locations anyway before using more pins to mark the victims' home addresses.

Taking another look at his results, he pursed his lips. Again, there was no discernible pattern. The only way to tell for sure if there was a link would be to visit the sites themselves.

They were also going to need to canvass each area for witnesses, he thought, but that was a job that uniform could handle. He'd arrange it once he'd seen the locations. He grabbed his jacket from the back of his chair and headed out.

*

As he drove down the side of the station, a lorry from one of the supermarkets went past, heading out of town. He stopped to let the stream of traffic behind it pass.

Glancing to his left, he saw the poster on the lamp-post again. This time, he could read it. A band called Whiplash were promising to 'rock your world' on Thursday night at a local pub venue. Pete thought of the posters he'd got in production right now, for Tommy. A few hours from now, he'd have them in his hand and, soon after that, they'd be going up all over the city.

He hoped to God Tommy would see one and get in touch.

The question was, where to put them. He'd spent weeks, back in the summer, cruising the city night after night, hoping against hope to spot his son or to run across someone who had.

The traffic cleared and he pulled out, turning right.

Maybe it would be down to someone else spotting Tommy and calling it in, rather than Tommy himself getting in touch. In which case, it couldn't hurt to get the case back into the papers, he thought. But how? The police had very strict rules about dealing with the press. They had a full department that specialised in just that, so to do it officially he'd need the DCI's approval.

He shook his head, slowing for the roundabout and signalling left. There was no way Silverstone was going to help him on this. It would have to be unofficial. Which would blot his copybook yet again, but he'd cross that bridge when he came to it. This was for Tommy, so he'd do whatever it took, regardless of what Silverstone thought about it.

He thought of Lee Birch, a young reporter from the *Express & Echo* who had been inspired by the recent abduction of young Molly Danvers and its aftermath to apply to join the force. He would help, if Pete went to him. But would his boss, Angela Davis? Recalling their last conversation, Pete seriously doubted it.

Still, if he spoke to Lee, maybe they could work out an angle that she couldn't resist.

He crossed the river and turned right, heading for the first stop on his search for possible links between the victims or the locations.

There had to be something that tied them together.

Chapter 14

The third new victim had been found slumped over with a needle in his arm, sitting cross-legged in the tent that he had lived in – one of three in the fenced-off site of former garages that had been pulled down to make way for new housing that never got built.

When Pete parked in front of the place and eased through a gap in the hoarding, he found the site covered with rubble and weeds and littered with rubbish. The stink of human waste assailed his nostrils as he saw the three tents still standing at the back of the site, a man in a black anorak and filthy jeans leaning over a camping stove, stirring the contents of a battered saucepan.

Pete raised his phone and took a quick snap of the site. The man in the tent glanced up uninterestedly then went back to whatever he was cooking. As Pete put his phone away and started towards the man a thought struck him like a blow to the gut.

Was this the way Tommy was living now? Was he out there somewhere, as vulnerable to these killers as this guy's late friend had been? More vulnerable, in fact. He was both physically smaller and so much younger and less streetwise. If they found him, as they had so many others, he wouldn't stand a chance. They'd kill him – probably torture him first – and dump him like so much rubbish.

Pete's throat clogged, his eyes growing hot and sore. He took a deep breath and tried to calm himself before stepping forward again to talk to the guy in front of him.

He stopped before he got too close, the sour stink of unwashed skin too much for his nose.

'Morning.' He took out his warrant card. 'Did you know Wayne Adams?'

'Snake? Yeah.'

'Do you know if he had a particular problem with anyone? Anyone take against him bad enough to do something about it?'

The guy gave a derisive snort. 'You're saying he was killed now?'

'It's a possibility we're looking into. I'm guessing he didn't have anything that anyone would want enough to hurt him for it.'

The man let his eyes roam the site around them. 'Prime bit of real estate, this.'

'I can see. Who's using his tent now?'

'Mick Duggan.'

Pete glanced across at the unoccupied tent. 'How's that work, then? He know Snake, or did he come along after?'

'They knew each other.'

'Any idea where I could find Duggan?'

The man shrugged. 'Said he was going to try to score today, but he had to make some cash first.'

'And how does he do that, as a rule?'

'Busking. Got a harmonica.'

A memory stirred in Pete's mind. Foot-tapping country and blues music echoing along a wide street. 'Long blond hair and a big beard, wears a curled-up Stetson and a long coat?'

'Yeah.'

'OK. Thanks. And what's your name, if you don't mind me asking?'

'They call me Ziggy.' He pulled off his hat. His ginger hair was a couple of inches long and completely wild.

Pete grinned.

'Alfie Bowens.'

'Thanks.' Pete nodded and turned away, walking a lot quicker on the way out of the place than he had on the way in. He pushed the loose hoarding back into place behind him and took a deep breath of clean air before climbing back into his car. An image of Tommy surviving in those same conditions, his small frame hunched over a fire, just like Ziggy had been, filled his mind. At least Ziggy had a tent. Did Tommy? And did he have company, like Ziggy, or was he alone?

They had to get those posters up, had to get him home before it was too late.

Pete shook his head, climbed into the car and was reaching for the ignition when his phone buzzed in his pocket. He took it out and checked the screen.

'DS Gayle.'

'Hi, boss.' It was Jill. 'Those papers you brought back from Brigit Mostova's flat. The bank statements don't show any payments for the flat.'

'As you'd expect. She'd have been paying in cash or kind or maybe a combination of the two.'

'Be good to find out which, wouldn't it?'

'In the meantime, you could put a call out for Mike Duggan. Busker with a harmonica, wears a long coat and a battered old cowboy hat. Just spot and report. I only want to ask him some questions.'

*

Duggan was spotted as Pete was heading back to the station. The radio crackled and a uniform call-sign was quoted over the airwaves. 'Somebody was looking for Mike Duggan. He's busking outside the railway station on Queen Street. Should we bring him in? Over.'

'Christ,' Pete muttered. That was the last thing he wanted. He snatched up the radio and keyed the mike. 'Negative. This is DS Gayle. Do not apprehend. Repeat, do not apprehend Michael Duggan. Leave him be. I'll be there in a few minutes. Just go on with your patrol. But thanks for finding him. Out.'

He hit the lights and siren, swung the car around and headed for the city centre.

Duggan was on the wide pavement outside the station, tucked back against the wall, far enough from the entrance not to cause an obstruction, but close enough to catch the attention of anyone passing in or out. Pete drove past and pulled up twenty yards further down the road, towards the clock tower. As he stepped out of the car, he could hear the breathless notes of 'Orange Blossom Special' echoing along the street. He walked up, dropped a two-pound coin into Duggan's open violin case and surreptitiously showed him his warrant card.

'Need a word,' he mouthed.

Duggan's striking blue eyes met his and he nodded. A few final notes on the harmonica and he wound up the tune, slipped the instrument into his coat pocket and pushed the battered and stained hat back on his head. 'What's up?'

'Best shut your case.' Pete nodded to the open instrument case on the ground between them. 'Won't take long, but you don't want to leave temptation lying around, eh?'

Duggan shrugged and gave the lid a kick, knocking it closed. He left the foot on top of it while he waited for Pete to tell him what he wanted.

'I understand you took over Wayne Adams' tent when he died.'

Duggan nodded.

'How come? Why you?'

He shrugged. 'He was a mate. He didn't need it no more.'

Pete tilted his head, acknowledging the point. 'Do you know how he died?'

'OD'd, didn't he.' It was a statement rather than a question.

'He did, but not in the way you think. He was poisoned.'

'What, bad shit?'

Pete nodded.

'Deliberate?'

Pete waited.

'Shit, man. That's evil.' He met Pete's gaze. 'Who done it?'

Pete smiled briefly. 'That's what I'm trying to find out. Do you know who he got his gear from?'

'Nah. Not into that stuff, am I? Baccy and booze – they're my things.'

'OK. But, if you find out, let me know, eh?' Pete handed him a card.

Duggan took the card and shook his head. 'That's twisted, man.' He took out his harmonica and blew a mournful wail that morphed into a slow, lamenting blues tune that Pete didn't recognise as he stepped off, glad of the fresher air, even just a few feet from Duggan's sour, unwashed body.

*

'So, Mr Perkins.' No point beating about the bush, Pete thought as he sat across from the man in an interview room at the station once more, an hour later. 'We've made a discovery that puts a bit of a new light on your relationship with Miss Mostova.'

Perkins' eyebrows rose.

'The rent on her flat. How was she paying it? Because it wasn't coming out of her bank account.'

Perkins nodded. 'I gave her a discount and she paid cash. It went straight in my wallet.'

'And have you got the same arrangement with any of your other tenants?'

'No, just Brigit. You only need so much cash in your pocket.' He shrugged.

'And how long had this been going on?'

'Ever since she moved in. She was paid cash, so she just put some aside for the rent. That's what she told me, anyway.'

Which was pretty much the answer Pete had expected, true or not. He would have to check with Dave when he got back from talking to whoever he'd found from the company. But, in the meantime . . . He leaned forward, elbows on the table. 'And she never paid the rent any other way, Mr Perkins?'

'What's that sup—? No, no, no.' He sat back, his hands flat on the table. 'I told you before, Sergeant. I'm a married man. I don't get up to that kind of thing. No way.'

Pete was nodding slowly. 'Gives you a possible motive, if that's what had been going on, though, doesn't it?'

'I . . .' He closed his mouth. 'I suppose it would, if that's what had been happening. But it's not.'

'What, you weren't even tempted? Pretty girl like that. Yours for the asking, if she didn't actually offer? Come on. What man wouldn't be?'

Perkins' lips thinned and his face darkened as Pete spoke. 'I was once told, Sergeant – "Don't judge others by your own standards." You might be temptable. I'm not. Not that way, at least.'

'Then, which way, Mr Perkins? What does tempt you, if not easy sex?'

'As I said, Sergeant, I'm happily married. I can be tempted with sex. Just not by anyone other than my wife. I also enjoy good food, good wine and scenic travel.'

'And where were you, the night of the fourteenth of October?'

'I don't know. That's weeks ago. Where were you?'

'At home. With my wife and daughter. But it's not me that needs an alibi, Mr Perkins.'

'I'm her landlord, Sergeant. Not her lover, boyfriend, business partner or anything else. I'm also innocent until proven guilty, not the other way round, so I don't need an alibi – *you* need proof of guilt. And you won't find it for me because I'm not guilty, so I suggest you move on and look at someone else.'

Pete pursed his lips. 'See, that's a mistake a lot of people make,

Mr Perkins. The courts assume innocence. I'm the police. We assume guilt. We have to. We're involved in a process of elimination in cases like this. So, once we've narrowed the field of suspects, then yes, we have to prove guilt. But until then, we're simply looking at means, motive and opportunity. So, until we establish that you didn't have the opportunity, you're stuck with being a suspect and we're stuck looking into your affairs in as much detail as we have to, to establish the truth. So, I suggest you have a careful think about that and see if you can't tell me where you were on the night in question after all.'

Perkins held his gaze. Gradually, the anger faded from his eyes, the lids narrowed slightly as his brain finally kicked into gear and he thought about the question. Then he blinked. 'Which day of the week was it?'

'Wednesday.'

'Tuesday, we were out to dinner with friends. Wednesday, I'm sure we stayed in.'

'No visitors?'

'No. Just the two of us, a bottle of wine and the TV.'

'Mm-hmm. Do you have a Sky TV box, Mr Perkins?'

Perkins shook his head quickly at the change of subject. 'Yes.'

'And would you have been using it that evening?'

'I expect so, yes.'

'Would you object to me or one of my colleagues checking it?'

'Of course not. Why?'

'Because it might help establish your alibi.'

'How?' He shook his head in confusion.

'When I watch something off the Sky box and don't want to keep it, I delete it, but those deleted programmes are kept for a certain length of time in another file on the hard drive. With the date and time that they were deleted. Is your wife likely to be in now?'

'Yes. Why?'

'She can corroborate which programmes you watch together,

so whether you were in to watch them with her and delete them that night, if they'd been pre-recorded. I'm looking to get a killer off the streets, Mr Perkins, not for an easy arrest.'

*

When Pete walked back into the squad room, his whole team were at their desks. He dropped his coat over the back of his chair and sat down.

'Evening, all. Let's have a quick summary of where we are, shall we? Who's first?' He looked around for volunteers, but there were none. 'Jane. You've been out all day. What can you tell us?'

'Petrosyan left between two and three in the morning. No van. One witness. Old lady a few doors down had got up for a pee, heard the car engine and looked out, saw a dark-coloured Mercedes driving away. Angle of view wasn't ideal, but she saw twelve DAJ on the plate. I've run it and it comes back to a Davit Achabahian.'

'Is that DAJ a private plate, then?' asked Dave.

Jane shook her head. 'No, just a coincidence. He lives in Exwick, so I went round there. The car was in the drive, but there was no movement in the house all afternoon.'

'We could give him a knock, though. Keep the pressure on,' Dave suggested.

'On what pretext?' Pete asked. 'We've got nothing to get a warrant on. Might as well leave him be. At least we know where to look for him when we need to. What have you got?'

Dave pulled the papers on his desk into a pile, picked them up and tapped them into a neat stack. 'I've spoken to Bill Williams, the transport manager at the bakery. He doesn't have any link to Trent and Sons and wasn't aware of anyone else at the bakery having one. He does remember Andrew Michaels though. A plodder was what he described him as. Slow but reliable. The reason he remembered him was that he was often the one to bring the trolleys out from the bakery.'

'OK, but did he say anything about him that'd be cause for concern?'

'No. But then I moved on to the model railway club. It was like I was talking about a different bloke. Outgoing, popular, a mover and a doer. Helped organise the annual exhibition and the Christmas do. In fact, the exhibition was his idea. He'd been to one in the Midlands, somewhere, and thought there ought to be one down this way.'

'You're right. That sounds completely different from everything else we've heard about him. Who did you talk to from there?'

'Club secretary Marion Keyes, the chairman, Vince Gavin, and a couple of the members – old boys that have been involved in it since the year dot.'

Pete was nodding.

'I've also looked into the earliest victim that the doc's identified. Bloke called Mark Fergusson. He lived down Bartholomew way. Had a little flat down there. He was a recovering alcoholic. Been dry for about a year until nineteen months ago. Then he polished off a bottle of whisky, laid down on a bench just a couple of minutes from his front door and never woke up. He was found by a passing milkman, next morning, stiff as a board. Seems like his dad died a couple of months before that, then his brother was killed in a car crash, along with his wife and kid, leaving our boy all alone in the world.'

'OK. Where's the suspicious element in there?'

'The fact that he was found with just the one empty bottle and he'd drunk at least two. More than anyone could drink on their own – even an alky. You'd black out long before you got there.'

Pete nodded slowly. 'So, he was fed the stuff. Good work. Jill?'

'I've looked into Brigit Mostova. She hasn't had a regular job since Trent and Sons closed down. Did a bit of temping, but the timing wasn't great for her. It dried up after a bit. The agency went through a bad patch, apparently. Barely survived, but they pulled through. Brigit left them, though, and I can't find any employment records for her after that. Regular deposits into her bank account though. Mostly cash.'

'So, that's when she went on the game,' said Dave.

'You reckon?' Dick said ironically.

'I can't find any other source for the income,' Jill resumed. 'I checked with the employment agency while I was on with them, to see if they'd ever had any dealings with Andrew Michaels or Jerry Tyler. They hadn't.'

'Good thought, though,' Pete said.

'I couldn't find any police records for her, so she never got nabbed for prostitution or made a complaint against anyone. And there's no links in Jerry Tyler's file to any of the other victims.'

'Dick, what did you dig up on the Prof?' Pete asked next.

Dick swallowed, Adam's apple bobbing in his narrow throat. 'The rumours were true. He did work at the uni. He was a professor of applied biology.'

'Science link noted,' Pete said.

'He lost his wife to cancer nineteen years ago. The grief got too much for him. Affected his work. He took to drinking too much. Eventually, the university had to let him go. They got him onto a rehab programme, but he dropped out. Then he gradually dropped out of society in general. Wasn't paying the bills, so his house got repo'ed. He's been homeless ever since. In and out of here, as we said before, on a frequent if not regular basis. Never did anybody any harm, just couldn't get off the sauce. Didn't want to, I reckon.'

'So, no links to any of the other subjects?'

'Not that I could find, but you never know. I mean, these homeless types wander about all over, don't they? He could have run across any of them at any time and made a connection, if only a fleeting one. We'll never know unless any of their friends or relatives were aware of it.'

Pete's eye was caught by the big clock at the far end of the squad room. Three minutes past five. Damn. He had to pick up those posters by half-past. 'OK. Next thing I need you to do is check Anthony Perkins' financial records for any significant outgoings or groups of outgoings that add up to a significant sum. I've confirmed his alibi for when Brigit Mostova was killed, but the fact he wasn't there doesn't mean he had nothing to do with it. Ben: edited highlights. I've got an appointment I can't miss.'

'How is the wife, boss?' Dave asked with a grin.

'It's not with her. Ben?'

'Boss. With the name of the guy at HQ who compiled the lists for Natterjack, I got hold of copies of the files they were composed from. He didn't include Petrosyan's lot because he wasn't given the info on them. No Armenians or similar on any of the lists. I did confirm who sent our list to him though.'

'And?'

Ben leaned forward in his chair, glanced over his shoulder, and spoke in little more than a whisper. 'I expected it to be Jim, but it wasn't. It was Simon Phillips.'

Chapter 15

'Wow, Dad! Twice in a row?'

Annie's hands were on her hips as she stood squarely in the front doorway, but her face gave the lie to her stance with the grin that was playing around her mouth and twinkling in her eyes. 'Are you going to be making a habit of coming home at this sort of time?'

Pete tossed his briefcase past her into the hall and scooped her up in his arms, playfully nuzzling her neck as he growled mock-anger back at her. He pushed the door shut behind him with his foot before putting her down. 'Certainly not, young lady. What kind of example would that set?'

He heard Louise say something in the sitting room, but didn't catch what it was. Picking up his briefcase, he stuck his head in there. As usual, she was curled up on the sofa, eyes glued to the TV, a game show on the screen.

'What was that?' he asked.

'I said, "A caring one. For your family,"' she said without taking her eyes from the screen.

'I'm home early *because* I care for my family,' he said, stepping into the room and nodding for Annie to follow him. He opened the briefcase and pulled out a stack of papers, dumped them on the coffee table and said, 'What do you think, both of you?'

Annie's eyes widened as she took in what they were. 'Brilliant! Where can we put them?'

The posters had come out better than he'd hoped, the lettering bold and high-contrast, the photo clear and sharp.

'Wherever we want to, Button. Wherever we think Tommy might see them or anyone else might see him.'

'I could take some copies to school, in case anyone's seen him.'

'You could. But you'd need to get the head teacher's permission before you put them up.'

'Yes!' She punched the air then gave him a hug. 'Thanks, Dad. Now I'll get tea.'

She scampered off to the kitchen and Pete turned to Louise. 'Hey. Was I being held to ransom there? She wasn't going to feed me until I gave in?'

Louise shrugged. 'She's your daughter.'

'So, what do you think of them?' he asked, motioning towards the posters.

'They should do the job, if you can get them out and about.'

'Yeah, what about that? What we talked about before.'

She looked up at him with a frown. 'I told you: I'll go out when I'm ready. I don't need to be pushed.'

He raised his hands, palms up. 'Hey, I just thought maybe, if you've got something to go out *for*, it'd help, that's all. I mean, with this case to deal with and . . .' He stopped himself with a shrug. She didn't need to know about the other thing. She wouldn't say anything to anyone, of course, but Silverstone had made it perfectly clear – nobody outside of his team was to know about it. And Pete knew he meant absolutely nobody.

'And what?'

Damn. She wasn't any less observant, was she? 'The fact that Annie can't be left alone.'

She stared at him in silence.

'Well, she can't, can she?' He spread his hands wide. 'She might be grown up way beyond her years, but the fact is she's still only ten. I know it's sometimes easy to forget, but . . .'

Louise pursed her lips, not entirely convinced.

'Do you want a cup of tea?'

She grunted. 'OK.'

*

'Lee. You still with the *E. & E.*?'

Pete had called the young reporter from his mobile, as he had the number programmed into it from two weeks ago, when he'd witnessed a young victim of abduction and rape running into the hospital. It was just past nine in the evening. Annie was in bed. Louise was in her usual seat on the sofa, eyes glued to the TV while he went out to the hallway to make the call.

'Yes, for a bit longer,' Birch said. 'I'm joining up as a PCSO in January, then going into training on the next intake.'

After his experience outside the hospital and its aftermath, Lee had decided to quit journalism and join the police.

'Well, while you're still there, I've got a little something for you. You're the only one I'm calling.'

'Oh, yes? What's up?'

'There's going to be flyers appearing round the city, aimed at bringing Tommy Gayle back home. We've got a witness statement that, not only is he still in the area, but he was another victim of the guy who took Rosie Whitlock.'

'Wow. He's been gone how many months? And he's still around?'

'Mm-hmm. I've typed something up for you. I'll read it, shall I?'

'OK.'

'It has emerged that another potential victim of the alleged Exeter child-rapist Malcolm Burton, thirteen-year-old Thomas James Gayle, is still at large having escaped his captor near the Co-op on Dunsford Road. Thomas, known as Tommy, is believed to be on the run, assuming that he is somehow implicated in Burton's crimes, though surviving victim Rose Whitlock, also thirteen, refutes this categorically. Anyone spotting Tommy, who may be living rough, should not approach him, but should contact the local police by calling 101. A trained officer will then be dispatched to provide the assurances necessary to bring him home to his family.

'Tommy went missing in May of this year. It was reported at the time that his father was local detective sergeant Peter Gayle, the man behind the recovery of Rosie Whitlock and the subsequent arrest of Malcolm Burton. His mother, Staff Nurse Louise Gayle, thirty-seven, is reported to be still off work with the stress of his disappearance.'

'Wow. Anybody would think you read the papers, Sarge. Maybe we ought to just swap jobs, eh?'

'Huh. Once this comes out, I might well be looking for another job.'

'Get out of it. They can't sack you now. It'd be a PR disaster.'

'I hope you're there to tell DCI Silverstone that when he reads that piece.'

Lee laughed. 'Not likely. I've only met him once, but I don't think I'd want to cross him.'

'Ah, you flutter your eyelashes at him, you'll be fine.'

'Jesus. My sphincter's clenching at the thought. He isn't, is he?'

'I'm saying nothing.'

'Now, that would be a scoop! But, talking of bosses, how am I going to sell this to mine? You're not exactly her favourite person after the other day.'

Pete had had to make a brusque and demanding phone call to her after Lee saw the young girl running into the hospital – the kind of call that she was far more used to making than receiving – and it had not sat well with her.

'Like I said, it's an exclusive. Flyers will be going up around the city, starting tomorrow. And the Burton case is still news.'

He heard the younger man sigh on the other end of the line. 'I'll see what I can do, but I can't make any promises, Sarge.'

'All I'm asking is that you try.'

'Will do, Sarge.'

Pete ended the call and returned to the sitting room.

Louise hadn't moved and didn't now as he sat down next to her. 'So?' she asked.

'He'll try.' He shrugged. 'It's all I can ask of him. Whether Angela Jennings will run it, we'll have to wait and see.'

'Why wouldn't she? It's news, isn't it?'

'Yes, but she might see it differently, just to be difficult. I spoke to her last week, after Molly Danvers was attacked, and I had to be a bit sharp with her, to get what I needed. Just depends how thick-skinned she is, I suppose.'

'She's running a newspaper. How thick-skinned does she need to be?'

Pete nodded slowly. 'Good point, well made.'

*

He had no idea what the time was and didn't want to know, but it was deep into the night when he got up to go to the bathroom. He came back to bed, slipped under the duvet and lay there, listening to Louise's soft, regular breathing.

It must have been a full minute or more before Louise released a long sigh.

'I've decided. I'll do it,' she said.

Pete stiffened then turned towards her. 'Really?'

He sensed rather than saw her nod in the darkness. 'If I can't make the effort, I can't really say anything about anyone else, can I?'

'Except anyone else hasn't got the same issues that you have.'

'That's not the point, though, is it? I'm his mother. Mothers go through hell and back for their kids. You've seen it and so have I.'

Pete nodded, remembering the case she was talking about. A case they had both worked on – he to investigate the cause of the fire, she to treat the twenty-nine-year-old mother who had crossed a blazing landing to reach her two young children. She had suffered horrific burns, but had saved her kids, smashing a double-glazed window to be able to drop them to a couple of neighbours with a sheet that she'd thrown down first. She had then jumped, breaking one ankle and the opposite hip when she landed on a concrete drive. But her first concern was for her babies. Unable to stand, she had still insisted on holding them both until the ambulance arrived.

With nothing he could say, Pete simply leaned over and kissed her.

Chapter 16

'Jesus! What time did you get in this morning?' Pete asked as he dropped his coat over the back of his chair.

Ben glanced around the big, open-plan room, but they were the only two in there.

'Half-six. Had to be sure to have the place to myself for a bit.'

'And what have you found?'

'I've been tracking where DS Philips compiled the list he sent to Middlemoor from. He used several sources. Custody records, confidential informants, information from other CID officers – primarily Jim Hancock's team, of course – and from the uniform branch.'

'Talking of Jim, why didn't he compile the list?'

Ben grimaced. 'Don't know. Independent eye, I suppose. He's the usual suspect on drugs, so DCI Silverstone obviously decided to have someone do it who's not normally connected. I looked at the original documents he drew the list up from, too. Couldn't see anything having been deleted from them.'

'How'd you get hold of them?'

'They're still on his computer over there.' Ben nodded towards Simon Phillips' desk.

'You didn't?'

'I said I needed to be in early.'

Pete shook his head. The boy had nerve to spare. 'Anything else useful?'

'A Twitter feed from his missus. Her dad died. That's where the fifteen grand came from.'

'And you've confirmed that?'

'Yes.'

'So, back to square one. No financial motive. But, if that's the case, what *is* the motive? What else could it be? Whether it's Simon or not, someone's corrupted the law, put their whole career in jeopardy and even risked jail to let a drug dealer stay in business – and expand his operation into the gaps left by us sweeping up all his competition. You can see why Petrosyan would want to push someone into a stunt like that, but it would take a pretty significant motive to get a police officer of any rank to risk everything.'

'Yes, but . . . I've already checked and no one in the station here has any links to Eastern Europe, never mind Armenia, so . . .'

'Sounds like a bloody stupid question, but has anyone in the station got any links to outstanding crimes? I mean personal links, not professional.'

'What, like . . .?' He tilted his head appreciatively. 'I don't know. I'll check.' Turning back to his computer, he began tapping rapidly at the keyboard.

*

Pete checked the time. It was 8.35 a.m. A couple of other people had come into the squad room, but they were towards the far end, members of Mark's and Jim's teams. He picked up the phone and dialled.

He had almost given up waiting when it was finally answered. 'Whipton Secondary School. How can I help?'

'This is Detective Sergeant Gayle of Exeter CID. I need to

speak to the head, please.'

'I'm afraid he's preparing for assembly just now, sir. Could it wait an hour?'

'The point of the call is to speak to him before he goes into assembly.'

There was a pause. 'Very well. One moment, please.'

The ringing tone returned as she put him through. Again, it rang several times before being picked up.

'Whipton Secondary. Brian Sherburne speaking.'

'Morning, Mr Sherburne. Detective Sergeant Gayle here. Exeter CID. I'm glad I caught you before assembly. There's something I need you to announce to your students before they see it in the local paper.'

'Indeed. And what might that be, Detective Sergeant? Gayle. Do I take it you're Tommy's father?'

'That's right. It's about Tommy that I'm calling. If you could just tell your pupils this morning that he's known to be alive and still in the area and that we're looking for him as a missing person rather than as a suspect in any crime, that could be very helpful. You may know from the press already that he's been linked to the abduction, the week before last. The young girl from Risingbrook School. But he's being sought purely as another victim.'

'I see. And what benefit do you see from that, Detective Sergeant?'

'For one thing, it'll give your pupils a heads-up before it appears in the papers. For another, if any of them are in touch with him somehow, it might help us find him so that he can act as a witness against the perpetrator of a child abduction. We have the primary victim's testimony, of course, but the more evidence we can provide, the more certain we are of putting a dangerous man in prison, where he can't harm any more kids.'

'Very well. I'll include something in my morning address.'

The door to Pete's right opened and he glanced across to see Jim Hancock enter, followed by Simon Phillips. They continued a conversation that he couldn't hear as they crossed towards their desks and he felt the slump of disappointment.

'OK. Thank you, Mr Sherburne.'

He ended the call. How the hell was he going to talk to Jim now, with Simon there, too? Then he looked down at his right hand, which was still resting on the telephone receiver. He picked it up again and dialled.

'Jim,' he said when it was picked up. 'It's Pete. Don't let on. Give it half a minute and meet me in the kitchen, yeah? I'll explain in there.'

'OK . . .'

He put the phone down again and stood up. 'Nature calls. Back in a minute,' he said to Ben. 'Stay sharp.'

*

'Jim.'

'What's all the cloak-and-dagger about?' Hancock asked as he closed the door of the little kitchen behind him.

'Operation Natterjack. You're the one who specialises in drugs cases, so how come Simon handled the arrest lists?'

Jim's eyebrows shot up. 'I was busy. He was less so. Why? What's up?'

'You ever come across a bloke known as the Armenian?'

Jim shook his head, the corners of his mouth pulling down. 'Just a rumour, isn't he? A bit of scary fiction put about by some of the dealers to keep their clients in line.'

'How about Zivan Millic?'

'One of said dealers. I've had him in the cells a couple of times, but nothing ever stuck.'

'The Armenian was his supplier. Boss, even. Was, because Millic is dead.'

Jim's eyes widened. 'How?'

'Car accident that wasn't. His brakes had been tampered with.

I'm trying to find out who did it.'

'Well, whoever it was, they did the city a favour.' Jim leaned back against the worktop and crossed his ankles.

'Yeah, that's the impression I got. But the point is, he and the Armenian weren't on the arrest lists for Natterjack.'

'We could never pin down where Millic lived, for one thing, so that kind of kept him out of the picture. And the Armenian – well, he's just a bogey-man type of thing.'

'Gagik Petrosyan.'

No reaction.

'Who's he?'

'The Armenian. I spoke to him yesterday, but he did a midnight flit last night.'

Jim grunted.

'Still, he won't have gone too far. He's got a business to run.'

Jim grimaced again. 'So, what's all this leading to, then?'

'That Petrosyan's apparently the head of a whole organisation. Family business, you might say. But none of his crew were on the lists that Simon sent in, so I'm wondering why.'

'What, you think . . .? No.' He shook his head. 'He's got his faults, we all know that, but no. You've been out of the office too long, mate. Simon's not bent. No way.' He pushed away from the worktop.

'So, what is he? Because the facts are there, for whatever reason.'

Jim sighed and reached out to clap Pete gently on the shoulder. 'I know he's not got anywhere with Tommy, mate, but even you don't get your man every time. It doesn't mean you're not good at your job. Sometimes we just don't have the information. Simple as that.'

Pete pursed his lips. This had got him nowhere, except for confirming his suspicion that Jim had had nothing to do with the matter. Either that or he was an Oscar-worthy actor. 'I don't need to ask you to keep this conversation between us, do I?'

'What conversation?'

Pete clapped him on the shoulder and stepped past him to the door. 'Thanks, mate.'

He headed back to his desk in the squad room. Several more people were in now, including Dave and Jill of his own team. He shared a glance with Ben, who shook his head slightly, then sat down and switched on his computer. The windows logo was still on the screen when he felt a presence at his shoulder and Simon Phillips muttered in his ear. 'What the hell's your game, Gayle?'

'Eh?' He spun around. 'What's the matter with you?'

'This morning's *Express & Echo*. Page two. "Boy still missing." That piece has got your fingerprints all over it.'

'I wouldn't know. I haven't seen it.'

Phillips slapped the paper down on Pete's desk, folded to show the offending article. Pete picked it up, looked at it, then back up at Simon. 'You know as well as I do, I'm not their editor's favourite person. No way she's going to do me any favours.'

'If this is you deliberately undermining my case, I'll have your badge. So help me.' Simon snatched the paper back and stalked off. Pete watched him head back towards his desk, then turned to face his own. Dave was looking across, one eyebrow raised.

'Dissent in the ranks, boss? That's not setting a good example to the troops.'

Pete shrugged. 'I'm just sat here, minding my own business, Dave.'

'That's your story and you're sticking to it, eh? Nice piece. Short and to the point. Should be effective, if he sees it. But what's with the posters? There's a by-law against that, you know.'

Pete spread his hands. 'Do you see any posters about my person? No. And they're not in my desk or in my car, either. But, if they were to appear, they'd only be a few among thousands around the city. Even the bloody lamp-post outside here's been done. Some band or other.'

'If you can't beat 'em, join 'em, eh?' Dave laughed. 'I don't think that's quite the line we're supposed to take, officially.'

'And you're such an expert on sticking to the rules.'

'You gotta know them to know how to break them.'

'Sergeant Gayle,' Silverstone's voice barked across the big room. 'My office. Now, please.'

Pete grimaced and Dave tossed a phone book over to him. 'What's that for?'

'Back of your trousers, boss. Takes the sting out of the cane wonderfully.'

Ben snorted, trying not to laugh in case the DCI was still in earshot. 'Don't do that,' he said to Dave. 'You could choke a body.'

'That's all right. Jill's trained in CPR, aren't you, Jill?'

'Don't bring me into your sordid little games, Dave Miles.'

As Pete stood up, he saw Dave wink at Ben.

'She loves me, really.'

'I could slap you, really.'

Pete headed for the door, but still heard Dave's reply. 'Now who's getting sordid? I've told you before, we've got to keep those kinds of games private.'

He fought to suppress the grin that was pulling at the corners of his mouth. He didn't know what Silverstone's problem was, but he was certain that grinning like an idiot wouldn't help.

As he stepped into the corridor, he focused on what the DCI might be about to bollock him for. Had he seen the newspaper, as Simon had? Had Simon gone to him already to make a complaint? Or was there something else? He didn't know, but by the time he reached Silverstone's door, the grin had been replaced by a frown.

He knocked.

'Come.'

Pete opened the door and stepped in. 'Morning, sir. I'm glad you shouted. I wanted to talk to you this morning. The issue with Operation Natterjack. There's a couple of things with it, at this stage. One, I need to ask why you had Simon, rather than Jim, compile the lists for the arrest teams. And two, I need to ask you to speak to Simon about it.'

Pete was watching Silverstone's face closely as he kept talking, not allowing him to get a word in while he focused on a subject that he knew the senior officer would want to hear about.

'The thing is, we've managed to discount any financial or familial motive for whoever we're looking for, so we're trying to find any other motive that might exist. But, at the same time, there doesn't seem to be any tampering or deletions between what Simon sent to Middlemoor and what came back in the final arrest lists, so now we need to know where Simon got his information from before we can go any further. And a question like that would be less likely to alert anybody who had something to hide if it came from you, wouldn't it? The whole operation being your idea, as I understand it. You see what I mean, sir?'

Silverstone's expression had gone from anger through frustration to reluctant interest. Pete hoped he'd done enough to diffuse the worst of the DCI's mood, whatever the reason for it.

'None of which alters the reason for my calling you in here, Sergeant.' He slapped the morning newspaper down on his desk, opened to the article about Tommy. 'I want an explanation. And it had better be a good one, if you want to stay a detective sergeant. Or a police officer, for that matter.'

'I don't know what you want me to say, sir. As you've made abundantly clear, it's Simon's case, although he's got absolutely nowhere with it, as far as anyone outside his team can tell. I can't comment on what he may or may not have released to the press, but Simon showed this to me himself, a few minutes ago, and I can't see that it can do any harm. It doesn't say anything that could compromise either his case or the one against Malcolm Burton. And it looks pretty much designed to encourage a potential witness in the latter case to come forward and provide extra testimony, which can only be a good thing, I'd have thought.'

Silverstone's lips had compressed into a thin line, the muscles at the corners of his jaw clenching. 'Simon tells me he didn't release anything to the press. He feels this is a deliberate attempt to undermine him and interfere directly in one of his cases. And you know perfectly well that that is not permitted and will not be tolerated, Sergeant. Now, did you, or did you not, speak to this Lee Birch character?'

'Yes, sir. I saw him downstairs in reception on Friday. If I recall correctly, we discussed the relative merits of journalism and policing as career choices.'

Silverstone stared fiercely at him for a long moment. 'If I find out that you talked to a reporter about an open case, Sergeant, you'll be back directing traffic in Okehampton before you know what's hit you.'

'Sir.' *And that will be something for the press to get their teeth into*, he thought, but kept to himself. 'I think Bob was on the front desk when I spoke to Mr Birch. He may have heard what we talked about. Will you talk to Simon about where he sourced his information from, regarding Operation Natterjack?'

Silverstone leaned forward, arms on his desk. 'I am not completely stupid, Sergeant. I can see exactly what you're doing and it won't work. I'm not going to tolerate breaches of clear and established rules and regulations. Mark my words. There will be consequences.'

'Of course, sir. I . . .' Pete had an idea. He let the fact show on his face. 'I wonder if all this isn't some sort of attempt, on Simon's part, to deflect us away from a more serious matter. Like the one I came in to speak to you about.'

Silverstone sighed. 'I'll talk to him, Sergeant. I'll also talk to Mr Birch.'

'Thank you, sir. Oh, and why did you ask Simon to compile the lists, rather than Jim?'

'A simple matter of workload. Simon's was less intense at the time than Jim's. He had the time to do it when Jim didn't. Now, get out of my sight before I lose what little patience I have left.'

*

'There's got to be some sort of link, however tenuous.'

Pete signalled and pulled over to the side of the road thirty yards short of the turning bay where it ended.

'Yeah, but what if it's just the killer?' Jane said as she unclipped her seat belt. 'He *is* somehow the link.'

The atmosphere on the industrial estate was completely different to how it had been after all the businesses were closed up for the night. Cars, vans and lorries were coming and going. Across the road, a sign-written van had pulled up on the pavement and the driver was chatting with a couple of guys who had come out of the business premises beyond. A man had just gone back into the tyre place next door, having been standing outside, smoking a cigarette. The hum and whine of machines came from various points around them as they opened the car doors and stepped out.

'You're a cheerful sod, this morning.' Pete stepped out of the car and closed the door.

Jane shrugged, smiling. 'You know what they say. Life's hard and then you die.'

Pete locked the car and they stepped away towards the end of the road. 'Yeah, so what's the point of making it harder than it is already?'

'I'm just pointing out the possibility, boss.'

A compressed-air drill rattled in the tyre fitters' nearby.

'All right. So, if it was true, how would you deal with it?'

Jane pursed her lips, frowning. 'With no physical evidence, it's going to come down to profiling, isn't it? I mean, who would be likely to be in all the places where you'd run across the various victims, and at the right times of day?'

'Well, Andrew Michaels limits that for a start,' Pete pointed out, as they crossed the turning bay towards the high metal fence that screened off the shrubby, weed-choked waste-ground beyond. 'He was a home bird except for when he went out to the dole office or the model train club.'

'And we've seen what happened to him. But how would that tie in to Brigit's lifestyle? She'd have been a night owl, wouldn't she? So, what are we looking for?' she asked, changing the subject.

'Anything the killer might have left when he was carrying out the attack on Brigit.'

'Well, we ain't getting over there,' she said, looking at the pointed tops of the two-metre metal uprights that made up the fence.

'There'll be a way around somewhere, if we need it.'

'You hope.'

'Well, if not, I'll toss you over. How's that for a plan?'

'Charming.'

'That's me. You start at that end, I'll go left and we'll meet in the middle.'

'OK.'

They split up and Pete went around the curve into the turning bay as far as he thought a hosepipe was likely to reach, plus a few paces extra just in case. He looked around. Pavement, road, fence. A few oil stains on the tarmac. Nothing else within reach. He checked the gutter then moved across to look through the fence. Began moving back around the curve towards Jane.

There had been all kinds of weather in the weeks since Brigit Mostova died, so he wasn't expecting to find much, but that made the need for care even greater. Pete took his time, searching everywhere for the smallest of details. A bloodstain. A cigarette butt. A scuff mark. Anything could be significant. He could afford to miss nothing.

He had barely moved ten feet towards her when Jane shouted. 'Hey, boss. I think I've got something.'

Pete made a mental note of the exact spot he'd reached then went to meet her. She was standing beside the fence, waiting for him.

'What have you got?'

She nodded towards the fence. 'Looks like a bit of white cord.

The type of thing she might have been tied with.'

He reached where she was standing and peered between the metal stanchions but saw nothing. 'Where?'

'About three feet in, right by that bunch of dock leaves.'

He looked again but could still see nothing white until he ducked down closer to Jane's eye level.

'Ah. Got it.' The quarter-inch thick strand was curled in under the wide, leathery leaves. 'Good find. Now, how do we get at it?'

'I've said before, I leave the clever stuff to you.'

Chapter 17

'Find anything, boss?' Dave asked as they walked back into the squad room.

'Jane did,' Pete said, taking his jacket off and hanging it over the back of his chair. 'Don't know if it'll be any use after a few weeks out there in the weather, but we took it to Forensics anyway. What about you lot?' Leaning both hands on the back of his chair, he looked from one to another of his team.

'We've been searching for links between the victims,' Dick said. 'And come up totally empty. There's nothing. We can't even find any proof that they went to the same supermarket.' He shrugged. 'They might have, but we can't prove it.'

Pete nodded. 'So, where does that leave us?' He had his own ideas, but he wanted the team to think about it.

'Right back where we started,' Dave said glumly.

'Not quite,' Jill said. 'If the victims didn't know each other, the link between them has to be the perp. Even if they're random choices, for whatever reason, he had to find them somehow.'

'So, are we looking for a spree killer?' asked Ben. 'Shit, they're almost impossible to track down unless they make a mistake.'

'That's not the only other option,' Jill argued. 'Could be just one of the victims is the true target. We need to check if any of the victims had a problem with anyone.'

'Although, playing devil's advocate,' Dick said, 'it could be that he hasn't killed the real victim yet.'

'Jesus! You're a real ray of bloody sunshine this morning,' Dave shot back sourly. 'Come on then. You've put us in it, now get us out of that particular shit-hole.'

Dick shrugged. 'I was just saying. But all we've got apart from what Jane found down on Marsh Barton is the CCTV footage from the High Street. The gang of lads that were larking about around Andrew Michaels before he died.'

'Ben's already been to the uni. Where else do we try looking for them?'

'We need to narrow it down, that's all. I mean, they probably are from the university – it's just a question of which part.'

'Well, they're not going to be in the Humanities faculty, are they?' Jill said.

'I still think we've got to be looking at medicine, pharmacy or the sciences of some sort,' Pete said.

'What is this then?' asked Dick. 'Some sort of experiment?'

'Could be. We just don't know what sort yet. So, we need photos of the gang from the High Street. Then we need to revisit friends, family and neighbours of the victims as well as the university again to see if anyone recognises any of them and find out if any of the victims was having problems with anyone. And, in the meantime, we wait and see what Forensics comes back with, if anything, on the rope from Marsh Barton. Dick and Jill, you can take the university. Jane, you go down to the High Street and up Castle Street where they looked like they came from. Dave, you and I'll check with the victims' families. Let's see if we can actually get somewhere today, eh?'

*

Pete knocked on the dark blue door of the house opposite Jeremy Tyler's. This was the fifth one he'd tried since he left the station after spending two hours on the phone. So far, he'd got two no-answers and two who had come to the door but not seen anything unusual on or around the night that Tyler died.

He saw movement through the frosted glass, heard a chain being slid into place and the door finally opened. A woman, probably in her mid-seventies with silvery-white hair, peered through the gap.

Pete held up his warrant card. 'Afternoon, ma'am. DS Pete Gayle from Heavitree Road CID. I wonder if I could ask you a couple of quick questions.'

'What about?'

'The fire across the road. Did you see or hear anything out of the ordinary around the time it happened or just before?'

'Don't think so, no. Which night was it?'

'Tuesday.'

'Tuesday.' She nodded slowly. Then her blue eyes lit up. 'Yes, of course. Tuesday. I always watch *Holby* on telly. Just before it, there was—'

Pete's phone rang abruptly and she stopped, frowning.

'Sorry,' he said, taking it out and glancing at the screen. Surprise jolted through him. It was Louise's mobile number. Why wasn't she using the landline? He glanced up at the old lady. 'Hold that thought, would you? I need to take this. Won't be a moment.' He turned away and took a step back down the path. 'Lou? What's up?'

'Pete? Can you come and get me? I'm . . .' She broke down and he heard her sobbing quietly over the phone.

'What's going on, Lou? What do you mean, "get you"? Where are you?'

'I'm . . .' She choked and sobbed again. 'Oh God. I'm on St David's Road. I went out to put some of these damn posters up and I . . .' Again, she stopped, crying. 'Pete, I can't move.'

'OK. Just take it easy. Stay put and try to relax. I'll be there in a few minutes.'

He ended the call and turned back to the old lady. 'Sorry about that. Bit of an emergency. You were saying about Tuesday evening, just before *Holby City* started.'

She frowned. 'Was I? What about it?'

'Something happened. You saw or heard something out here.'

'Tuesday?'

Get on with it, for Christ's sake. 'You were just about to settle down in front of the telly.'

'Oh.' She brightened suddenly. 'Yes, that's right. The night of the fire. I'd just put my cuppa on my tray, came across to shut the curtains – I never bother until I actually come into the room, you know – and I looked out and saw a couple of young lads coming out from Mr Tyler's place, over there. I thought it was odd because he never gets visitors, you know. Keeps himself to himself. Nice enough chap. He's helped me with a couple of things now and then. But—'

'What did these lads look like?' Pete interrupted before she could go too far off on a tangent.

'I don't know. It was dark. One of them looked like he had a leather jacket on. Light brown, it looked. The other might have had a waxed coat. Dark, curly hair. You could see it shine under the street lights.'

Pete pictured the High Street CCTV of Andrew Michaels at the moment he died. The lads larking about round him. It could be a couple of them.

'Laughing and joking as they went off up the street, they were. Then I closed the curtains and that was it until all the fuss and bother over there, sirens and blue lights and all that.'

'OK.' He took the sheet of photographs of the lads on the High Street from the folder in his hand and held it out to her. 'Do you recognise any of these people?'

She frowned, peering closely at the pictures. 'Bit blurry, ain't they?' She looked up at him. 'Hmm. No. I couldn't say. Not from them.'

Pete grimaced, disappointed, but he couldn't blame her. The pictures weren't very sharp and, at her age, she'd need them to be pin sharp and enlarged a lot more than the three-inches high that the A4 format of the printout allowed. 'Well, thanks anyway. You've been very helpful. Now, I'd better go and answer that call I had a minute ago.' He turned and headed quickly back down the garden path.

St David's Road was at the far end of the estate where they lived, towards Whipton, where Tommy's secondary school was located. Louise had obviously had the idea to put a few posters up around there in case the kids saw them and knew anything. Good idea, he thought, as he reached his car and hopped in. It was a shame it had turned out to be too ambitious for her first foray outside the house in months.

He started the engine, hit the throttle and the blue lights.

It might not be an official call, but it was certainly urgent.

*

Pete saw Louise from fifty yards away as he turned into the end of the street. She was sitting on a low, crenellated brick wall at the front of someone's garden. He turned the flashing lights off and drew to a halt in front of her, double-parking in the middle of the road. It wasn't until he stopped the car that she looked up. He got out and went over to her.

'Where've you been?'

'Where . . .? I've been working, is where I've been.' He took a breath. 'What happened here?'

Her eyes looked haunted. She sat stiff-backed on the bricks, hands deep in her coat pockets.

'Bloody cold weather, I suppose. I was . . . down there. See all those leaves all over the place?' She pointed to a spot about thirty

162

yards away where a large buddleia overhung the footpath from one of the gardens. 'I slipped on them, nearly fell. Looked down and they were all around me. And then there was somebody behind me. I heard his footsteps. I panicked and froze. I couldn't move. I waited until he'd gone and I still couldn't move so, after a bit, I phoned you.' Her face crumpled. 'God, I feel like such an idiot. I was stuck there for ages until I got the courage up to move. Then I tiptoed out of there like some sort of cartoon burglar.'

Pete took her in his arms and held her, unable to say anything until his mind cleared of its initial reaction. 'It's OK,' he finally muttered into her hair. 'I'm here now.'

'God, I'm so bloody pathetic!' she sobbed, clinging to him.

'Rubbish. You walked here from home?' He stood back, still holding her as he looked around them.

'Yes.'

'Well, that's an achievement on its own. It's got to be nearly half a mile.'

'Yeah, and six months ago it would have been nothing. Look at me! I'm a mess. A snivelling, useless mess.' She stepped in, clinging to him again.

'No, you're not.' He gathered her into his arms as she broke into tears. Let her cry for a while before giving her a squeeze. 'Come on, let's get home, eh? We can get the posters up another time.'

'And what good will that do? You've already told the paper they're going up today. If they don't, you'll lose credibility *and* it'll be another day wasted when we could have contacted Tommy.'

'So I'll put some up later, myself. I'm out and about this afternoon, anyway, trying to track down witnesses.' He settled her in the passenger seat and closed the car door, wishing he had the time to do the job thoroughly himself. But, with this case to deal with . . .

'What, and they're not missing you in the squad room?' she said, as he climbed in next to her.

He ignored the jibe. 'We're all out and about this afternoon. A lot of ground to cover and not much time to do it in.'

He started the car and moved off. Had just turned the corner at the end of the road when his phone rang in his pocket. He used the car's Bluetooth system to answer it. 'DS Gayle.'

'Pete, it's Andy. We just had a call I thought you might be interested in. Homeless guy died down on the Quay.'

He glanced at Louise, but she was staring straight ahead. 'Died?'

'Yeah. Took a dive off the bank above the arches. Didn't go quite to plan, we're guessing.'

'Why?'

'It looks like he was trying a belly-flop onto the flagstones down there, but one of those iron posts got in his way. Direct hit. Nasty mess, apparently. A few very queasy-feeling tourists for witnesses.'

'Oh, thanks. Who's on-scene?'

'Mick Douglas and Sophie Clewes.'

'OK. And why am I likely to be interested?'

'Well, I know the guy's homeless, but even they don't tend to get that bloody high during the day, do they? So I thought there might be something dodgy in it, although I gather he went down quietly. No yelling.'

'Mm.' Pete pursed his lips and glanced at Louise again. 'OK. I'll be there shortly.'

'Right. I'll pass that on.'

He closed the call. 'I'll drop you off, then head down there.'

Louise said nothing for a moment, then: 'How about you go straight there. I'll ride along. You can take me home after.'

She was facing forward, her expression closed.

'You sure?'

She drew a breath. 'I could do with the company for a bit, all right? And it's not like I haven't seen blood before, is it?'

He tilted his head. As a nurse, she'd probably seen more than he had. 'OK.'

At the next junction, instead of turning right towards home, he turned left, heading back towards the main road.

*

When Pete drove down onto the Quay, the wide paved area was crowded with people. Two patrol cars were already parked to either side of Doc Chambers' black estate car and a line of police tape was strung across from the far end of the antique shop to the tourist information centre opposite. Two uniformed officers stood behind the tape, keeping the crowds back.

Pete pulled up the handbrake and turned off the engine. He looked across at Louise. She was staring out at the milling people around them with an expression of mixed horror and distaste.

'I won't be long.'

She grunted.

He squeezed her hand and stepped out of the car. After weaving through the crowd, he nodded to one of the uniformed officers at the tape and ducked under it. To his left, a bunch of people sat around the white cast-iron tables outside a café. They looked subdued, several of them pale and ill. Sophie Clewes and Dave's five-a-side mate Mick Douglas stood near them. He saw them exchange a few words and Sophie headed towards him.

A white canvas screen had been erected about thirty yards further down the Quay. Two pairs of plastic-covered feet showed beyond it where two of the crime-scene technicians were working – or perhaps one of them was Doc Chambers.

'Hello, Sarge. How's it going?'

He turned back to her. 'You tell me, Sophie. What have we got?'

'Looks like a jumper. Witnesses over there.' She waved a hand back towards the tables where she'd come from. 'They say they didn't hear anything. No scream or whatever. The first anyone knew about it, he was flying through the air. Hit one of those metal posts along there with the chain going through them.' She grimaced. 'Right mess. Nearly cut him in half.'

Pete sucked air through his teeth. 'Any idea who he is?'

She shook her head. 'His clothes suggest homeless, but beyond

165

that . . . I don't recognise him and nor does Mick.'

Pete sighed. 'Best go see if the forensics chaps have found anything useful, then. Thanks, Soph.'

'Sarge.' She turned back to her colleague and the witnesses while Pete headed along the old quayside.

The windbreak in its heavy metal feet was about four feet high so he could see nothing until he was just two or three steps away. The smell reached him first – the ferrous tang of blood over the unique nose-curling smell of fresh death.

Blood and gore had sprayed out across the flagstones. The blood was already beginning to brown as it clotted, but still pooled red in the gullies between the pavement slabs. The body, as Sophie had said, was impaled on one of the round-topped black iron stanchions. The face was turned away from him, the body wearing old and filthy jeans and a black anorak, the hood flipped up over his head.

Something stirred in Pete's memory as he stopped on the far side of the windbreak and the man working over the body looked up at the sound of shoes on the pavement.

It was Doc Chambers, togged up in white overalls, shoe covers, a plastic protective hat and purple nitrile gloves.

'Peter. I hope you haven't just eaten. I'm afraid this looks like another one for the list.'

Pete frowned. 'How come?'

Chambers stood up and stepped back towards him raising a hand towards the line of shops in the arches at the base of the high wall. 'Look at the distance from here to there. A body arcs outwards as it falls, of course, but not that far. From that height, you'd expect him to be perhaps ten feet from the wall. This is closer to thirty.'

'So, he took a run at it.'

Chambers shook his head. 'Look at the slope up there. It's far too steep. Plus, it's covered in shrubbery. How's he going to run through that and not leave a mark in it?'

'OK.' He looked up at the bushes and trees along the top of the wall. 'If he was thrown, it would have taken more than one of them.'

'Quite.'

'I wonder if they might have been seen. We'll have to check up there for witnesses and physical evidence. Any indication who the victim is?'

'No ID on him. Looks like a homeless person.'

Behind him, one of the technicians took a swab from its plastic sleeve and lifted the hood back from the dead man's head. Pete saw the wild red hair and felt a swoop in his stomach. 'Ziggy.'

Chapter 18

'You knew him?'

Pete nodded, meeting the doc's gaze. 'Real name Alfie Bowens. I spoke to him about one of your victims: Wayne Adams. Ziggy lived in the tent next to him, in the old garage site on Temple Street.'

'A potential witness then.'

'As it turned out, no. But he was helpful.'

'And now he's . . .'

'Yeah. The second time that's happened this week.'

'Really? Who was the first?'

'Zivan Millocovic.'

'Ah, yes. Tampered brake pipe. Nasty coincidence that.'

Pete raised an eyebrow.

Chambers paused. 'Surely, you don't think it's any more than that?'

'Whatever it is, I don't like it. You'll do a full tox screen on this one?'

'Of course.'

'I'll go see what I can see from up there, then.' Pete nodded at the high brick wall behind him. 'Talk to you later.'

*

The row of smart old brick-built houses that overlooked the Quay and the river from above had mostly been converted to business use now. Pete drove past the line of cars parked in front of them to where they ended and the narrow strip of open grass and manicured trees and shrubs opposite extended to both sides of the road. Here, the parking continued, but was less densely occupied. He found a space and pulled in.

'I'll just have a look up here then I'll take you home, OK?'

Louise nodded, looking past him towards the edge above the quayside arches. 'He jumped from up here?' She shivered.

'Whether he jumped is open for debate, but yes, this is where he went from. About there, I'd guess.' He pointed a short way further along to the left.

'Well, he didn't slip and fall.'

A tarmac footpath ran along the far side of the narrow stretch of parkland, bordered by a green-painted, cast-iron barrier. *He didn't take a running jump, either*, Pete thought.

'No. But, he may have had help.'

She opened her mouth to speak then stopped, staring at him wide-eyed. 'That's horrible.'

He tipped his head. 'Welcome to my world. Back in a minute.'

After checking the door mirror, he stepped out of the car and crossed the road and the grass beyond.

The shrub-covered ground sloped steeply away from the far side of the guard rail, ending with a sheer drop at the top of the wall. In total, it was about six floors – something like eighty feet – down to the flagstone and cobble quayside below. Easily enough to kill someone, even without the metal stanchion that Ziggy had landed on. But there was no way you'd jump from here.

Pete pictured an anorak-clad figure climbing over the cold metal barrier that his hand now rested on and running down the slope that was so steep that you'd barely be able to stand on it, to leap off the edge. Someone high enough on drugs could possibly do it if there was a clear path, but there wasn't. There were too many bushes in the way.

He'd definitely had help. And there was no way that a single person could have thrown him off here. He felt a waft of breeze from behind him and the acrid stench of puke reached his nose.

He looked around on the path and just over the fence, taking a couple of steps in either direction, but could see nothing. He felt the breeze in his hair again, the stomach-churning stink of sick coming with it. He turned around and headed slowly back towards the road, eyes to the leaf-littered, autumn-shaggy grass.

He found it seven paces from the path. There wasn't much. Barely a cupful. But it might contain the DNA of whoever left it there. He took out his phone and hit a speed-dial number. It was picked up on the second ring.

'Doctor Chambers.'

'Hey, Doc. I'm up above you. I've found where Ziggy was thrown from. Looks like someone wasn't too happy about having done it. Threw up in the grass. Can you send one of the forensics chaps up here?'

'Of course. They'll be there in a few minutes.'

'Right. I'll wait.'

*

As Pete drove back to the station after dropping Louise at home, he mulled over who could possibly be responsible for the deaths he was investigating. From the CCTV of Andrew Michaels' collapse on the High Street, he was clearly looking for a bunch of young lads. Whether all, some or just one of them was another matter but the old lady had said she saw two and Ziggy's death supported that. So, perhaps a pair of them with the brass balls to operate under the noses of people who could identify them. Which suggested a level of arrogance – or certainty that their friends would not say anything, even if they saw something – that beggared belief.

The other big question was, did they really have a source of information that was leading them to his witnesses before he could get them to testify? They weren't getting their information from the press because they were acting on facts that hadn't been released. So did they, like Petrosyan, have someone in Heavitree Road station feeding them information?

He shook his head.

Two leaks in a station like theirs seemed highly unlikely. Were they perhaps linked to the Armenian? He hadn't called them before Millocovic's death, but . . .

'Jesus.'

This was becoming too much to get his head around. But what other alternatives were there?

He signalled and pulled into the station entrance. He parked at the rear, went in and climbed the stairs to the squad room.

'Somebody give me some good news,' he said, sitting down heavily.

'Coffee's fresh,' said Dave. 'Red just made it.' Red was his nickname for Jane, referring to her hair colour.

'About the case,' Pete said, giving him a look.

Dave shrugged and lifted his mug to take a sip. Jane's arm snapped across to jab him in the ribs so that he almost spat the drink over his desk.

'Hey!' He put the mug down among the mess of papers in front of him.

'There's three pubs between the High Street and the castle,' she said to Pete. 'I went into all three. Nobody recognised the lads in the footage. However, there's also a café and a Starbucks and the Starbucks manager did recognise them. Couldn't put any names to them, but they go in there at least once a week, he said, though they don't have a regular day or time.'

'If they're at the uni, it'll depend on when they get their free periods, won't it?' Dave suggested. 'What have you been up to, boss? You've been gone a while.'

'I've been dealing with another new victim. Alfie Bowens, aka

Ziggy. Homeless chap. He was thrown off the top above the arches, down at the Quay. Landed on one of those cast-iron stanchions.'

'Oh!' Dave made it sound almost like praise for a goal. 'That'll have hurt.'

'Briefly,' Jane put in flatly.

'The interesting part is that he lived in the tent next to Wayne Adams. He's one of the blokes I spoke to about him the other day.'

'How many tents are there?' Dave asked.

'Three.'

He grimaced. 'Makes you wonder who wants to develop it, now the market's picking up again, doesn't it?'

Pete raised his eyebrows, nodding. That was an angle which hadn't occurred to him, but one worth pursuing. 'I'll check with the council, see if there've been any planning applications or enquiries about the place.' He picked up the phone and dialled.

When the connection was made he asked for the planning department. The phone began to ring again. Pete waited. And waited. He was just about to hang up, redial and ask if the department had closed early when it was finally picked up.

'Planning department. Sorry for the delay. How can I help?' The voice was brisk, bright, young-sounding and female.

'This is DS Gayle, Exeter CID,' Pete told her. 'There's a site on Temple Street, used to be garages but it's now just a vacant lot. Would have been number fifty-four to fifty-six. I need to know if you've had any activity on it recently. Planning applications, enquiries, whatever.'

'OK. Hold on, I'll check.' He heard the rapid clicking of a keyboard, a pause, then: 'Here we are. Yes. An enquiry was made with Land Registry in July this year, then one with us in September and we have an application pending the next planning meeting, which is next Wednesday, for the building of a block of twelve flats on the site.'

Pete felt the thrill of interest. 'And who put in the application?'

'Pickering Construction. They're a local building firm. Small

172

but good quality. Can I ask, why the interest?'

'I'm afraid I can't answer that. It's in regard to an ongoing investigation. But thanks very much for your help.' He ended the call.

Dave was looking across the desks. 'Got something?'

'Pickering Construction.'

'What about them?'

'Have you ever heard of them?'

'No.'

'Well, they're the answer to your question – who's been interested in the site where Wayne Adams and Alfie Bowens were living.'

Dave nodded slowly. 'Nice one, boss.'

Pete logged into the Police National Database and searched for Pickering Construction. There were no entries, so he tried a Google search instead. The company had pages on LinkedIn, Facebook and Twitter as well as a website of its own. He clicked into that and found a professional-looking page featuring a very tasteful wide shot of a short-street development, which looked new but at the same time fully occupied and established. Clicking onto the About Us page, he found that the Seaton-based company was run by two brothers and they specialised in small- to medium-sized developments that fitted comfortably into the local areas. They made a point, the site said, of building a mix of executive and affordable homes, though the pictures on the site concentrated on the more expensive ones.

It all looked very glossy and family friendly. But then, of course, it was supposed to, being the company's own website.

Pete returned to the search engine and scrolled further down the results page, to see if there was anything listed from the press. He was on the third page of search results before he found anything. Then he saw the headline: 'Violence brings controversy to building site'. The *Midweek Herald*, an East Devon newspaper, had carried the story three years before. He clicked into it and began to read.

A council member in Sidmouth had been attacked while out walking his dog late in the evening and threatened if he didn't see to it that a site in the seaside town had its planning application passed at the next meeting. The five-acre site was owned by a local man who was trying to sell it to Pickering Construction for the building of a small estate. Police had interviewed the man, who wished to remain anonymous – *I bet he bloody does*, Pete thought – but he had been unable to provide them with a description of the assailant, apart from the fact that he was male, heavily built and at least six feet tall. With no other evidence and the landowner and both Pickering brothers having solid alibis, no further action could be taken, but the site application had, of course, been rejected.

His interest piqued, Pete clicked out of the page and continued his search, but came up with nothing more of interest.

Still, it was worth pursuing, he thought.

Seaton had its own small police station, much like the one he had come from, some years ago, in Okehampton. He phoned them, introduced himself and asked the desk sergeant, 'Does Pickering Construction mean anything to you?'

'Family firm, based here in Seaton. There was some controversy with them a couple of years ago, but nothing before that and nothing since, that I know of. And no charges were filed on that occasion, either.'

'That was the Sidmouth thing?'

'That's right. Somebody threatened a member of the council planning committee or something. Never did find out who it was. Wasn't either of the Pickering brothers. Apparently, they run a tight ship, but I expect, with these builder types, you need to, eh?'

'Probably. What do you mean by a tight ship, exactly?'

'Not the type of chaps you mess with, so I've heard. Do as you're told, when you're told, kind of thing. Haven't seen any direct evidence of it, mind.'

Maybe there is none, Pete thought. *Doesn't mean they're angels, though.* 'OK. Thanks for that.'

He hung up and sat back, thinking. Were the Pickering brothers as squeaky clean as they wanted everyone to believe or were they the type who used intimidation and pickaxe handles to get their own way?

*

Colleton Crescent was back to being quiet and peaceful as normal when Pete got back there. He found a space at the near end of the row of old converted houses and parked. The first house was divided between a graphic design studio and an accountant's. He rang the bell for the ground floor. A buzzer sounded and a tinny voice came from the speaker. 'Yes?'

'DS Gayle, Exeter CID. I need to speak to someone about building security.'

There was a buzz as the lock was released and he pushed the door open. Inside, the conversion was modern and open, the walls all white. A pale wood stair rose up to the first floor with a sign for the accountant's while desks and drafting tables were spread around the lower floor. A man in his twenties looked up from behind a computer. He had spiky dark hair and a tiny goatee beard and wore an Iron Maiden T-shirt.

'Can I help?'

'Yes.' Pete stepped forward. 'Do you have security cameras in this place?'

The man shook his head. 'Only the one covering the door.'

'Does it record?'

'Don't think so. It just comes on with the buzzer, so we can see who's out there.'

'OK. Thanks.' Pete turned to leave.

'What's happened? I saw the white overalls over the road earlier.'

Pete pursed his lips and turned back. He was going to get a lot of this. It was human nature. 'Someone died, down by the arches.'

'What – went off from up here?'

'Yes. You didn't see anything in relation to that?'

The young guy's eyes opened wide in horror. 'No, mate.'

Pete left the building and moved on. Next door was a dentist. The young receptionist was regretful, but couldn't help him. He moved on again. A tanning studio was followed by a computer repairer, then a lithographic printer. None could help. He was over halfway along the row, his hopes flagging, when he entered the dark, old-world wood-panelled reception of a firm of solicitors that he hadn't even registered the name of.

The receptionist was in her forties, stylish with blonde hair and just the right amount of make-up. She looked up from her computer screen as he entered and a professional smile widened her lips. 'Can I help?'

'I hope so.' He showed her his warrant card. 'DS Gayle, Devon and Cornwall Police. There was an incident out here this morning. I'm hoping to find someone along here who has CCTV coverage of the road.'

Her smile widened a touch. 'Then you've come to the right place, Detective Sergeant. We have full security coverage. Let me see if one of the partners is available to help you.' She tapped at a console near her right hand and spoke into the subtle headset that she was wearing. 'Mr Franklin, do you have a few minutes? I have a police officer in reception who needs to see our CCTV footage from this morning.' She paused. 'Thank you.' She looked up. 'Mr Franklin will be down shortly. Would you like to take a seat?' She indicated the curve of a soft-looking leather sofa in the window behind him.

Pete returned her smile. 'I spend far too much time sat down as it is.'

'Very well.' She returned to her typing and Pete leaned one elbow on the high-fronted desk to wait.

Moments later, a door opened to one side of the reception area and a large, solidly built man in his fifties walked briskly in and stuck out a large hand. 'Dan Franklin. Detective . . .?'

'Gayle. Pete.'

The man's grip was firm and dry as they shook hands.

'And you're looking for CCTV coverage of the Crescent?'

'That's right. There was an incident this morning. About three hours ago. I was hoping to find a clue as to the perpetrators.'

Franklin was nodding. 'I see. Well, I can't make any promises but, as a firm of solicitors, we have to take security very seriously. We hold some very sensitive information here and some very valuable documents. Come this way.'

He raised a hand towards the door he'd come through and Pete followed him into a corridor, one side of which was covered in dark oak panelling while the other was white-painted plaster, broken with a series of windows.

'We have camera coverage of both the front and back of the building,' Franklin went on. 'I don't imagine you spotted the cameras out the front. Tiny little things.' He opened a door and led Pete into a small, dark room where the wall to the left featured four small screens showing what appeared to be live feeds, in colour, from different cameras, two at the front and two at the rear of the building. One of those at the front looked to be right beside the door but, as Franklin had guessed, Pete hadn't spotted it when he'd come in. He pointed to the screen, which was showing a view, at head height, across the road towards the grass beyond.

Franklin grinned. 'It's in the door frame. Looks like an old, defunct bell push.'

'And it looks like it might give me exactly what I'm looking for, if you record the feed from it.'

'We do indeed. We're a small firm. We don't have the where-withal to employ someone to sit in here all day, watching.'

'Could we spin it back to about 11 a.m.?'

'Mm-hmm.' Franklin leaned over a desk in front of the screens and moved the mouse of a computer, bringing its screen to life.

A few clicks and the feed from the front door camera was on the computer screen. Another and Pete saw the time stamp in the bottom right corner start to flick backwards.

Chapter 19

'Stop.'

Pete peered at the screen, straining to make out more detail as the image froze then slowly backed up. A silver Peugeot hatchback came back into view, heading across the top half of the screen from right to left, a single figure in the front and what looked like two in the back. The driver was definitely male, but in silhouette. In the back, at least one of the figures was also male. This one could be seen in more detail, though the buildings were reflecting in the glass, degrading the image. He had dark hair and wore a jacket that pretty much matched it, but he was turned away from the camera, towards the third figure, seated behind the driver. Pete could not make out any detail on that one. He or she seemed to be slumped at an odd angle.

As if they were drunk or drugged.

But at – he glanced down at the timestamp in the bottom corner of the screen – 11.22 a.m.? This had to be them.

He recalled the image of the car in the footage from the Marsh Barton estate. The shape was the same. He was sure of it.

But being sure in his own mind was not enough.

'Could I get a copy of this section?'

'Of course. I'll burn you a DVD. Should we check further, first?'

'Yes. Better had, just to be sure. Thanks.'

Franklin made a note on the yellow pad at his elbow.

The dark grey Aston Martin that was parked in front of the solicitors' at the time blocked any possibility of getting a registration off the target vehicle, of course, but it was still a step forward, Pete thought, the thrill of the chase sparking in his gut.

He would check the rest of the row, to see if anyone else had any better footage, but this was a start. He could feel it. He had no idea how many silver Peugeot hatchbacks there were in Exeter. Dozens, at least, he imagined. But it was more information than they'd had ten minutes ago.

A step in the right direction, if only a small one.

*

'Did you find anything, boss?' Jane asked as he took his seat back in the squad room.

'Yes. Hold on, though. I need to fine-tune it a bit.' He switched on his computer, brought up the internet and started an image search. A couple of minutes later, he closed the web page and looked up to see his whole team staring at him. 'Have you lot got nothing to do?'

'Plenty, thanks,' said Dick. 'We're just wondering what you're doing.'

'Discovering that our perp drives a silver 2010 Peugeot 308. And you?'

'I'm looking into Tony Perkins' finances, like you wanted. Jesus, what a mess! It'd take a whole team of Inland Revenue experts a bloody month to make sense of it. And that's just the month we're interested in.'

'But, miracle-worker that you are, you've done it on your own in an afternoon, right?'

Dick tilted his head. 'I wouldn't go that far. And, of course, I can't guarantee that all of it's traceable with him taking cash payments from some tenants. But what I can say is that the end result of his October finances is consistent with the previous few months and last month. There's no trace of the kind of difference that would want explaining in the circumstances.'

'So, we're no further forward with him.' Pete was about to say more when his phone rang. He stopped and picked it up. 'DS Gayle.'

'Peter. It's Tony Chambers. Thought I'd keep you updated. I just got the toxicology report back on our friend from the Quay, Alfonse Bowens.'

'Hello, Doc. What's it say?'

'Entirely negative. No drugs or alcohol in his system.'

'So . . . why didn't he yell when he went over?'

'He'd been punched in the throat, or, at least, hit with a blunt object with similar characteristics to a fist. There are also marks on his scalp consistent with his head being pulled up and back to facilitate that and fresh scrapes on his knees that aren't from the fall, so . . .'

'Mmm. Thanks, Doc.'

'Doc Chambers?' Jane asked as he put the phone down.

'Yes. Results on the guy who went over the top, down at the Quay. Sober and conscious. Knocked down to his knees from behind, head pulled back, punch to the throat, then thrown over.'

'So, at least two of them.'

'Exactly two.'

'How do you know?'

'The silver car,' Dick said.

Pete allowed himself a smile. 'Three people in it, one of them slumped over, possibly incapacitated in some way. The timing's right and there were no other likely candidates.'

'Did you get a reg or a facial shot?'

'Yeah, right. If life were that easy I wouldn't need the likes of you, now, would I?'

'So, why two from the same location, all of a sudden?' asked

Jane. 'Unless Dave was right about the developing angle.'

'I wouldn't fancy living in that third tent right now,' Dave said.

'Me either, Dave, so get yourself down there and warn him. Mick Duggan's his name. Get him to move on, take the tent somewhere else. Dick, we know Perkins doesn't drive a Peugeot, but he's old enough to have a son who does. You could check on that. And Jill, look into the Pickerings. Family members, employees, anyone with a link to them. I'm going downstairs.'

He pushed his chair back and stood up.

Having thought it through, there was only one way that anyone could be taking out potential witnesses in this case. He had to find out if he'd been followed when he went to the site where Ziggy and Snake had lived.

*

It was almost five-thirty-five by the time he got back up to the squad room, but his team were all still there and working, apart from Dave, who was out looking for Mick Duggan to persuade him to move.

'Anybody found anything?'

Dick shook his head and Jill grimaced.

'Nothing useful,' Jane said. 'How about you?'

'Nope. Which, in my case, is a good thing.'

'How come?'

'It means I wasn't followed to Temple Street. And there's no other way that Ziggy could have been targeted because of this case.'

Dick looked up from his screen. 'So, Dave's gone there for nothing. He'll love you for that.'

The door opened and PC Sophie Clewes entered. She glanced at the board as she passed. 'Huh. Two silver hatchbacks in two days. How's it going, Sarge?'

Pete's eyes narrowed. 'What do you mean, two silver hatchbacks?'

'There was one on the hill when Millic had his accident. Couple of lads in it. I stopped them, told them to find another way around because of the accident.'

'Two lads in a silver hatchback and you didn't bother to report it?'

'It wasn't relevant. They were headed *towards* the accident. Why would they be doing that if they knew about it beforehand?'

'Damn! Did you get a registration?'

'No. Why would I? I just waved them down, told them to go another way. That was it. There was no problem. What's all the fuss about?' She looked from Pete to Jane and back again.

'The one in the picture up there is on Colleton Crescent, just before that bloke went off the top above the arches,' Jane told her.

'So . . . Shit.'

'Yes,' Pete said heavily. 'Shit is right. What can you tell us about the one over the river?'

Sophie began to redden. 'Not much. It was a ten reg Peugeot, but other than that . . .' She shrugged helplessly.

'What about the occupants? Do you remember what they looked like?'

'I'm not completely useless, Sarge.'

'Then, how about getting a Photofit done ASAP, eh?' Pete switched his gaze to Jane. 'Dave's got the software, hasn't he?'

'Yeah.'

'Log her onto his computer then. She can use it while he's not here.'

'I was just . . .' Sophie started.

'About to give us the first useful pictures we've had of our perps,' Pete said over her. 'Yes. Thanks for that, PC Clewes.'

She muttered something he didn't catch as she went around towards Dave's desk.

'Don't mind him,' said Jane. 'He's had a bad day. If he was female, I'd blame it on PMT, but I don't know what the male equivalent is.'

Pete took a breath. He'd been harder than he needed to on Sophie. She didn't know the ins and outs of the case. Hell, she wasn't even part of his team, officially, and she was good at her job. 'Men suffer from PMT, too,' he said. 'Especially those of us who're married. By association, if nothing else.'

Jill looked up from her screen. 'That's called bringing your personal problems into the workplace, boss.'

'No, it's called nagging.'

'Don't let Fast-track hear you talking about that,' said Dick. 'He'll have us all on courses about self-discipline before you can wag a finger.'

'Isn't that some weird sort of religious masochism?' Ben asked. 'I'm sure I read about it in *The Da Vinci Code*. Or was it another one . . .?' He yelped and ducked as Dick swung an open hand at the back of his head.

Sophie smiled despite herself.

'Sorry, kiddo,' Pete said to her. 'I was a bit harsh there.'

'I thought so,' she said. 'But I'll get over it. In time.'

Pete saw the twinkle in her eyes. 'Glad to hear it. Just out of interest, these two lads – what were they wearing?'

'One had a . . .' She paused and looked across at the board. 'One had a brown jacket, just like that one.' She pointed at the CCTV image from the High Street of the bunch of lads who had been larking about around Andrew Michaels at the time of his death. 'The other had a denim jacket, T-shirt and dark trousers on. Like the one next to him, there.'

'Which one was driving?' Pete was fully serious again now.

'The one in the denim.'

Pete paused for a second to see if there was any doubt in her mind. There wasn't. 'OK. Give us a couple of Photofits and you're forgiven.'

'Well thanks.'

He saw Jane smile and couldn't help joining her. The girl showed a lot of promise. But what was he going to do now? He really needed to get off home, to help Annie and Louise with the posters of Tommy, but how was he supposed to up and leave now that he'd insisted that Sophie stay on and compile pictures of the two lads she'd seen? Everyone in the squad room knew that the fresher the memory of anything, the more accurate it was.

Damn it.

He rubbed his hands down his face and looked across the cluttered desks. 'If you want to get off home and do that in the morning, Sophie . . .'

She looked up. 'No, that's OK. I'll do it now, while I've got the chance.'

'It's up to you,' he said. 'I'm out of here, though. I've got something else to see to.'

Jane looked up. 'You want me to come along?'

'No. But, if Sophie comes up with anything, you can send me the results.' He grabbed his jacket and headed for the door.

Chapter 20

'Where've you been? Don't answer that. At work. I thought you were coming home early tonight.'

Louise was in her usual spot on the sofa, but she was dressed in jeans and a thick sweater, ready to go out.

'It's not just work, like any other job. You know that. And we caught a possible break just as I was about to come home. I couldn't just leave the guys to get on with it. What kind of example does that set? Where's Annie?'

He heard the gush of water from the bathroom and, moments later, her small feet came thundering down the stairs. 'Dad! Are we going, or what?'

'Jesus, I've only just got in! Don't I even get a hug?'

'You would have at five o'clock, but it's nearly half past six. You're too late.'

'Don't you start, young lady. I get enough of that from your mother.' He took a swipe at her backside as she dodged past him, heading for the kitchen.

'There's laws against physical violence these days,' she said as she went from sight. 'Especially to kids.'

'Ah, only until we get out of the EU. Then they'll be repealed. We'll bring back the birch and all sorts. Have a bit of discipline back in the country.'

'You're so old-fashioned sometimes,' she said.

'Yes, and one thing I remember from way back in the ancient times is, "Spare the rod and spoil the child."'

'You've never got time to go fishing.'

He shook his head. 'You're too clever by half, young lady. Come on, get your coat on. You'll want gloves and a hat too, tonight. It's bloody nippy out there. You coming, Lou?'

He was answered by silence from the sitting room as the TV was switched off.

'Where are we going?' he asked.

'Up around the swimming pool?' Annie suggested. 'We've already been round by school, and round the big school.'

'You have? Who with?'

'Mum, of course. And Hayley and Milly and Christy came, too, and their mums.'

Pete paused. Louise had been out again? After this afternoon, he'd doubted she would, especially on her own. 'Good,' he said. 'Well, that's two places we don't need to go then.'

He turned back towards the front door as Louise appeared from the sitting room. The expression on her face was unreadable. Not blank, but closed. He felt a swell of pride and love for her. Clearly, she was determined to get this done, whatever the emotional cost. 'All right, let's go and do this. Fish and chips afterwards, to warm us up again.'

'Yay,' Annie cheered.

He reached out and ruffled her hair.

'*Dad!*'

'Well, put your hat on then. Who's got the posters?'

'They're on the side,' Annie chimed. 'And the stapler and the tape.'

'Grab them up, then. And brace yourself. It's winter out there.'

*

With the protection of the early evening darkness, Louise seemed completely oblivious to the fact that she was out in public while they put posters up around the swimming pool and its car park, then moved on to the nearby sports field and its clubhouse. Cars and pedestrians passed them as they worked. A couple of people even stopped and asked what they were doing, what the posters were for, and she didn't react – simply let Pete and Annie speak.

They put more posters up along the roads bordering the front and side of the sports field and around its small car park. An arcade of shops, including a mini-supermarket, a hairdresser's and a Chinese takeaway, was just a couple of streets away. Pete parked outside the hairdresser's, which was in darkness at this time of night, and they got out, Annie bringing the posters, tape and stapler.

'I'll see if they'll take one in the Spar and the Chinese,' Pete said, taking a few of the posters.

'Right. We'll start over the road.'

They parted company and Pete went into the mini-mart first. There were a couple of posters on the glass door as he went in. Two people were waiting at the till. Pete spotted a noticeboard at the far side of the tills, only one of which was in operation. Small cards filled it, other posters covering the wall above and below it. He looked around, but could see no more staff so joined the short queue.

The customer at the front took his change, picked up his items and left. As the woman in front of Pete stepped forward, he saw the door at the back of the shop open and a woman emerged. He left the queue and stepped across to meet her.

'Excuse me. I was hoping you'd be able to put one of these up in the shop. It's my son. He went missing back in May and the police haven't had any joy finding him, so we thought it was time we took the job on ourselves.'

'Well, I don't . . .'

'Please. He's only thirteen,' Pete said quickly, seeing the

reluctance in her expression. 'His mother's at her wits' end and we don't know what else to try.'

'Mmm. Well, all right. Give me one and I'll put it up later, when I get a minute.'

'Great. Thanks ever so much. Anybody that sees it might be the chance we've needed to find him.'

'OK.' She took the poster he held out.

Pete wasn't sure if she'd put it up or had just agreed to get rid of him, but it was one more chance for someone to see it, however slight. He had to accept that. He shook her hand and left the store.

As he stepped outside, he heard a laugh from across the road and looked towards the sound. Annie was ducking away from Louise, who was taking a playful swipe at her. He smiled. It was too long since he'd seen them play together like that. Maybe this was just what Louise needed.

He headed for the Chinese takeaway, next door but one to the little supermarket. Pushing open the door, he saw that there was no one in the place, on either side of the counter, but then a door opened behind the till and a stocky Oriental whose age Pete couldn't guess stepped through.

'Hello. What can I get you?'

So often, Pete had been into places like this and been greeted by a surly, almost unwilling assistant. This guy's small, rimless hat, Donald Duck T-shirt and smiling manner were a pleasant surprise.

'Sorry,' he said. 'I was just—'

His phone rang abruptly in his pocket and he took it out to check the screen. *Jill*. He nodded to the man behind the counter and turned away.

'Hello, Jill. What's up?'

'I've found something,' she said. 'I was looking into the Pickering brothers, like you asked, and I came up with a link between them and a Danny Dyer from here in Exeter. He used to work for them. And he's got a record for drugs offences and violence. GBH. Assault with a weapon. Ron Pickering's bailed him out more than once.'

'Is there any connection from Dyer to any of our victims?'

'Not that I've found yet, but I'm still looking. Oh, and Sophie's done those two composites.'

'Great. Either of them got a name yet?'

'Not yet. Dave's running them through the PND now,' she said, referring to the Police National Database. 'We do know neither of them is Danny Dyer.'

'All right. Might be worth running them against his known associates though. I'll be in in a bit.'

He ended the call and turned back to the man behind the counter. Unsure of how much he'd heard, he thought it would probably be best to use the more direct approach here. He took out his badge. 'Sorry about that. DS Gayle. We're going for a second push on a Missing Persons case from back in May. Young boy, thirteen years old. I wondered if you'd be able to put up a poster for us.'

The man took the sheet Pete offered. 'Of course. No problem.'

'Thanks. I'd best get back to the station, by the sound of it.'

Pete left the shop and looked around for Louise and Annie. At first, he couldn't see them, then he looked further down the street to his left and saw movement in the shadows between the pools of light cast by the street lights. Two figures emerged from the darkness, hand in hand. He saw Annie look up at her mother and smile. As he stepped forward, he thought he saw Louise's response, but couldn't be certain at that distance.

Either way, though, she wouldn't smile at what he was about to say.

'Hey, girls,' he called. 'How's it going?'

'Daddy!' Annie ran forward, dragging Louise with her by the hand. She grabbed Pete's hand when they met and swung both wildly back and forth. 'This is cool. I'm going to see parts of the city I've never been to before.'

He laughed. 'And parts you'll never see again, with any luck.' He looked to Louise. 'I've got a poster up in the Chinese and possibly another in the Spar. I'll have to check on that one, though. She seemed a bit iffy with the idea.'

'And we've put them up on the lamp-posts and telegraph poles over the road and down that way.' Annie let go of his hand to point back the way they'd come from. 'So, there's just up there and then we can move on again.'

'Actually, Button, I got a call while I was in the Chinese. I need to pop back into the station.'

Her little face fell.

'We can do these few up here first, but then I'm going to have to call it a night. I'm sorry, pet. We'll do some more tomorrow, though. You and your mum can sort out where and I'll take you.'

'Oh, Dad . . .'

'Come here.' He drew her into a hug and looked up at Louise, whose face had reverted to its now-normal blank expression. 'That crime scene earlier. We've got pictures of the two suspects.'

'So, you ID them and the case is closed?'

He tilted his head in agreement.

'You'd best go do it, then.'

*

'So, have you identified them?' Louise asked as he walked into the sitting room two hours later.

'Not yet, but we're getting close. What we have determined is that the silver Peugeot that was up there just before the guy went over isn't a local hire car. It may be stolen or it may belong to one of the perps. There is a stolen one locally that matches the details. And another in Dorset. It could be either. And the faces we've got don't match any convicted felons, but I'm going to get Silverstone to put them out to the media in the morning and we're going to have a strong push on the university.'

'Pile the pressure on too much, they might shut down and clear off,' she said.

Pete nodded. 'It's possible. But it's a win-win, isn't it? Either they'll stop killing or we'll identify them. Then, even if they've done a runner, it's just a matter of time before we catch them. Anyway, how're you doing? You seem brighter.'

'Mm. I feel it, somehow, too. Don't know why.'

'Perhaps because you've got something to focus on and do. Annie in bed?'

She grunted. 'Went up forty minutes ago.'

'I won't disturb her then. I expect you talked about where we should go tomorrow night?'

'She didn't want to talk about anything else. We thought to stay out of the city centre for now – focus on the places dotted about in the estates and so on.'

Pete instantly pictured the Co-op on the Dunsford Road, where Tommy had last been seen. 'OK. Although you'd be surprised at how many places there are in the city centre that people can disappear into, so we do need to get some posters up there, too.'

'There's only three of us. We can't be everywhere at once. And with you at work all hours, there's—'

'Hey,' he broke in, raising his hands. 'Sorry. I just had a thought: the hospital. We could put some up there. A&E. The main reception. The café. Anywhere else?'

'Any of the reception and waiting areas,' she said. 'Outpatients, X-ray, Pathology, you name it . . .' She paused. 'You want me to do that during the day, don't you?'

He pursed his lips. 'Kind of awkward, you being off sick from there. I just thought, with the number of people who go through there every day . . .'

She sighed. 'Mm. Changing the subject, do you want a cup of tea?'

Wow! That's a first in a hell of a time. 'Yeah. Why not?'

'Go on then. I'll have one, too.'

He saw the twinkle in her eyes and could not suppress a laugh.

*

The kettle had not even boiled, Pete had put the tea bags in the mugs and was spooning in the sugar when the phone rang. He dropped the spoon into one of the mugs and snatched it up before it disturbed Annie, but, even as he did so, he heard Louise from the sitting room.

'For God's sake. You've barely been home ten minutes.'

'Hello?' he said.

'Boss? It's Ben. I think I might have found something.'

'You're still in the office?' He looked at his watch. It was just after ten and Ben had been there since 6.30 that morning.

'Yes, well . . . Like I said, this sort of stuff's better done with less company, rather than more. I was just going to pack it in for the night, but I found a Facebook page for DI Underhill's daughter, Christine. She's a vet in Tavistock. Anyway, she was having a rant about her nan, basically. The DI's mum. She's got rheumatoid arthritis. Had it for ages. Trouble is, the usual treatments don't work for her any more. The only thing that does is one of those super-expensive drugs that the NHS won't use, so they have to be supplied by some special department that was set up by the government a couple of years ago, mainly to deal with cancer drugs. Well, now, apparently, things are changing. A lot of the drugs they supply are being withdrawn from use, even that way. Insufficient benefit efficiency or some bollocks like that. So, an eighty-four-year-old lady who served her country in two wars, is left to suffer in agony. Christine is obviously not impressed.'

'Can't say I blame her, but I can't believe Colin would be involved in anything like this, no matter what the reason. I've known him for years. He's as straight as a die.'

'I'm just giving you the facts, boss.'

'I know. Thanks, Ben. Get off home now, yeah?'

''Night, boss.'

Pete put the phone down slowly, his mind in turmoil. Colin Underhill, Pete's mentor, teacher, friend and professional father figure . . . He shook his head. He couldn't believe Colin would get involved in something like this. Apart from anything else, how? There'd been no mention from either Jim or DCI Silverstone of Colin's being involved in the process. And to be able to alter them without it showing up in the searches they'd already done, he'd have had to get hold of them before Simon did. Could they have passed from Jim through Colin to Simon? But why would they, unless Colin was supposed to do the compilation and he passed it on to Simon? He frowned. No, Fast-track had specifically said he'd allocated the task to Simon because Jim was too busy, so that didn't work.

And anyway, the fact that his mother was suffering unnecessarily didn't affect anything at work. Unless . . . Was it even possible?

He headed for the stairs. He'd need to check on the internet.

'Pete?' Louise called from the sitting room.

'Give me two minutes,' he said, turning onto the stairs and taking them two at a time.

In his office, he powered up his laptop and logged onto the internet. A quick search gave him the name of the drug Ben had been talking about. But how would anyone get hold of it without going through their doctor? Even legitimately, it was incredibly expensive. Surely, any illegal source would be prohibitively so, unless . . .

'Shit.' His eyes closed as he absorbed the idea.

Unless you had a drug dealer who you could blackmail into getting the stuff.

And, if you were doing that, you wouldn't want them getting arrested.

Chapter 21

Back downstairs, he finished making the tea and took it through to Louise.

'So, what was the call?' she asked, as she took her mug from him.

'Ben. He's been looking into something on the quiet. Thought he'd found something, but . . .' He shook his head. 'I can't see it.'

'Why?

'It's just not credible. I'm . . .' He ran his bottom lip across his teeth as he struggled with the decision until . . .

What the hell? There is no downside. Who would she tell?

'Fast-track tasked us with looking into why a whole section of the community – namely, Armenian immigrants – were excluded from his drugs raids, week before last, regardless of the fact that they include a whole gang of dealers. Ben was looking into who could have had a hand in that and why.'

'And what did he find? If you can tell me.'

'A Facebook page. You know Chrissy? Colin's eldest. She was on there about her gran, Colin's mum. Seems like she's got RA. The usual drugs don't work for her any more and the NHS won't pay for that new one, Tocli-something, so she's left to suffer.'

'What's that got to do with Colin and a bunch of drug dealers?'

'Well, if he was getting the stuff for her through the Armenians by misusing his position, he'd want to steer any police attention away from them, wouldn't he? I mean, I can see the logic. I just can't credit the idea, that's all. Not Colin.'

'You've still got to check it though. In the morning. It'd be negligent not to.'

'Yeah, but . . .'

'But me no buts, my old gran used to say.' She took a sip of tea.

Pete grunted, knowing she was right. 'Seems a bit dishonest, though, looking into him while he's away in Bristol.'

'Best time, I'd have thought. Do it right and, if he's innocent, he'll never even find out you did it. Nobody else fits the bill, I suppose?'

'Not that we've found so far. Had a few tentative leads, but they've all proved false in the end.'

'Well, knowing Colin, I dare say you're right: this one will, too. And he'd probably be more pissed off if he found out you'd excluded anyone without checking them thoroughly – including him – than he would be at the fact that you'd done it.'

Pete took a slug of tea, set his mug down and leaned across to kiss her. 'And there you go again. Being right.'

She sighed. 'Not going to help you sleep tonight, though, is it?'

'Probably not.'

'Is there anything you can do about it before morning?'

He shook his head. 'Not reliably, no.'

'There you go then. What you can't do, there's no point worrying about. Deal with what you can, when you can.'

He laughed. 'You found a batch of those Chinese fortune cookies they talk about on telly?'

She tilted her head and put her hands together. 'Ancient Chinese proverb say, "Wisdom come in all shapes and sizes."'

*

By ten to nine the next morning, Pete was getting desperate. He and his whole team plus the city's full roster of uniformed patrol

196

officers had been in place and working for over half an hour and had come up with nothing.

They were spread around the university campus, plain-clothes officers with their badges on lanyards around their necks, asking everyone they could if they recognised either of the two faces that Sophie Clewes had come up with, especially in connection with a silver Peugeot 308.

Pete was feeling fuzzy-headed and sluggish, his eyes gritty after a night of poor sleep as he nodded his thanks to one young woman and turned to a group of three others who were approaching the entrance to the biology faculty. 'Girls, can I ask you if you recognise either of these two faces? One of them may drive a silver hatchback.'

The willowy redhead walking slightly behind and between the other two glanced at the computer-generated drawings but showed no reaction. The other two – one of them chatting animatedly, the other laughing at something she'd said – paid no attention at all.

'Ladies. Two seconds. These are potential serial killers. Have you seen them?' he asked more forcefully.

'What?' The one who had been laughing turned towards him, ponytail swinging.

'Do you recognise either of these two? Maybe in connection with a silver Peugeot hatchback?'

She grimaced, shaking her head.

'They look like Dom and Josh,' said the chatty one, taking a brief glance. 'So, what are you doing tonight, Amy?'

'No . . .' The redhead shook her head.

'Dom and Josh who?' Pete asked, the thrill of discovery tempered by irritation with the three girls and their self-centred dismissiveness.

'Don't know. Don't even think they're in this faculty.' The chatty one again. 'We just meet them in the pub sometimes.'

'Which pub?'

She shrugged. 'The Blue Boar. The Coach and Horses.'

Both student bars. 'Have you got last names for either of them?'

'It's not them,' said the redhead. 'That one's nose is too big. And you never see Dom with stubble like that.'

'Nevertheless, so that we can talk to them and eliminate them . . .'

She shook her head.

'As I said,' the other one said, 'we only know them from the pub.'

'OK. Thanks anyway.'

He let them go, ignoring their giggles as he quickly wrote the new information in his notebook and turned back towards the increasingly intense influx of students, most of whom were female. It was now less than ten minutes before lectures would start. They were unlikely to get any more positive responses from the hurrying students, but there was one more thing he could try, even though it carried the risk of alerting the suspects to his search for them.

He held the two pictures up above his head. 'Has anyone seen these two people? One of them wears a brown leather jacket. Has anyone seen these two?'

*

As the flood of arriving students tailed off just before 9 a.m., Pete keyed the mike of his radio. 'Delta Sierra Papa Golf. Has anybody got anything on our two suspects?' He released the button to a burst of static followed by silence. After a pause, Dave's voice came over the air. 'Sounds like a negative, boss. Should we stick at it or head back to base?'

'Give it ten for stragglers, then you take the Blue Boar, Dave. I'll head to the Coach and Horses. We've got possible sightings at both. Jill can stay on here with half the uniformed team while the rest of us get back to normal duties.'

'All received.'

'Received, Sarge.' Jill's voice followed Dave's.

Even a city pub was not going to be open at nine-thirty in the morning, but Pete used a phone listing website and called ahead so that, when he knocked on the closed door of the Coach and Horses public house, it was opened almost immediately by a woman in her fifties with tightly curled blonde hair and far too much make-up.

He held up his warrant card. 'DS Gayle. I phoned a few minutes ago.'

'Yes, come in.' The woman's dry, husky voice reminded Pete of whisky and cigarettes.

She stood back then closed the door behind him. The place smelled strongly of old beer. The low, beamed ceiling and dark furniture gave it a claustrophobic feel. Chairs were upturned on the small tables and a vacuum stood in the middle of the floor, a bowl of soapy water and a washcloth on the bar.

'What can I do for you?' She leaned one elbow on the bar.

'You're the landlady?' Pete asked.

'Monica Devlin.' She extended a hand. Though small, its grip was firm and dry.

'We're trying to trace two men who we've been told come in here sometimes. They're in their early twenties, we think. One's been seen in a brown leather jacket.' He checked the bar was dry before laying the two pictures out side by side.

'Yes. They come in once or twice a week, I suppose. Have for the last year or so.'

'Excellent.' Pete felt the thrill of progress. 'You don't know their names, I suppose?'

She shook her head, large hoop earrings gleaming as they swung. 'I think that one might be called Josh, but that's about all I can tell you.' She tapped one of the pictures with a long, pink fingernail. 'It gets pretty loud in here most evenings. I don't hear too much that's not directed specifically at me.'

Pete nodded. 'And I expect they always pay cash?'

'Most do, in this trade, unless you do food. Which we don't so much.'

'Anything else you can tell me about them?'

'Not really. They come in, chat up the girls, occasionally join in a game of darts or play pool.' She shrugged. 'That's about it.'

'When was the last time you saw them?'

'Last night, actually. They must have come in about nine, stayed for an hour and a half or so.'

'Anybody they spent time with, chatted to, whatever?'

She shook her head. 'I don't know. Sorry. It was pretty busy. I didn't have time to see what was going on away from the bar.'

'Fair enough. Thanks anyway.' Pete picked up the pictures and slipped them back into the folder he was carrying. 'I'll let you get back to it.'

She crossed to the door, flipped the button on the Yale lock. 'Don't suppose you can tell me what they've done?'

Pete grimaced. 'Sorry. Ongoing case.'

She nodded and opened the door for him. 'Best of luck with it then.'

'Thanks. And for your help.' He shook her hand again and stepped out, feeling glad of the chill sunshine after the dim and sour-smelling pub. He stopped, looking up and down the narrow lane. Which way would they have come from? If they had driven into the city, where would they have parked? Or were they in digs, close enough to walk? Uphill, to his right, led to Fore Street, where he knew there were CCTV surveillance cameras. Downhill led out onto the Western Way, at either end of which were major junctions with more cameras.

He took out his phone, brought up the contacts list and tapped a number.

Moments later the connection was made. 'Dave Miles.'

'Dave? Pete. Where are you?'

'Just about to leave the Blue Boar.'

'Any good?'

'Not much. Landlord recognised them. Couldn't put names to either of them, though, and he hasn't seen them since sometime last week.'

'They were in the Coach and Horses last night. Still only got a first name, though: Josh. I'm going back to the station. See if you can give Jill a hand.'

'OK.'

*

'Graham,' Pete said, sticking his head into the windowless CCTV room, 'I need to have a look at the Fore Street footage from last night around nine o'clock. Probably best start about twenty-to, to make sure.'

'Failed. I heard the door latch.' The CCTV operator didn't bother to turn away from his screens.

Pete stepped into the room, which was kept in semi-darkness to help the operator concentrate on his screens. 'Don't know what you mean,' he said, as the door closed behind him with a soft click. He didn't see that much of Graham, but with the fat man being of a somewhat sensitive disposition, when he did, he enjoyed the opportunity to try to make him jump. This time, he had clearly not succeeded.

'What are you looking for?'

'Two lads. One of them tends to wear a brown leather jacket.'

'What – those same ones from the High Street? That gang?'

'Yeah, that's them.'

'Hang on a tick.' He focused on the main screen, tapping at the keyboard beneath it. 'Fore Street, 8.40 p.m. yesterday. Which end?'

'About halfway down,' Pete said with a grin.

'You would, wouldn't you? Well, as it happens, we have got one. Here we go.' He hit the Return key and the screen changed from day to night. 'Fast-forward, shall we?'

201

'OK.'

The image blurred, then steadied, people walking up and down the street in Charlie Chaplin super-speed, cars and busses whizzing by. 'Do you know if it was just the two of them?' Graham asked, concentrating on the screen.

'No, I don't.'

'Shame. It'd make it easier to spot them.'

The camera was pointing up the hill, towards the High Street, the entrance to the snooker hall close by on the left of the screen, the gambling arcade just beyond it, reminding Pete of the discovery he had made a few days ago that a young witness in the abduction of Rosie Whitlock had spent time in there and may have known his son, Tommy.

He shook the thought from his mind. He had to focus.

'There,' said Graham. 'Is that them?' He slowed the replay back to normal speed, the yellow glow of the street lamps shining from the jacket worn by one of a pair of men walking down the street towards them. Pete waited, watching as they drew closer, but they were still too far off when they abruptly turned left, down the side street that led past the Blue Boar.

'Could be. Back it up a bit.' He peered over the stocky man's shoulder, watching as the two figures went into reverse, re-emerging from the shadowy entrance. 'Stop.'

They both stared at the screen. As a historical recording, rather than a live event, there was nothing Graham could do to let them see the image any more clearly.

'It could be.'

Pete grunted and glanced at the time stamp. 'That was at 8.56. Go on a bit, see if there's any more likely candidates.'

Graham complied. The two figures on the screen turned into the side road and disappeared and he sped the replay up again. A couple of minutes later, they had reached 9.20 p.m. on the time stamp.

'That'll do,' Pete said. 'No point going any further. If we go back to the two at 8.56, have another look at them, can we try to track them back, see where they came from?'

'Yes.' He hit Pause, then rewound rapidly. Hitting the pause key again, he froze the image on the screen with the two figures a few feet short of the turn. Pressing Play, he let them walk forward and paused the image once more, just before they made the turn. 'Print that, shall I?'

'Ta.'

He hit a few keys and a printer in the corner of the small room began to whir. 'Right. We've got another camera at the end of Queen Street. We'll try that one next.'

Moments later, the image on the screen changed. Now they were looking up Queen Street from the far side of the junction with Fore Street and the High Street, the time stamp saying 8.56. He hit a button and the figures on the screen began to move slowly in reverse. He sped up the replay. At 8.54, two dark heads passed close under the camera, the far one's shoulder gleaming briefly.

'There,' Pete said quickly.

Graham hit Pause, then eased the replay forward in slow motion. The two figures came back onto the screen, right at the bottom edge, but the angle was such that there was no shot of their faces.

'Looks like they came from the High Street, but go back a bit further to make sure,' Pete said.

The image started to move again. The clock ticked back another minute, but the two figures didn't return to the screen.

'OK. Where next?'

'Across the road, looking up the High Street. The camera you got them on before, when they did for that fat lad.'

Pete laughed shortly. 'And you go on at me! You're about as politically correct as Dave Miles.'

'Well, you're his boss. He must have got it from somewhere.'

'I dare say, but it wasn't me,' Pete said, as the other man switched cameras again.

The High Street was quiet at that time of night. The shops were all closed, of course, and there were not many nightspots up that way. After a few seconds, he saw the two figures they'd been tracking walking in reverse up the far side of the wide, paved street. The jacket now showed up as a pale colour, though it was hard to tell exactly what under the yellow street lighting. The two dark heads bobbed and turned as they chatted, reversing up the street. At one point, the one in the dark, anorak-style coat raised a hand to wave. Pete looked to the far side of the screen and saw a group of girls in short skirts and high heels, coming out of a side street. Two of them waved back — except, he realised, they hadn't. He was watching in reverse, so they had waved first.

The guy in the pale jacket turned his head to look across at them, giving a full-face shot, though too distant to be useful.

Still, that was more girls who knew them. They had to be somewhere close at hand.

The image on screen continued moving, the two figures walking backwards, away from the camera until they disappeared abruptly from view.

'Hold up.'

Graham hit a key and the image froze, then eased forward, the two men emerging into view again. 'Princesshay,' he said. 'Maybe they parked there.'

'Have we got anything round there?'

Graham shook his head. 'It's NCP. They have their own. I can ring them.'

'Please.'

'I'll give you a buzz when I've got it, shall I?'

'That'd be great. When d'you reckon — ish?'

Graham glanced at the clock on the wall. 'Don't know. You might be lucky and get it today, but I'm not going to make any promises.'

'Do what you can, eh? Use your undoubtable charm on them.'

Graham laughed.

'OK, wish me luck. I'm off to the headmaster's office. Again.'
'Will you never learn, boy?'
'I keep trying.'
'Yes, that's the problem. My patience, Alan's, His Lordship's . . .'
Pete spread his hands. 'What can I say? I am what I am.'

He headed upstairs trying to figure out how the hell he was going to put his question to Silverstone without mentioning any names.

Chapter 22

'Sir.' Pete stood stiffly before the DCI. 'We're making progress on the issue of the Armenians, but I need to see a copy of the plans for Operation Natterjack.'

'Why?'

'I need to track certain information from its original source to its ultimate destination without alerting anyone along that path to what I'm doing. The plans will tell me the route to follow.'

'I see. Would it, perhaps, be quicker to simply ask me?'

'Possibly, sir. But I'd rather not cast aspersions at anyone until I've got some evidence to back them up.'

'Hmm.' Silverstone continued to stare at him for a long moment. 'It's no small document.'

'Of course, sir.'

'Would an email be private enough?'

'Perfect.'

'How's the pathologist's case coming?'

'Slowly, sir. But we're making headway. We seem to have two subjects. Young males, early twenties at a guess, known as Dom and Josh. No last names yet. One of them appears to drive a silver Peugeot 308, but Swansea tell us there are three hundred and twelve of those registered in South Devon. We can narrow it a bit by the fact that it's a 2010 model, but that still leaves us with eighty-three, assuming it hasn't been nicked and brought in from another jurisdiction. They frequent two pubs and a coffee shop that we know of, on an irregular basis, and they're known informally among the student population in the city. We haven't found anyone who knows where either of them lives or works yet, though. Of course, they may well be students themselves. We're following up on that as we speak.'

Right. And how many victims now?'

'Ten confirmed, sir, including at least two more this week.'

'Then it's time we stopped buggering about and caught them, Sergeant. Get on it, for God's sake.'

'Sir.' *That's what I've been trying to bloody do, you useless tit.* 'And the email, sir?'

'What? Yes, I'll do it now.'

'Thank you, sir.' Pete turned and left before he could get himself into any more trouble by saying what he was thinking.

As expected, Ben was still beavering away at his screen, the only one of his team in the squad room. He sat down heavily and flicked on his computer.

'Hey, boss. How's it going?'

'There's an old song called "If I Were a Carpenter", Ben. Well, if *I* was, I'd be sorely tempted to bring in a bloody big mallet and hit Fast-track over the head with it repeatedly until he either showed some semblance of intelligence or pegged it.'

'I'm not absolutely certain, boss, but I think there might be a law or two against that.'

'For now, maybe. But there's been some chatter again about legalising euthanasia.'

'Eh? That's assisted suicide, isn't it?'

'Otherwise known as putting someone out of their misery. And that would put him out of a hell of a lot of people's misery. Talking of which, have you got anything off that bloody computer yet, to put me out of mine?'

Ben's laugh turned to a grimace. 'Only what we talked about last night, boss.'

'Well, if you'd known . . .'

Slap.

Pete's head whipped around to see a hand on top of a sheet of paper on the far side of his desk.

'What the fuck is this?' Simon Phillips demanded.

Pete looked up into a pair of brown eyes that were blazing with anger. 'I don't know,' he said. 'I can't see it.'

Phillips shifted his hand to expose the contents of the sheet. It was a brief letter, addressed to Simon, from his bank. 'I'll tell you what it is,' he said, his voice low and angry. 'It's a letter informing me that my account has been examined by a police computer. That's not what it says, of course, but that's certainly what it means. What the hell are you trying to pull, eh? Just because I haven't brought your precious boy back to you, you're trying to dig up anything you can to discredit me? Well, you won't bloody well find anything. Because there's nothing *to* find. I wonder why it is that little Tommy so clearly doesn't want to come home or even be found. Perhaps you should be looking closer to home, rather than trying to throw the blame at others. Have you thought about that? You try anything like this again and I'll have your bloody badge off you, d'you hear me?'

Pete fought to stay in his chair rather than surge up out of it and floor the man. 'All I can hear,' he said, low and tight, 'is a lot of hot air from an incompetent bullshitter. You need to go and sit down before you get in some real trouble.'

Simon barked a laugh. 'What, you're threatening me now?'

Pete shook his head. 'Grow up, mate. This isn't a playground.'

'Oh, I'm not playing. You can trust me on that.' Simon snatched up the letter and marched back towards his desk.

'Sorry, boss,' Ben said quietly. 'Did I . . .?'

'Don't worry about it,' Pete said, turning towards him. 'It wasn't your fault.'

'But . . .'

'Well, yeah. *That* was. But if it hadn't been that, he'd have found another excuse, sooner or later. I trod on his toes, so to speak. He doesn't like it. Makes him feel inadequate.'

Ben nodded and returned his attention to his computer screen.

Pete focused on his, opened his email and found a message from DCI Silverstone with the promised attachment. He saved and opened it.

'Christ,' he muttered when he saw the page count. 'Bloody *War and Peace* wasn't that long.' He sighed. At least he didn't have to read all of it. He scrolled down to the list of contents.

*

'Right,' he muttered and began to read.

An independent officer at each station, i.e. one who has no connection to drug-related arrests or suspects, will compile all available intelligence on dealers, suppliers and users of illegal drugs within the area covered by that station and send it to the relevant officer at Devon and Cornwall Police Headquarters, Middlemoor, Exeter.

So, if this had been adhered to . . .

Pete grunted.

One thing Ben had achieved was to clear Simon of any involvement in the actions they were looking at. Which meant he had to talk to the man. Privately. He sighed and turned in his chair. Simon was concentrating on something on his desk. His team were working away individually. Pete picked up his phone and dialled.

'DS Phillips. How can I help?'

'Simon, it's Pete. Do not put the phone down. We need to have a conversation and it needs not to be overheard.'

There was a pause. Then: 'OK.'

'Yes, we were looking at your bank account. Along with a lot of others in the station, on the orders of DCI Silverstone. You can check with him, if you haven't already. It was in connection with Operation Natterjack. He asked me to do it specifically because I wasn't here while it was all being set up. Now, you're the person who compiled all the intelligence that went from here to Middlemoor, so I need to ask you who dealt with that or had access to it, apart from you and Jim.'

'And I need to tell you to mind your own bloody business. But I won't. The answer is nobody.'

'It went from Jim to you to Middlemoor with no other input?'

'That's correct.'

'OK. Thanks for that.' He put the phone down, turned around in his chair and caught Simon's baffled glance. He nodded once, then turned back to his desk.

So, once more, they were without a suspect.

'Ben,' he said. 'We can narrow the search down to Jim and his team and whoever dealt with it at Middlemoor.'

'And I've already cleared Jim and his team. So, that leaves Middlemoor. Except, you already established that what went in there is what came out.'

'There's only one answer to that,' Pete said. 'We missed something.'

*

A little over an hour later, Pete was working through his case notes, trying to figure out what they could have missed, when the door opened and CID's newest recruit walked in, a tray of steaming mugs in her hands.

Sandy Dennis had moved upstairs from Patrol just three weeks ago, while Pete was still at home on compassionate leave, but he had known her as a beat cop. She had had a special affinity with the homeless, the drug- and alcohol-dependent – those who felt abandoned and ignored by society – so she was a perfect fit with Jim's team when Frank Benton retired.

'Damn.' He slapped his hand on the desk.

'Jesus! Do you have to, boss?'

'Frank Benton,' he said. 'I don't remember seeing him on the list of people you checked out, Ben.'

'Well, he's gone, isn't he? And no great loss, either.'

Frank had retired, having served the last twelve years as a DC because he'd never earned a promotion – or much else, for that matter. He'd simply bided his time, putting in the minimum required effort, until the first opportunity to slip off and take his pension. And, in the meantime, he'd taken great pleasure in goading the junior staff, including Ben, at every opportunity.

'Maybe, but he was here when the plans for Natterjack were being drawn up, wasn't he? And, if I know Frank, he'd have jumped at the chance to put his name to something that didn't take much actual work. Like a list of suspects, for example. He might even have volunteered.'

'Yes, but Simon drew that up.'

'From data supplied by Jim and his team as well as Uniform. I'd lay odds that Frank had a hand in Jim's contribution. Especially just before he retired. He'd have wanted to keep his arse on that chair as much as physically possible, rather than doing any real work.'

'True.' Ben nodded.

Pete turned in his chair. 'Jim,' he called. 'You got a sec?'

Jim nodded and got up to come over to Pete's desk. 'What's up?'

'The data you provided to Simon for Operation Natterjack. Who actually compiled it? Was it you or one of your team?'

'Well.' Jim shrugged. 'Mostly, it was Frank. I passed him the files, let him get on with it. There wasn't much he could screw up, was there? And it saved him getting tied into an ongoing case just before he finished.'

'Did you check it before you passed it on to Simon, though?'

'Well . . . no, actually. It took him longer than it should. No surprise there, I suppose. By the time he got it finished, Fast-track was already squawking for it.'

'Right.' Pete was nodding. So, there had been no opportunity to check Frank's work before it got passed through Simon and on to Headquarters.

'What's . . .?' Jim's eyes widened as realisation dawned. 'Ah. So, Frank missed the Armenian off the list.'

Pete tilted his head, eyebrows rising. *And engineered the perfect opportunity to get away with it by not finishing the job until the last moment.* 'It's a good theory, at least. Thanks, Jim.'

'No trouble.'

Jim headed back to his desk.

'You got something, boss?'

'Could be.'

Pete keyed in Frank's details from memory and hit the Search key. In moments, the program had thrown up a bank account and a building society savings account under the name of Frank Benton. Pete opened up the latter. Its latest total was just two thousand, six hundred and forty-two pounds. He scanned backwards through the last couple of years. The account had been used very little, no major amounts coming in or going out. He closed it and checked the bank account, which was in joint names with Frank's wife, Sylvia. Its current total was just under a thousand pounds more than the building society one, with an assortment of deposits and withdrawals that showed it to be Frank's main account. He combed through the last four months. Nothing suggestive of corruption showed up. But, if there was one thing Frank wasn't, it was stupid.

Pete returned to the search screen and replaced Frank's name with that of his wife. He hit the Enter key and sat back. This time three accounts came up: the same joint bank account, another with just her name on it and a savings account in a different building society to Frank's. Pete opened the individual bank account first. As he'd expected, the total was small, the activity minimal. Her wages from her job at the tourist information office were paid into it each month then, almost immediately paid back out again, into the joint account and her savings account. He switched to that one.

'Ooh.'

A current total of just under seventeen thousand pounds showed on the screen.

'Nice.'

He scanned up through the deposits and withdrawals. There were few of the latter, generally of the sort of size that their exotic style of holidays would account for, and the deposits were steady at five hundred a month, going back over the past three years. Then a large lump-sum appeared, listed as a cheque. Where had that come from? He checked the exact date. The twentieth of September three years ago. He cast his mind back. What had happened then . . .? He'd never been close to Frank. As Ben had suggested, the bloke was a waste of space. But one thing he wasn't was quiet. If something significant happened in his life, everyone in the squad room knew about it. It was just a question of whether you paid any attention.

Pete wished he had.

Although . . .

He really didn't want to call Jim over again, but he couldn't recall what had been going on in Frank's life three years ago, no matter how hard he tried. He picked up the phone instead.

'Jim,' he said when the connection was made. 'Me again. Sorry. What was going on with Frank, three years ago in September?'

'Three years? How the hell can that be relevant to—'

'I'm not saying it is,' Pete interrupted quickly. 'It's just I've come across something out of place and I wanted to make sure it's not related.'

'OK . . . When did they move house?'

'That was it. Thanks, mate.' He remembered Frank going on and on about how they'd moved into a bigger house and still made a profit on the deal.

Putting the phone down, he went back to his screen. He scanned back further but found no more anomalies in the account so he closed it and sat back again, thinking. If he'd had a lot of money from somewhere he shouldn't have, where would he have hidden it? Frank hadn't ever been one for ostentation. He'd never spend twenty quid on a watch, never mind the ten or twenty grand that you could spend on some, if he could get one for two. His car was a beat-up old Vauxhall. At least he'd bought British, Pete thought with an internal shrug. And the house, though bigger than their last one, had needed of a lot of work doing.

'Mmm.' *I wonder*, he thought. That amount of work had to be paid for and tradesmen weren't cheap, these days, even without the materials. You could spend a fortune on a place like that. But, had he? It wasn't as if there was anyone in the station that Pete could ask. As far as he knew, no one was likely to have stayed in touch with Frank after he'd left.

'Ben, turn that thing off and come with me.'

Chapter 23

Frank and Sylvia Benton's house was in a village just outside Ashburton. An old farmhouse, it was built of local stone with a red-tile roof and expansive lawns to either side of a lavender-edged flagstone path.

'Cor, that must be worth a bob or two,' Ben said, looking up at the place as Pete parked in front of it.

'Best part of a million, I should think. Especially round here.'

'Where the hell did a DC get that kind of dosh?'

Pete tilted his head, one eyebrow raised. He locked the car as Ben opened the wrought-iron gate and they went up the path. Pete rang the bell, the scent of lavender mixing with that of the pink and maroon roses to either side of the doorstep.

'Place belongs on a chocolate box, doesn't it?' Ben said, looking around.

There was the sound of a bolt sliding and the door opened in front of them.

Sylvia looked radiant. At fifty-three, she was grey-haired but immaculately turned out, even at home, her hair and make-up perfect. She was one of those women who could make even jeans look stylish.

'Peter,' she said, her eyes widening in surprise. 'How nice to see you. Come in. And this is . . . Ben, am I right?'

Ben nodded. 'That's right.'

'Well, don't just stand there.' She stepped back, holding the door wide. 'This is a surprise. To what do we owe the honour?'

Pete stepped inside, followed by Ben. 'We were out this way to interview a potential suspect and thought we'd stop by, see how you and Frank are doing, how the house is coming along.' He looked around. The hall was large and well lit, the floor tiled in a black and white check, woodwork all a rich mahogany colour that matched the sparse but smart old furniture.

'Oh, it's coming along,' she said. 'We've still got a bit to do, but we'll get there. Through here.' She indicated a door to the right. They went through into a cosy sitting room with armchairs arranged around a wood-burning stove, bookshelves covering the walls to either side of them and a TV angled out from one corner. 'Take a seat, both of you. Do you fancy a drink? Tea? Coffee?'

'A coffee would be great,' Pete said. 'Thanks. What's Frank up to?'

'Oh, he's out, I'm afraid. Fishing. He's got quite keen lately. Not very good at it, mind.'

'Slippery customers, these fish,' Pete said.

Sylvia laughed. 'Yes. Any news on Tommy?'

'Nothing concrete.'

'I'm sorry. How's Louise coping?'

'She's up and down, you know. Good days and bad. Still more bad than good, but I think she's gaining ground, slowly.'

'Poor woman.' She shook her head. 'I'll get the drinks. Won't be a minute. Make yourselves comfortable.'

She bustled off towards the back of the house and they sat.

Ben looked around and raised an eyebrow. 'Very nice,' he said.

'Need the grand tour, though, don't we?' He nodded towards the wood burner. 'Warm yourself up a minute, I'll go see if she needs a hand with the tray.'

As he stepped out into the hall, he heard the explosive hiss of boiling water being blasted through a small opening. He followed the sound through an open doorway to the left and behind the stairs. 'Do you need a hand, Sylvia?' he called.

'Through here, Peter.'

A short passage led past two closed doors and an open one to a stable door at the back of the house, the small window in the top section showing a glimpse of garden. The sounds were coming from the open doorway. He went into a large, bright kitchen, at once modern but suitable to the size and style of the building, the cupboards were an eggshell blue, the walls bright yellow.

Sylvia was working at the side of the room, near the Belfast sink that was cut into the solid wood worktop beneath a large window that looked out over the back garden. She looked up as he appeared in the doorway. 'You could grab the biscuits if you like. Second from the end.' She nodded towards the cupboards to his right.

'OK.' He stepped in, opened the cupboard she'd indicated and found a large cut-glass biscuit barrel filled with a mix of digestives, cookies and chocolate-dipped shortbreads. 'Wow. Looks wonderful.'

*

'Well, it's been lovely to see you,' Sylvia said as they stood up an hour later.

'You, too,' Pete said. 'It's just a shame Frank wasn't here, eh, Ben?'

'That's right.'

'Still, maybe next time, eh? Don't know when that'll be, of course. But perhaps, if we get ourselves organised, we'll ring ahead.' He headed for the hallway, Ben following.

'I'm sure he'd be glad to see you.'

'Well, thanks for the coffee.'

'My pleasure.'

Pete opened the door, stepped out, then paused on the step to let Ben move past him. He gave Sylvia a hug. 'See you soon.'

'I hope so.'

He stepped away and caught up with Ben. They waved from the gate, Sylvia waving back. Pete waited until they were in the car, his hand on the ignition key, before he said anything to Ben.

'So?'

He turned the key, starting the car, and put it into gear.

'Well, there's no way I could afford a place like that.'

They waved once more to Sylvia, who was standing in the open doorway.

'You should have seen the kitchen,' Pete said, as he pulled away. 'They've splashed some serious cash in there.'

'Keep the little lady happy and she won't ask too many questions.'

'You sound like a married man,' Pete laughed.

'Research and observation, boss.'

'Talking of which, we need to research every penny that's come into Frank Benton's hands in the last few years because I can tell you already, that place wasn't paid for through their current accounts.'

'Well, solicitors don't take cash so it'll have had to go through an account somewhere.'

And the land registry would tell them which solicitor Frank had used, but they wouldn't get a warrant for the details of the deal just based on suspicion.

Pete stopped behind a short line of traffic as a set of lights in the narrow streets of Ashburton turned red in front of them. He looked around at the ancient buildings. To his left, were an optician's, a chemist's and an estate agent's.

'Hmm.'

'What?' asked Ben.

'I wonder how helpful an estate agent might be, if we approach them in the right way.'

'How d'you mean?'

'Well, for Frank to buy that place, someone had to sell it. Which usually involves an estate agent. And they'll know all the details we need.'

Ben smiled. 'We just need to find out which agent and ask them in the right way.'

'Yep.'

'A quick search on the web should tell us that.' Ben took out his phone. 'I could even do it on here.'

'Now, there's a plan.'

The lights ahead of them turned green and Pete slipped the car back into gear, easing forward with the traffic, flicking on his indicator to turn right at the junction, following the sign for the A38, Exeter and Plymouth.

*

By the time they got back to Exeter, Ben had discovered that the house had been bought through a local Ashburton estate agent, though not the one Pete had spotted by the traffic lights. He had the price paid and the solicitor Frank used – Diehl and Slaughter of Exeter.

'I've come across that name recently,' Pete said, as he drove through the outskirts of the city. 'Damned if I know where, though.'

'The other week, on the Rosie Whitlock case?'

'I expect so. I'll think of it in time. I don't imagine it's important. What we need now is some way of persuading them to tell us how that six hundred and seventy-eight grand was paid and where from.'

'Good luck with that.'

Pete grunted. 'I suppose what we can do in the meantime is eliminate a few possibilities.'

'Like what?'

'Well, the rich maiden aunt's bequest, the big pension payout, the lottery win, the long-term savings account.'

Ben was nodding. 'Don't know about the rich maiden aunt, but the rest shouldn't take long.'

'OK, I'll see about the old aunt, you delve deeper into their financials.'

*

Back in the squad room, they found the team's desks still deserted.

Pete left Ben to his financial checks while he checked Frank's HR file for his date and place of birth, then typed them and his name into an ancestry search program. Almost immediately, it came up with the names of his parents and Pete began to build a family tree. Searching on the parents gave him their births and the names of Frank's grandparents, then he found Frank's aunt who had died at just three years old and his brother, who was still living. He went back one more generation, filled in the siblings of Frank's grandparents then did the same for Sylvia, whose details he had found through their marriage in 1989.

It turned out that Frank didn't have any unmarried aunts or uncles. Not even any great-aunts or uncles except for two who had died in childhood, like his aunt. He did, however, have an uncle who had married but had no children – an elder brother of his mother, called Robert Wilson, who had lived in Paignton and had survived his wife by three years, dying in 2012.

And wills were a matter of public record.

Pete looked up Robert Wilson's.

He had changed his will after his wife's death to leave everything to another single beneficiary. His nephew Frank Benton had missed out in preference to a hospice in Brixham.

'Huh,' Pete grunted. There was some justice in the world, after all.

He checked through the rest of the family tree he had compiled, but found no sources of inheritance for Frank or Sylvia. He printed all he'd found and closed the program. 'It wasn't the old aunt or uncle,' he said to Ben.

'He hasn't had any big wins or insurance policies paying out, either. And there's no way he bought the house out of his savings, never mind doing it up like they have.'

'So, where did he get the money? We really need to find out from his solicitor. I'll go and have a word with His Lordship while you dig back as far as you can in his and Sylvia's financials.'

'Right, boss.'

Pete switched off his computer and headed for Silverstone's office. He knocked on the closed door.

'Come.'

Pete went in, closing the door carefully behind him.

'Peter. Do you have some news?'

'We've got a suspect, in regard to the Operation Natterjack oversight. Need a warrant to question his solicitor, though, about exactly how he paid for a property transaction.'

'Who are we talking about?'

'Frank Benton.'

'And when was this property transaction?'

'Three years ago.'

'Presumably you've checked all the usual sources? Savings, bequests, winnings, mortgage?'

'There's no legitimate source for the money. Between the purchase price and the renovations, he's got to have spent getting on for a million.'

'I know he was far from the most conscientious officer in the squad room, but what are we accusing him of?'

'Well, he won't have earned that much through Gagik Petrosyan, that's for sure. He hasn't been here long enough – not by a long chalk. So, there's got to be something else going on, but we don't know what yet.'

'Then, I suggest you find out, Peter. And pronto. *Then* we can apply for a warrant for the solicitor's records.'

'Sir.'

'And, what of the other matter? These killings.'

'We're swamping the university, searching for information on the two suspects, sir. Getting their pictures in front of everyone we can in the hope that we'll come across someone who knows them by more than first names.'

'And you're not worried that'll get back to them and scare them off?'

'Doesn't matter if it does. They've got to keep on living as normal or we'll hear about it. They might stop killing, but that's no bad thing, is it?'

'Very well. Make sure you do hear about anyone who changes their habits suddenly and, in the meantime, find out what Frank Benton's been up to – where he got all that money from.'

'Yes, sir.'

Before returning to the squad room, Pete headed downstairs. One of the few people in the station who had known Frank in any more than a passing sense was Bill Matheson, the big semi-retired desk sergeant who worked alternate days with Mike Desmond. And he had seen Bill when he went out earlier.

The reception area appeared to be deserted. Bill was chatting with the two women on duty behind the high-topped counter.

'Hey, Bill,' Pete said. 'Have you got a sec?'

Bill looked up. 'Hello, mate. Yeah, of course. What's up?' He stepped forward to lean his elbows on the counter between them.

'Have you spoken to Frank Benton since he finished?'

'No, why?'

'Somebody said he'd taken up fishing. What the hell's that about? He's got all the time in the world to spend with his missus and he buggers off out to play with a bunch of maggots.'

'First I've heard of it. He did used to get out and about now and then, but he was always into birds, as far as I know.'

'Oh? Bit of a twitcher, was he?'

'Yeah. Used to be into birds of prey and that, big time. Why, you thinking of going down the river with him, are you? He's moved away, you know. Gone inland, for some reason.'

'I know. Ashburton. Fair old place he's got himself. No, I just thought, with the two of you being mates, you'd perhaps have stayed in touch, that was all.'

'I expect we will. It's only been a few weeks, though. Got to let the bloke get settled.'

'Fair enough.'

'What d'you want him for, anyway?'

'Oh, I just want to ask him about a case.'

'I've got his new number if you want it.'

'Ah, that would be handy. I'll give him a quick bell.'

He had no need of Frank's number, but it would support his subterfuge to accept it.

'Hang on.' Bill went back behind one of the desks in the area behind the counter, opened one of its drawers and took out a pad of Post-its and a small address book. He copied something from one to the other, put the book away and brought the note over. 'Here you go.' He handed it over.

Pete checked the note and raised it in a wave. 'Thanks for that.'

He headed back upstairs. Ben was still tapping away at his keyboard.

He glanced up. 'One of the things they taught us on that IT course last spring was tracking traffic to and from an IP address.'

'Right.'

'Well, that's what I'm doing now. I started with Frank's old one, before he moved. Nothing unusual there. But, since he's gone out into the sticks, he's had several emails to an account in the name of Eagle Enterprises. So, I tried to find out where Eagle Enterprises were doing business from before he moved, or if it was a new thing. Turns out, it's not new, but, until a few weeks ago, it was doing everything online through two addresses here in Exeter. One was the university library, the other was that internet café on Broadgate.'

'OK. I don't suppose you've got into the actual emails, to see what kind of business we're talking about?'

'Can't do that without a warrant, boss.' He winked. 'I'm still working on it.'

Pete nodded. 'And I don't suppose a simple search comes up with anything on Eagle Enterprises. It's not a registered company?'

'No such luck.'

'Interesting, though. I was just talking to Bill on the front desk. He reckoned that Frank was well into birds before he left here. Birds of prey like kestrels, ospreys. Eagles. Yet, Sylvia said he'd gone fishing rather than bird-watching. They're not mutually exclusive, of course, but they are both time-consuming so, why the change?'

Ben shrugged. 'People do get bored. Change hobbies. Especially with a change of location. Different opportunities.'

'Yes, but I can't see Frank as the waxed jacket and wellies type. Sitting for hours, yes, but having to work at it? Out in the cold?' He shook his head. 'No. Not unless he's getting a lot more than enjoyment out of it.'

'Gotcha,' Ben said triumphantly. He paused, reading. 'Yep, he's getting a hell of a lot more than enjoyment.'

'Whatcha got?'

'Emails arranging the sale of eggs and chicks of peregrines, merlins, hobbies and goshawks.'

'Nice one.' Pete slapped him on the back. 'Best come out of it, then, and I'll get us a warrant to go in legally.'

Chapter 24

'What I don't get is why he'd tell Sylvia that he's changed hobbies from bird-watching to fishing,' Ben said as Pete drove out of the city once more.

'Christ knows. Maybe we'll find that out when we find him. Just make sure we stay on track to do that, eh?'

'Right, boss.'

Once Pete had obtained the warrant they needed to make their discoveries admissible in court, Ben had once more accessed the Eagle Enterprises email account and saved several of the email exchanges from it while Pete got Frank's mobile number from his HR file and put a trace on it.

The location had come up as a couple of miles west of Bovey Tracey, in a heavily wooded area near the eastern edge of Dartmoor.

'One thing we can be sure of,' Pete continued, 'he's not out nest-raiding at this time of year.'

'No. He could be scouting them, ready for spring, though. Here you go.' Ben passed him an opened Mars bar.

Pete accepted it gratefully and took a large bite. It was almost mid-afternoon and they had not stopped for lunch. 'Thanks.' He handed the bar back to Ben as he accelerated down the entry onto the southbound A38 trunk road.

Ben was tracking the location of Frank Benton's mobile phone on a tablet computer on his lap.

'As long as he doesn't talk to Sylvia before we get to him. She's bound to tell him we came round and there's no telling what he might do then.'

'Yeah, but . . . he's a bit old for doing a runner, isn't he?'

'Some of the Hatton Garden bunch were in their seventies. Frank's only in his fifties.'

'I suppose.'

'No supposing needed. What we do need is to find out what he's been up to and who with. And whether there's anyone else in the station up to the same, now he's retired.'

Ben grimaced as Pete sped along the dual-carriageway. 'It's a horrible thought, though, isn't it? Someone we worked with . . . The betrayal of it.'

*

'There's got to be a way across there.' Ben peered across at the thick woodland to their right as Pete drove up the narrow, tunnel-like lane with tree branches meeting overhead. Frank's mobile phone signal was coming from just a few hundred yards away through the trees, on the other side of the River Bovey.

'Zoom out a bit,' Pete suggested.

Ben had zoomed in tight on Frank's location as they got closer. He tapped the minus sign on the bottom right of his tablet screen and the satellite photograph of tightly packed trees zoomed out one stage. He tapped it again. 'There. Keep going, there's a road going in up ahead. A bridge goes over the river. He can't be far off that footpath or whatever it is, going down through that skinny little field there.'

Pete glanced down at the screen. 'Probably in those trees to the left of it.'

'Hey! This is my job. Yours is the road.'

'For a young lad, you're a lot like my old gran sometimes.'

'Yeah, well. I've still got my whole life ahead of me, unlike you old folks.'

'At least I've got there. You make many more comments like that and my driving won't matter.'

'Just round this bend, it should be.'

'Yes, Nan.'

'If I had another Mars bar . . . There it is,' Ben said as they rounded the curve in the road.

It was little more than a farm track. The tarmac was broken and pitted, grass growing up the middle. Bushes and ferns brushed both sides of the car and the trees were so close that it looked like the road would give out at any moment.

'Are you sure this is right?' Pete demanded.

'Yes.' Ben looked down at his screen. 'It shows our position right here. Don't look,' he added quickly. 'The bridge is just a couple of hundred yards further.'

'And where does this *road* go after that?'

'There's a couple of farms further up, then it just ends by the look of it.'

'Right. And where's Frank?'

'Off to the right, just beyond the river. We'll have to find somewhere to pull over and—'

'Do what?' Pete broke in. 'There isn't room up here to swing a cat, never mind get off the damn road.'

'We haven't seen Frank's car yet, boss. He didn't walk all the way here.'

Pete grunted.

The road curved to the left in front of them, then the bridge appeared. It was an ancient hump-backed structure, the brick sides dotted with tiny ferns and tufts of grass.

'Bloody hell,' Pete said. 'There might be farms further on, but they're not going to get a combine harvester up here, are they?'

He drove up over the bridge and, as they crested it, they saw that the verges widened at the far side. There was a double gateway on the right with a dark red four-by-four parked in it and a swing-gate leading down to the river.

Pete pulled gently onto the grass at the base of the bridge, the far side of the car brushing the hedgerow. He drew up the handbrake and stopped the engine. 'He's still there, I take it?'

Ben checked his screen. 'He's moved a little bit further downstream, but he's still in there.'

They looked across. Beyond a high, overgrown hedge was a narrow strip of grass, the far end bordered by mature woodland like that on the far side of the river. Frank Benton was somewhere among it.

'How far?' Pete asked.

'Half a mile or so.'

'Come on then. Sitting here won't get us any answers.' He opened the car door and stepped out. All he could hear was birdsong and the soft ripple of water. Behind him, Ben closed his door, loud in the stillness. Pete stepped through the swing-gate onto the path down to the river.

It was little more than a stream here, flowing swiftly over gravel and red dirt, the water crystal clear. Pete could see leaves and stones on the bottom as he started along its bank.

Behind him, Ben cursed softly.

Pete glanced over his shoulder. 'What?'

'I've lost my signal.'

'I'm surprised you didn't lose it a couple of miles back. You might as well turn that thing off.'

'Oh, great. How are we going to find him now?'

'The old-fashioned way. By being quiet, for one thing.' Pete turned back to the path, concentrating on where he was putting his feet.

'Yeah, but . . . there's a lot of country out here. He could be anywhere.'

'He could, but one thing's for sure. He'll be coming back this way. His car's there, behind us.'

*

The river had cut a deep gorge through the rock thousands of years ago, making a steep-sided valley that was now thick with deciduous woodland which had been cut into here and there with long, narrow fields of pastureland. The path left the side of the river a few hundred yards downstream from the bridge and cut up and across the steep side of the valley. Under the trees, the ground was dotted with ferns, grasses and butcher's broom among swathes of dog's mercury and large patches of bare earth that perhaps in spring would be filled with bluebells or wood anemones but for now held the odd tiny patch of green where a red campion or a foxglove clung to life in a spot of sunlight.

The rich soil was damp and soft with winter rain and past frosts so that, here and there, tracks were left in it. Pete saw the toe of another boot print just before a long, black smear where the wearer had slid in the mud. A thin branch was snapped off at the side of the trail, the broken end showing pale in the dappled light.

'Careful here,' Pete said quietly. 'It's slippery.'

Up ahead, a break showed in the trees, a stile crossing the path where it emerged into the thin sunshine.

Coming from the opposite direction, Frank reached the stile before they did. Pete stopped, putting a hand up to stop Ben behind him. He watched Frank swing his two rods over the stile then climb over, readjust the tackle bag over his shoulder and catch the binoculars swinging across his chest.

As Frank lifted his head to carry on, Pete stepped forward. 'Afternoon.'

Frank jumped. 'Damn! You scared the bejesus out of me. Pete?' He frowned. 'What are you doing out here?' He paused. 'And Ben?'

'Looking for you,' Pete said.

'Why, what's up?'

'Need to ask you about a case.'

'And you had to come all the way out here to do it? Must be bloody urgent.'

'Well, we thought it'd be better to catch you on your own if we could, save Sylvia overhearing anything she shouldn't.'

'About what?' Frank had stopped in the path, twenty feet from Pete. He glanced around as if he wanted to put down the rods and the bag in his hands.

Pete stepped forward, closing the distance between them. 'An ongoing case. A bunch of raids on drug dealers and so on, week before last. I know you were gone before it happened, but Jim told me you were involved in the organisation of it. Drawing up the lists of addresses and so forth.'

'That's right. I didn't know you were back at work. Any news on Tommy?'

Pete shook his head. 'No, nothing firm yet. I started back because of these raids. They needed someone to babysit the squad room while everyone else was out hauling pushers out of their beds.'

Frank was nodding. 'So, what do you need from me?'

'Well, the thing is, there was a bit of an oversight in the Exeter operation and, as you were involved in drawing up the lists, I thought maybe you'd be able to shed some light. Only, this isn't the first time the person in question was overlooked. In fact, his whole gang has been, ever since they came to the city four years ago. It's like someone in the know has been making sure they stayed under the radar all along. But then one of them was killed a couple of days ago. Brake line was cut so he couldn't stop. Went straight out in front of a lorry.' Pete clapped his hands together and saw Frank blink. 'Splat. Never knew what hit him. Or, if he did, it was only for a second. Zivan Millic.'

'Yeah. Big, ugly bugger. Pusher in two or three of the pubs, or so we suspected. Never could prove anything. No one willing to testify. He's dead? That's one less nasty bastard in the city then.'

'That's right. His boss isn't too happy about it, though. Feels let down, disappointed, apparently. Of course, he didn't say as much, but I wouldn't be surprised if he's looking for whoever did it and whoever allowed them to. In terms of our side of things, I mean.'

'His boss?'

'The Armenian. Millic had just come from his house when he died. We had it under surveillance.'

'Eh? I thought the Armenian was just a bogeyman type of thing. You've identified him? And he implied he'd got someone on the force?'

'He's not quite daft enough to say so, but he did have, yes. Of course, you know that as well as I do, don't you?'

Frank frowned. 'What's that supposed to mean? Christ, if I didn't know better, I'd think you were accusing me of something.'

'And, if I didn't know better, I might think you were innocent,' Ben put in from behind Pete. 'But I do and you're not.'

A flash of anger showed on Frank's face. 'You want to keep the boy under control, Pete. You and me can discuss this like men.'

'Yeah. Thing is, you didn't pay for that house with peanuts, did you? And doing it up as well . . . That kitchen alone must have cost well over ten grand. Didn't come out of your wages, did it? Or Sylvia's. And it was way more than the bit you'd have got from Petrosyan, so where'd it come from, eh?' He sighed. 'One thing Ben's good at is computers. He's been tracking your phone all the way here so we know exactly where you've been for the past half-hour. The question is, what are we going to find when we get there? I'm thinking it might be a nest site, considering what we saw in the Eagle Enterprises email account. Don't know which species, of course. Ben thought maybe goshawk – these valleys and woods.'

'The boy a twitcher, is he? I know he twitched fairish in the squad room. All you had to do was walk past too close behind him.' Frank laughed. 'And, as for reading people's emails, that's illegal, that is. Could get you charged. Drummed out of the force.'

Pete shook his head. 'Not when we had a warrant.'

'On what basis?' Frank demanded.

'Other evidence. Anyway, we can talk about it in the car. It's getting cold, stood about here.'

Frank chuckled. 'You've got soft, mate.'

'Maybe.' Pete stepped forward. 'Come on, put the rods and the bag down.'

'You aren't going to handcuff me?'

'You know the rules, Frank.'

Frank's head was shaking slowly. 'No, I mean you *aren't* going to handcuff me.' He dropped the rods, threw the bag at Pete's head and leapt off the path, down the steep, wooded slope.

Chapter 25

'Shit.'

Pete batted the bag aside, surprised by its weight. 'Ben, head him off. Get back to the car.' He started down the steep, thickly wooded slope as, in front of him, Frank threw aside his binoculars.

Frank dodged around a large tree then yelped as, jumping back across, he went straight into a thin, whippy young trunk.

'Frank,' Pete called. 'Don't be bloody stupid. You're not going to get anywhere. Shit.' His foot caught on a root and he lurched forward, then caught a low branch with his arm and swung himself back upright, jumped down a short drop and landed hard, just yards behind the older man. 'We're between you and your car and Ben's half your age and twice as fit.'

'Yeah, but you don't know where you are and it'll be dark in another hour.' Frank crashed through a stand of dark, spiky butcher's broom as Pete swung himself around a narrow trunk towards his quarry.

Frank was surprisingly agile for his age, leaping and dodging, ducking and weaving through the trees and brush. The slope was getting dangerously steep. Pete couldn't see the river, but he knew it was a good fifty feet below them, if not more. He put out a hand to bounce off a thick, old oak tree and, seeing the tangle of brambles ahead, gave himself an extra push so that his foot landed on rather than behind the strong, trailing stems. He jumped sideways from there, his other foot landing on the bole of a small tree that gave him a firm, clear push-off. Careering downhill, he had no idea what was in front of them. He just knew he had to catch Frank and stop him before one of them had an accident.

He was closing the distance, though. He was almost ready to make a flying leap, taking the man down, when he spotted a horizontal branch across his line of flight and stopped himself with a grunt.

He kept running instead, breathing hard now, arms flailing as he struggled to maintain balance in his headlong downhill pursuit. Frank laughed and dodged left around the far side of another big tree. When Pete saw him again, all he saw was his back. He was too far to catch again. As he watched, Frank's foot slipped out from under him and he went down on his backside, sliding down the steep slope. Then his foot jarred on something and he was upright again, feet flying as he concentrated on what was in front of him, ignoring his pursuer.

He hit an animal track and switched direction again, cutting across to the right, stretching out his legs as he ran downhill, his path clear for several paces. Pete had to put out a hand and bounce off a small tree to stay behind him. He saw the trail cut back to the left, a few yards ahead, but Frank kept going in a straight line. A thicket of tight-leaved wild box stood ahead of him, a twin-trunked tree to its right. Pete saw him aim for the trunks, leaping at full speed towards them.

'Fuck,' he yelled, hands stretching out to either side as he closed in on the gap. He yelped as one arm gave way and he went feet first through the gap between the trunks, his shoulder bouncing hard off the one on the left. Then he seemed to be falling. He cried out.

Pete let his feet hit the ground harder, digging in as he tried to slow himself, a flash of fear jolting through him.

There was only one way.

He went down hard on his back, feet out in front. Both feet slammed into the base of the right-hand trunk and he grunted as his legs absorbed his momentum, bending almost double. He got quickly to his feet, hands on the twin trunks as he peered through the gap between.

Frank was about twenty feet below him, lying in a crumpled heap across an awkwardly angled slab of dark rock, one knee bent at an unnatural angle against the twisted trunk of a red-berried hawthorn.

He wasn't moving.

Pete pushed himself back and looked around.

The twin-trunked tree stood at the top of a low cliff that stretched away to the left for perhaps twenty feet, but ended much closer at the other side in a dangerously steep slope. Thin trees dotted the slope densely enough to provide hand and footholds.

He looked down again. Frank was still not moving. In fact, he was very still.

Pete stepped across to the far side of the big tree, jumped across the steep slope and grabbed the trunk he had been aiming for, then began to ease himself hand over hand, trunk to trunk, down towards where his former colleague lay. Reaching the rocks, he clambered back along, the rustle of wind in the twigs above mingling with the sound of the water below him in a wintry chorus.

'Frank.'

He paused. There was no movement at all. Frank's ribs were motionless. Was he holding his breath or . . .? Pete reached out tentatively, found the side of Frank's neck and felt for a pulse.

There was a flicker. A pause. Another flicker.

He was alive, but only just.

'Ben,' Pete bellowed. 'Ben.' He took out his phone and checked the screen but there was no signal. 'Shit.'

Then faintly, he heard a reply. 'Boss?'

'On me,' he yelled.

'Coming.'

Pete checked Frank's right eye. The iris tightened as the light struck it. He checked the broken leg for blood but saw none. Taking out his phone, he photographed the scene from several angles. There was no way he was going to move the man. Awkward and potentially uncomfortable as his position was, it was far safer to leave him be than to move him and risk aggravating some internal injury.

'Boss?'

Ben sounded much closer now.

'Down here. Frank fell. Get a phone signal and get an ambulance here ASAP. He's unconscious, his pulse is weak and irregular, but his irises are still responsive.'

'Hang on. I'm nearly there.'

Then Pete heard the sound of running feet in the leaf litter. 'Boss?'

'Down here.'

'Ah.' Ben's head appeared between the two trunks of the split tree. 'There you are. Is he . . . alive?'

'Yes, just. Did you hear me before?'

'Bits of it.'

'He's unconscious. Weak, irregular pulse. Broken shoulder and leg. Probable broken ribs. Other injuries unknown. Get a signal and call an ambulance. You can guide them in; I'll stay with him.'

'Did he . . . confess?'

'Not yet, now move!'

Ben ducked back and Pete heard him running back up to the path. Holding a hand over Frank's nose, he felt the light waft of a tentative breath.

'Hold on, Frank. Help's on the way. Won't be long now.' *And, after that, you've got some questions to answer, old mate. And a cell with your name on it.*

'Sir.'

Pete stood loosely to attention before DCI Silverstone's desk.

The immaculately uniformed station chief looked up from his papers. 'Situation report, Sergeant?'

'One leak plugged, sir. Frank Benton has been illegally taking chicks and eggs from the nests of birds of prey around Dartmoor for years. I've got his notebook, which goes back six years, detailing nests, acquisitions and sales. Seems like he made one of those sales to Gagik Petrosyan, who recognised him as a police officer, took a punt and managed to blackmail him into providing information that would keep him and his gang off our radar.'

'It seems like or we can prove, Sergeant?'

'We've got proof of the illegal nest raiding and so on, both from his own notebook, which he had in his possession this afternoon and from an email account that we traced back to him. As for the Armenian, we have several contacts between them among Frank's mobile phone records and, if he recovers, I'm sure he'll tell us whatever we need. Trying to run like that was the act of a desperate man. He'll take whatever deal we're willing to offer, I'd imagine.'

'And what are his chances of recovery?'

'The hospital wouldn't say, sir. He was still alive by the time he got there, but only just. He has several broken bones, including four ribs, two of which punctured a lung. He's also got a ruptured spleen and one kidney that's seriously damaged. They're doing what repairs they can, but he's still in theatre and will be for some time.'

'A nasty fall, then.'

'Sir.'

'Self-inflicted though.'

'Exactly.'

'And the Armenian. Do we know if, when DC Benton retired,

he replaced him with anyone else in a similar role?'

'No, sir, we don't. Not yet.'

'It hasn't been long so, possibly nothing would show up yet.'
Pete nodded.

'Something to keep an eye on though.'

'Yes, sir.'

'And the other matter. Any news?'

'Nothing yet, sir. The team should be coming in any time now.
They wouldn't have bothered getting in touch unless they found
something significant.'

'Which suggests they haven't.'

Pete tilted his head in agreement. 'Nothing that'll lead directly
to an arrest, at least.'

'Very well. Carry on, Sergeant. And, good work.'

'Thank you, sir.' *Bloody hell! Good work? That's a first.* Pete
turned and opened the door, leaving Silverstone's office before
he said something he shouldn't.

Back in the squad room, he sank into his chair and said to
Ben, 'Where's the smelling salts? I'm in shock.'

'Why's that, boss?'

'I just got a "good work" from Fast-track.'

'Jesus, you're really on a roll. You'll be getting a promotion
next. Remember us on your way up, won't you?'

'I'll remember your bloody cheek, matey. You've been spending
too much time around Dave Miles, I reckon. We'll have to do
something about that.'

Ben's face took on an almost nervous expression.

Pete laughed. 'He hasn't taught you how to spot a wind-up
yet, though, has he?'

'Yeah, well. Between him and you, I'm up against two of the
best, aren't I?'

Pete laughed. 'Where the hell are they, anyway? Have you
heard from them?'

Ben shook his head. 'No. Do you want me to ring one of them?'

Pete grimaced. 'No. They'll turn up presently, I expect.' He checked the time. It was after five. Pete really wanted a team brief before they knocked off tonight, but he didn't want to interrupt them if they were still busy at the university.

He unlocked the bottom drawer of his desk and took out a file, opened it to where he'd placed a marker, about a quarter of the way in, and took up reading where he'd left off on the last occasion he'd had the opportunity.

Case No 1746/sp/16. Thomas James Gayle, Missing Person.
Witness interview.
Miss Deborah Jenkins, pool attendant, Exeter Indoor Swimming Pool.

This was a copy of the file that Simon Phillips had compiled on Tommy. The same copy that he'd handed back to Colin Underhill a week and a half ago after Jane had provided it to him without official sanction. He'd got it back, on the strict understanding that he was to remain nothing but an observer in the case, because it directly overlapped with his own inquiries into the abduction of Rosie Whitlock, the previous week.

He read on.

SP: What can you tell me about your impressions of Tommy Gayle?

DJ: He's focused. A bit of a loner, maybe. Doesn't interact with anyone while he's swimming, but he has got a friend he hangs around with afterwards. I suppose they're waiting for their parents to pick them up. Rosie. I don't know her last name. I've never dealt with her directly. She always comes in before my shift starts. Good swimmer though. Again, very focused, but she's . . . better trained, I think, than Tommy. He's more of a raw talent.

SP: And what about after? You said they hang around together. What do they get up to?

DJ: Oh, just normal stuff. Chatting. They sometimes have a Coke

*between them, or a coffee in winter. Sometimes they go outside for
a bit. Maybe to smoke, but I couldn't say for sure.*

SP: OK. But nothing else inappropriate for their age?

*DJ: Not that I've ever seen, no. He sometimes watches her when
they're not together, as boys will, but that's all.*

SP: So, you'd say he's aware of the opposite sex as being attractive.

*DJ: Oh, yes. He's small for his age, but not developmentally
backward.*

*SP: And this Rosie is the only person you've seen him interact
with?*

DJ: Pretty much, yes. He'll speak if he needs to, but . . . Shrug.

SP: Conclusion of interview.

So, Simon had evidence that Tommy and Rosie Whitlock knew
each other and hadn't said anything last week, when Pete took
Rosie's case. What was he playing at?

'Hey, boss.'

Pete snapped back to reality with a jolt, went to slap the file
shut but stopped himself just in time as he looked up to see Jane
shrugging her coat off opposite him and Jill stepping past her
towards her own desk.

He closed the file more gently than he'd been about to and
put it away.

'Ladies. How's it gone, today?'

'Do you want the detailed review or just the edited highlights?'
asked Jane.

'Edited version will do for now.'

'OK. We've covered about two-thirds of the university. Left the
more obscure and the more general areas for tomorrow. And, so
far, we've got bugger all.' Jane plonked herself down in her chair,
opposite Pete.

'Except, we've confirmed what we already knew,' Jill put in, as
she draped her long, black coat over the back of her chair.

Pete felt the shift of air as the squad room door opened again.

'Like I said: bugger all of any use.' Jane leaned back, stretching. 'And my legs and feet are killing me.'

'Terrible, these heels, aren't they?' Dave said as he walked in with Dick Feeney. 'That's why I never wear them to work.' He put one hand on his hip and flounced across the room, hips swaying widely.

'We really don't need to know about your personal habits,' Jane said.

'I am what I am.'

'Yeah, a pain in the arse,' Dick added, as he crossed behind Pete.

'I told you to keep that as our secret.'

'Will you never learn?' Jane asked. 'Never trust a copper.'

Pete winced inwardly. 'All right, kids. Calm down. Park your backsides and let's wind this up, shall we? Dave, Dick, what have you got?'

'A partial plate on the Peugeot,' Dick said. 'But I ran it and it didn't go anywhere.'

'I'll do the jokes,' Dave said. 'Your delivery needs work.'

'So does your timing,' Pete told him. 'Now's not it.'

Dave threw him a salute and Pete turned back to Dick.

'A young lady told me it was HB 747 something. She's an art student. HB pencils.'

'Yeah, yeah. It'll never fly,' said Dave.

Pete glanced at him. 'Dick?'

'I ran it and there aren't any silver 308s with that reg.'

'They're not daft, then, whoever they are,' Dave said. 'As long as they don't get caught by a vehicle check.'

'You're a chatty bugger this evening,' Pete said. 'How about doing something useful? Put an alert out on that registration if you haven't already. You never know – someone might spot it.'

Chapter 26

'All right, so where do you want to go tonight?'

Pete aimed the question at Louise, but it was also designed for Annie to respond to. He picked up his knife and fork, cut into a roast potato and transferred half of it to his mouth.

'We thought about the other side of the city. Over where he was last seen. That Co-op on the Dunsford Road and the area round it. Just to knock it off the list. Then, if there aren't many opportunities over there, maybe go down towards the industrial estate,' Annie said.

'I don't know about that last bit, after dark.'

The last thing he wanted Annie seeing at her age – or at any age, come to that – was a string of prostitutes walking the streets and picking up punters.

'There are one or two other places over that side that we could look at though. Round the sports field, for instance, and a few shops in the estates over there.' He stabbed a cube of beef from the casserole on his plate and lifted it. 'Mmm.' The meat was surprisingly tender, almost falling apart in his mouth.

'Why not Marsh Barton? The MacDonald's and the ice rink would be worthwhile, if nothing else. And there's bound to be at least one burger or kebab van round there.'

Pete swallowed, glancing at Louise, but she was looking down at her plate, pretending to sort through the runner beans with her fork.

'I'm glad we're raising such a clever and caring daughter. I really am. But I'm not taking you down there after dark, Anne Elizabeth. There's things that go on down there at night that aren't for young eyes like yours to see.'

'Like what?'

'Like things children don't need to know about.'

'Like sex and drugs?'

Pete was glad he hadn't refilled his mouth as he coughed in shock. 'Yes, like those. Now, eat up. We haven't got time to waste on talking about things that don't matter to us.' He stabbed a bunch of beans with his fork.

'Of course they matter. I need educating on how to deal with them responsibly.'

He stuffed the beans into his mouth and began to chew. 'What you need,' he said around them, 'is to stop winding me up and eat.'

*

By the time Pete and Annie finished their meals, Louise had eaten barely a quarter of hers. She was sinking into another trough of depression. Pete's first thought was to protect Annie from this, but she had lived with it for the past several months, just as he had and, if anything, she probably coped with it better than he did.

Certainly, she could get through to Louise in this condition better than he could.

He caught Annie's eye and gave a small nod towards her mother.

She picked up on it immediately. 'Mum. Hurry up. We need to get going.'

Louise looked up from her plate, gave her a hint of a smile. 'I'm . . . not particularly hungry, pet.'

243

'You will be by the time we get home. All that walking, you'll be famished.'

Pete saw something shift in Louise's eyes. He reached out to stop Annie, but it was too late.

'Do not baby me. I'm your mother, not the other way round.' She pushed the plate away.

Annie's face started to crumple, but then she rallied. 'So, try acting like it,' she snapped back. 'Instead of sulking like a baby who's lost its teddy bear, get out there and help us find him.'

'Annie Elizabeth Gayle, you will not talk to me like that,' Louise shouted. 'Go to . . .'

'I will, when you make me,' Annie shouted over her. 'This depression thing has gone on longer than it ought to. Longer than's good for you, me or Dad. It's time you snapped out of it and never mind the excuses.' She slammed her hands on the table as she stood up and pushed her chair back.

Pete reached out, put a hand on her arm. She glanced at him. 'No, Dad. It needs saying.'

He smiled.

'Are you going to let her talk to me like that?' Louise demanded.

'We all know it's not as simple as that, Lou, but, in essence, she's right. It is time to do something about the situation.'

'Well, thanks a bloody bunch and sorry for malingering, I'm sure.' She pushed herself back from the table and stood up.

'Nobody's suggesting you're malingering,' Pete said. 'We're just trying to find a way of getting you motivated that's all.'

'Like my son being missing isn't enough. Yeah. Thank you.'

'That's not what we're saying and you know it.' Pete grasped Annie's hand. 'We know how much you care for him. We're just trying to find a way of focusing that into useful action, in . . .' He stopped himself before he said something that would undo anything they'd achieved so far, but it was too late.

'Instead of what?' she demanded. 'Instead of useless inactivity? Instead of self-destructive anger? Instead of feeling constantly like someone's torn a big hole in my chest and pulled out everything that gave me purpose in life and thrown it away?' She broke down and started to sob, spun away and hurried out of the room.

Stricken, Annie looked to Pete.

'It's all right, love,' he said softly. 'You did well. Let her cry it out for a bit while we tidy up.'

'Are you sure?'

They could hear Louise sobbing in the next room as they took the dinner things through to the kitchen.

'Yes.'

In fact, he was far from it, but he didn't want to let Annie know that. She had tried her best, had shown remarkable maturity for her age, and he didn't want anything to spoil that if he could help it.

Minutes later, he heard Louise go upstairs. He glanced down at Annie and she met his gaze with a shrug. Pete finished washing up and tipped the water away as Annie folded the tea towel and slipped it over a nearby cupboard handle.

'Let's go . . .'

He stopped, hearing feet on the stairs again, coming down.

They met Louise in the hallway. Her eyes were dry, her face composed if a little blotchy and she had changed into jeans and boots with a thick jacket.

'Right, then,' he said briskly. 'Get your coat on, Annie, and grab your bag.'

*

An hour later, they had put posters up around the Co-op on the Dunsford Road as well as two other places on that side of the river and were climbing into the car again.

'Is that it over here then?' asked Annie.

'Apart from down by the playing fields, yes.' Pete shut his door. Further up the hill was the set of shops where he'd met Petrosyan, but he didn't want to go there. If the Armenian learned that Pete's son was missing, there was no telling what he might do in order to take advantage of it.

He heard the snap of her seat belt being fastened, clipped his own into place and started the engine.

'We could do the ice rink while we're down that way.'

'Yes, we could do that. But that'll be it for tonight.'

'OK.'

With no traffic visible, he swung the car around and headed down the hill towards the playing fields and rugby ground. It would take some time to do a thorough job of putting their posters up around there – a quick stop-off at the ice rink and it would be past Annie's normal bedtime before they even started towards home.

*

Pete turned into the drive at just after a quarter to ten. He pulled up the handbrake and switched off the engine.

'Well, that was a good night's work, wasn't it?' he said, as he slipped off his seat belt.

'Just have to see what response we get, won't we?' said Annie from the back seat.

'Yeah. We can't expect it to be instant, you know.'

'I know,' she said, her tone adding, *I'm not an idiot.*

'Past your bedtime, isn't it, or you'll be getting up before you've gone to sleep and what are your teachers going to think of me then?'

'How would they know?' she demanded, as they stepped out of the car.

'They'll know when you start snoring on your desk.'

'I don't snore!'

'Oh, yes, you do.'

'I don't. I'm a lady. We huff, don't we, Mum?'

'Definitely.'

'Is that like glowing instead of sweating?' Pete asked, as he opened the front door and let them go in ahead of him.

After stepping inside, he closed it again and the kitchen door slammed behind him.

'Damn.'

'I thought I felt a draught,' Louise said. 'You left a window open in there?'

'At this time of year?' He stepped past them and opened the kitchen door. Louise was right – there was a cold draught. He flipped on the light.

'Shit.'

Broken glass was strewn across the floor from the back door, fractures radiating across what was left in the frame.

They had been burgled.

'Call the station,' he said.

'What?'

'Call the station – 101. We've been broken into.'

A breakfast bowl stood on the table, a spoon in it along with the faintest dregs of milk and cereal.

Instantly, Pete knew. It could only have been one person.

Tommy.

A chill ran through Pete's body.

He'd been in here while they were out. Had broken in while they were out, in order not to meet or speak to any of them.

The air slid out of him. He squeezed his eyes shut, head dropping forward as he leaned on the edge of the table with both hands. His eyes were hot and sore, his throat clogged with a lump that hadn't been there moments ago. A lump that he just couldn't swallow.

Why?

He must have seen them go out. Didn't he know why they were going? What for? Had he not seen and read any of the posters they'd put up?

Where was he? Where had he been living for the past ten days or more? *How* had he been living?

Pete shook his head, straightened up and went to the fridge. He opened it with a finger and thumb. Milk, bread, spread and jam were missing along with his last two stubbies of beer, a bottle of lemonade and a pack of mini pork pies.

'Annie, go upstairs. Check your brother's room.'

'Why? What's wrong?'

He closed the fridge and reached for one of the food cupboards. 'Check his wardrobe. See if anyone's been in there.'

He could hear Louise on the phone as Annie met his gaze. He saw understanding dawn and she turned quickly away. Her feet thundered up the stairs as he opened the cupboard and saw that it, too, had been raided.

'His wardrobe's been gone through,' Annie yelled moments later. 'There's stuff missing.'

'Thanks, Button.' He stepped forward, saw Louise put the phone down and turn towards him. She looked utterly bereft. Stricken.

'He's . . . He's been here while we were out?' she whispered. 'He . . . didn't want . . .'

'We don't know,' he said gently, closing the kitchen door behind him.

'Of course we bloody know! He's been here while we were out, he's taken food and clothes and he's gone.' She broke down and Pete stepped forward, taking her in his arms. 'What did we do that was so awful?'

'We didn't do anything,' he said. 'Ask Annie.' He glanced up. Annie was at the top of the stairs, unsure what to do, where to go. He tipped his head, beckoning her down.

'Oh God. I don't know if I can stand much more.'

'Shh,' Pete murmured as Annie joined the hug. 'It'll be all right. You'll see. He'll see those posters and he'll come back to us.'

Still facing the front door a minute or more later, it was Pete who saw the blue lights outside. The car pulled up, the lights were switched off. He gave Annie and Lou a squeeze. 'They're here.'

Louise turned away and Annie followed her into the sitting room while Pete went to the front door. Two uniformed officers were coming down the path.

'Nicky. Mick. You were quick.'

Nicky French and Mick Douglas looked like Little and Large walking down the drive, except much neater in their uniforms.

'We were only a couple of streets away, Sarge. Somebody's shed got broken into. Some tools nicked.'

He nodded. 'We were out. Just got back and found the glass in the back door smashed. They raided the fridge and the food cupboards, Tommy's wardrobe. As far as we know, that's all. We haven't checked. Thought we'd best wait for Forensics with their fingerprint dust. Obviously, we suspect we know who it was, but it would be good to get confirmation.'

'Best have a quick shufti then,' Mick said, pulling a pair of purple nitrile gloves from his pocket and pulling them on. 'You need a pair?'

'Yes. Thanks.' Obviously, his prints would be all over the place, but gloves would help prevent him smearing any fresh ones that had been left during the break-in. 'Louise and Annie are in there.' He nodded towards the sitting room as they passed it on the way to the kitchen.

'We'll talk to them in a bit,' said Nicky. 'Check the scene first.'

They went through into the kitchen.

'Yours?' Mick asked with a nod at the cereal bowl.

'No. Whoever broke in.'

'OK. Anything else gone? Cash, maybe?'

Pete shook his head. 'We don't keep any here.'

'Did Tommy have a bike?' asked Nicky.

'Yeah. In the garage. The door's down. I never checked it.' Pete headed outside, checked the up-and-over garage door. It was locked and there was no other way in. He looked at them with

249

a grimace. 'Getting bloody cold tonight, isn't it? Let's go back in. Forensics on the way, are they?'

'Yes. In the meantime, we'd best take a statement.'

*

The last of his team to leave, Harold Pointer paused in the hallway. 'We did find prints on the back door handle. And on the fridge, the banister and the wardrobe door in the room upstairs.'

Pete glanced to the side and saw the grey fingerprint dust still smeared over the banister and the newel post at the bottom of the stairs.

'We have exemplars from the whole family, of course,' Harold went on. 'Who should I report any results to? Obviously not yourself.'

'It will be, actually. We suspect this is related to the Rosie Whitlock abduction, so . . .' He shrugged.

'Very well,' Harold said, his tone clearly indicating otherwise.

'What can I say? Your only other option is Simon Phillips, but do you see him here?'

'No.'

'There you go then.'

Harold sighed. 'I'll be in touch.'

Pete laid a hand on his white-overalled shoulder. 'Thanks, Harold.'

They had been halfway through giving statements to Mick Douglas and Nicky French when Harry and his team had arrived. The statements had been completed and the uniformed pair gone on their way forty-five minutes ago. He saw Harold out, closed the front door and went back into the sitting room where Louise and Annie waited for him. They both looked up as he came in, but it was Annie who spoke.

'Why did he do it, Dad? Why did he break in while we were out, rather than face us?'

Maybe that's exactly it, he thought, surprised once more at Annie's insight. *Maybe he just didn't want to face us.* 'I don't know,' he said. 'It could be he was trying to protect us. If he hasn't seen the posters yet, and thinks he'll be wanted in connection with Rosie's abduction, he might have thought it was the best way.'

'But we're his family.'

'Exactly. Which is why he'd want to protect us. I'd best get on.'

Pete turned away, heading for the shed and his toolbox in order to repair the back door, at least temporarily. He hoped that what he'd said was true but, deep in his heart, he knew it probably wasn't. At least, all he'd read so far in Simon's file suggested it wasn't. He shook his head. Where had he gone so wrong?

Chapter 27

Pete finally sat down with Louise at 11.15 p.m.

He had sealed the back door and put away his tools and Annie was in bed, exhausted but refusing to admit it. He sighed. 'That'll be safe for now, but I'll get a glazier to come in tomorrow and put a new unit in. Tomorrow night, if we're not all too knackered, perhaps we'd best cover the estate shops between here and the Topsham Road. There's no telling where he's holed up, but it looks like he might not be too far away so, the more local places we can get the posters up, the better his chance of seeing one of them.'

Louise was frowning. 'I don't want some stranger coming here while I'm on my own.'

'That's why I said I'd arrange it. That way, I'll know when he's coming so I can pop back for a bit. It won't take long to stick a new unit in there, as long as I can give him accurate measurements when I phone him. I've seen it done. You can have one of those double-glazing units out and replaced in a couple of minutes, literally.'

She hugged herself and shivered. 'Don't tell me that.'

'You've got to know how and the modern ones have to be done from the inside, so we're safe in here.'

She looked at him. 'Really?'

'Promise.'

'Hmm. Is it bedtime, then?'

'I . . .' He stopped as the phone rang in the hall. 'Shit. Who's that?' He got up and stepped out to answer it. 'Hello?'

'DS Gayle?'

'Yes.'

'It's Mick Douglas. A while after we left your place, we got another call. The multistorey on King William Street. There's been a . . . well, a hanging. We're not sure if it's suicide or what. I'm calling you because of the car that's up here, near the body. Silver hatchback with HB 747 in the plate.'

Pete felt a wash of ice run through him. 'And the victim?'

'Young chap. Early to mid-twenties, at a guess. We haven't ID'd him yet. Can't reach his pockets safely until Forensics haul him up or let him down. They're here now.'

'Who? Harry and his team?'

'Yes.'

'OK. I'm on the way.'

'Thanks, Sarge.'

Pete went back into the sitting room.

'Go on then,' Louise said heavily.

'Looks like one of our suspects has become a victim.'

She frowned sharply.

'That was Mick Douglas. He's found the silver Peugeot we've been looking for in relation to Alfie Bowens' death. Alongside another body.'

She grimaced. 'Guilt trip, you reckon?'

'We'll see. Harold's there now with his guys. Don't wait up.'

She gave him a brief smile. 'I wasn't going to.'

*

As Pete drove up towards King William Street he could see police tape fluttering across the end between two lamp-posts, a uniformed PC standing guard at one end.

There was little traffic around at this time of night. He slowed the car and pulled up beside the officer, powered down the passenger window and showed his warrant card.

'Evening, Sarge.'

The man lifted the tape so that Pete could drive under it and up the narrow, twisting street. Further up, another strand of tape stretched across the road beyond the six-floor multistorey car park. He turned in and drove around to the back of the building. Blue lights reflected off the surrounding buildings. The place was full of emergency response vehicles. An ambulance, three patrol cars, a Forensics van and even a fire truck were parked haphazardly on the small, odd-shaped patch of tarmac. A few feet from the wall of the multistorey, a small white evidence tent had been erected and was glowing in the night with the lamps that illuminated its interior.

As he got out of the car a black estate car came around the corner behind him. He recognised Tony Chambers' VW Passat and stood waiting for the silver-haired pathologist to park up and join him.

'Hey, Doc. How's it going?'

Chambers, his battered black leather medical bag in one hand, stuck out the other in greeting. 'Peter.' They shook. 'I'm certainly keeping busy.'

'Have they told you anything they didn't tell me?'

'Just the basics. Gender, age range and race, when he was found and who by. The fire team were about to cut him down when I was called.'

'I thought you like to see them in situ, before they're moved.'

'Generally, yes. This one was a little less practical in that respect. Not so keen on heights.'

Pete's eyebrows rose. 'I didn't know that.'

'It's not something I brag about. Anyway, I told them to take pictures before they cut him down so, hopefully, we'll get what we need from them, the body and the general scene.'

'And his car,' Pete said as he lifted one side of the tent opening and let Chambers precede him inside.

'Indeed. Thank you.'

The body was laid out neatly on a plastic sheet. The face was purple above the thin, white cord that was pulled tight enough around the neck to dig deep into the flesh. In death, the lad looked like a teenager with his tousled dark hair, clean shave and closed eyes. Neither his feet nor hands were bound. Pete looked at the fingernails. They all appeared intact. All of which made it look, at least at first glance, like a suicide. But was it? Or was it just staged that way? While Chambers put down his bag and crouched beside the body to begin his work, Pete stepped out and looked around for the first responders. He spotted them standing together, off to one side. He headed towards them.

'Busy old shift you've had. Who reported it?'

'Security guard,' said Mick. 'He was on his regular rounds. Saw the cord, looked over and saw the vic. He wasn't moving, so he left him and called it in. He's in the patrol car over there.' He thrust his chin at one of the cars parked a few yards away. Peering through the glare on the window, Pete could make out the figure of a man in a dark uniform sitting in the back.

'I'd best have a word then. Get some details. Thanks, guys.'

Pete walked across to the car and climbed into the back, beside the big man. 'Evening. I'm DS Gayle. And you are . . .?'

'Brian Collins.'

Pete could see the company logo on his uniform above his ID badge. He took out his notebook and clicked out the tip of his biro, ready to write.

'So. The PC said you were on your regular rounds?'

'Yes. The car park's not closed at night. Some staff use it. We come around every three hours or so. Cover a few sites. The NCPs, the ice rink, swimming pool, this one, a couple of others.'

'So, where's your vehicle?'

'Up top, where I left it.'

'Is there any CCTV around here?'

The big man shook his head. 'Not that I know of.'

'OK. Many other vehicles up on top?'

'Just mine, the one near the victim and one other. Red Nissan Micra, over towards the far side.'

'And you didn't see any others coming down as you went up? Or coming out of the end of the street as you arrived, anything like that?'

'No.'

'Did you notice the time when you found him?'

'Of course. Standard procedure. It was two minutes to eleven.'

Pete made a note. 'And you didn't touch anything up there?'

The man shook his head. 'I watch enough TV to know better than that. And there was no point trying to save him or anything. He was dead. No doubt.'

'OK.' Pete thanked him and headed back to the evidence tent.

Ducking inside, he saw that Doc Chambers was just closing up his bag. 'What have we got?' he asked.

Chambers glanced up. 'Without the previous cases, it would be easy to call this one suicide. But, as with them, there are signs that a sleeper hold was applied, incapacitating the victim before he was suspended over the railing up there. Makes him heavier to handle, of course, but it saves having him struggle or shout.'

Pete nodded. Rendering the victim unconscious was unusually humane for this guy, but it would have made his task here a lot easier. 'Any ID on him?'

'No. Age is early to mid-twenties. He's well nourished, had a fairly comfortable lifestyle. Student, office or shop-worker. Something of that nature.'

'OK. Thanks, Doc.' Pete ducked out. A white-overalled Forensics technician was working at the base of the wall a few feet away. He headed that way. 'Who's up on top?' he asked.

'The boss is up there with a couple of the guys.'

'Right. Thanks.'

Pete turned away and started the long trudge up the exit ramp to the top of the car park.

The wind up there was bitingly cold. He fastened his coat up to the neck and shoved his hands deep into its pockets. Three figures in white were working near the edge of the building around a pale hatchback. One of the figures stopped what he was doing and looked up as Pete drew closer. He stepped away from the car.

'We meet again, DS Gayle.'

'Hello, Harold. How are you doing?'

'Almost done, actually.'

'Found anything useful? A VIN number, perhaps?'

Harold opened one of his aluminium cases and lifted out a small plastic bag. 'Exhibit A is a petrol receipt from a local supermarket, dated three days ago. It was paid with a MasterCard.'

'That'll do nicely.'

Harold tilted his head. 'Wrong card type, Detective Sergeant, but point taken.'

'Anything else that might lead towards an ID for whoever's been in the car recently?'

'There are plenty of fingerprints on the driver's side of the car, the steering wheel, handbrake and so on, but the passenger side was wiped down with alcohol wipes, inside and out. Said wipes were then set alight on the passenger seat, along with an amount of alcohol which had been poured down the seat-back and around the floor of the car beneath it.'

Pete glanced across at the car. 'It doesn't show,' he said.

'Your perpetrator may be forensically aware, but he's not a skilled arsonist.'

An image of Jerry Tyler's house popped into Pete's mind. *I'd beg to differ on that*, he thought.

'His mistake was to close the car doors,' Harold continued. 'The flames ran out of oxygen, so the damage is purely superficial.'

Pete smiled. 'I love it when a plan like that doesn't come

together.'

'We also have the possibility of DNA from the number plates. They're home-made. Computer printed and laminated, then stuck over the real ones with double-sided tape. I hope you're going to catch someone soon, Detective Sergeant. My team and I are going to need a holiday at this rate.'

Pete clapped him on the shoulder. 'We like to make sure you're earning your wages, Harold.'

*

After switching on the lights that covered his work area, Pete unzipped his coat and stood staring at the case board, focusing on the two composite pictures that Sophie had provided them with.

It wasn't an exact match, but the victim on the multistorey looked a lot like the first image – the one she said had been driving. At least, it was a close enough match to give him a working theory.

The doc said it hadn't been suicide. A sleeper hold had been applied, the rope placed around his neck, tied to the safety rail and he'd been tipped over. How the doc could tell about the sleeper hold, Pete didn't know, but he hoped to God the lad hadn't woken up from it. That would have been a horrible way to go.

But a suicide was what it was meant to look like, the idea no doubt being to make it look as if he couldn't stand the guilt. The parallels between Alfie Bowens' death and his probably being deliberate, in the hope that the police would focus on that and not think about any alternatives.

Pete shifted his gaze to the other picture.

'So, you're on your own now and feeling paranoid. You know we're coming for you, don't you? Want to make sure there's no one to drop you in it. Well, you've done that yourself, buddy boy. All we've got to do is get your mate's ID, track down his known associates and we'll have you.'

At least, he hoped it would be that easy.

To be fair, it rarely was and, even if it did lead them to him, they would need a lot more than they had now to get him to trial. And, judging by the lengths he had gone to already, he wasn't likely to confess. Which left them with precious little. Sophie had seen him in the car, but she couldn't place him at a crime scene. They had the CCTV from the High Street, but it was too distant to be identifiable. There was the old dear across the road from Jerry Tyler's who'd seen the pair leaving just before the fire, but she was far from the most reliable of witnesses. She would be torn apart in short order on the witness stand. And the CCTV from Colleton Crescent gave a glimpse of the passenger in the car, but not of his face.

All told, they were way short of a conviction.

'Right. Let's see if we can't get a bit closer,' he muttered, turning away from the board. He went to his desk, switched on his computer and took off his coat. First, he would check on the car. He sat down and keyed in the details, hit Return. The response was almost instant. The original number plate matched the VIN. Ownership came back to a forty-three-year-old man in Poole, Dorset. He had reported it stolen three months ago. So, there was question one: where had it been since then?

He took out his phone and brought up the picture he'd taken of the petrol receipt Harold had found. He stared at the little screen, calculating backwards in his head. The purchase had been made at 9.42 a.m. on Tuesday morning.

The morning that Zivan Millocovic was killed.

So, he might be able to put the lads together half an hour before Sophie could. On the way *to* where it had happened. He would have to check the forecourt CCTV. But in the meantime, he could get the name and address of the card holder.

He switched programs on his computer and entered the trans-action details.

The answer popped up in seconds.

The card belonged to a Joshua Parker, date of birth 25 April

1994, from Kettering in Northamptonshire.

Josh.

Pete switched programs again, called up Joshua Parker's credit card history and printed out his last two statements then went onto Facebook. Searching for Joshua Parker drew a blank. He tried Josh Parker and immediately got a hit.

The dead youth looked back at him from a close-up photo taken at a steep angle as he leered drunkenly into the camera.

Pete sighed.

Another family had to be notified of the death of a loved one. Another set of parents had to bury a child. He glanced at the time. He'd let them sleep. Morning was soon enough to deliver the bad news. Let them sleep while they could.

He printed out the Facebook page then fetched everything from the printer, clipped it together and stuck it to the case board with a red line to it from the Photofit that matched Parker. Then he grabbed his coat, shrugged it on and turned off the lights, throwing the squad room back into darkness.

Chapter 28

'I wish to God we hadn't taken all those posters with us tonight.'

Pete turned his head on the pillow, not surprised that she was still awake. He'd have been surprised if she wasn't after what had happened tonight.

'If we'd only left one on the kitchen table or something, he'd have seen it and known he could stay.'

He'd come straight upstairs when he got home, checked on Annie and come to bed. He lay down with a sigh and that's when Louise spoke.

'I know,' he said. 'Which is why, when I fixed the back door, I stuck one on the outside of it. In case he comes back.'

'And I put one on the lamp-post over the road after you'd gone.'

'I saw there was something there. Didn't see what. I was thinking of putting one on the garage door in the morning.'

'Mmm. I wish we could, but best not, eh? Don't want to get into trouble with the council.'

'True. I'll get some up round the hospital tomorrow, though, if I get a chance.'

'No need. I called Jenny. She's picking some up on her way to work in the morning. She'll do it for us.'

'What shift's she on?'

'Seven till three.'

Shit. Pete squeezed his sore and gritty eyes shut. It was almost two now. They had about four and a half hours until Lou's colleague turned up on the doorstep. 'Best get some sleep, then, while we can.'

*

Pete went straight to the station after dropping Annie off with her friends. When he walked into the squad room, he saw that several of Simon's, Jim's and Mark's DCs were already beavering away, as well as Jill and Dick of his own crew. He hung up his coat, took the notes on Josh Parker down from the case board and carried them to his desk.

Jill looked across. 'I saw you'd got some more info up there. You identified one of them?'

'Yes. But we won't have to track him down. He's in the mortuary.'

'Saves the cost of a trial,' Dick said, as Jane walked in, followed by Ben.

'What does?' she asked.

'One of our suspects is dead, apparently,' Dick told her.

She grimaced. 'What happened?'

Pete brought them quickly up to date.

Jane sucked air through her teeth. 'So, where's he from?'

'Northamptonshire.'

'You want me to get onto the local force, send the info up there so they can send someone round in person?'

'Yes. Ben, get onto Facebook, see if you can track down anything useful on his friends and so on. His account's under "Josh Parker".'

Dave walked in as they were pulling up their chairs. 'Blimey. Looks like a hive of activity in here. What's to do?'

'Get on to the university,' Pete told him. 'Find whatever you can on Joshua Parker and let them know he's deceased.'

'Is this Joshua as in Dom and Josh, our suspects?'

'Yes. Looks like Dom dangled him off the side of a car park last night.'

'Damn, that's not friendly.'

Both Dave and Jane picked up their phones while Pete powered up his computer. Almost as soon as the home screen appeared, a message popped up in the bottom-right corner to tell him he had an email from Harold Pointer.

He clicked on it.

Prints, as promised.
Car contains one set. The victim.
Other site, one set again. Thomas James Gayle.
Regards,
Harold Pointer, Chief Forensic Officer.

Pete sighed, eyes closing. Thank God. His son might not be home yet, but he was close by and he was OK. It was just a matter of time until he saw one of the posters and then he'd know he could come back without fear of reprisal for acts that weren't his choice or fault.

He picked up the phone and dialled. After five rings, the answerphone kicked in. He wasn't surprised. She rarely answered the phone. He waited for the beep. 'Lou, it's me. I've just got confirmation. Last night – it was who we thought.'

She might well call back when she heard that, but, either way, the knowledge would be a huge relief for her, as it was for him.

He put the phone down, picked a highlighter pen from the mug on his desk and started going through Joshua Parker's latest credit card bills.

By the time he'd determined that there was nothing useful there, Jane and Dave were off the phones and Ben had announced to anyone willing to listen that Josh didn't have a girlfriend, but

Dom did and her name was Mandy Taylor. What he didn't have was a Facebook page of his own, though the girlfriend did and hers was filled with pictures of them and her friends. What Ben hadn't found was any new information on Dom apart from his connection to the girl.

'OK,' Pete said. 'So, how do we find Mandy Taylor?'

'Well, she's reading marine biology at the uni. We could track her down there.'

Marine biology? Pete had been outside that building the previous morning, searching for anyone who recognised their two suspects. He pushed his chair back abruptly. 'Let's have a look at her.'

Ben turned his screen.

'Shit.' Pete wished there was something handy enough to punch, but there wasn't. 'Not only was I there, I actually spoke to her and her mates.'

The three girls who had been in too much of a hurry to talk to him. The red-haired one – the one on the screen in front of him now – had claimed that the pictures couldn't be a match to the Dom and Josh that they knew. What had she said? *His nose is too big.* Christ, as his girlfriend, she ought to know.

But why had the others backed her up when she said they only knew them from the pubs in town? If they knew differently . . . He'd clearly said that the two faces belonged to potential serial killers. Was it a thrill to them? Some sort of joke? He shook his head, at a loss.

'One of her friends is called Amy. See if you can find her on there.'

'OK.' Ben started scrolling through the dozens of pictures on the site. Then he stopped abruptly. 'Here we go. "Me and Amy at the Firkin pub." How's that?'

The two girls were leaning into each other, both grinning into the camera, which was too close to allow anything else into the picture.

'Great. Now, see if you can find out what Amy's last name is.'

'Easy.' It took him just a couple of clicks. 'Here we go, boss. Amy Fellows, age twenty, of Burnham-on-Sea, reading applied biology.'

Pete snapped his fingers and pointed at the screen. 'She's our way in. She knows Dom and Josh. And she'll talk if we get her on her own. Dave, take Jill with you for the sake of form, but don't be gentle.'

'I'll send you the details,' Ben said.

'Righto. Josh Parker was no longer in the halls of residence, boss. Must have had a private let somewhere. And he was studying medical laboratory science.'

Pete tilted his head. 'There's our medical link, then.'

'Yep.'

'Ben, see if you can track anything down on Dom.' He returned to his seat as Dave and Jill left the squad room. 'I'll have to go see Fast-track and keep him up to date.'

He followed Dave and Jill out of the squad room and headed along to the DCI's door. He knocked.

'Come.'

Pete went in. Silverstone was standing at the side of the small room, pouring himself a cup of coffee from the cafetière on the sideboard. He turned, cup in hand. 'Peter.'

'Morning, sir. Just wanted to keep you up to date on the case. We've got one of our suspects in the mortuary. Looks like a falling-out with his partner-in-crime.'

'Mm-hmm.' He set his cup and saucer on his desk and looked up at Pete. 'While you're here, perhaps you could explain something to me?'

'What's that, sir?'

'How the *bloody* hell . . .' his hand slapped his desk '. . . you thought you could get away with putting posters up around the city, trying to persuade your son or anyone who's seen him to get in touch.'

'Sir . . .?'

'One, it's illegal and you're a bloody police officer, for God's sake. And two, as I've pointed out several times before, it's interfering in another officer's ongoing investigation. Did you imagine that, somehow, I wouldn't get to hear about it, Detective Sergeant? Or did you just think I'd be too soft to do or say anything about it? Because, if either of those is the case, let me tell you now, you're sadly mistaken.'

'I didn't think either of those things, sir. And nor did I think it was interfering in any way with Simon's investigation. If anything, I thought it might assist it. After all, he hasn't got anywhere so far, has he? But . . .'

'What Detective Sergeant Phillips has or has not achieved to date is beside the point and you know it. You cannot and will not involve yourself in his ongoing case – in any way whatsoever. Is that clear?'

'Sir, you're aware that my wife is still off work since Tommy disappeared. She's clinically depressed, although she hasn't had an official diagnosis yet because she refuses to see a doctor. So . . .'

'So, you're a medical expert now, as well, are you? My God, Peter, does your arrogance have no bounds?'

'I've never claimed any expertise in the medical field and nor would I, sir. What I do know about is my wife. She wanted to put those posters up. I thought it would help her depression – which it has, by the way – and I'll continue to do whatever it takes to help her and my son. If you can't understand that, then you're clearly not a . . .' he hesitated, changing what he was about to say '. . . family man. But there was no intention of hindering or undermining Simon's work. On the contrary. As I said, we thought, if anything, it might help. Certainly, it can't do any harm.'

'Except to the reputation of this force and this station. How the devil do you expect anyone to take us seriously when we can't even be seen to obey the law ourselves? Tell me that.'

It was a fair point that Pete had been aware of all along. He drew a breath and moderated his tone. 'I take your point, sir, and for that I do apologise. But there didn't seem to be any other way forward until last night.'

Silverstone had drawn a breath to continue, but stopped abruptly. 'What happened last night that's relevant?'

'Tommy broke into our house while we were out, sir. His fingerprints were found.'

Silverstone let the air out of his lungs in a long, slow sigh. 'Which constitutes proof that he's still alive and in the immediate locale. You matched the fingerprints yourself?'

Pete shook his head. 'No, sir. I called it in, made it official. Harry Pointer found and identified them.'

'Right. Go and send Simon Phillips in here.'

'Sir.'

*

Pete walked briskly back to his desk. 'Right, we're in. You take her email, Ben, I'll take her phone.'

When he'd returned from Silverstone's office, Ben had announced that he'd found both Mandy Taylor's email address and her mobile number. Pete had gone immediately back to the DCI's office to arrange for a warrant on the basis of her lying to him yesterday and thereby perverting the course of justice.

He sat down and stuck a Post-it note of the young woman's mobile number to the top corner of his screen. 'OK, Mandy, let's see who you've been talking to lately.'

It took a matter of moments to access her account and download the call log. He printed it out and once again plucked a yellow highlighter from the mug of pens and pencils on his desk. A quick scan through the printout showed that she used the phone a lot, but there were a few numbers that she called frequently. He chose what looked like the most frequent and began highlighting the contacts with it. Many of them lasted just seconds. They would be texts. The longer calls would be conversations and there were at least three of these a day. He put down the highlighter, picked out another, this one orange, and used it to mark the contacts with a second number. This one was less frequent, but the calls tended to be longer.

He did a reverse number look-up and, as he expected, found the first number belonged to Amy Fellows. The second came back with the name of Dominic Hardy.

'Got him.'

And she had texted him yesterday morning at three minutes to nine. Minutes after Pete had spoken with her and her friends. What had she said?

It took him a matter of seconds to find out.

What have you done? Police looking for you.

Moments later, he had replied.

Trust me. Not a problem. In lecture now. Will deal with it later.

And he'd certainly dealt with it, Pete thought. Maybe not immediately, but certainly effectively.

He pictured the body laid out at the base of the multistorey car park last night. The one person who they knew could firmly implicate Dominic Hardy in a whole series of murders, silenced for ever. Was the method of killing symbolic? Closing his throat once and for all. Permanently trapping the information inside him.

Or was that just his own mind attaching symbolism and pattern to an essentially random choice?

Either way, he had what he needed: a name.

He went back to basics, called up the internet and googled the lad's name. It came back with a whole series of hits, the first few of which were clearly nothing to do with his target, though one was local. There was nothing from any of the social media sites.

He sat back in his chair. 'What have you got, Ben?'

'Dominic Hardy, boss. She's been exchanging some pretty raunchy emails with him.'

'No law against that,' said Dick. 'Let's have a look.'

'Perv,' Jane accused.

'You keep saying all men are. Might as well be hung for a sheep as a lamb.'

'I've got him as well,' Pete said, ignoring them. 'Let's track him down, shall we?'

'Student roster?'

Pete nodded. 'Good man.'

A couple of minutes later Ben grimaced. 'That's no kind of biology.'

'What?'

'He's a design engineer.'

'Eh?' Pete stared at him. 'You sure?'

'Yep. I recognise him from Mandy's Facebook page.'

'Right. Get hold of the uni and find out his timetable. We need a word with young Dominic.'

Chapter 29

'Come on. We've got two minutes.'

Pete snatched the door open and ran into the three-floor brick building with Ben close behind him. The corridor led straight ahead, but they knew already that the lecture theatre they wanted was on the first floor. Where the hell were the stairs?

He started forward, searching.

All was quiet for now, but in moments the place would be heaving. They could easily lose him in the seething tide of humanity – especially if he spotted them before they saw him.

A set of doors on Pete's left had glass in the top sections. He saw stairs leading up. 'Here.'

He pushed through and started climbing, taking the stairs two at a time. On the next floor he saw the label beside the door across from him: 2B.

They wanted 2E.

A bell rang loudly.

'Shit.' Pete ran for it. He was passing 2C when the doors opened and the first students emerged. Thankfully, it was just a trickle. This was a university, not a school.

The first students emerged from the next door along. He concentrated on them, waiting and watching. Their target,

Dominic Hardy, should be somewhere among this crowd. The flow thickened, the noise level increasing. Still, Pete and Ben waited. Most of the students coming out of the lecture were male, several were dark-haired, but none of them wore or carried a brown jacket and none matched the photo of Dominic and Mandy that Pete held in his hand.

The flow tapered off. The last couple of students emerged. Pete and Ben glanced at each other. Pete shrugged and stepped forward through the doors. A man in his thirties stood alone behind the desk at the front of the big room. He was slipping books into a leather briefcase.

'Morning,' Pete said, holding up his warrant card. 'DS Gayle. This is DC Myers.'

'How can I help?'

'We're looking for one of your students. Dominic Hardy.'

'Actually, he was notable by his absence this morning.'

'Ah.'

'Anything I can help you with?'

Pete shook his head. 'No, thanks. We've just got a few questions to ask him. Nothing related to his studies.'

'I gather his father's a GP somewhere locally. I don't know which surgery, but I don't imagine it would be too difficult to find out.'

'Mmm.' Pete nodded. 'That's useful. Thanks.' He put away his warrant card and ushered Ben out of the room.

'On his toes, d'you reckon?' Ben asked when they were back in the corridor.

'Possible. Let's track down his dad and find out, shall we?' He checked his watch. 'Meantime, I've got an appointment I can't miss. I'll drop you back at the station.' The glazier would be arriving at his house in less than an hour. If he didn't make it there first, Louise would create merry hell.

*

271

Ben found the surgery address before they got back to the car. They were walking across an open-sided quadrangle between three university buildings, Ben tapping and swiping at his smartphone when he suddenly looked up. 'Got him. Dr R. Hardy. Chapel Lane Surgery, Topsham.'

'Sure?'

'He's the only Dr Hardy that comes up in the area.'

'Right. Best give him a ring, then, tell him we're coming to see him. Don't want to go wandering in there while he's got a patient in her underwear, do we?'

'No, boss.'

Pete smiled. If he'd said that to Dave, the answer would have been more like, 'It depends on the patient, doesn't it?'

Ben still had some confidence-building to do.

Back in the car, Pete had just pulled out of the parking space when Ben made the connection on his phone.

'Hello, yes. I hope so. My name's Detective Constable Myers. I'm with the Major Investigations unit at Heavitree Road police station. My sergeant and I need a brief word with Dr Hardy. It'll only take a few minutes, but it is urgent that we speak to him. It's concerning his son.'

He paused.

Nice one. Pete nodded. That would get his attention.

'Yes, that's right. If you could let him know to expect us, we'll slot in between his patients.'

He listened again. 'Great. Thank you.' He ended the call. 'All set,' he said to Pete.

'Well done.'

'I've been thinking, boss: how would he have found out about some of the victims? Like Jerry Tyler, for example. I mean, they wouldn't have run across him in the pub or met him on the street and known, would they?'

'Yeah, I've wondered about that, too.'

'So, how can I help you, detectives?'

Dr Richard Hardy was a tall, lean figure in a navy blazer, his check shirt held closed at the neck with a burgundy tie. His hands were large and bony, but disappointingly limp when he shook Pete's hand.

'Please.' He indicated the patient chair across the desk from his own. Ben leaned against the wall beside the door, notebook and pen in hand while Pete took the chair.

'We were at the university earlier,' Pete told him. 'Looking for your son, Dominic, but he wasn't in the lecture he was due to attend. The professor said something about him being ill.'

'Yes. Self-inflicted, I expect. You know what students are like. Out all hours of the night and then can't get up in the morning. Claimed he had a headache. I told him to drink plenty of water, but what can you do?' He spread his hands.

'I know what you mean.'

'So, why the need to speak to Dom? And how, exactly, can I help?'

'We need to speak to him about what he was doing yesterday and a couple of days before that. Or, more particularly, about what a friend of his was doing. Joshua Parker.'

'Josh? What's he been up to? I can't see it being anything too untoward.' He gave a forced laugh.

'Well, we'd ask him if we could, but I'm afraid that's no longer possible. There was an incident last night, just before midnight, which I'm afraid he didn't survive. I'm sorry, did you know Josh well?'

'God, how awful. No, but Dom did. They'd become quite good friends. He'll be devastated.' He shook his head. 'My God. What happened?'

'Actually, it looked like a suicide.'

'No! Not Josh, surely? He was such a . . . well, he seemed . . .'

Again, he shook his head. 'I thought he was quite happy. Quite positive about his studies, his future career, you know? This is . . . a huge shock, Detective.'

'So, there weren't any signs beforehand then? Changes in behaviour? Increased signs of stress? Nothing like that?'

'No.'

'And Dom. He's all right, is he? Apart from not being able to get up in the morning.'

'He's fine. Same old, same old.' He sucked air over his teeth. 'This is going to hit him hard, though. They hadn't known each other all that long, in the scheme of things. A couple of years or so. But they'd become like brothers, you know?'

Pete was nodding. 'Sometimes two people just gel, don't they?'

'Exactly.'

'OK, well, thanks for your time, Doctor. We'd better let you get on.' Pete stood up and nodded to Ben that it was time to go. Then he turned back to Dr Hardy. 'Just one thing, while I think of it. You haven't had any break-ins here, recently? Or any unexplained incidents with the pharmaceutical side of things?'

Hardy frowned. 'No, not that I'm aware of. Why?'

'It's a question we've been asking lots of surgeries and so on, the past few days. There've been some cases of things popping up in unexpected places recently. Digoxin. Insulin. Suxamethonium.'

Hardy grimaced. 'As I say, I'm not aware of anything like that here.'

'OK. Thanks again.' Reluctantly, Pete shook his hand again. The grip was no more pleasant than before.

He ushered Ben out and they headed back up the short corridor and through the reception. He waited until they were in the car with the doors shut before asking, 'What was the doctor's home address again?'

'Number three, Estuary Lane.'

'Right. Let's see if Dom's still at home then.'

He started the car, was part-way through backing out of the

space when his phone rang. He paused, then hit the button for the Bluetooth and continued the manoeuvre. 'DS Gayle speaking.'

'Morning.' The distinctive West Midlands accent told him who it was before the man said anything more. 'It's Colin Mason from Forensics. How are you doing, Detective Sergeant?'

'Fine, thanks, Colin. What can I do for you?'

'Wrong way round. It's what I can do for you this morning. The crime scene last night. The multistorey car park. Harold was surprised, given the victim's age and so on, that there wasn't a mobile phone either on his person or in the car, so he sent someone to search for it. And they found it. Unfortunately, the SIM card and the battery had been removed and then the phone itself had been thrown off the far side of the building and fallen six floors.'

'Ouch,' said Ben.

'The good news,' Mason went on, 'is that, although the phone is probably not going to be repairable, the internal memory chip survived intact. So we've had someone put it into another, intact, phone in order to extract the information from it. You may be aware that they hold the last half a dozen or so calls or texts on-board on a rolling basis.'

'Yes,' Pete said. 'So, what does it tell us?'

'Well, I was about to email you the results and you can see for yourself.'

'Perfect. Thanks, Colin.'

Pete ended the call and handed his phone to Ben. 'Here. See what he's got for us.'

'Right, boss.'

Moments later the phone 'pinged' and Ben opened the arriving message.

'Well?' asked Pete.

'Text received at 11.13 last night. "Cunning plan. Let's do a recce while the coast is clear. Meet at car in five." Then, a minute later, he sent a reply. "Too soon, surely?" Next one came in almost straight away. "Recce only, for future use." He sends back "OK", and that's it.'

'And the texts were from . . .'

'Our friend Dom.'

'Luring him to his death.'

'Yeah. Cold bugger, isn't he?'

'I think you'll find the term is "Suffering from antisocial personality disorder".'

'So, he's a psycho.'

'Hmm.' Pete tilted his head in acceptance. 'Which means, if we corner him, he's dangerous. To anyone in range.'

'So, should we be going after him, just the two of us?'

'I'm not planning to corner him. We see if he's there, see what state he's in and take it from there. If we can get the cuffs on him by surprise, fine. If it looks risky, we walk out and call in the heavy mob.'

'Fair enough. It's just round the corner here.'

Pete let the car slow down as he rounded a bend in the road on the edge of Topsham. Sure enough, a junction showed on the left. He indicated and turned into a narrow lane with tall field hedges at either side.

'Are you sure?'

'Trust me. Google Maps.'

'OK.' He kept going. The road bent to the left then the right, left again, then dead-ended at a wooden fence that overlooked the river. But there was a side road far enough back from the end to allow for a large stone-built house and its gardens. Pete took the turn and, beyond the big old mansion was a short row of four or five detached bungalows backing onto the river, each in its own large garden separated from the others with high laurel hedges. They were old cottagey homes with tiled roofs that almost matched the tone of their walls.

'Should be the second one along,' Ben said.

Pete turned into the open driveway and stopped the car. A

gabled dormer looked out over the front door, giving the old bungalow a Cyclops-like appearance.

Pete went up to the front door and pressed the doorbell, producing a deep chime from within.

They waited, but there was no reaction. Pete tried knocking heavily on the door. Still nothing.

'Go and have a look round the back,' he said and followed Ben as far as the lounge window, where he peered in. There was no need for net curtains in a location like this. The inside was dark and cosy, the furniture mostly antique, a lot of dark wood and leather. There was no sign of life. He stood back and waited. Ben did a full circuit of the house and emerged from the right-hand side.

'Doesn't look like there's anyone home, boss.'

Pete's phone rang again and he checked the screen. 'Dave. What's up?'

'Just got notification that Dominic Hardy's phone's active. He's currently setting up a date with his girlfriend for this evening.'

'That's handy. Can you triangulate it?'

'They're texting. You've got no chance.'

'OK. We're at his house and there's no sign of life here so we'll have to catch up with him later. See where they're going and when.'

'Will do.'

*

'What do we know, then?'

Pete dropped his jacket over the back of his chair and sat down.

'Our boy's booked a table for 7.30 at Rigoletto's,' Dave told him. 'Amy Fellows wasn't much help. She talked, but she doesn't know much.'

'Neither of the lads has got a record,' Dick added from his left.

'Figured that much when their prints didn't pop up. Any news from the hospital?'

'I rang them,' Jane said. 'Frank's still out of it.'

'I had a thought, boss,' Dave said.

'Steady.' Jane reached out and put a hand on his arm. 'Don't overdo it now.'

'Up yours, Red. Seems to me, if Dom's willing to do that to his best friend, he's not going to worry about who else gets hurt if he can see a way out of trouble.'

'True.' Pete nodded.

'So, we need to get him as alone as possible and take him by surprise.'

'Mm-hmm.'

'Well, I happen to know the owner of Rigoletto's, and . . .'

'Why doesn't that surprise me?' asked Jane.

'Because you know him too well,' Jill said with a wink.

'I'm happily married, thanks.'

'If you've quite finished, ladies, us gents are trying to have a serious conversation here,' Dave said imperiously.

'Ooooh!' Jane cooed.

'Since when were you ever a gentleman?' Jill asked.

Dave stuck two fingers up at her. 'As I was saying, boss. I know the owner there, so I could get him to give us the heads-up when the target's about to leave and we could pick him up as he comes out.'

'You sound like you've thought this through.'

'Yes, well, contrary to rumours put about by certain people . . .' he stared at Jane '. . . I do that sometimes.'

Chapter 30

Rigoletto's was in a narrow side street that ran steeply down off Fore Street, just beyond Cathedral Square. With the Christmas lights being switched on in three days' time, it would get a lot brighter down here at night, but, for now, it was dark and underlit, apart from the light spilling from the few businesses that remained open – a wine bar, the restaurant and a fish and chip shop.

They had checked with Swansea that afternoon. Dominic Hardy owned a bright red Honda Civic Sport. Pete glanced at the side mirror on Ben's side of the car. The Honda was parked on the other side of the road, about twenty yards up from the restaurant. Plenty of space in which to arrest him before he reached it when he came out. Dick and Jill were in another car, parked out of sight on Fore Street. Sophie Clewes and Mick Douglas, in uniform, were waiting across the street from Pete's position, down the hill from the restaurant, while Dave and Jane were waiting by the Honda.

Hardy and the girl had nowhere to go.

He hoped.

The arrest warrant had not been easy to get. Silverstone doubted that the evidence they had was sufficient, plus he wanted to bring the Operations Support team in on the arrest as Hardy was clearly a safety risk to anyone he felt threatened by and anyone else within reach at the time. Pete had finally persuaded him on the basis that Operations Support officers would be placed at a table near the door of the restaurant with orders to act like they were enjoying themselves and strictly avoid talking shop, however long they had to stay in there.

They had booked the table for 8 p.m. to minimise the chances of being spotted by the subject.

It was now 9.23 and the cold of the night had seeped into Pete's bones. Surely, they couldn't be much longer? They'd been in there almost two hours, for God's sake. How long did it take to fill your belly?

His own stomach grumbled with hunger. It was a long time since he'd snatched a baguette and a Coke before coming down here.

The radio on the dashboard crackled and Dave's voice came over it. 'Subjects on the move. Repeat, subjects on the move. Stand by.'

The manager would have called him on his mobile, as promised, to let him know that Hardy and the girl were about to leave the restaurant.

Pete looked past Ben at the side mirror. 'Look sharp. We don't want them to see your face. They're sure to guess something's up, else.'

'What's that supposed to mean? They don't know me from Adam.'

'True, but a face shows up pale, whereas the back of your head might be shiny with all that gel in it, but at least it's dark. And when they spot Sophie and Mick over the road . . .'

The door of the restaurant opened.

Pete reached over and keyed the radio mike. 'Target emerging.'

'Affirmative.'

He saw Dave and Jane start down the hill towards the opening door as a slim red-haired woman in a short black dress stepped down to the pavement. She was followed by a young man in a brown leather jacket as headlights showed from the top of the street. The young man saw Sophie and Mick coming up the hill towards him and hesitated almost imperceptibly then turned away, steering the girl uphill, towards his car. Jane and Dave were holding hands as they walked down the hill towards the young couple.

As Pete watched, Dave said something to Jane and they paused, looking at the menu in the restaurant window.

With the headlights getting closer, the two couples approached each other.

'Let's go,' Pete said, reaching for the door handle.

He stepped out of the car and started around it on the downhill side. Ben closed his door and Pete pressed the remote, locking the car with a clunk. They crossed the road briskly, in front of the approaching vehicle.

He saw Jane turn and say something to Dave then they appeared to pull apart, though their hands stayed linked for a moment. He heard a feminine giggle and Jane released Dave's hand and stepped past Hardy and Taylor on the girl's side. Then there was a shriek as Jane grabbed the redhead around the waist, yanking her away as Dave stuck out a foot and slammed his elbow into Dominic Hardy's back. Hardy stumbled but somehow didn't go down. His hands touched the pavement, then he was off and running up the hill like a sprinter out of the starting blocks.

Pete heard Dave's shout as he turned and ran after the younger man. He gave chase too.

'Call Jill and warn her,' he yelled. *Damn it, why hadn't he brought his radio out of the car?*

*

God, this hill was steep! He was keeping up with Dave, but Hardy was pulling away from them, he saw, and drove himself harder still, hoping that someone had called or radioed Dick and Jill who were waiting at the top.

Then Hardy dodged to the right and was gone from sight.

'Shit,' he cursed.

The problem with this part of the city was that it was riddled with footpaths and alleyways that cut through it like a rabbit warren in every conceivable direction and Hardy had just dodged into one: Bear Street was a dead end for vehicles but provided a cut-through in two different directions, one of them leading to Cathedral Square, which would give Hardy all sorts of options.

He saw Dave turn after the younger man and hoped he could keep him in sight for long enough to at least see which way he went.

God, he was getting too bloody old for this. Or too unfit, anyway. At least the latter option gave him the chance to do something about it, though he doubted he'd have the need to, if they lost this suspect. He wouldn't have the job any more.

He reached Bear Street and turned in. Dave was just disappearing into the narrow alleyway at the far end. Pete ran after him. Could hear the echo of running footsteps coming back to him from up ahead.

At least that was something.

Chest heaving, throat raw, he felt the burning in his legs as he pounded onward, still going uphill. Was that deliberate? Was the young bugger aware that the two men chasing him were so much older and less likely to be able to keep coming after him if he went this way?

He saw Dave pass under the street light at the far end of the alley then disappear to the left. Towards the Square.

Damn. Just what he hadn't wanted to happen.

He pounded through the alley, footsteps echoing loudly off the high, constricting walls. At the far end, it opened out again into a narrow street that curved away to the right while, to his left, another alleyway led through to the bottom end of the cathedral enclosure. The way Dave had gone. Again, he could hear running footsteps. Panting now, his chest burning, he followed. He was just about to turn into the alley when a young couple stepped out of it, right in his path.

'Whoa.' His hands went out, grasped the girl's shoulders and pushed her towards her companion, who stumbled sideways against the stone wall as Pete scooted past them.

'Hey! Careful!'

'Sorry,' he called back, bouncing off the far wall with one hand. He kept going. Couldn't afford to stop and risk losing Hardy. He was too far behind already. Feet slapping the flagstones, he ran on. The alley twisted left then right. Briefly, he thought he heard the footsteps in front of him once more, then they were gone again. But were they Dave's or Hardy's? Or both?

He hoped both, but it was hard to tell. Then he could see the far end, where the alley opened out into the square with its concrete paths criss-crossing the grass. Shops and restaurants faced the squat bulk of the cathedral from the far side. The skeleton of the old hotel near the opposite corner stood stark against the night, dark and almost menacing among the lights to either side of it. Trees provided a filigree frame to the scene.

Movement.

In the shadows to his right, over towards the side of the cathedral. He caught the slap of shoes on stone, just two steps then quiet again. Peering into the darkness, he thought he saw the pale flash of hands as a figure ran away from his position.

There was no way out that he knew of over there. He started towards the front of the big, Gothic church, the wide flagstoned area in front of it lit by small, Victorian-looking street lights.

Something moved at the corner. Pete kept going, jogging steadily across the grass. In front of the cathedral, people milled about, enjoying the evening. He saw an arm raised near the far side, pointing towards him. Then a flicker to the right again. A pale shape that he hadn't seen before. A man stepped into the light, jacket slung over one shoulder to reveal a pale shirt. He sauntered across towards the doors of the cathedral, looking for all the world as if he was simply out for an evening stroll, as innocent as the day was long.

But even in the light of the street lamps, Pete could see that his jacket was brown. His dark wavy hair confirmed it.

Dominic Hardy was trying to hide in plain sight.

Pete angled across towards the big doors, which were closed at this time of night, aiming to intercept him.

'Hey!'

The shout came from his right. He recognised Dave's voice.

'Dominic Hardy. Stop.'

The figure looked over his shoulder. Saw Pete too and started running again, across the front of the cathedral, as Dave emerged from the darkness, chasing him, and Pete sped up, adjusting his line so that he still might intercept Hardy, though now it would be on the hard stones in front of the cathedral doors.

Hardy dropped his jacket and seemed to speed up. Pete pushed harder. He heard shouts from around the square, but ignored them as he adjusted his angle of approach again. He wouldn't catch the guy now until he was on the grass near the far corner of the cathedral that was now looming over them, huge and dark and solid.

He could hear Dave coming in from his right, closing the gap until all three of them were just feet apart as they reached the edge of the paved area.

Hardy jumped up towards the grass, which was a foot and a half higher. Pete matched him, almost close enough for the tackle. A couple more paces . . .

'Shit.'

Hardy's foot hit the raised stone edging that bordered the pavement and he bounced off backwards and sideways, dodging between Pete and Dave, who cursed too, and taking an acute angle towards the west side of the square. Pete's foot slid on the grass as he tried and failed to change direction.

Dave was more successful. From behind the fleeing man, he could match his move.

As Pete slid on a foot and one knee, Dave hit the low wall with one foot, arms outstretched, and pushed off against it, turning in the air. Pete thought for an instant that he was going to attempt the dive, but it was too far.

'No,' he shouted.

But Dave had more sense than that. He landed on his other foot and launched himself forward at a full run.

Pete gained both feet again, looked where he was going and yelped as he tried to raise his hands, but he was too late. He slammed into the stone wall of the cathedral.

'Dammit.'

God, that hurt!

He shook his head, looked up and saw Dave twenty yards away, still close to Hardy, but not close enough. They were both still running hard. Pete had no chance of catching them before Hardy reached the shops and cafés at the far side of the square and, beyond them through one of the short connecting alleys, the lights and bustle of Fore Street. He took out his phone and hit speed-dial 4. It rang once. Started the second ring and was answered.

'Boss?'

'Get up Fore Street, Jill. He's aiming to come through past the pizza place. Dave's behind him, but . . .'

'On the way.'

Pete ended the call, put the phone away and started after Dave and Hardy. As he jumped down off the grass, he saw movement at the far side of the square. A figure moving quickly up past the shopfronts.

Ben.

'Good lad,' he muttered.

As he jogged forward, he saw Ben speed up, aiming to cut

the fugitive off before he reached the opening through to Fore Street. Hardy stiffened, finally seeing the young officer too. He glanced to his right, towards the top corner of the square, past the burned-out hotel, but a crowd of tourists were standing there, staring up at the ruined building.

He tried the same move as before, cutting back at an angle between Ben and Dave, sprinting across the grass, heading back the way he'd come. Dave changed direction, so did Ben, but, being further back, Pete had the best chance of cutting him off.

He could already taste blood in the back of his throat from his earlier run, but he sped up regardless, running for all he was worth. Now was no time to wimp out.

He could see the bright entrance to the alleyway leading through to Bear Street. A figure appeared, coming towards them, then another. Two more. An arm was raised. A shout rang out. 'There!'

Was this Special Ops at last?

'Go, boss,' Ben shouted.

Hardy's head was moving right and left as he sought an escape route.

'I'm going,' Pete called back hoarsely.

'Stop. Police,' came from in front of them.

That decided Hardy. He dipped into a crouch, one hand reaching down as he made a sliding turnabout. His head came up. He was going to come through between Pete and Dave again. But he had misjudged. Dave was closer than he'd thought. As he surged upright again with a bellow of rage, Dave's arms went out and he dived.

The tackle connected, Dave's left arm wrapping around the kid's waist, taking him backwards off his feet. Dave hit the ground, Hardy rolling backwards over the top of him, arms splayed as he tried to break his fall. Dave pushed the roll further so that Hardy ended up on his face with Dave lying across the backs of his legs.

He bucked, trying to escape.

Dave came up off him, but he was in control. One knee came down hard on Hardy's left kidney as he leaned over, grabbed his right wrist and twisted it into a hammer lock.

'Ow! What the fuck?'

Dave snapped a handcuff on his wrist then grabbed the other one and clamped them together behind his back. 'Dominic Hardy, you're under arrest, matey. You do not have to say anything, but anything you do say may be used in evidence . . .'

'What are the bloody charges?' Hardy demanded, struggling to twist over onto his back.

'Murder,' Dave told him, standing up while keeping hold of his cuffs.

'Rubbish! I've done nothing wrong.'

'You can explain that to the judge. Come on, up you get.'

Chapter 31

'Why am I here?'

Dominic Hardy slouched back in his chair, the sleeves of his thin sweater pushed up towards his elbows. His tan leather jacket had been retrieved from where he had dropped it during the chase last night, and had been bagged, tagged and sent to Forensics along with his blood sample. Now he sat in Interview Room 1, having refused breakfast, opposite Pete and Dave Miles with his solicitor at his side, the soft whir of the digital audio and visual recorder just enough to break the silence.

'That was explained to you at the time of your arrest,' Pete reminded him. 'DC Miles here was quite clear about it. I heard him myself.'

'Humour us, Detective Sergeant.' Mr Bartholomew Merriman, solicitor-at-law, was small, plump and balding, wearing an expensive-looking grey suit and a dark green tie with a brightly coloured logo embroidered onto it. 'For my benefit, if not Mr Hardy's.'

'You're here, Mr Hardy, for questioning regarding the unlawful killings of Joshua Parker, Zivan Millocovic, Brigit Mostova, Andrew Michaels, Alfie Bowens and Jeremy Tyler, among others.'

'On what basis, exactly?' asked Merriman, adjusting his tie as if its logo was meant to mean something to Pete.

'On the basis of an arrest warrant issued this afternoon following the discovery of evidence of Mr Hardy's presence at a number of the scenes of the aforementioned deaths and other evidence of his undoubtable links to the remainder of them.'

Merriman's eyebrow rose imperiously. 'Undoubtable, Detective Sergeant? I hardly think so.'

'You haven't seen the evidence, Mr Merriman. And we're not here to discuss your opinions, except where they pertain to what your client should or shouldn't say to my colleague and myself.'

'And, in that regard, Detective Sergeant, I humbly suggest to my client that he invoke his right not to say anything to you in respect of these matters.'

'Be that as it may, we're still obliged to ask the questions that we've prepared, as you well know.'

Merriman inclined his head slowly.

'Right, then. If we're all sitting comfortably, let's begin. Where were you between 11 p.m. and 1 a.m. the night before last, Mr Hardy?'

With the slightest hint of a smirk, he glanced at his solicitor, then met Pete's gaze. 'No comment.'

'And the previous day, between 11 o'clock and noon – where were you then?'

'No comment.'

'OK. Do you recall the night of the fourteenth to the fifteenth of October this year?'

'No comment.'

'Where did you spend that evening, Mr Hardy? And how?'

'No comment.'

'Your best friend, Joshua Parker, has been driving around in a stolen car with false number plates for the past few weeks. Do you know anything about that?'

'No comment.'

'Because we've got one of your fingerprints on that car.'

Which wasn't true, but Hardy didn't know that.

He frowned briefly.

'We've also got a witness who saw you leaving the home of Jeremy Tyler, this past Sunday evening, along with Joshua Parker,' Dave said, leaning forward, elbows on the table. 'How do you know – sorry, how *did* you know Mr Tyler?'

Pete noticed the muscles at the sides of Hardy's jaw clench and relax. 'No comment.'

'Because we've got two choices,' Dave continued. 'Either you knew him somehow. I don't know, maybe you've got the same proclivities? Or else you got his information from your mum. And we know she wasn't his parole officer, so my guess would be the former.'

Hardy's lip curled. 'Don't be disgusting.'

'Oh, sorry. So, it was your mum then. Was she complicit in what you've been doing or did you get hold of the information without her knowledge?'

Hardy stared back at him silently.

'If you don't tell us, we'll just have to question her,' Pete said. 'And if she is complicit . . .' He shook his head. 'That's going to be a hell of a thing. A parole officer in prison?' He gave a long, low whistle. 'I wouldn't fancy her life in there.'

'She knows nothing,' Hardy said flatly. 'And I'm admitting nothing. But if she was so overworked that she had to bring a laptop home one day, it would be easy for me to pull a file off onto a USB stick while she was in the loo, wouldn't it?'

Pete tilted his head in a small shrug. 'Talking of your parents, there's a full audit of the pharmacy at your father's surgery being done as we speak, so I don't suppose he's going to be too thrilled with you either. I wonder what we're going to find there, eh? A few things missing? Like digoxin, insulin, maybe suxamethonium? Or some vials with needle marks in? The wrong weight of contents in them? Like water instead of the marked contents, for example?'

Hardy's face remained carefully expressionless.

Pete pursed his lips, nodding. The boy didn't appear to give a damn about his father. 'Are you bisexual, Mr Hardy?'

'What?'

'I hardly think my client's sexual orientation is relevant here, Detective Sergeant. If you're merely trying to provoke a reaction then . . .'

'I'm not trying to do anything, Mr Merriman, apart from get to the truth.' His shifted his gaze back to Dominic Hardy. 'Answer the question, Mr Hardy. Are you bisexual?'

'You don't have to . . .'

'No comment.'

The words were the same, but the tone had altered. Arrogance had given way first to tension and now anger. Good.

'My reason for asking is that, although we arrested you in the company of a young lady, we found your DNA on the backside of a homeless man's jeans, so . . .' He shrugged. 'You can see my confusion.'

'What I can't see,' Merriman said, 'is the relevance.'

Pete turned back to him. 'The relevance, Mr Merriman, is that said homeless man was dead when we found your client's DNA on his person. He'd been taken up to Colleton Crescent in your client's best friend's car and thrown off the top of the embankment to land on one of the metal stanchions down on the quayside.'

Merriman grimaced slightly and swallowed, but laid a hand briefly on his client's arm.

'So, Mr Hardy. Shall I repeat the question?'

But the pause had given Dominic time to regroup and regain his former confidence. He shook his head. 'No comment.'

'I wonder what your girlfriend will think about it, though, eh?' Dave said. 'And the fact that you consort with prostitutes. I bet she doesn't know about that yet, either, does she? I hope you haven't given her anything nasty. I'll have to warn her about the need to get checked. My moral duty. I don't imagine she'll be quite as supportive then, eh?'

Hardy's eyes narrowed, his lips pressed tight together as he sucked in a deep, slow breath and let it out again through his nose.

'Of course, the clincher is the phone records,' Pete said. 'We found Josh's phone. Don't know what you did with the SIM card, but we didn't need it anyway. The phone itself stores the last few calls and texts, so we've got you enticing him to the car park where you killed him. And you may have tried to make it look like a suicide – like he'd got a conscience, unlike yourself – but we have a very good pathologist. He picked up on the sleeper hold you used on him first. So, we don't need you to say anything, Mr Hardy. We've got you, either way. You're going to prison for a very long time. The only real question I've got is why? You had everything in life. Every advantage. Why throw it all away like that? What for?'

Hardy smiled. 'You're a working man, *Sergeant*.' He laid heavy emphasis on the title and, by implication, its deliberate incompleteness. 'You wouldn't understand.'

'I've surprised you once. You never know – I might do again.'

Hardy sneered. 'No. Or you wouldn't be here. You'd have realised how pointless your life is.'

'I don't see how putting the likes of you away where you belong is pointless.'

'Of course it is. You put one away, how many more spring up in their place? There's a never-ending supply, like the Hydra's heads. Just like the skivers, crackheads, hookers and criminals you're sitting there calling victims. And what's the point of this, eh?' He looked around the room. 'I'm only talking now because I choose to. I'm under no obligation. It's up to you to prove I did anything wrong. And the whole system is stacked in my favour.'

Dave laughed. 'The legal one might be, but the prison one certainly isn't. Not unless you *are* bisexual, that is. Nice young lad like you, ripe for the plucking – you'll be ever so popular in there.' He laughed again.

'Are you threatening my client, Detective Constable?' Merriman shifted in his seat.

Dave sat back, holding his hands up. 'Nooo.'

There was a knock on the door and Jane stuck her head in. 'Sorry to interrupt, boss. I thought you'd want to know. Just got a call from the hospital. He's awake.'

'Excellent news.' Pete stood up. 'Interview suspended at—' he looked at his watch '—11.37 a.m. No point wasting any more time here. It's not as if we need a confession.' He reached over and stopped the recorder. 'Put him back in his box, Dave, and charge him with first-degree murder for Josh Parker, Alfie Bowens and Jerry Tyler. That'll do for now. We can always add more later.' He looked at the solicitor. 'You'll be earning your money on this one, Mr Merriman.'

*

Frank Benton was in a side-ward all on his own. He had tubes coming from his nose and his arm, wires from his chest and handcuffs from his right wrist to the bed frame.

Pete smiled as he stood at the end of the bed, looking at his former colleague.

'There's no need to gloat,' Frank said sourly.

'No, but it feels bloody good. How are you feeling, now you're awake at last?'

'As if you bloody care.'

Pete shrugged. 'True, but if I'm going to gloat, I might as well go the whole hog, eh?'

Frank said nothing. Just stared at him.

'So, anyway, now you're awake, I thought I'd best come and have a chat. I've been doing some reading while you were napping. Fascinating stuff, that little brown book of yours. I'd have thought you'd know better than to give us all the evidence we need. But, then again, I suppose you'd need to keep records. No good killing off the golden goose, eh? The only thing I haven't figured out yet is whether Sylvia knew about it all.'

Frank still said nothing – no doubt waiting to see how much trouble he was in, Pete thought. Well, that was OK. The answer was a lot.

'I'm guessing not, but we'll have to prove that, won't we? If it's true and if we can. They say you can't prove a negative, though, so . . .' He shrugged. 'Either way, she's going to be in for a shock. From a million-pound house to none in one easy step. Well, not so easy from her perspective, I suppose, but from ours . . . I mean, there's no way you bought that place on your salary, is there? And, as for doing it up . . . Still, it'll sell easy when we come to it. And, looking on the bright side, at least you'll have a roof over your head for the next several years, even if Sylv doesn't. Might have bars on the windows, but at least you won't have to pay the bills, eh? Rates alone must be a bomb on that place.'

'She hasn't got a clue,' Frank said dully. 'Never has had. She thought we bought the place on an advance pension payout.'

Pete nodded. 'I thought as much. Only thing I could never figure out is what she saw in you. But that's by the by. The reason I'm here is the Armenian.'

A frown flashed across Frank's face and was gone almost instantly.

'After all you've done for him over the years, he might be your ticket to a lighter sentence.'

'He won't do me any favours. Not now I'm no use to him any more.'

'No, but we can if you tell us all about him.'

'I do that, I won't be in prison long enough to have a shave. I'd be dead meat and so would Sylvia.'

'I don't get why everybody's so damn scared of the bugger. He's not even that big. And a few years' solitary followed by deportation will keep him nicely out of harm's way anyway.'

Frank was shaking his head. 'You've got no idea, mate. He's got connections all over the place. He wants something done, it gets done before he even asks for it. Otherwise, the bloke who should have pays the price.'

'Well, if that's the case, do you reckon Sylvia's safe now you've been arrested, anyway? I mean, if he wants to make sure you stay schtum, surely he'll have his eyes on her already.'

Frank shifted in the bed, handcuffs rattling against the metal bed frame as he tried to sit up. 'Then you need to make sure she's safe. Now.'

'No, you need to tell us what we need to know. *Then* we'll see about Sylvia.' Pete leaned on the end of the bed with both hands, staring at his panicked former colleague.

'Get her safe or you'll get nothing from me,' Frank shouted.

A nurse appeared to Pete's right. 'I'm sorry. I'm going to have to ask you to leave, Mr . . .'

Pete pushed himself upright. 'Last chance, Frank. I get Petrosyan or you and Sylv are on your own.'

'Detective,' the nurse snapped.

Frank went to raise a hand to her, but couldn't. He raised the other one. 'It's OK, nurse. All right,' he said to Pete. 'What do you need?'

'I don't expect you can help on the drugs side of it, but you can give us him for corrupting a police officer. That's enough to get him put away and we can go from there.'

'OK, but you've got to make sure Sylvia's safe first.'

Pete smiled. 'I knew you'd see things my way in the end.'

Chapter 32

'In position.'

The two words came clearly over the radio despite being muttered softly so as not to alert anyone inside the house.

All traces of the fatigue that, under any other circumstances, would have seen him asleep at this hour were gone as his concentration peaked. This was it. Redemption, if it were needed. As SIO on the case, it was his call. He keyed the mike. 'Go, go, go.'

Subtlety vanished. The big guy at the front of the group of helmeted and body-armoured officers slammed the Big Red Key into the front door with all the force he could muster. Once. Twice. Three times. The frame splintered, the door swung free and they charged in, yelling.

'Police! Stay where you are. Don't move.'

The whole team was shouting at once, a cacophony of voices, the same thing happening out of Pete's sight at the back of the house, adding further to the shock effect. The words lost all meaning, became just a jumbled mass of sound, but would instil instant terror in all but the most hardened soul as the Special Operations squad spread quickly through the property, searching out and securing its occupants while Pete waited on the doorstep.

Special Ops had been only too keen to redeem themselves after the debacle at the Italian restaurant the previous evening. Pete had contacted them as soon as the warrant was issued. A meeting had been organised within the hour, a standard plan of attack agreed and the decision made to go ahead immediately, rather than wait until the early hours of next morning, as they often did.

Not that it was far off the early hours anyway, by the time everything had been organised and they'd got into position. He checked his watch as the shouted reports started.

'Secure.'

'Secure.'

Correction, he thought. It *was* the early hours. Just earlier than usual at 1.10 a.m.

'All secure,' the final report came over the radio.

That was his cue. He pushed his shoulder off the door jamb and walked in. 'Subject location?'

'Front bedroom.'

Pete started up the stairs of the 1930s semi. Eight men in heavy black uniforms made the place feel claustrophobically crowded even to him. At the top of the stairs, he turned along the landing and crossed to where two of the team were standing oppressively in a doorway. He stepped between them.

Gagik Petrosyan was sitting up in the single bed. He was naked from the waist up, his lower body covered by a sheet.

'Knock, knock, Gagik. Lovely evening,' Pete said. 'Sorry: morning. Get your pants on, you're under arrest.'

The Armenian's top lip twitched. 'What for?'

'Blackmail. Corrupting a police officer. We'll see what we can do about adding to that by the time your solicitor gets out of his bed and down to the station.' He paused. 'I take it you're going to want your solicitor?'

'What do you think?'

'I think you're mine for the foreseeable, Gagik.' Pete read him his rights then keyed the mike on his radio. 'Dave, Dick. Come on in. Let's turn this place inside out, see what we can find.'

'No comment.'

Pete had no idea of the number of times he'd heard those words out of Gagik Petrosyan's mouth since he'd started this interview, forty-five minutes ago. He pressed on regardless.

'No problem. Because we've got the evidence we need without your comments. The only difference they'd make is to the length of your sentence. We've found your books, Mr Petrosyan. And you can't deny that they're yours because we've also got your DNA and an exemplar of your writing from when you were booked in here. You didn't imagine it was standard procedure to have a prisoner fill in a form, did you? Giving someone in your position a sharp object – a pen?' He shook his head. 'Far from it, Gagik. But it worked out nicely. And the fact that the books are in Armenian or whatever isn't going to be a problem either. You can get some brilliant translation programs, these days.'

He could see the rage and frustration building in Petrosyan's face. Any moment, he would come surging up out of his chair, wanting – needing – to wrap his hands around Pete's throat. Not that he would get anywhere near, handcuffed to the table as he was, but it would demonstrate his violent temper and lack of control nicely when it was played back in court.

As long as Pete could avoid the accusation of goading him . . .

He changed the subject. 'Are you familiar with the name Frank Benton, Mr Petrosyan?'

The Armenian stared at him, eyes blazing, but said nothing.

'Frank Benton is a former police officer. But, of course, you know that, don't you?'

Still, Petrosyan maintained his silence.

'We have evidence that you've had extensive contact with him. Calls and emails made both from him to you and from you to him. Can you tell me what those calls and emails concerned, Mr Petrosyan?'

The Armenian sucked air in through flared nostrils.

His solicitor, a tall, stooping hawk-like figure in a grey suit similar to what Dick Feeney was wearing on Pete's side of the table, only a lot more expensive, cocked his head on one side and peered down his nose at Pete. 'I believe my client has made it perfectly clear that he has no wish to talk to you, Detective Sergeant. Is it not time we concluded this charade and acted like gentlemen?'

'Went for breakfast, you mean, Mr Savage?'

There was a knock on the door and Dave stuck his head in. 'Boss?'

'DC David Miles has entered the room,' Pete said for the recording. 'What's up, Dave?'

'Can I speak to you outside for a sec?'

'Sure. Mr Savage here is pining for a bacon butty anyway, so I was just going to wind it up for a bit. Interview suspended at—' he checked his watch '—8.35 a.m.' He stopped the digital recorder and stepped out into the corridor. 'Back already?'

Dave and Jane had been to Topsham, to the Hardy residence, with a search warrant.

'Yeah, and bearing gifts. Dom's laptop.' He paused.

'And?'

'There's a file on it called "Clean-up" that consists of downloaded articles from the *Express & Echo*, the *Western News* and the *Exeter Daily*. Articles about the deaths of Andrew Michaels, Brigit Mostova, Donald Tennyson, etc., etc., etc. Starting with an alcoholic who was found dead on a bench down on Bartholomew Street eighteen months ago and ending with Alfie Bowens.'

Pete felt the grin spreading across his face. 'Marvellous.' He slapped Dave on the back. 'Bloody perfect in fact. We've got him good and proper with that.'

'With what, Detective Sergeant?' The imperious, nasal voice came from behind him.

He turned. 'Not your concern, Mr Savage. A different case. Although, with what we've got on your client, I think the same applies.'

The lawyer's thin lips twitched and he turned away to walk down the corridor towards the custody desk.

'Looks like today might be a good day, despite the early start,' Dave said with a grin.

'Doesn't it?'

*

'Solicitor,' Hardy said flatly.

'He's on the way, Mr Hardy. I could just fill you in, in the meantime, though. Save us all some time. If you don't object?' He raised an eyebrow, but got no response from Hardy so carried on. 'My colleagues tell me you don't have a password on your laptop. I'd have thought, these days, with all the dodgy things which go on around computers that would have been essential. Or don't you believe things like that can happen to you?'

Hardy stared at him coldly.

'No matter.' Pete shrugged. 'It wouldn't have made a difference. We've got some top-notch experts in that field, up at Headquarters. But, with what you've got on yours, I'd have expected you to at least try to keep it secure.' He shook his head as if disappointed in the younger man, then fixed him with a calm stare. 'We found the "Clean-up" file, Mr Hardy. All your handiwork nicely filed and recorded for us. Even a couple we didn't know about.' He leaned back and sighed. 'Thirteen deaths. Fourteen, counting Josh. What happened there, eh? Going to spill the beans, was he? We found where he'd spilled his guts on the grass up on Colleton Crescent after you send Alfie Bowens off there. Grew a conscience, did he?'

Still Hardy said nothing.

'Did he actually threaten to come and talk to us or did you just suspect he would?'

He paused again, staring closely at Hardy.

'I think you just suspected it. Couldn't afford to take the chance.

300

Didn't want to end up here. Where you are. And, you know, it was that killing that got you here. Without it, yes, we had some clues. We were making progress. But there was no guarantee we'd have ever got enough evidence to charge anyone. Maybe not even to identify you. But, with it . . .' He shook his head. 'With it, we identified Josh, then you and . . .' He spread his arms. 'Here we are.'

He pushed his chair back. 'Still. I'll leave you to ponder that while we wait for your brief, shall I?' He stood up and left the interview room, leaving Hardy alone with a uniformed custody officer and his thoughts. Heading along to the high-fronted booking desk, he leaned an elbow on it.

The sergeant looked across at him from his seat behind a computer screen. 'You must be about knackered, aren't you?'

Pete felt a wave of fatigue wash over him. He'd been on the go since seven the previous morning. It was now nearly nine-thirty. 'Yeah. Just finish this off and I'll be off home for some kip.'

'Still, productive night's work, eh?'

He grinned. 'We like to keep you occupied, down here in the bowels.'

Bob grunted. 'Bowels is right. The amount of shit that comes through here . . .'

The door opened behind Pete. Bob glanced across. 'Talking of which . . . Hello again, Mr Merriman. What can we do for you?'

He ignored Bob, fixing his attention on Pete. 'I understand you wish to continue interviewing my client, Mr Hardy, Detective Sergeant.'

Pete nodded. 'He's in room two. After you.' He extended a hand in invitation. 'It won't take long.'

'I'll have a minute with my client before we commence, Detective.'

'Be my guest.'

There was only one thing Pete really wanted to ask Hardy about anyway: how and where they had acquired the drugs they'd used on their victims. And even that wasn't essential to the case.

301

Whether or not they could charge him with every one of the killings, they had enough to put him away for life. Or, at least, a life sentence.

And this was one of those cases where Pete fervently believed that life ought to mean life. There were no extenuating circumstances here. No excuses. Hardy was a cold-blooded killer who planned his kills carefully and meticulously and had no more motive for them than a hit man would. Not even as much, as he wasn't getting paid for them.

He did it because he enjoyed it. And because he could. No more and no less. Anything else was just excuses.

The door to interview room two opened and Merriman peered out. 'My client is ready for you, Detective Sergeant.'

Pete stepped forward with a smile. *That's what he thinks.*

Nowhere To Run

A missing child. A dead body. A killer on the loose.

Returning to Exeter CID after his son's unsolved
disappearance, Detective Sergeant Peter Gayle's first day
back was supposed to be gentle. Until a young girl is
reported missing and the clock begins to tick.

Rosie Whitlock was abducted from outside her school. There
are no clues, but Peter isn't letting another child disappear.

When the body of another young victim is found, the hunt
escalates. Someone is abducting young girls and now they have
a murderer on their hands. Time could well be running out for
Rosie, and when evidence in the case relating to his own son's
disappearance is discovered, the stakes get even higher . . .

No Way Home

A dead body. A mysterious murder.
A serial killer on the loose.

A taxi driver is found murdered in a remote part of Exeter.
He is a family man with no enemies to be found.

The only physical evidence is dozens of fingerprints inside the
cab. How will DS Peter Gayle ever track down his killer?

Then another cab driver is found dead. Now this isn't just
a case of one murder, but a serial killer on the loose . . .

Acknowledgements

As always, I could not have completed this book without the assistance, in so many ways, of my wife, Prunella. Former Thames Valley Police officer Rick Ell once again gave invaluable advice when it was needed, as did my editor, Victoria Oundjian at Harper Collins. Without them, this would not have been the book that it is. I would also like to take this opportunity to thank the in-house artwork team at Harper Collins, who I think have excelled themselves with the cover art for this novel. The location is instantly recognisable, though it has never, to my knowledge, looked quite so dramatic. Thanks also go to all those who provided such wonderful reviews of the first novel in this series. I hope you all enjoy this book as much as its predecessor.

Dear Reader,

We hope you enjoyed reading this book. If you did, we'd be so appreciative if you left a review. It really helps us and the author to bring more books like this to you.

Here at HQ Digital we are dedicated to publishing fiction that will keep you turning the pages into the early hours. Don't want to miss a thing? To find out more about our books, promotions, discover exclusive content and enter competitions you can keep in touch in the following ways:

JOIN OUR COMMUNITY:

Sign up to our new email newsletter: http://smarturl.it/SignUpHQ

Read our new blog www.hqstories.co.uk

https://twitter.com/HQStories

www.facebook.com/HQStories

BUDDING WRITER?

We're also looking for authors to join the HQ Digital family!
Find out more here:

https://www.hqstories.co.uk/want-to-write-for-us/

Thanks for reading, from the HQ Digital team

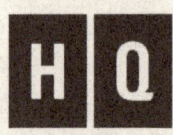